KEN CLATTERBAUGH

THE FREEDOM OF WILL

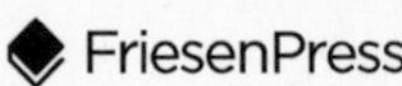

Suite 300 - 990 Fort St
Victoria, BC, V8V 3K2
Canada

www.friesenpress.com

First Edition — 2016

Cover Icon Credits:
Full Moon by MarkieAnn Packer from the Noun Project
Hamster Wheel by Olivier Guin from the Noun Project
Place Setting by Lilit Kalachyan from the Noun Project
Nun by David Peña B from the Noun Project
Tornado by misirlou from the Noun Project
Prisoner by icon 54 from the Noun Project
Face by Mauro Lucchesi from the Noun Project
Thought Bubble by irene hoffman from the Noun Project

ISBN
978-1-4602-8302-8 (Hardcover)
978-1-4602-8303-5 (Paperback)
978-1-4602-8304-2 (eBook)

1. FICTION, SATIRE

Distributed to the trade by The Ingram Book Company

TABLE OF CONTENTS

HOME

Will, dressed and lying on his back in bed, was talking to God. Will and God exchanged thoughts frequently.

"It's exciting God. We're going on a road trip!"

"I can't go on a road trip."

"Why not? If you can do anything, surely you can go on a trip."

God chuckled. "Going on a trip implies there is a place that you are not and a place that you are, and a *trip* is going from the place you are to the place that you are not. However, since I'm supposed to be everywhere…"

"Oh, spare me," Will groaned as he turned onto his stomach and looked out his dormer window. Sometimes God was just a smartass.

The day was already warming, and Will was starting to perspire despite his recent shower. He noticed, not for the first time, that the bed was too small for his large frame. It was a happy moment, the kind that schoolchildren experience the first day of summer vacation, anticipating endless days of reading, playing, and, of course, no more school. In Will's case, it was the end of high school and the beginning of a new adventure. Packed and ready to travel to a job in west Texas, Will lingered for a moment, enjoying his anticipation in spite of the knowledge that his aunt and uncle were waiting for him downstairs.

Memories held him at the window. For the past fifteen years, he, William James Tillit, had lived in this house in this room. The house belonged to his Uncle John and Aunt Rita, who had been his guardians.

Four generations of the Tillit family had lived in the same location, overlooking the Red River Valley south of Shreveport, Louisiana. The first structure was a twenty-by-twenty foot cabin. Will's great-great grandfather, an itinerant preacher known for his singing sermons, had claimed the land and built the cabin sometime around 1840. His son, a shouting Methodist, turned the dwelling into a dogtrot house by adding a similarly sized cabin, connected by a breezeway, to the original structure. Uncle John and Aunt Rita's father, a pastor of a local congregation, built a new house with a second story following a fire in 1954. Uncle John took over the premises shortly after his father died, and Aunt Rita, after a career as a sixth-grade teacher in a private Christian school, took up residence with her brother shortly before Will joined the family.

The front porch sat directly below Will's dormer room. Looking out, he could see a circular drive that brought visitors to the front steps. The drive circumscribed a rich green lawn, a favorite place for firefly chasing when Will was much younger. Flanking the porch to the north and south were smaller gardens, well tended thanks to his horticultural talents.

Without his labor, Will wondered what would become of the gardens. Aunt Rita was always too busy, either with her bookkeeping or household chores. She justified her lack of interest in the garden by her steadfast belief that the end of time would precede significant production from the vegetable patch. Her apocalyptic vision had infected Will when he was much younger. Sometimes, he would carry tasty young carrots, a vegetable of which he was particularly fond, in his pockets just in case he, too, was called unexpectedly to heaven. He discontinued the practice after he learned from a friend that his pants might be left behind along with the sinners of this world. Uncle John, for his part, limited his gardening commitment to doing some early spring spadework in an effort to work off his winter fat and to justify his prodigious consumption of the lush, red tomatoes produced in the Louisiana heat.

This approach to the house had been indispensable during Uncle John's brief foray into the funeral business. Highway 71 ran along the Red River about a mile below the house. A narrow lane left the highway and led straight to the bottom of the circular drive. On either side of the lane were cow pastures that Uncle John had decided to convert into the Red River Cemetery as a complement to his Christian Funeral Home business. The plan was that a hearse would pick up the deceased at the house and, following a short trip around the drive, deliver the departed to a burial site.

Will smiled at the recollection that things had not gone as planned.

The fields had proved as unsuitable for a cemetery as they were for cow pastures. The noxious weeds and poor fencing encouraged the cattle to exercise their freedom to roam, and the spring flooding and high water table encouraged the corpses to do likewise. Many a family came to visit their beloved, only to find the headstone covered with silt or in quite a different location from the one they remembered on the day of interment. Will wondered sometimes if those who prayed at the site of a dead relative or friend would have done so had they realized the remains were on a cruise in the Gulf. The cemetery was relocated after a couple of years.

Sprays of bougainvillea and cypress vine climbed the walls of a small garden shed that sat among the tupelo trees, live oaks, and magnolias of the north side of the house. From the right angle, one could see the nose of an abandoned hearse parked behind the shed. Heliotrope and confederate rose bloomed profusely next to the house, and already the tomato plants were burdened with their fruit in the vegetable patch to the south.

"Will?" Aunt Rita called from the kitchen.

"Right there!" Will picked up his bag and paused for a final quick look at his relatively clear desk, occupied only by his high school annual.

The kitchen smells were delightful this mid-June morning. Ham, eggs, and his aunt's special biscuits filled the breakfast table. Uncle John was already seated. Aunt Rita was preparing a plate for Will. A couple of cats, Foxy and Delilah, stared at Will from one corner of the kitchen, and Bubba, part mastiff and part hound, snored in another corner.

"Morning, Will," Uncle John said as he patted the chair next to him.

Aunt Rita smiled and also gestured toward Will's customary seat. "Are you packed and ready? It's going to be one syrupy day."

"Syrupy" was Aunt Rita's favorite term for a hot, muggy Louisiana day.

Aunt Rita and Will took their places at the table. They all joined hands and bowed their heads for their customary round robin prayer. Uncle John was brief. He asked God to watch over Will on his journey, and then he nodded to his sister to continue. Aunt Rita asked Jesus to watch over Will and that Will would keep his personal relationship with Jesus. She squeezed Will's hand, indicating it was his turn. Will was clear about what he would say.

"Thank you, God, for my Uncle John and Aunt Rita, and the gift of their love."

Will realized that if the cats and Bubba could pray, they would offer the same thanks. The Tillit house was always filled with orphaned kittens, puppies, and, occasionally, children.

Will remembered one young woman, who was very afraid of someone, who had stayed for a few days. He was quite young at the time, and he never got the whole story. The woman slept in Will's room for a few nights, and he was relegated to the couch in the front room. Although Will was a bit grumpy about this turn of events, his aunt and uncle made it clear he was doing a good thing. Will's favorite dog at the time, Laddie, a small terrier mix, was allowed to sleep with him on the couch, something that would not have been allowed but for Will's sacrifice.

In many ways, Will was also one of the needful creatures his aunt and uncle took in. Will never knew his father or even who his father was. His mother, Mary-Rose Tillit, was the youngest sister in the family. Aunt Rita was the oldest child and Uncle John the second. His mother was much younger than her two siblings. She never married and refused to identify Will's father when she became pregnant. Her choice in men was consistently bad. Will barely remembered his life with her. She was rarely home, and she left Will with a series of babysitters. Slightly younger than his mother, the babysitters were mostly high school girls who worked cheap.

Late one evening, Uncle John and Aunt Rita turned up at the rental apartment in which Will and his mother lived and took him back to their home. It turns out his mother had called them and said she wasn't coming home. She had an opportunity for a new life if she chose to exclude her child. Aunt Rita's anger at this abandonment led her to rarely acknowledge that she had a younger sister. At the same time, she never condemned her either, at least not to Will.

Uncle John, who had taken the phone call, told Will that his mother had left with a dentist who did not want a young child in the deal. "Your mother is a good woman who likes to laugh and have a good time," Uncle John said. "She loves you, but the temptation of a new start was too much for her."

Will wondered often about his mother, but he had so little information that his wonderings were mere speculations and fantasies about a reunion with her. Meanwhile, he was immersed in a world of care and love, and that soothed his sense of loss.

Will's theology was hardly fully developed, but neither was he theologically naïve. The morning prayers from his aunt and uncle revealed to him the canyon between their theological positions. To say that the Tillit house was religious was to note an obvious fact; to say that this religion contained an abyss was an understatement. Still, the house was practically harmonious, a healthy environment for a young boy.

Religion was the Tillit family business, and Uncle John and Aunt Rita were an unstoppable tag team of pious enterprise. When Uncle John was a young man, he took his tent revival on the road. He traveled largely throughout Louisiana, Mississippi, and North Texas. But the revival business had become too grueling and televangelism too attractive to those who used to attend the revivals. There was also the problem with the IRS. After years of audits of Uncle John's revenues, the IRS was about to levy a large fine for his failure to file in 1982 and 1984 and for incomplete returns in 1985 and 1987. However, Aunt Rita, who had just retired from teaching and moved in with Uncle John, took over his bookkeeping and lent enough order to the chaos that the IRS was happy to escape without putting a likable man of faith on trial. They accepted Aunt Rita's offer to pay a smaller penalty and to keep honest records in the future.

After Will's arrival in 1990 at the age of five, Uncle John and Aunt Rita turned to what they called "backyard religion," and Will became an under laborer in the family business. They held local revivals on the banks of the Red River near their home. For a couple of years, they sold resting places in the Red River Cemetery, and they provided religious books, both wholesale and retail, from their small True Word Bookstore. Uncle John also hosted a weekly revival hour on a Shreveport-Bossier City radio station, and he was a frequent guest speaker at local churches.

As Will grew older, he became more familiar with his aunt and uncle's specialized roles in their various enterprises. Uncle John was a bit casual, to say the least, about financial details, whereas Aunt Rita operated with the precision of an accountant. Besides holding the purse strings in the family, Aunt Rita contributed to the backyard religion business by singing in her sweet alto voice on the weekly radio show, overseeing the bookstore, and lining up musicians for the local revivals.

The division of labor between the siblings extended to their responsibilities in raising young Will. Aunt Rita fed Will, treated his scratches and bruises, made certain he had a decent wardrobe, and tried fervently to explain the glories of the end of time to him. She was a devout fundamentalist and believed firmly in the inerrancy of the Bible. She believed that every proposition in the Bible was true and came directly from the mouth of God and that the entire history of the world was recorded or prophesied in the books beginning with Genesis and ending with Revelation. Because she was waiting anxiously for the end of time, she lived with an intensity that reminded Will of a small bird hunting for food for its chicks with one eye out for hawks.

Aunt Ruth's faith in the Bible extended to her own edition. Early on, Will came to realize that although Aunt Rita read the Bible regularly and was very fond of citing it, she had a terrible memory for text, and her interpretations of scripture tended to be eccentric. For example, having read about flying "rolls" in Zechariah 5, she refused to have dinner rolls at the table, seeing them as a source of evil. When Will pointed out that she was taking a misprint—the passage was about flying *scrolls*—to be literally true, she replied, "God put this copy of the Bible in my hands for a reason. I wouldn't be surprised if it was because your uncle eats too fast. It probably saved his life not having dinner rolls at the table."

Aunt Rita's small, thin busyness contrasted sharply with her large, affable brother whose movements were always deliberate and unhurried. When Will thought of his Uncle John, what came to mind were dog-attended walks in the woods, early morning fishing trips, and debating some idea in his uncle's extensive library. Uncle John was more like an older brother, while Aunt Rita was Will's loving supervisor.

To Uncle John, the Bible was a vast store of metaphors, myths, and allegories. As far as he was concerned, there were only two commandments: to love your neighbors, which he took to be all creatures, great and small, and to exercise your God-given grey cells. He boiled these down to the pragmatic code: "Do the best you can." He was the quintessential evangelist whose focus was to bring people to belief. As a practitioner of conversions, he knew that different stories appealed to different folk. By nature, he looked to the future and was always planning some outing for the family. Whereas Aunt Rita tried to instill the right theology in Will, Uncle John would, as often as not, simply hand Will a pile of books as an answer to his questions, whether they had to do with God, how to embalm a body, or how to build a greenhouse. Reading was always followed by a "mental exercise" in which Will and his uncle had a critical discussion about the reading. As a result, Uncle John turned Will into a voracious, reflective reader.

Whenever Will asked Uncle John if he shared Aunt Rita's apocalyptic vision, he would reply that no human truly knew God's will. Uncle John's favorite Bible passage was Isaiah 55: 8–9: "For my thoughts are not your thoughts, nor are your ways my ways, says the Lord. For as the heavens are higher than the earth so are my ways higher than your ways and my thoughts higher than your thoughts." To Uncle John, God was an ineffable entity, something that the religions of the world pursued but never captured. Uncle John commented often that a lot of folks had tried to second-guess God, and they had been about as successful as the Chicago Cubs in winning the World Series. "But the Cubs are engaged in an appropriately human task," he added, never failing to hide his disappointment in them year after year. Uncle John never spoke directly against his sister, nor did he try to prevent her Bible lessons.

When Will was quite young, he became fearful as a result of his Aunt Rita's story telling. At age six, he thought that Magog and Gog lived under his bed. He imagined Magog to be a horned beast with large, upward-jutting teeth. Gog was more of a slithering, slimy glob. Both lay in wait for him to turn out the lights, which made Will unwilling to go to bed at night. Uncle John solved the problem with a Bible-nightlight from the family's bookstore. Will never could see the difference between the frightening tales from Revelation and the stories of Stephen King, whose books he had to sneak into the house and read on the sly in his room.

As he grew older, Will tested his aunt's peculiar take on things. At one point, he searched diligently in what he took to be the most prophetic passages of the Bible to see how Robert E. Lee Consolidated High School would do in football that year. Will was no more successful in finding a relevant prediction than Robert E. Lee was in winning a game that year.

When Will asked God about this failure of prophecy, God quipped, "Football scores must have been in one of those gospels that did not make it into the Book." God's comment left Will with the distinct impression that looking for football outcomes in the Bible was probably not an appropriate use of scripture. He also concluded he did not like God in his sarcastic mode.

By early high school, Will planned to follow the male tradition in his family and become a pastor. Will had a good presence—he practiced sometimes on his aunt and uncle—and an excellent memory for texts. He even revealed to them that he talked to God sometimes—something they considered quite natural—although he did not reveal just how unrelentingly sardonic God was.

But Will's pastoral ambitions were dashed quickly. The discovery came in football. Will was quick and powerful, built just like his uncle. The Robert E. Lee offensive and defensive coaches fought over whether to make Will a defensive back or a tailback. He ended up playing both ways. However, much to his embarrassment, in his excitement over the first big game, Will was beset with a violent case of the hiccups. Nothing would make them go away, and they prevented him from breathing properly. A similar attack came with each game. It also happened during a drama club production of *Arsenic and Old Lace*, in which Will was supposed to be poisoned. Instead, he lay hiccupping helplessly on the floor, much to the amusement of the audience. After these incidents, and after experiencing the nasty side effects of the anti-hiccup medications he had tried, Will withdrew from all activities that involved public performances, including the debate team, of which he was the most promising member. Will was fine when he was doing research for debate or in football practice; his body just could not deal with the excitement of being before the public. His aunt and uncle took his disability in stride. It was less disturbing to them than to Will.

When Will apologized to God for abandoning his ambition to become a pastor, God seemed unconcerned.

"You know, Will, you don't have to be a pastor to be a good person." Then, God added cryptically, "In fact given the clerical temptation to abuse power, it probably helps."

Breakfast was over. The three faces at that table all reflected sadness that a chapter was ending. Will, the abandoned child who had been taken in by two childless, older adults and loved as their own, was leaving home. He had just turned nineteen and was on his way to work for a casual acquaintance of Uncle John's from the touring days. Reverend Shister was opening a Christian theme park in west Texas, located off Interstate 27 between Amarillo and Lubbock. With jobs scarce for young people and a severe decline in family finances, Will had leapt at the chance to earn some money and be on his own. A good student, Will was on a one-year delay before attending Tulane University. The work in west Texas—in addition to the grants for which he was eligible—promised to pay for a good chunk of his college tuition.

Will's aunt and uncle had come to support his delay in going to college. Initially, his aunt wanted him to go straight to Tulane, but his uncle thought he would benefit from the experience of working at the theme park.

"You know Rita, that boy is smart, kind, and naïve as a gerbil about life," Will overheard his uncle say. "I really think he will get more out of college after a year of seasoning on his own."

Whereas Will did not think he was particularly naïve, he also supposed such a belief was typical of naïve people.

Breakfast ended with another short prayer of thanks. Then Will loaded his duffle and a pile of books into his ten-year-old S-10 pickup. Hugs and goodbyes were short and tearful. As he turned onto the lane at the bottom of the circular drive, he waved back to the two figures standing arm-in-arm on the porch. Will's excitement at leaving warred with his regret of the same.

"Well, God, we're on our way—and no smart remarks about being everywhere."

"My lips would be sealed—if I had lips," God replied.

Will cranked up his favorite country and western radio station, which was playing the current number one hit, a tale of lost love entitled "When You Were Here, I Was There."

PROSPERITY

Driving north, listening to country music, and watching the familiar countryside slide by left Will's mind awhirl with ideas, excitement, and not a little anxiety. He had spent virtually no time away from home before. While he looked forward to college, the idea of spending a year making money and seeing a bit of country had immediate appeal. He wondered what he'd major in. He had considered everything from oligochaetology to philosophy.

"Wow," God intruded. "You've considered everything from 'o' to 'p'. There are other letters in the alphabet, twenty-five to be exact, that are the beginning of other subjects of study."

"Twenty-four," Will grumbled, all too familiar with God's deliberate misunderstandings. He responded in kind, "Maybe I'll study acupuncture or perhaps zymurgy. Is that sufficient alphabetical range for you? Still, I like the idea of oligochaetology. Oligochaetologists spend more time outside than philosophers do, and I like to dig in the dirt."

God was silent.

A few miles north on Highway 71, Will approached the mammoth golden gates of the New Word Prosperity Apostolic Life Congregation. A large silver cross, entwined with a dollar sign, adorned the roof of the church, which served as a hub for a private school, a conference center, a shopping mall and a sports stadium. All of this, together with the parking lot, took up some 120 acres of good Red River farmland. A rash of billboards, electric signs, and official state markers announced the upcoming glories of the New Word church. A gigantic sign topping the columns that supported the four-lane entrance read, "Trust in the Lord—Guaranteed."

Will was in his junior year of high school when the area south of Shreveport had been transformed by the opening of the megachurch, or the mega-megachurch, as some called it. Construction of the facility took three years. Its opening on Easter Sunday the previous year was heralded by a barrage of television advertisements, posters, and balloons. Prayer wagons with incredibly annoying speakers saturated every small community and most of Shreveport. New Word restaurants advertised two meals for the price of one. The stores offered comparable bargains on clothing, toys, and anything else one could want. Gas at the New Word gas station was a dollar off the regular price. The opening of the church proved to be an instant financial disaster for local businesses and an even worse calamity for local churches.

Will had a vivid recollection of his guardians' reaction to the opening. Uncle John was especially quiet that Easter Sunday. He was not preaching that day, so the family attended a nearby Baptist church led by Uncle John's friend, Pastor Bob Williams. It was a miniscule gathering, barely two pews, as many of the congregation had gone up the road to attend New Word.

After the service, Uncle John and Pastor Bob engaged in a quiet but intense conversation while Will and Aunt Rita walked in the small garden maintained by the Women's Committee. Will remembered taking his aunt's hand. He sensed sadness in her and felt it in himself as they ambled among the flowerbeds.

On the way home, Uncle John revealed some of his feelings about the new church. His anger, a rare thing, was evident. "That new minister, Reverend Ted Steady, actually offered me and Bob positions as associate pastors. It would be our job to minister to the flock. I guess he doesn't have the time. We both declined; it felt wrong. Prosperity theology is the discount store of religion. Steady hires the old and nearly retired to work for peanuts and to peddle his product. New Word has already offered us ten cents on the dollar for our bookstore inventory—they already control our suppliers—and our radio show has been canceled so they can broadcast Steady's services. Steady worships mammon, not God. Unless God is a banker, he's not welcome in that place. It's a business venture, pure and simple. There's no compassion, no community, and no history! Bob said that the poorest and sickest parishioners are actually screened out. They have security people who cull the crowd and put them in a special corner away from the cameras. Their presence is considered incompatible with their precious appearance of *prosperity.*"

In the silence that followed Uncle John's outburst, Will realized that the comfortable, familiar days of their backyard religion had just taken a tragic turn.

As he passed the complex, Will's memory flashed back to the nightmare of his one and only visit to New Word. The week after the opening, Will and two high school friends, Wilma Williams, Pastor Bob's daughter, and Denny Crais attended New Word. Wilma wanted to shop for bargains in the mall, and Denny, who was thinking of joining the army, planned to talk to the recruiters who were always available in the complex.

Will had discussed his visit to New Word with Uncle John and Aunt Rita. His uncle encouraged him to experience the church for himself and make up his own mind. Aunt Rita was of another mind. Perhaps she saw the impact of this new church on the family's finances more clearly than her brother.

When they walked into the church, Will had had an indelible sensory experience. The air itself was scented with lilac and citrus. Once inside the church, he realized just how cavernous it was. Multiple stages dotted the front, with the largest center stage containing the pulpit. Two balconies hung over the first level seating. And everywhere, there was room for movement.

In front, a gigantic screen had been lowered. On it were messages for the Prayer Center, Christian dieting, Christian books, insurance, car dealers, and Christian social groups, such as teen dances and singles groups. It was, Will decided, just like Wal-Mart. Products everywhere. The whole atmosphere felt secular and alien to his love of small churches, fellowship, and listening to someone who knew him.

Reverend Steady, known popularly as "Reverend Ted," was the main attraction. As with any big show, he was preceded by several warm-up acts. Will and his friends watched two bands followed by videos that were more like professionally done commercials. In particular, Will remembered a video for the Prayer Center, which said that, for a modest cost, you could have twenty-four hour a day prayers said by a computer. For a little bit more, you could have a prayer said by an entire congregation in Africa or India. The video showed a family purportedly mourning the death of a grandfather. They drove up to the center's drive-in window in a van purchased from the New Word car dealer, judging by its plate frames. Then they deposited their prayer—the text was shown on the screen—into a capsule together with a small, childish clutch of flowers that had been presumably picked by a teary-eyed granddaughter of about eight. They placed the capsule inside a vacuum tube. As they closed the little window, it shot straight up as if it had enough momentum to go directly to heaven. The little girl looked up, her eyes bright with joy. "For you, Grandpa." The commercial ended with a fade away of the Prayer Center and the words, "A place for those who care."

By that point, God was unable to restrain himself. "See what happens when Spielbergian techniques are applied to religion? I haven't cried so much since *ET*."

Will did not disagree. The whole commercial seemed self-serving, saccharine, and insipid. Throughout the commercial, Wilma made a gruesome face that gave Will the giggles. Denny, who loved the sentimentality, glared back at their lack of appreciation.

The video ended, and the congregation stilled. Will glanced at his friends. Wilma shrugged. Denny was tense. The anticipation and silence continued.

Reverent Ted's appearance was so amazing that Will actually jumped in his seat. One minute there was no one in the pulpit, and then there was a loud noise, smoke, and Reverend Ted, like Dracula, arose out of the mist.

"Look, it's a money vampire," God quipped.

Behind the pulpit, the giant screen came to life with an ear-shattering explosion—the sound system would rival the best amphitheater—and images of what looked like US soldiers fighting somewhere in a desert. Reverend Steady was wearing a military camouflage outfit and waved a fully automatic rifle in the air. Later, Denny texted Will informing him that it was one of the latest models, which he identified as an M-21.

"Are you a warrior for Jesus?" Reverend Ted shouted.

The congregation had been waiting for this moment. "Yes!" they roared in response.

"Will you die for him like he died for you?"

"Yes!"

"Welcome, troops of the Lord."

The reverend slipped his rifle into a holster on the side of the pulpit. Behind him on the screen an American flag waved with an image of a saluting soldier superimposed over it.

Will's jaw actually dropped at that point. Denny, in contrast, was so pumped that he wiggled in his seat and kept repeating "Yes!" over and over again. Wilma cringed beside Will and buried her face momentarily in his shoulder.

"I hope he shoots himself in the foot," God said with delight.

Reverend Steady launched into his sermon. "All this is mine," he said, spreading his arms wide. "I own a controlling interest in this church, this mall, and all its facilities. I am a wealthy man. With my investments, I'm probably in the top point one percent of Americans. I travel by private jet. I own four homes in various parts of the world. And each day, I am wealthier than I was the day before. Why do I enjoy these gifts from the Lord? As it is written in Deuteronomy eight, verses seventeen and eighteen, 'Do not say to yourself, "My power and the might of my hand have gained me this wealth." But remember the Lord your God, for it is he who gives you power to get wealth. . . .' The bottom line, my friends, is that I am rich, because Jesus wants me to be rich."

Reverend Steady paused and scanned the congregation, including those in the balcony. The audience became hushed. Behind him, the image of the flag gave way to an actuarial sheet with some very impressive numbers on it. When he spoke again, Reverend Steady's voice turned into a shout. "And Jesus wants you to be rich as well!"

The audience resounded in affirmation. They wanted to be rich, too. That's what they had come to hear.

"You know," Reverend Ted continued, "they say that Jesus was a poor man. But how could a man be poor who is the Son of God? I'll tell you a secret. Jesus was humble, but he was *not* poor. Adjusted for inflation, Jesus was a millionaire. That's right, Jesus was a millionaire, maybe even a billionaire."

God was unable to restrain his sarcasm. "Jesus must have been a general contractor, not a simple carpenter. Maybe he dealt in derivatives."

Will smiled. He liked God's perspective on prosperity theology.

Reverend Ted eyed his flock like a hawk looking at chicks. "You are asking yourself, how can I become wealthy? I can't even get out of debt. I have to pay the insurance, my credit cards, the doctor bills, and braces for the children." Steady was silent for a moment. "Well, I don't have any insurance. I don't have any doctor bills, my children's teeth are perfect, and I pay all my credit cards when they're due. You, too, must trust in the Lord. If you believe, Jesus will take care of you. If you believe, you will have even more than you ask for. If you believe, every need will be taken care of. Why do you need insurance? Do you doubt in the Lord? You are sinners who do not enjoy the things you want, because you do not believe that Jesus died for you and you are unwilling to let Jesus guide your life. But you say, 'I do believe,' well let me tell you, and hear me now, you do not believe enough! Let your wealth be the measure of your faith. My faith is great, and so, therefore, is my wealth."

Reverend Ted paused. There was not a riffle of movement in the audience. Will and his friends felt his eyes on them.

"I've just told you the secret to wealth. Now I'm going to ask you for money. 'What?' you say. 'Get a load of this guy! He's already rich, and I'm not rich. Perhaps there should be a reverse collection.'"

The congregation laughed.

"Let me begin with a passage from Luke six, verse thirty-eight, 'Give, and it will be given to you. A good measure, pressed down, shaken together, running over, will be put into your lap; for with the measure you give will be measure you get back.'"

Collection plates were passed around. Will rummaged automatically through his pocket for loose change until God interrupted him.

"You're not actually considering giving him money, are you?"

While Wilma searched her purse, Denny wrote a check.

"Did you come here to get right with the Lord, or did you come here to steal from God?" Reverend Ted asked. "You know the commandment: Thou shalt not steal. And believe me, stealing from God is the worst kind of stealing, because he knows right away, and he knows where you live."

His warning was met by nervous laughter. The screen behind Reverend Ted changed to show mission workers in Africa and South America.

"If you steal from me by not giving, you steal from God. I have already given you the secret to wealth, so tear up that insurance check or that check to the dentist, and make your checks out to me, Reverend Ted

Steady, and believe me, you will be rewarded a thousand times over. I will talk to God personally for you. Guaranteed."

"Maybe I should 'Job-ify' him," God grumbled in Will's ear.

"What?"

"You know, *Job-ify* him. Allow his investments to deteriorate, allow his children to die, and take away his health."

"That's disgusting."

"Are you shocked that I would allow such things?"

"No." Will was feeling like a bit of a smartass himself. "I'm shocked at your abuse of English. Turning a noun into a verb."

"Oh," God replied. "Maybe I should become a sportscaster. After all, I do admire his *athleticism*."

Even sitting in church, Will laughed out loud at God's sarcasm.

Will took the collection plate and pretended to make a donation. He simply could not bring himself to give one penny to this man. Denny was of another mind and dropped in a check for one hundred dollars. Wilma followed Will's example, her face growing red with anger. At the time, Will could not help but recall Uncle John saying, "Do not lay up treasures for yourself on Earth except the good will of those you can help."

Suddenly, there was another explosion, and the image on the screen behind Reverend Ted changed to a street scene followed by a glimpse of what was probably a gay pride parade where two women embraced while standing on a float. The audience gasped at such an "obscenity." Reverend Ted stood rock still for the next few moments before resuming.

"In case you didn't notice, I just changed the subject," he announced to twitters among the faithful. "It's time to talk more about being a warrior. Do you know how when you go down into a damp basement at night and turn on the lights, the floor moves with unhealthy roaches and water bugs? They're everywhere. They pollute the room, your house, and your neighborhood. Then you go out to the dumpster, and it's filled with rats. Vermin. Well, I hate to be the one to tell you, but we all live in that basement and in that dumpster. God's enemies are everywhere. They seek our destruction at every turn. They, the secular humanists and the atheists who deny us prayer in our schools don't even want a little prayer before a football game! Are they afraid to hear the truth?" Steady paused and glared at his audience. "Women want to marry women, men to marry men. They don't care about the sacrament of marriage. They're an abomination!"

The congregation moaned, and some wept.

Will remembered another of Uncle John's observations that every argument for inserting religion into public life could be used to justify inserting a specific sect of religion into public life, and that's why religion belonged in the heart and the church and not in schools or legislatures.

Wilma turned to Will. "Had enough?"

Will nodded, and they slipped out of the pew and headed for the exit.

Reverend Ted continued. "What can we do about this enemy? As Christian warriors, there are many ways we can fight. Home school your children or send them to our New Word Christian School. Do not expose them to Satan's thoughts. Vote for genuinely Christian candidates who care about Christian values. How can you tell the pretenders apart from the real Christians? I'll talk to Jesus and then tell you who they are. That is my Christian duty. Now, let us sing 'Onward Christian Soldiers'."

"So now I'm supposed to be a political consultant?" God asked rhetorically.

Will and Wilma exited from one of the side doors.

"Denny said to go on without him," Wilma said. "After they call for those saved to come forward at the end, they also have a call to those who want to join either the army or the marine corps, and the recruiters take them away. Denny is planning on joining today and figures a recruiter will give him a ride home." Wilma sighed, "Will, I will never set foot in that place again. I need a shower!"

Will realized that he, too, was very upset. The service, the space, and Steady's words all felt so wrong. He slipped his arm around Wilma whose friendship went back to second grade. "They're such bigots and pretenders," he said. "What's your dad's take on all this?"

"He's...we've...talked about it a lot," Wilma said thoughtfully. "He was on the planning commission for the county when the deal for the New Word complex went through. The land on which this place was built was supposed to be used for a state park. The governor, however, sold it for a song to Steady in exchange for a substantial campaign contribution. The legislature granted a property tax exemption to Steady's corporation. The New Word private school gets vouchers under the new state plan, and the taxpayers are paying for electricity, sewers, and roads to this place. And, you won't believe it, but Steady got a sales tax deferral for ten years on all the businesses in the New Word complex. The taxpayers are getting screwed."

"Mom has also heard some additional dirt on Reverend Teddy from her sister in California. Steady pretends to be a big family values guy, but in California, he's been charged with bigamy. He has three wives, one in northern California, one in southern California, and one in Nevada. When they found out about each other, they launched a civil action against ol' Teddy. And the attorney general is following up with criminal prosecution. But Teddy has friends in high places, so who knows how it will turn out. I wish I hadn't come today."

"Three wives. That's certainly biblical," God remarked.

"Buy you an ice cream at the DQ?" Will asked, wanting to make Wilma feel better.

"Yes," Wilma said with a wan smile, "forget the shopping."

After he dropped Wilma off at home, Will asked God if he had any further thoughts about the visit to New Word. God was quick to answer.

"It makes me think I'll become an atheist."

Will laughed. "Just how can *you* become an atheist?"

"I'll just stop believing in myself," God said with a divine chortle. "But seriously, this whole experience raises the issue of how religion and money always seem to be close neighbors. Look at the cathedrals and statues of gold that are considered sacred."

"I haven't thought about that enough," Will responded, "but I suspect religion would not survive long if it was a money loser, at least not here, but whatever is going on in that place, it's not healthy."

Will pulled out of his reverie long enough to realize he was well past the New Word complex and on the interstate heading almost due west toward Dallas. He began to think about finding a place to stretch his legs.

As Will drove steadily westward, another drama had already begun in the Gulf of Mexico and the Canadian prairies. From the south, a large, swirling mass of warm wet air was moving rapidly north and a bit east, pushing inland. At the same time, from the north a cold front was dropping toward Oklahoma and north Texas.

At the National Weather Center in Dallas, John Carey, a weather analyst, looked up from his computer. "Oh shit," he said to no one in particular. "I've run the data five times, and it's always the same. An ugly convergence in the Dallas area, a mother of twisters." Then, as he realized he was talking to himself, he added another, "Crap" for emphasis.

He rose stiffly from his desk, took a last sip of cold coffee, and headed to the public notification office.

Let them deal with the bad news, he thought.

HAM

Will exited the freeway a few miles west of the Texas state line. He was already tired of driving in the heat. He had gotten up at four in the morning out of sheer excitement, and saying goodbye had taken longer than planned. The thought of a rest and maybe a nap in the shade appealed to him. He was in no big hurry, since his job did not start for another week.

After consulting his road atlas, he turned north toward Greenville, Texas. He definitely wanted to avoid the Dallas/Fort Worth congestion, and he was near a turnoff to Lake Tawakoni State Park.

After parking, he decided to leave most of his stash of cash—the $400 he had started out with—under the carpet behind the driver's seat. He put $100 in his wallet. Will felt more secure with this arrangement for the simple reason that he had a penchant for losing his wallet, and the small slit in the carpet where he tucked the money was virtually invisible.

"Good idea," God said. "You're much more likely to lose your wallet than your truck."

Will locked the truck and struck out on a trail. The sign promised a moderately rigorous walk of about 2.5 miles. Will was used to a lot of exercise. Besides digging in the gardens, he took off frequently for long rambles with his uncle or long runs with one of the dogs. At the moment, his knees felt tight from sitting.

The undergrowth along the lake was green, and there were enough cottonwood trees to provide shelter from the sun. Will completed part of the loop and then stopped to enjoy the lake.

Careful to avoid a patch of poison ivy, he sat on the edge of a cottonwood stump. It was too late in the day for fishermen, but powerboats and personal watercraft dotted the water. The faint smell of gasoline hung in the air along with the shouts of those at play. Will, like his uncle, was a nature lover, not someone who enjoyed churning across the water or the land on a gas-powered machine. In his rambles with Uncle John, they usually took along bird or plant guides so they could identify whatever species they came across.

The nearby poison ivy took Will's mind back to his home and one of his earliest conversations with God. He had been seven years old and sitting in his treehouse in a live oak that was plagued by poison ivy at the base. As he nestled atop his old sleeping bag, it occurred to him to ask after God's whereabouts.

"Where are you, God? Are you in heaven? Are you here?"

To his surprise, God answered. In fact, God seemed amused. "I'm here *and* I'm in heaven."

"How can that be?" Will asked while scratching at a poison ivy scab on his leg. "How can you be in two places at once?"

"Lots of things can be many places at once."

"Like what?"

"Like a bit of gossip or the color red," God responded and then departed.

"Oh." Will realized that God was going to let him figure it out.

When Will told Aunt Rita and Uncle John that God came into his head and talked sometimes, they did not object, although Will was naturally inclined to keep the content of his divine conversations to himself. Aunt Rita thought that God spoke through the Bible and had doubts that God was the great conversationalist Will found him to be. Uncle John probably had similar doubts, but he did not seem to think Will's God talk was harmful in any way. Will knew that both his aunt and uncle regarded him as a good boy, and they were proud of him.

"He loves all God's creatures," Will had overheard Uncle John remark. "He's a bit overly imaginative, but he is loving, trusting, and smart as a whip. Maybe too trusting, but I do love that boy." Aunt Rita added that of all the blessings in her life, Will was the best.

Of course, thinking of his aunt and uncle also reminded him of the hard times that had come. Wilma's dad was right. New Word church was just like Wal-Mart or Cabela's or any of those big chains. First, they made big promises about jobs and added business in exchange for big subsidies from the community. Then they asked for property tax relief or even sales tax relief or else they threatened to go elsewhere. Wilma's dad had noted that we all paid for their profits with our taxes, and all the little businesses contributed as well. In Will's community, the same amount of money was being spent, but more of it was going to the megachurch now.

Will felt his anger growing as he stood up and pitched a rock far out into the lake. These thoughts had intruded on his refuge, so he trudged on toward the parking lot.

Will was almost back to his truck when he saw the cat. It was a burly, orange, tomcat, and it did not move when he approached. Instead, it studied the ground and pounced on something in the grass. Will had seen cats catch mice before, and he never liked to watch them play with their prey. From his reading of natural history, he knew that Charles Darwin had also been troubled by nature's cruelties.

As Will approached, the cat tossed its prey into the air, and then, holding the wiggling victim in its mouth, glared at Will. The cat's prey was light colored, and it was too big to be a mouse. Maybe it was a baby rat.

Will picked up a dry branch and struck a nearby tree. The stick made a sharp crack as it broke. At the same time, he took a step toward the cat, which abandoned its prey and bounded into the taller grass along the lake. Will knelt down to see what the cat had dropped. Lying quietly in the grass was a blond hamster. Will had seen these little rodents at the pet store in Shreveport where they bought food for the assorted strays and adopted animals that lived at his aunt and uncle's house. He called them palomino hamsters and loved the way they filled their cheeks with food.

When he retrieved the small creature from the grass, Will noted that one of its back legs was hanging by a thread of skin. Otherwise the little animal seemed free of external wounds. The hamster's small dark eyes studied Will. He was pretty sure it had to be in shock. Seeing some rocks nearby, he thought momentarily of putting the small creature out of its misery, but that seemed too drastic.

Back in his truck, Will drove on toward Greenville and stopped at the first small animal clinic he saw. The attendant took the small bundle from Will, wrapped it in a clean towel, and told him the doctor would be right with him.

Dr. Charles, a fit fiftyish woman, appeared shortly. "You have two choices young man. You can let me stitch the wound where the leg was—of course the leg is lost—and give him some antibiotics, or I can put him out of his misery. We need to do something right away. What do you prefer?"

"How much would it cost to treat him?" Will asked, ever mindful of his limited supply of money. "And what are his chances?"

Dr. Charles studied the earnest young man. "For you and this little guy, how about twenty five dollars? If I treat him now and he hasn't lost too much blood, he has a good chance of recovery. He's in shock, but he's still strong. Missing a leg, especially a back leg, should not slow him down too much."

"Let's treat him," Will said as he wondered what in the world he would do with a hamster.

"I'll leave a little hole for the wound to drain, so don't worry unless it begins to look inflamed," Dr. Charles added as she headed toward the back room where she would treat the hamster.

Fifteen minutes later, Will was back in his truck with a package of hamster food and the small creature lying on the terry cloth towel the vet had provided. The day was sweltering; it was late afternoon by then, and Will was tired of the heat. He also doubted it was doing the hamster any good.

A few blocks down the highway was a "decent" motel, according to the vet's assistant. Will headed there, took a room, cranked up the air conditioner, and moved the hamster into the top drawer of the bureau beside the ubiquitous Gideon Bible. He cut down two plastic cups with his pocketknife and filled one with water and the other with hamster food. Then he lay on the bed and fell fast asleep.

He awoke a couple of hours later. The room was getting cold as the overworked air conditioner rattled in the window. The worst heat of the day was over. Will checked on the hamster; he was curled up just as he had left him. There was a small amount of blood on the towel, but the creature was not chewing on the stitches, something Dr. Charles had feared.

A barbecue house across the street advertised real Texas beef and Lone Star beer. After his nap, Will felt more like breakfast. Further down the road was a pancake house, which served him a good omelet. Back in the room, he did not bother to disturb the hamster. Will knew the creature was weak and feared that the little guy might not make it through the night.

Feeling a bit at loose ends, Will considered calling his aunt and uncle. They would have just finished dinner and be sitting on the porch probably talking about him and wondering how he was doing. Aunt Rita had given him a cell phone before he left, but something inside him told him to wait before calling home. He was lonely, and that was not the best time to call.

In a moment of growing homesickness, he even thought about turning around and driving home, but that would be a betrayal of all his enthusiasm for being on his own.

The motel room also contributed to his sense of isolation. It smelled of stale smoke and the window opened only a crack. He tried to engage God in a conversation, but God was elsewhere.

Television had never been a serious temptation for Will, but he turned on the room's TV anyway. The weather report was just wrapping up. There was a possibility of severe thunderstorms in the Dallas/Fort Worth area the following day. Then, as if to torment him further, in the final segment the news team took their audience on a tour of the New Word church and its facilities. Will switched channels. An advertisement informed him of a new scent for men that would cause him to be assaulted on the street by multitudes of beautiful women.

I'll bet you can get it cheap at the New Word drug store, Will thought as he turned off the TV.

Finally—he could not wait any longer—he peeked fearfully into the drawer. At first, he thought the hamster was dead, but then he saw the creature's little chest rise and fall. The hamster food was untouched, as was the water.

A long shower washed away the stress of the day and the sticky feeling of driving in the east Texas heat. Will turned back the bedspread and sank onto the Bounce-scented sheets. Their smell made his eyes water, but he was too tired to care. A catalogue of fishing lures in his duffel caught his eye, but as he reached for it, a faint grinding noise distracted him. At first, he thought something was wrong with the air conditioner, but then he realized the sound was coming from the top drawer.

Will crept over to it and looked inside. The food and water remained untouched, but the hamster's two black, beady eyes looked up at him. It was seated, standing—with hamsters, it was hard to tell—near the back of the Gideon Bible. The hamster had made significant progress in eating the glue that bound its pages. As Will watched, the little guy returned to work with atheistic enthusiasm.

"Hi Ham," Will said, realizing he had just christened his traveling companion. He could not resist asking, "Ham, are you an atheist?"

Ham made no reply as he attacked a new spot on the binding, but God released an involuntary "Huh!" God rarely did that. Usually, he announced when he was in Will's mind and wanted to talk. But he was either bored or surprised by Will's question.

"Well," Will said, "Ham doesn't believe in you. So, does that make him an atheist?"

"While I concede that Ham is putting a major hurt on that book—it isn't a very good edition in any case—he is certainly not an atheist. True, Ham doesn't believe in me, but neither does he believe in the Easter Bunny. In fact, he doesn't even believe that he himself exists. The reason is simple: Ham does not have any beliefs whatsoever."

"So?" Will was pretty sure where this was going, but he wanted God to make his point.

"To not believe in something is ambiguous. In one sense, one might not believe in whales, because one does not have any beliefs about anything. In a second sense, one might not believe in whales, because one has the belief that whales do not exist. An atheist has a belief, namely, the belief that God does not exist."

Will nodded. "So to be an atheist one must hold beliefs, and among those beliefs must be the belief that God does not exist. Then maybe Ham is an agnostic." Will was unwilling to give in completely. "An agnostic is someone who neither believes in God nor disbelieves in God, and since Ham has no beliefs, he neither believes in God nor disbelieves in God, so he must be an agnostic."

"You're testing me," God grumbled. "An agnostic is someone who believes there is no compelling evidence or reason either way or that the evidence or reasons for and against the existence of God is equally balanced."

"Does an agnostic have to believe that he has no belief either way?" Will asked innocently. "Does someone have to be aware of his or her agnosticism?"

"Yes."

"Are there no agnostics who do not know they are agnostics or who do not believe they have no beliefs one way or the other? Can there be unconscious agnostics? If so, then Ham is an unconscious agnostic."

Will felt triumphant. He almost never won arguments with God.

"No," God returned to the offensive. "An agnostic, like an atheist, must be capable of believing or not believing. And an agnostic must believe something about the evidence. A person who is in a vegetative state does not have beliefs, but that does not make that person an agnostic. Ham lacks the capacity for belief."

Will smiled to himself. He usually enjoyed talking to God, and this conversation certainly picked up the evening. He thought of another wrinkle in the discussion. "Would someone who claimed not to know if there was a God but believed in God anyway be a believer or an agnostic? It would seem that he would be agnostic, because he did not know that God existed, but he would be a believer because of his belief in God. One can believe in things that one does not know, after all."

At that point Will had a vision of God downing four Aspirin with a God-sized glass of water.

"If you believe in God, then you are a theist even if you have doubts or don't think the evidence is conclusive," God replied. "However, you make a useful distinction between knowing and believing. And here I will make a concession to you. We should define an atheist as someone who knows that God does not exist or believes that it is probable that God does not exist and an agnostic as someone who does not claim to know either way—or claims to know that she does not know—because either there is no evidence or the evidence for and against is equally balanced. If this is right, then, unlike the theist, the atheist or agnostic must have specific beliefs about the nature of the evidence for God's existence. But we are a long way from home here. The point is that you must be *capable* of belief in order to claim to know anything, even to know that you do not know. You cannot be classified as an atheist, an agnostic, or a theist if you don't have the capacity for belief. So, can we just agree that Ham is a hamster, not an atheist hamster or an agnostic hamster, just a hamster with a craving for glue?"

"I yield," Will said. "I will go further and agree that we need to amend our concept of an atheist as someone who believes God does not exist, because the evidence points against it, whereas an agnostic is someone who believes no evidence exists that can tip the matter one way or another."

Will also realized that he was a theist simply because he believed in God, but he had no real grasp of any of the reasons why. Furthermore, he had no real understanding of why one might be tempted by atheism. He worshiped the God that his aunt and uncle worshiped. That was automatic. He had not really examined these questions; he had simply grown up with two steadfast believers. He promised himself sleepily that he would revisit these questions sometime later that summer. For the moment, he was quite content with his God.

Will felt God withdraw from his mind. As he left, Will felt the equivalent of a divine slap on the back.

"I knew you were lonely tonight, Will. Sleep well."

As Will slept, the faint grinding noise continued unabated.

HARRY AND REV

Harry Grime sat nervously on the corner of 6th Avenue and Marginal Way, which marked the center of a wealthy suburb in Serenity, Texas. Looking out of place in this oasis of affluence, he sat at the wheel of a ten-year-old, beige, two-door Mazda sedan. Harry stared straight ahead toward an elegant brick home three houses away. The odor of his cheap cologne seeped into every corner of the car's interior.

Harry straightened his beret and studied his boots. They were clean and shiny, and his uniform was newly pressed. Rev had insisted that he take his uniform to a professional cleaner. The cleaner had removed the spaghetti stains and put a little starch into the green and black camouflage suit. It looked better than new, Harry thought. Although Harry was short—he stood only about five foot four—with his dark hair in a buzz cut and his restored uniform, he thought he looked like a real military officer, especially when he wore his dark glasses.

Rev, on whom Harry was waiting anxiously, was Reverend Oliver Newton, a.k.a. Smooth Sam Willingham. They had met at the Western Texas House of Correction or "WTHC," as its graduates like to call it. At WTHC, Rev had occupied the cell next to Harry's. Harry's cellmate was a large inmate named "Blink." Rev seemed to be everything Blink was not: articulate, charismatic, and a successful career criminal. Blink rarely talked, and rumor was that he could be violent, although no one had ever witnessed it. Harry got on well with Blink, whose mere presence protected him from predatory guards and inmates. But Rev was Harry's mentor, the person Harry sought to emulate.

Harry needed a mentor. A lifetime of attempted criminal activity had simply introduced him to the wide variety of jails and prisons available to those easily caught. Even as a child Harry had been included in shoplifting trips, because he provided an easy diversion for the police or store security. While the others left with various items, Harry could be counted on to lead the police on a short and successful chase. Of course, those who took Harry along told him nothing, not even their real names.

He was also a failure as a car thief. He stole cars that had little market value, and when he did try for a Beamer, he got caught when he made an illegal left turn. Harry was a poor driver. That's how he came to be housed next to Smooth Sam who, at the age of fifty-eight, was doing only his second short prison term for selling fake prescription insurance to desperate, elderly citizens—desperate because Texas had cut so much from its medical programs. He had told them that his prescription drug card, TEXPHARM, was good at every pharmacy in Texas and twenty-three other states. In fact, the drug card was useless under any insurance program, private or public, but by the time the seniors found out, Smooth Sam was long gone.

Rev emerged from the brick house, which boasted immaculate, professional landscaping and a slate front walk, approached the car, and slid into the passenger seat. He noticed the odor of Harry's cologne immediately.

"Jesus, Harry, you stink!"

"Whatchamean?"

Rev took Harry's water bottle from between the seats, doused his hanky in water, and wiped Harry's face vigorously. "It's that damn cologne. Where did you get it?"

"I stole it from Valarie." Harry was hurt. He had taken the bottle from his girlfriend's dresser at the same time as he stole some of her loose change. He liked the cologne; it reminded him of Valarie. Besides, the incredible flowery odor smelled nothing like the inside of a prison.

Rev, always well dressed and orderly, got out and deposited his wet hanky in a trash container. "That's the best we can do for now," he said regretfully as he climbed back in the car. He could not help but wonder what had possessed him to take on Harry as an accomplice. "Let's go have coffee someplace, do a little rehearsing, and then look for a place that will allow us to test drive a Hummer."

As Harry started the Mazda and headed out of the plush neighborhood,

Rev clutched the door handle. "Pay attention to your driving."

"How did it go?" Harry asked.

"It was smooth, very smooth." Rev's ruddy complexion fairly glowed with self-satisfaction. "He is definitely a ready-to-believe." A ready-to-believe was what Rev called a mark who was hooked. "I want to give him some time to think it over."

When it came to conning, Rev had just the right amount of patience; he never pushed a mark too hard. Rev had begun to work out his latest con while in prison. In a moment of boredom, he attended a meeting of "the Corinthians," a group of inmates who had found religion since being incarcerated. The Corinthians were better known among the inmates as "Players for Parole." It was there that Rev first got to know his neighbors Harry and Blink. Harry was there to flesh out his case for parole, and Blink was there because Harry was there. But over the course of a few meetings, Rev encountered other prisoners who had become true believers, and it was from his observation of these conversions that a new "game" was born.

Rev realized that many prisoners were attracted to the book of Revelation for a couple of reasons. The first was the level of violence and mayhem described in its pages. The idea of hail and fire, a sea of blood, falling stars, all leading to massive torment and death had their appeal, especially to the socially pathological, whose personal apocalyptic visions needed to be fed. One prisoner, for example, read and reread the parts about the angels' trumpets blowing and how the third trumpet killed a third of the animals in the sea and destroyed a third of the ships. That prisoner had a history of killing animals before he killed two men in a bar fight. Violent literature was generally denied a place in the prison library, but the Bible was considered to have redemptive qualities.

The second came from the promise at the end of Revelation that the Lamb was coming soon, which gave a sense of urgency to those whose lives were weighed down with the repetitious, spirit-killing ennui of incarceration. What impressed Rev, however, was the sheer power of belief of those in the group who seemed to be genuinely caught up in the tale. Since Rev did not find a great difference between the fears and needs of those inside prison and those outside, he realized the potential for raising money by exploiting such beliefs.

Once out of prison, Rev changed his name, bought an appropriate wardrobe, and became a congregant in several churches in small and large Texas communities. He also became an active volunteer in every charity or program that would bring him into contact with wealthy churchgoers. His seemingly selfless activity ingratiated him to the local pastors and the lonely parishioners who were attracted by his pleasant manner and sandy-haired good looks.

It was at one of these events, a church supper in Dallas, where he met his current mark, Seymour Smythe. Seymour was a banker who lived in Serenity near the compound Rev had rented in order to set up his mock militia. Seymour also owned a condominium in Dallas. Seymour's many banks and businesses were spread across the northern part of the state and up into Oklahoma. Seymour made his money buying up land from drought-devastated farmers and selling it to developers of shopping centers and corporate warehouses. When downtown businesses went bankrupt because of the new malls, he bought up the downtown buildings and applied for federal renewal grants. After some healthy contributions to local congressmen, he received government grants to rebuild the downtowns, much of which he pocketed. Sometimes these government-backed urban renewals actually reversed the process and left the malls gasping for customers.

Seymour's much younger wife—he had divorced his first wife and left her penniless after he made his first million—had disappeared. Seymour worshiped his child bride and was convinced she had been taken to heaven. He even had a dream in which two angels carried her aloft in her chaise lounge. (She had spent most of her time by the pool reading graphic novels.) In truth, Rev happened to know she had run off with the pool maintenance man, a handsome college dropout from Galveston. But Seymour believed that his lovely wife had been taken to heaven during an early Rapture. He, on the other hand, being unworthy, had been left behind to face the Tribulation. At that point, he decided he needed to upgrade his standing with the Lord. The Reverend Oliver Newton was there to oblige his deepest religious desires.

Harry and Rev arrived at Kitty's Coffee Corral, where they slid into a back booth well away from the other customers, of which there was only one, who was up front talking to Kitty.

"Harry," Rev said, still hoping to make Harry a more knowledgeable accomplice, "do you remember much from those Bible study classes in prison?"

Harry thought hard for several minutes. "Well, I...first, there was the Garden of Edam."

"Eden," Rev interjected. "Edam is a cheese."

"Yeah, that's what I meant." Skipping a great deal of history, Harry added, "Then there was, like, a time of contest between good and evil, a rupture when the good people are saved and taken to heaven. There are lots of bad people left over, especially in government. Then..." Harry was at a loss for words.

"Rapture," Rev supplied.

"Yeah," Harry said. "Then...we fight the bad people."

"Yes. And what is that time called?"

"The Titillation," Harry responded promptly.

Rev sighed. "Not quite. Tribulation. And you are a tribulation trooper in the Tribulation Army trained to fight the bad people during the seven years' war."

"Whatever," Harry said. He did not really care about this stuff now that he was on parole. "Then Jesus comes and snuffs all the bad people, and we go to heaven." Harry grinned as he wrapped up the end of history.

Rev leaned across the table. "Look, Harry, this con depends on our looking like we are a military force—disciplined, devout, and ready to battle the Antichrist and his minions. I need you to do just what you're doing, being a good soldier. And we need to make the others look like soldiers as well. So, be an example." Privately, the Rev thought it was unlikely his ragtag band could ever pass muster.

"Jesus, Rev..." Harry said, unaware of the message Rev was trying to send.

"Quit saying that, Harry. Tribulation troopers don't take the Lord's name in vain." Rev wondered often about his ability to succeed with such a flawed instrument.

"If we're soldiers, why can't we have real guns?"

"Because we're felons on parole," Rev said for the hundredth time.

Rev's cell phone rang. He talked for a few moments. He concluded the conversation with, "We'll be there promptly at fifteen hundred hours."

As he closed his phone, he turned to Harry, who looked puzzled. "Now, let's go pick up that Hummer." Rev rose from the booth.

Harry had considerable trouble exiting the booth, first, because he was trying to figure out what time 1500 was, and second, his Leatherman was caught in a tear in the plastic fabric. Harry always wore his Leatherman and his dark glasses. In his mind, they made him look more like a real soldier, especially considering he wasn't carrying a gun.

At three o'clock sharp, Harry and Rev arrived on Seymour Smythe's street in a borrowed, black Hummer. The Hummer salesman sat in the back seat. In hopes of a sale, he had cheerfully put on a beret like Harry's and a camouflage shirt. The two "soldiers" made the Hummer appear military.

As Rev got out, he noted that Seymour was peeking out of his window. "Keep the air conditioning running. I may be awhile, and stay at the wheel," he remarked as he headed toward the front door.

Harry remained silent, staring straight ahead, as instructed. The Hummer salesman curled up with an old copy of *Car and Driver*.

At the door, Seymour, pale and paunchy, greeted Rev. His faded blue eyes were questioning. Rev knew he still had doubts about this investment, doubts he was there to dispel.

"Hello, Mr. Smythe." Rev's tone was both kind and somewhat conspiratorial, suggesting that they were going to be comrades in arms.

Seated in Seymour's library with coffee in one hand, Rev waited for his mark to express his doubts. They were not long in coming. Seymour's eyes narrowed, and he took on a cunning look. Rev knew that where money was involved, Seymour was no fool.

"What makes you think that now is the time to form your Tribulation Army?" Seymour asked as he sat back and sipped coffee, his eyes never leaving Rev's face.

Rev knew he had to find the right words and display the correct level of confidence. It was to his advantage that he knew some of Seymour's theological convictions. Most importantly, he did not intend to contradict Seymour if he could help it. While Rev was no Bible scholar, he had read enough that he knew the book of Revelation could be taken to mean anything.

He began carefully. "I don't pretend to know God's plan, or to know the actual dates of the critical periods—the Rapture, the Tribulation, Armageddon, and the Millennium." Rev did not want to repeat the mistake of the Millerites (and many other millennialists) who gathered to welcome the end of the world on October 22, 1840, only to discover, to their great disappointment, that the world clunked on as usual.

Seymour showed some annoyance at this cautious beginning, so Rev dove a little deeper, grasping for the right apocalyptic vision. "Of course, we have been approaching the end of time since the beginning." That seemed safe enough. "The little things, the subtle things promoted by the Antichrist, have been gathering momentum. The presidency of Bill Clinton, the nine eleven attacks, the destruction of Katrina, the persecution of Christians in the United States and overseas, the gay marriage movement, the earthquakes, the growing strength of the United Nations and the World Trade Organization, the growth and power of the federal government..."

Seymour's little eyes glittered; Rev knew he had hit a target somewhere in his list.

"America is special. We are a Christian nation. That is why we were attacked on September eleventh, two thousand and one. Four years ago God gave us a glorious sign, fire from the heavens to warn us that he was fed up with our secular humanism, our teaching of evolution, and our tolerance of false gods. I call that disaster the 'Wake Up America Event'. It demonstrated God's wrath clearly. It is time to prepare."

At that point, Rev, who was running out of things to say, noted that Seymour was nodding vigorously and mouthing the word "Amen." Rev did not buy this version of events, but he was on a roll. He decided to wrap things up. "The trumpets are sounding, and the visions are clear enough even to the theologically blind."

"Exactly!" Seymour shouted, jumping out of his chair. "I've been saying that for years." Sitting down again, he slurped his coffee noisily and then refilled his cup. "We Christians must take control and spread the word to all corners. The souls who have been slaughtered for believing the word of God demand revenge."

Seymour was referring to Revelation 6:10. Then he jumped to Matthew 28:19. "'Go and make disciples of all nations.' We must support Israel against the infidels and pagans. Jerusalem will be restored." Seymour slid into Zechariah 8:8, "'I will bring them to live in Jerusalem. They shall be my people and I will be their God.' Surely Gog moves against Israel."

Seymour wandered off into an Ezekielian daze, and then he simply froze. Rev had to wonder at the sanity of his mark. *Never try to con a nut* was one of his guiding principles. Was he violating it here? And who was Gog?

Rev was not going to trade biblical passages with Seymour, first because he did not know enough, and second, because he feared misusing it according to Seymour's individual canon. Instead, he stuck to current events, mentioning the red horse of war and people slaughtering one another, the black horse of famine and the starvation in Africa, and then he ended with the pestilence of AIDS, which he suggested was transmitted to humans because of God's anger against promiscuity. Finally, pulling out his ace, he claimed to agree with Seymour that the Rapture had actually begun and that a few good people were already missing. Rev thought of this view as the "trickle up" theory of Rapture.

Rev was careful to explain that his Tribulation Army was not built from those who were freest of sin. "I use those who have lost their way and found it again. These soldiers, I believe, have been left behind to test their strength in the time of Tribulation. 'Their transgressions shall be forgotten.'" Rev hoped he had caught the spirit of at least one passage from Ezekiel.

Seymour did not move or respond for a long time. He still seemed to be lost. Finally, he roused himself as if he had made his decision. "You are wise to choose your army from those who have wandered from the path," he said. With that, he produced a check for $25,000 from his suit coat pocket. "Spend this well, and you will see more. I expect to visit your compound in two to three weeks. I want to hear more about your concrete plans and to see the merit of your army."

Rev pocketed the check calmly. He knew that once a mark had committed money, it was easier to talk him into further investments. "We thank you for helping us do the Lord's work," Rev said, oozing sincerity. "I do not intend to fail you or our Lord."

With that, he produced a small, silver pin that featured the letters "T" and "A" bundled together. He had found them at a second-hand store near the Texas Academy. Harry wore one on his beret. Rev handed the pin to Seymour. "Please wear this in honor of our faith, but reveal nothing to anyone unless I have checked the person out already. The Tribulation Army, at this point, must remain a secret army until we are stronger. The enemies of the Lord are everywhere."

Seymour nodded affirmatively.

Back in the Hummer, Rev told Harry to return to the dealership. He asked the salesman to be on the lookout for second-hand Hummers, preferably with little body damage, which Harry almost delivered to the present vehicle by just missing a bicycle rack on the curb.

The check was cashed easily at one of Seymour's banks. Then Rev had the money transferred to his Bermuda account.

Shortly thereafter, Harry and Rev approached a large, dust-covered sign that read, "Derelicts R Us: Pre-owned Car Parts." The sign sat just off Interstate 27 south of Amarillo. Behind the sign was an eight-foot cyclone fence topped with barbed wire. Tumbleweeds surrounded the perimeter fence. An equally tall gate stood wide open, leading into a few acres of dust, thistles, and every other weed that could survive in the arid conditions of west Texas. Beyond the fence lay even more sparsely-planted land. An emaciated cow watched disinterestedly as Rev's car pulled up to a double-wide trailer. Originally grey, it was turning a bright pink color, thanks to the efforts of Blink, who wielded a roller and brush. Two similar trailers sat at odd angles beyond the soon-to-be pink trailer. One was a faded pea green and the other a kind of brown algae color. An old Dodge Power Wagon sat alone in the weeds. Just behind all of the trailers stood two bright orange portable toilets, whose vivid color clashed seriously with the new pink.

Rev stepped out of the car and groaned. He should have seen Seymour's visit coming. "Harry, we have a lot of work to do and only a short time to do it."

Harry looked perplexed. It was an expression that Rev recognized well. Harry always look perplexed when Rev made a general statement, such as, "There is work to be done." Harry did much better if Rev said something like, "Take the barrel and put it right here," while standing on the spot.

Blink came over to greet Harry, giving him a manly slap on the back that left a pink stain on the back of Harry's crisp uniform.

Rev walked over to a pair of picnic tables and picked up a small bullhorn. "We have Kentucky Fried Chicken for dinner," he announced, an unnecessary act that only produced one more "soldier," Curt, who emerged from one of the portables. Harry broke out bottles of beer, iced tea, and pop.

Rev had finished his second piece of chicken when he noticed that one member of his "army" was missing. "Where's Chris?" he asked.

Chris was Rev's technical wizard. A hacker by profession, Chris had a knack for keeping generators, old cars, abandoned computers, and anything that was mechanical or electrical running. Rev wanted to know if his computer had been freed of a nasty virus that had infected it. He was afraid to turn it on without Chris's permission.

"He's out behind the last trailer," someone said.

Rev headed in that direction. As he walked, he noted the miserable condition of the compound. Small tracks in the weeds indicated trails that people walked, but it needed a thorough cleaning and reorganizing. He was already drawing up the orders in his head when he caught a whiff of the portable toilets, another item that needed to be cleaned up by the following week. Finally, he passed the last trailer house, but there was no sign of Chris.

Just as he was about to turn and leave, he saw a figure rise up out of the weeds. Actually, what arose from the weeds were two skinny arms. Rev approached the figure, who was kneeling with his back to the setting sun. A small washing basin rested on the ground beside him.

"There is no God but Allah, and Mohammed is His prophet," the figure intoned.

Rev approached Chris cautiously. "Chris, I need to talk to you."

"Burn in hell, infidel," Chris snapped, "I'm praying." Chris, who was costumed in a headcloth and false beard, glared angrily. Then his countenance changed suddenly. "But Allah is also merciful. What can I do for you?"

Rev shook his head. "I just want to know if the computer is safe to turn on."

"Absolutely," Chris said and then turned his back on Rev and resumed his prayer. "There is no God but Allah, and Mohammed is His prophet. There is no God but Allah, and Mohammed is His prophet. There is no God but Allah, and Mohammed is His prophet...."

Rev found he was walking back to his office in rhythm to Chris's cadence. Chris was an odd duck; Rev was not certain he was sane. Sometimes he was a horse possessed of the spirit of Guede, which made him frighteningly silent and mysterious. Fortunately, Chris was not possessed of his voodoo more than once a month. Talk about your identity crisis.

A well-meaning prison pastor had tried to convince Chris that it was prudent for him to believe in Jesus as his Savior. He had argued with Chris over religion for several weeks. Finally, he observed that even if we cannot prove that the Christian God exists or that God is more probable than any other god, we can at least know that either God exists or does not. If God exists and you believe in God, then you have everything (heaven) to gain and nothing to lose. If God exists and you do not believe in God, then you have everything (hell) to lose and nothing to gain.

Chris took this argument to heart, but after a brief period of trying to be a good Christian, he realized that the pastor's Jesus-focused personal god was a very different god from the Hebrew Bible's wrathful god, who was very different from the Church-oriented Catholic god, all of whom were most unlike the Voodoo spirit gods or the absolute Brahman of Advaita Vedanta Hinduism. Given this realization, and the realization that he could not prove one god more probable than another and that different gods rewarded different, incompatible lifestyles, Chris decided it was prudent not to believe in just one god. Instead, he tried to apply the pragmatic argument to every god. Unwilling to leave any divinity un-worshipped, Chris began a series of short-term religious alliances. On certain days of the month, he was a Pentecostal, and other days, Catholic. Sometimes he would sit meditatively contemplating Brahman. Other times he would pursue ancestor worship or go into a frenzy of dancing and speaking like a voodoo spirit. On each occasion, his practice of the religion seemed genuine and total.

At the same time—as a conman Rev knew a bit about how belief systems worked—Rev knew that Chris could not, even serially, hold such a diverse set of beliefs, which meant that Chris was probably crazy. However, in the interludes between religious enthusiasms, Chris was an amazing technician. The doors and windows on the trailers opened smoothly now. The Mazda ran better than new, and Rev's old computer just kept going. Yes, Chris was an asset, although Rev worried about his ability to maintain the pace, since the holy days when Chris was unavailable were beginning to pile up. And at the moment, Rev needed Chris more than ever.

He arrived at his trailer, went inside, and turned on his computer. While it was warming up, he opened the fridge and took out a beer. He faced a long night of planning what needed to be done to get the camp ready for Seymour's visit.

Seven in the morning found the entire cadre of Tribulation Troopers gathered around the picnic tables eating corn flakes. Rev's eyes swept over the group. In addition to himself, there was Chris, Blink, Harry, and Curt, all graduates from WTHC. *Too few*, Rev thought. With luck, he might be able to pick up a few more graduates to help out, but they never stayed.

Curt sat apart from the others. No one liked Curt, who returned the feeling. Of all those present, Curt was the one Rev thought might be dangerous. Curt was a convicted murderer who had gotten out of prison because the state of Texas had assigned a narcoleptic attorney to defend him at his trial. His prison rep was that he had no moral compunctions about doing anything to anyone, so everyone left him alone. Rev also suspected that Curt either had guns on the property—he had never found them—or that he had access to guns. Rev decided to keep a close eye on him.

As he got set to address the men, Rev realized he was engaged in a double con. First, there was Seymour Smythe. But Rev was also trying to fool the wider religious public. He wanted the law to leave him alone, he wanted access to the local churches, and he wanted to take money from those fools who believed his ruse. It occurred to him that just taking the $25,000 and leaving was probably the wisest course. But his pride kept him in the game. In fact, he was headed east to the Dallas area again soon to look for new marks—and maybe some cheap labor—at a Christian lifestyle fair.

CINDY

Cindy Norton sang loud in slightly accented Spanish. The song was "*Perfidia*" ("Wicked Woman"). She remembered the melody, and the Spanish language radio reminded her of the lyrics, although she could hardly hear the radio or herself above the grinding, popping, and rattling of her Volkswagen Rabbit. Her radio picked up only one station.

The day was cool for east Texas, for which she was thankful. She was alarmed, however, by the fact that the unseasonably cool temperature was due to the large, dark—indeed black—cloud mass that was gaining on her from the south. She pushed the Rabbit to its max, fifty-five miles an hour, which increased the noise and the engine's tendency to miss. Ending the day north of Dallas was her goal. News of her father's ill health had precipitated quitting her job and this flight home. Old feelings and memories slithered unwelcome into her mind as she fought fatigue and drove doggedly on.

What a change of circumstances she had endured over the past three years. Here she was—a kid from Ohio, an A-student, a high school homecoming queen, and, she reminded herself, a rebellious daughter—now driving from Mexico to Ohio. In Mexico, she had been an assistant manager at La Inspiracion, a Gulf Coast resort that catered to wealthy writers and artists. Indeed, she had effectively run the business for the past year and a half, since the manager spent all his time hobnobbing with the distinguished artists who came to work, play, and drink. It had been a good job and well suited to her quick mind, integrity, and easy grasp of Spanish. The absentee owners of the resort loved her and expressed appreciation for her proficiency. In spite of their rare visits to the facility, they knew her value and planned to make her manager within the year. Now that was history.

Mexico was not at all like Ohio, a fact for which Cindy was eternally grateful. She had grown up as Cynthia Norton in Oldstown, Ohio, a conservative community that had proudly cast 132 percent of its votes for George W. Bush in 2004. At that time, Cindy, who was still in high school, had irritated her family by her dedicated effort to see John Kerry elected president. Her mother disliked Kerry, because, as she said often, "I don't trust a smart man." Cindy smiled as she recalled that her mother never said this in front of her father.

Cindy's father was an extremely conservative pastor of a local evangelical church, which was losing membership due largely to a poor economy that had driven people out of the area. It was a stressful position with constant concerns about the budget and declining membership. Cindy had not helped the situation by attending the Unitarian Church and working in their food bank. According to her father, Unitarians were atheists.

Cindy's total alienation from her family came during her senior year. Her high school boyfriend, Jack Williams, was the star quarterback on the football team. He became fervently religious at one of Coach Winsome's pre-game chapels. The coach had brought in a charismatic young youth minister whose performance so impacted Jack that he came away ready to dedicate his life to Jesus. Jack also started going on a bit about how he expected to be swept up to heaven anytime now, but hopefully not until after the conference championship. Cindy had serious doubts about the likelihood of that event.

One passionate night in the spring of her senior year, she let Jack seduce her, something he had been trying persistently and clumsily to do since their first date. The whole delightful experience might have made her senior year, except that the backup quarterback, to whom Jack had boasted of his tryst, ratted them out in the spring. Word spread quickly throughout the community. In hindsight, Cindy thought her behavior had been childish and driven by a deeply adolescent curiosity about sex—something that was never discussed in her home.

The revelation of their contumacious behavior had devastating results, especially for Cindy. The patriarchal, conservative community of Oldstown reserved its real condemnation for the one who obviously corrupted "that fine young man." The other girls at school called Cindy a slut, as did her father, who felt she had humiliated him publicly. He declared her "dead" to him and refused to speak to her. The day he found out about her liaison, he attacked her and tried to throw her out of the house. Only her mother's intervention stopped his physical assault and allowed her to stay in her room until graduation.

At the end of the year Jack received a full athletic scholarship to the University of Florida. Cindy, based on her excellent academic record, received a small scholarship—not nearly enough to cover her expenses—to Ohio State. Of course, she could expect no help from her family. Cindy left Oldstown on the night of graduation, took a bus to Mexico, found a job at La Inspiracion, and worked her way from cleaning maid to assistant manager. Until recently, she had had no communication from her family, although she checked in regularly and let her mother know where she could be reached.

Now her father was seriously ill, heart attack. She needed to get home as soon as possible. The car that she had purchased from Reliable Ralph's was barely running, and her finances had taken a loss when the manager, out of spite, had refused to pay the salary she was owed, because she had to leave suddenly and he might actually have to work. Even though her father had treated her horribly, she wanted to be home to support her mother. A lot of forgiveness, especially toward her mother, had grown in her as the ugly memories of her high school days faded.

As Cindy raced northeast, Will was just checking out of the motel. Ham was relatively perky that first morning. Will realized he had to get a cage if Ham was to accompany him; he could hardly be allowed to run around in the truck's cab. The local pet store did not open until ten, so Will ate breakfast, wrote a letter to his aunt and uncle, and debated as to whether he should leave some of his precious money for the thoroughly decimated Gideon Bible he had secreted under the driver's seat. He was going to leave ten dollars until God spoke up.

"These bibles are donated, and it's a crummy edition in any case."

By late morning he was ready to travel west. Ham was ensconced happily in his cage, which was equipped with a water bottle, an exercise wheel, a dish of hamster food, and the remains of the Gideon Bible.

"Who says the good book doesn't have the power to heal?" God quipped.

Ham was feeling well enough that he even used his three legs to turn the exercise wheel.

Will charted his route going west; he hoped to avoid the freeway with its heavy traffic and giant trucks. The weather did not look promising, but Will was committed to getting to the theme park on time.

As Will skirted Dallas, the sky to the north looked reasonably clear. He had always enjoyed driving through the countryside. Cities made him uncomfortable. He was just starting to emerge to the west beyond the Dallas area when the wind picked up enough to buffet the S-10. The sky continued to darken. At that point, Will had no choice but to keep going, since the storm was developing all around him.

Less than a mile down the road, he realized he had made a mistake as darkness seized him, and a twister came down practically in front of him. He glimpsed swirling debris just before veering into the shallow ditch beside the highway.

"Get as low as you can!" God shouted.

Will turned off the engine, and started to open the door so he could lie down in the ditch when something struck him hard on the left temple. He was never able to recall just what happened over the next few minutes.

Cindy never saw the tornado that picked up her VW. Part of her rear-view mirror was missing, and she was focused on finding the road with only one headlight. Being airborne and upside down in a compact car over the Lone Star State is a rare experience, and Cindy could just as well have skipped it in her lifetime. She thought briefly that maybe her high school lover was right and the Rapture was upon her, until she realized that God would never want a junker like her car. Then the tornado did one of those strange things that twisters do: it set her down as gently as a butterfly on a willow. Except for being upside down, missing the driver's door, and having her suitcase resting against her back, all seemed well.

Cindy looked down and saw that her car was situated upside down on top of the extended cab of a small pickup. A young man lay on the ground beside the truck. He had some blood on his forehead, and he was moving a little.

"Hey, you!" Cindy shouted over the heavy rain that came in the wake of the tornado. "Are you okay?"

Her question got no response.

Will's head hurt, and his vision was lousy. He felt a bruise above his eyebrow and considerable nausea. And there was a voice from somewhere, above him. He thought it might be an angel, but angels didn't drive Rabbits and hang upside down struggling with a suitcase pressing on their backs.

"Could you give me a hand?" the angel asked as she wiggled violently. "I can't get out of this damned seatbelt."

Will's vision began to clear as the rain washed his face. "Just a moment, I'm not certain I can stand." He was sure his legs would not support him as he tried to gather them under himself.

The angel continued to flail about. Will managed to push clear of the door of the S-10 and was still trying to get to his feet when the seatbelt came loose, and the angel shot out of the car and landed right on top of him.

"Oops!"

Stunned, Will and the angel lay entangled on the ground for a few minutes. Then the angel spoke in a voice far too perky for Will's state of mind.

"Hi, I'm Cindy."

"Will," he managed to croak.

"Are we lucky or what?"

Will didn't feel so lucky at the moment. The rain was letting up, and the storm clouds had moved off to the northeast. Will knew that things were not quite right, but he had no idea what to do about it. His head hurt horribly, and his new acquaintance, Cindy, was scurrying about far too quickly. He glanced around but could not figure out where he was.

Cindy realized that Will could not focus, because he was disoriented. She also recognized that the Rabbit was in bad shape—the left rear wheel, a bumper, and a door were missing. The S-10 was relatively undamaged though, except for a slight concavity in the roof.

Cindy helped Will to stand and half dragged him around to the passenger side of the pickup. The possibility that the Rabbit might slide off onto them was a worry; it was tilting that way. Despite the fact he was a big man, Cindy managed to get him into the passenger seat, after putting the little rodent and his cage behind the seats. Then she closed the door, came around to the driver's side, threw her bag into the bed of the pickup, and started the engine. Taking a deep breath, she pulled the S-10 onto the freeway, hoping that the momentum would dislodge the Rabbit, which it did, leaving the little car to crash into the ditch behind them.

"We need to have a doctor check you out," Cindy said as she headed east toward what she hoped was the nearest hospital.

The emergency care clinic they found was busy with other storm casualties, but Will's head injury got them a nurse, who examined Will, asked him a bunch of questions, and then declared he had a serious concussion and needed to rest, not sleep, but rest. A couple of butterfly bandages and a $75 fee later, they were registered at a Motel 8, having split the cost. The motel was filled with storm refugees.

By early afternoon Will, Cindy, and Ham were relaxing in air-conditioned comfort. Will was not yet ready for food, although Cindy was ravenous. She had been sacrificing food for gas over the past few days. Will promised not to go to sleep if she would run out for pizza.

An hour later, they were sitting on the king-sized bed with a pizza box, plastic glasses filled with cola, and paper plates. Will was feeling better, although he still could not remember much of the event. He realized he had been in real danger of wandering disoriented down the highway. Cindy tried to cheer him up by telling funny stories about the eccentric writers who stayed at La Inspiracion. Will, whose head was much clearer, regaled her with his uncle's experiment into the funeral business. Each also revealed a good bit about their past, Will noting that he was raised by his aunt and uncle near Shreveport, and Cindy mentioning, without explaining why, that she was estranged from her family. Both hoped to go to college.

The weather had calmed down considerably. When they noticed that fact, the conversation returned to the incident in the ditch. Cindy knew that Will was getting better focus, but the nurse had also told her not to let him sleep until he was steady on his feet, which he was not.

"As long as I live, I will never forget being upside down over Texas." Cindy shuddered. "I've never been so frightened, so surprised, so…" Cindy was at a loss for words.

"I've seen some twisters from a distance," Will said. "But that one just seemed to pounce on me. We're both fortunate to survive. Do you think that was a miracle?" Will knew Aunt Rita would say it was.

Cindy had not thought in those terms. "I don't know. What is a miracle anyway? And how would we know if we experienced one?"

"I guess a miracle would be a vary rare, possibly unique, event. I doubt that many folks have flown upside down over Texas in a Rabbit," Will replied with a smile.

"Yeah, but tornadoes do lots of odd things. I saw a picture of a piece of straw driven through a telephone pole in an old *Life* magazine," Cindy said. "I doubt that that happened more than once, but that doesn't make it a miracle. And don't Catholics think a miracle occurs every time someone takes communion? So, miracles can be frequent as well."

"That's true," Will said. "And when I visited a Pentecostal church once, they had miracles every time a worshipper was seized with the spirit, had a fit, or talked in tongues."

"Maybe a miracle is something that goes against nature, a violation of a law of nature." Cindy was ready to move on to another definition. "And does a miracle have to be a good thing, a benefit to someone?"

Will, who was enjoying the conversation, wondered how to think about a law of nature. "If a law of nature is a regularity that never varies, then there can't be miracles. By definition, any violation would only show that the purported law is not a law. On the other hand, if a law of nature is just a regularity that occurs under normal circumstances, then God's stepping in would mean that circumstances were not normal. So once again, there would be no violation of the law."

Cindy, whose mouth was full of pizza, nodded her assent. "Does a miracle have to be a good thing?" she asked after she swallowed. "I thought so until I remembered that in the Bible, the devil often brought about visions and miraculous events that were not beneficial, Job's boils for instance. So I think we have to throw out beneficial along with violation of a law of nature. A miracle," Cindy speculated, "is an event brought about by a magical being. It may be rare, common, in accord with nature or not, and beneficial or not."

Will liked this definition and admired Cindy's ability to state it clearly and succinctly. He had no idea God was listening until he laid back on the bed to ease his head, which was beginning to throb.

"I was wondering if you would get there," God announced. "Congratulations. You know, the way some people think about miracles makes being a god easy. You get thanked for every good thing that happens and every bad thing that happens is blamed on someone else."

Will thought their last definition was right, but Cindy was not done with the inquiry.

"And how would we know when we have a miracle?" she asked.

Will was impressed. So was God.

"Good question," Will said. "Perhaps we have a miracle when God, or the supernatural being, tells us it's a miracle. But no, God telling us it's a miracle would itself seem to count as a miracle, and by this method we could not know that God was speaking to us unless God told us he was telling us and so on forever."

When Cindy got up to get some Aspirin for Will, God chuckled. "Even a presumably infinite being could never complete an infinite series, and *you* are merely finite. So I guess you never can know whether something is a miracle or not."

"It makes me doubt that there's any reliable way to tell if something is a miracle," Cindy continued after returning with the Aspirin. "People disagree about what counts as a miracle. They like to claim miracles that suit their religious agenda. I don't recall hearing about a grilled cheese sandwich that displayed the face of Allah, probably because grilled cheese is a part of the American diet and not something served in Saudi Arabia."

"As for human testimony," Will added, "the temptation to claim access to God's plans seems to be too much for many. Besides, we're way too inclined to believe amazing events and urban myths." Will was including himself in those so tempted.

Both Cindy and Will had enjoyed matching wits. However, Cindy looked alarmed suddenly. "Will, have you seen Ham? His cage door is open, and I don't see him anywhere near it."

They both searched the room, but Ham was nowhere to be found.

"Let's just sit quietly and listen," Will said. Cindy sat on the edge of the bed while Will rested his head. Soon, they both heard a grinding noise. Cindy opened the bedside table drawer, and there was Ham, well on his way to demolishing a second Gideon Bible. Cindy put Ham back in his cage with his new trophy.

Settling in on the bed, Cindy's face took on a serious affect. "Will, I have a big, big favor to ask of you. Think carefully about what I'm about to say. I hate to do this when you've been injured, but I think your mind is back enough for you to make a decision."

She paused and took a deep breath. "I called home when I went out for pizza. No one answered, so I called the hospital. They told me that my mom is also hospitalized now and in and out of consciousness. I'm a little low on funds, but I have gas money. I've checked on buses, trains, and planes. They're either too slow or too expensive. My car is a wreck, I'm out of time, and I need to make a beeline for Ohio. So, what I am asking is… can I borrow your truck and drive straight through? I will take good care of it and return it to you. You've only known me a few hours, so I know it's a lot to ask."

As Cindy sat there looking miserable, Will thought about his own resources. He also thought Cindy might well have saved his life when he was so disoriented on the highway. "I could give you the truck and what cash I can spare so you can drive to Ohio. I can still get to my job on time."

"I hate being so constrained by events," Cindy said.

"But it's clearly the best plan for you at this point," Will replied. He thought for a minute. "Maybe I should drive you and call the theme park to say I'll be late for work." Somehow, it felt wrong to be late for his first real job though.

"Absolutely not," Cindy said. "You have time to take a bus across Texas and begin work. It's a sweet offer, but no. Besides, I really feel like it's my duty to take care of this if I can just get there. I've been dealing with this mess at home off and on for years. You and I might have something if we had more time. But I don't want to start a relationship—if we're going to have one—by plunging you into my dysfunctional family."

Cindy told Will in more detail what had happened in her senior year. She thought it was only fair to provide that information before he decided whether or not to loan her his truck. What Will saw in Cindy's confession was her determination and strength. He thought she had been treated unfairly, to say the least. Girls in his high school had gotten pregnant and not been thrown out because of it. He knew that Uncle John had cautioned the parents of some of these girls against acting rashly and destroying a family. Will had never met anyone so close to his own age who was so self-assured and capable of taking control of her life.

"Take the truck, and take care of yourself, too," Will said with feeling.

Cindy's eyes filled with tears. "Will, I'll take good care of your truck, and I'll pay back every dime. I need to be on the road—now." She paused. "How was I so lucky to land on you?"

She leaned against his chest, and he wrapped her in his arms. They remained that way for some time. The afternoon came and went, and the first coolness of evening found them still entwined in bed. Both had slept briefly. Will had never experienced such a feeling of intimacy; he wanted the afternoon to last forever.

Cindy felt secure with Will. She thought he was handsome and gentle. "Will, I want you to know that I like you and...dammit, I want a rain check with you. I promise I won't hold your truck for ransom. But can we promise to reconnect in the future, spend some time together, and keep in touch in the meantime? I will see you again, even if I have to track you down in west Texas."

Will was feeling unfamiliar emotions; Cindy had already found a place in his heart. He held her tighter. "I must see you again, I ..." Will hesitated, worried about getting the hiccups at this precious moment. "I really want to have more time with you."

Since neither really had words for what was happening, and because of the urgency of Cindy's mission, they said no more. Cindy collected her things and prepared to leave.

Cindy made Will walk around the room a few times to test his strength. When she was satisfied, Will called the bus line to get prices and connections. They divided their money, and Cindy left in Will's truck. Each carefully stashed addresses and phone numbers. Will had a cell phone, but Cindy had lost her recharger in the tornado, so she would be out of touch until she could recharge. She had to save what battery was left to call home. Will never wanted to stay with anyone so badly in his life. And Cindy, whose concern for her parents had increased along with her affection for Will, wanted to tuck him into the cab with her.

As Cindy drove away, Will felt very alone; he was stranded, almost broke, and far from his destination. He wanted to call home but feared he would start to cry and his aunt and uncle would decide to come pick him up.

"I was wrong," God said, trying for humor. "You kept your wallet and lost the truck."

After an interval of talking to Ham and feeling sorry for himself, Will decided to call his future employer to see if someone could pick him up at the bus station in Amarillo. He was able to connect directly with Reverend Shister. After a stumbling explanation of his situation, the Reverend interrupted.

"Will, don't worry about getting here right away. We have a labor dispute going on, and I doubt we will open until mid to late summer. Give me a call in a month, and let's see where we are then."

"What happened to cause the delay?"

"It's a long story. I only hire Christian workers, actually, Protestant Christians who've been born again. I have a right to hire only true believers under the faith-based initiative that is indirectly funding this project through the Texas Commission on Tourism. I also use a lot of prison labor out here, but I saw these two guys cross themselves when the scaffolding they were on almost collapsed, so I fired them for being Catholic. The problem is, the other workers walked off the job, because the two Catholics are in the same union as them. That was a week ago. I'm negotiating with a prison right now for some new workers. So hang in there, and I will see you in four to six weeks."

Now Will's predicament was much worse. He was not only stranded, nearly broke, and a long way from his destination, there was no job in his immediate future. Shister's story about the Catholic workers torpedoed Will's excitement about his future employment. He thought of calling Cindy back, but she had been on the road for a couple of hours. That's when he saw a flier in the window of the motel. "Christian Lifestyle Fair – Hiring Workers." He called the number on the poster right away.

God chuckled. "Let's hope for a miracle."

PERFECTION

Will's work for the Christian Lifestyle Fair began shortly after he hung up the phone. The organizer of the fair, Carl Wetherspoon, needed workers right away. Specifically, he needed one good worker. He also agreed to let Will sleep in a small office in the back of the amphitheater that night.

When he arrived at the venue, Will stashed Ham, his bedroll, and his duffle. He also stole a moment to ask God what he thought of Cindy.

"I think you've met someone very special," God said, "but take your time; you're both young. You're kind of special yourself."

"I am?" Will responded. "Thanks."

By late that night, he and Carl had unloaded an amazing variety of commodities, including several large crosses (they were all on rollers), boxes of clothing, golf clubs, Heavenly Flight golf balls, and cosmetics, including Abstinence Perfume (Will wondered if it just smelled bad) for young girls and Virtuous Woman Perfume for their moms. There were also boxes of running shoes and flip-flops with the word "Jesus" written in the tread of their soles. Then there were the curtains, flags, tables, chairs, and food concession products, including boxes and boxes of biblical chocolates and refrigerator magnets to be given out free.

"More worthless plastic items for your home," God chimed in. "What, no dark chocolate?" Then God began to sing, "Hi ho, hi ho, it's off to unloading we go."

Will, who was engaged with trying to find a place to locate a pallet of chocolates, ignored God's running commentary.

He noted that a Christian militia, calling themselves the Tribulation

Army, had a display of replica firearms and weapons along with large pictures of their training camp. It showed large, green grassy areas, presumably for drills, a lovely white chapel, a small airfield and helicopter pad, and a nice recreation hall surrounded by Quonset huts, presumably sleeping quarters for the troops. Will saw that it was in west Texas, and decided to visit the booth later. The pictures did not look anything like the west Texas Will knew from geography, and the pictures never claimed to show the actual camp, but Will was too busy to think about that.

To Will's surprise, there was even a display from the Galilee Christian Theme Park, a giant two-dimensional ark featuring a pair of giraffes, a couple of elephants, and two dinosaurs looking over the deck railing. A small sign was also attached to the side of the ark announcing the delayed opening of the park.

The dinosaurs got a chuckle from God. "I can't tell if they're herbaceous or carnivorous," God said. "Maybe the carnivores on the ark ate the dinosaurs, and that's why none of them survived."

Surprisingly, getting the ark and its oversized passengers into the hall was not the biggest logistical problem of the day. That title went to a gigantic cutout Goliath and a smaller David. Goliath would not fit through the large doors, so they had to decapitate him and then reattach his head once inside.

By two in the morning, Will was so tired he hardly knew his own name. He was also dirty, sweaty, and he ached in every joint.

Carl thanked him and pushed a wad of cash into his hand. "Sleep in that room tonight; there's even a shower next door. Tomorrow and the next day, I'll pick up your motel tab." Carl gave Will a serious look. "Truth is, Will, you saved my bacon by coming in and working so hard, and now I find myself without a show manager to oversee things, troubleshoot, and run the information booth. Sherry had to pull out at the last minute because of family problems. Would you run the show for a couple of days? Mostly that means sitting in the information booth, passing out literature, and troubleshooting if something comes up, which is usually pretty minor. Like someone needs another chair or table. You already know the layout better than anyone. I'll pay you twenty-five dollars an hour and pick up your motel and meals. I'll be overseeing the cash receipts and the door."

Will was ecstatic, but he kept a straight face, too tired to respond immediately. Mistaking Will's slow response for hesitancy, Carl bumped the hourly rate to $35. Still operating with a delayed response, Will said he would be delighted to help out and told Carl he was going to sleep until just before the show opened at ten.

Ham was his usual bright nighttime self. He had removed the back from the Bible and was working on the last of it. Will, somewhat guiltily, chucked the Bible in a dumpster and left Ham with his chunk of spine. He fell asleep on the floor next to Ham as the hamster worked off his extra calories on his exercise wheel.

By nine forty-five the next morning, Will was showered and putting brochures and maps in the racks at the information booth. He was wearing a bright red golf shirt bearing a small cross on the left side and which identified him as staff and manager for the fair. The booth sat opposite the main entrance, and everyone who came into the fair had to pass by it.

Will finished sorting the free materials and looked at the long line of booths filled with busy tenders. It extended to the right and left of the doors and in a double, back-to-back line behind the information booth. Just to the left of the door, an earthy smell arose from the biblical plants booth. A sign above a set of pots containing small trees read, "'When Moses went into the tent of the covenant on the next day, the staff of Aaron for the house of Levi had sprouted. It put forth buds, produced blossoms, and bore ripe almonds.' (Numbers 17:8)"

"Not to mention that poor fig tree that Jesus cursed," God said. He seemed to be enjoying the exhibits.

Will began his circuit of the booths to see what the occupants might need. This trip was likely one of many over the next two days. The tender of the plant booth was watering its plants, and the dirty water was running across the floor. Will found a mop and cleaned it up. The Fishes and Loaves Savings and Loan—"We Multiply Your Money"—booth needed more electricity for their computers, and it took quite a while for Will to find the extension cords and a safe route to get them to the booth.

Christian Candies offered Will a free chocolate with the saying "'The Lord will help his anointed' (Psalm 20:6)" printed on it. After one piece and the temptation of a second free chocolate, God reminded Will of Proverbs 23:21, "The glutton will come to poverty." Will decided he was close enough to poverty already and took a second piece of candy.

A few paces took Will from the financial section to a car dealer that was holding a raffle on a new model of General Motors car called "The Sipper," which got close to sixty-five miles per gallon. Will spent some time looking it over and speculating that it might fit in the bed of his S-10 pickup.

Beyond the car dealer were more political booths. A couple of gun dealers promised guns to protect home and family. They were already attracting a largely male audience. These booths were filled with advertisements for all manner of guns, designs for in-home shooting ranges, pictures of fathers instructing their children on the use of firearms, and petitions aimed at various communities to make it legal for anyone over the age of sixteen to carry a gun. Colleges, seminaries, and high schools that banned guns were especially targeted. Lest some thought that these themes were un-Christian, a large sign in one booth quoted Matthew 10:34: "Do not think that I have come to bring peace to the earth; I have not come to bring peace but a sword." Someone had drawn a line through the word "sword" and written "gun".

Will hurried passed booths that were raising funds for legislation to ban abortions, birth control, pornography, homosexual teachers, homosexual marriages, and divorce, while many other booths promoted help for gays, prisoners, alcoholics, pornography addicts, Jews, Muslims, absent fathers, and witches. One booth featured signs deploring the influence of astrology and promised a campaign to have horoscopes removed from daily papers.

Finally, Will arrived at the booth for the Tribulation Army. A short man with dark sunglasses wearing a greenish uniform stood at attention beside the booth, a Leatherman attached prominently to his belt. As the man turned, Will noticed a pinkish stain on the back of his shirt. Behind the counter was a kindly looking man who introduced himself as Reverend Oliver Newton. Will asked about the group's purpose and origins. Reverend Newton, after giving Will his card, began a well-rehearsed speech about how select the group was and the nominal fee that was required to join, although he never really identified the purpose of the army.

Sudden, loud voices interrupted their conversation.

"Look out!"

"It's coming down!"

Will looked around in dismay. At first, he saw nothing out of the ordinary. People were just standing in front of booths, and they, too, were looking around. Then he looked up and was horrified to see that Goliath's head, a large, carefully painted cutout made of particleboard, was barely attached to the giant's shoulders and was moving in erratic circles in a generally downward direction. As Will watched, it came loose and sailed like a wounded Frisbee over the gaping crowd.

"Oh my God! Oh my God!" a woman shrieked.

The head seemed in no hurry to land. Perhaps it was the central air that kept it aloft. Will never knew. By then he was running, following the head and urging people to clear the aisle that he thought would be a likely landing place. He was the manager, after all, and visions of lawsuits, bloody injuries, and possible deaths flashed through his mind.

The head came close to the tops of the booths. Goliath's grim visage seemed to glare down on the unfortunate, who were about to be crushed. The good news was that the crowds were still limited to the early arrivals and tenders, and they were moving away from the flight pattern like a school of herring avoiding killer whales. With a grotesque midair twist, the head clipped the mast on the sailboat display and crashed into the Rapture insurance booth.

Will did not think anyone was in the booth when the head hit. He had walked by the display earlier. The company, Endtime Insurance, promised to protect loved ones who were left behind when the good people were raptured to heaven. Will wondered what would happen if the Endtime Insurance people were raptured. Would they still pay? And if they were not Rapture material, would they still pay? "Can your family afford to lose a breadwinner?" was one of their rhetorical questions on display. "Show your love to those less prepared than yourself," said the brochures that Will slipped on as he crashed into the booth near a small statue of a puppy with a sign under it that read, "Remember me when you are called."

Strong, helping hands belonging to a short plump woman lifted Will to his feet. The show badge attached to her gray smock read, "Sister Sara, The Social Gospel Mission." Her touch told Will that she had had some health care experience. She explored the gash on his forehead.

"Come over here and sit down," she said gently.

A tall, black woman, also dressed in gray and wearing a badge that identified her as Sister Ellie, joined Sister Sara in examining Will's head injury. The Social Gospel Mission, whose sign tilted dangerously now, occupied the last booth in the row just beside the Rapture insurance booth. Sister Ellie produced a bit of ice and, with a clean cloth, began to work on the bloody, tender spot on Will's forehead—the same place the tornado had bruised him.

"Just sit quiet for a moment and let me ask you some questions," Sister Ellie said.

Carl Wetherspoon arrived, sweaty and out of breath. "What the hell just happened? You're responsible here," as if Will had nailed Goliath with a sling and knocked his head off.

Sister Sara stepped between Will and Carl, who was red-faced and angry. "I've checked the other booths, and except for some damage to the stalls and that ugly statue, no one else is hurt. Several people, however, got a good scare."

Carl did not calm down; he was looking for a scapegoat. "Will, did you check to see if that head was secured after they took it off to get it in here?" He had a dangerous look in his eyes.

Will was slow to respond, having just experienced his second head injury in three days. But a response from Will was unnecessary.

Sister Sara's blue eyes took on the hard look of a basketball coach admonishing a player for a bone-headed play. "Carl, the boy just risked a mild concussion trying to clear everyone out. The contract, your contract, says that all exhibitors are solely responsible for the safety of their exhibits. You need to talk to the Bible camp that brought that monstrosity in here. It's not this young man's responsibility. He probably saved a few more concussions by warning us of what was happening."

Carl must have had experience with Sister Sara before, because he mumbled an apology, backed away, and ordered Will to get the booths in working order before the main crowds arrived. Will said he would try.

As Will started to rise, Sister Ellie put a firm restraining hand on his shoulder. "Young man, you are not moving for at least a little while. Let's see," she said, looking at Will's badge, "ah, it's Will."

For the next few minutes, she asked Will questions until she was satisfied he had only received a knock on the head and that he was reasonably functional.

"We have some staff here who can help you put things right," she said.

About that time, Sister Sara introduced Will to a young couple, Arie and Malcolm. Both were dressed in simple T-shirts, jeans, and gray baseball caps with "The Social Gospel Mission" written on the front. Arie was a beautiful young woman about Will's age. She had dark, naturally curly hair, a bronzed complexion, and a great smile. Malcolm was dark as well with alert, questioning eyes. Between them, they produced a complement of tools and set to work on the damaged booths. Will disentangled Goliath's head and returned it to the Bible camp director, who decided that enough was enough and stacked the cutout of Goliath and the cutout of David in an unused corner. The rest of the cleanup was easy. Will enjoyed the friendly banter between Arie, who was Jewish, and Malcolm who was Muslim. Both were enjoying the experience of the lifestyle fair. Through their joking conversation, Will gleaned that they thought highly of the two sisters.

Will was ready to head back to his information booth, but Sister Sara came by and took one more look at his eyes before releasing him. She also invited him back for an early afternoon lunch, which Will accepted.

Back at his booth, Will had a chance to note that a small seminary had set up a display next door. "Atheists Register Here, You Need Help!" read one of the banners. It got chuckles from those passing by. A young, very serious man nodded at Will as Will replaced brochures in the rack in front of his booth.

"What's the help you give to atheists?" Will asked out of curiosity.

"I just give them the old ontological argument," said the young man, whose nametag identified him as Jeremy.

Will had read some versions of the ontological argument, but he was not at all certain he could reproduce any of them at the moment, and he said as much.

"It's a very simple argument," Jeremy said. "God is the greatest being that can be conceived, a perfect being. If God did not exist, there would be a being greater than God, namely, the being who was just like God and existed. But there can be no greater being than God, therefore, God exists."

Will's head hurt, and contemplating this argument did not help. In fact it made him grumpier, as he was starting to worry that the accident might lead Carl to dock his wages. "So, just existing makes a thing greater?" he asked.

"I think so," Jeremy replied. "Suppose you had two equally talented artists or athletes, one of whom existed, and one of whom was fictional. Wouldn't the existing one be greater than the non-existent one?"

Will's intuition rebelled. "No, one would be actual and one would be hypothetical, but they could be equally great, equally talented, equally athletic."

Will thought of his childhood arguments about whether Superman was greater than Michael Jordan. Of course Superman was greater, and Jordan got no extra greatness points just for existing.

"Isn't the question of God about whether a being that great exists or not?" he asked. "If you assume that existence makes a contribution to greatness, then you essentially define God into existence. Besides, how many points does one get for existing? Is a being who exists for an hour greater than one who exists for fifty-nine minutes? We believe that God is great, and for other reasons we believe that such a great being exists. Why would we need revelation or grace if it were all a matter of definition?"

"But isn't a God who exists greater than one who doesn't?" Jeremy argued.

Will was in full philosophical debate mode now, and he was not about to back down. "Suppose we were to define the devil as the greatest evil being we can conceive. I'm not talking about the devil in the Bible, who is a fallen angel. I mean a being that is all-powerful, all-knowing, and all-evil."

Jeremy nodded. "Okay."

"An argument like yours would show," Will noted, "a perfectly evil being exists, because if the devil did not exist, a greater evil being could be conceived, namely one just like the devil but who actually exists. In fact, if you start with such a definition, then you seem to show that if we allow concepts like the greatest being that can be conceived, both God and the devil exist."

Jeremy seemed pleased. "So the argument works."

"No," Will said. "Your argument leads to the conclusion that two all-powerful beings exist, which is impossible. There cannot be two all-powerful beings, because each would limit the other. So, something had gone terribly wrong. The mistake is, I think, that you allow existence to contribute to the greatness of a thing. What makes sense is that we treat questions of existence separate from questions about a thing's nature."

"Wowser," God said. "Not bad for a guy with two recent head knocks debating a seminary student. Good job."

Jeremy was not happy with Will's failure to comprehend the genius of his argument, but he sat and mulled it over for a bit. Will, meanwhile, had a school group that had arrived and needed maps and directions to the food center. Just then, Carl showed up with a young woman in tow.

"Will, this is Mary. She will be taking over your position as manager of the show." Carl handed Will an envelope. "Here is your pay for the whole day of work and tonight's lodging. I think it better, given the accident this morning that you no longer remain as manager. Thanks for your work." Carl looked around furtively and then left Mary and Will standing there.

"I think he's afraid of Sister Sara and Sister Ellie," God said.

Will was furious. It was not his fault that Goliath's head came loose! But he realized Mary was an innocent here, so he showed her where things were and how she could access cleanup mops and brooms. Seeing that it was nearly noon, he headed down to the Social Gospel Mission booth for lunch.

When he arrived at their booth, he noted they had few visitors. The crowd was gathered at the partially demolished Rapture insurance booth. Will also saw that Arie and Malcolm were breaking out sandwiches and Cokes.

"Grab a chair," Sister Sara said. "Has Carl fired you yet?"

"He just did," Will replied as Arie handed him a tasty looking ham sandwich.

"Figures," Sister Sara remarked, taking a bite of her sandwich.

"Carl is a real piece of work, a shithead," Sister Ellie noted.

Will gasped at her language. "Great sandwich," he said to cover up his shock.

"Yeah," Arie said, "we got a good buy on ham lunch meat yesterday. Of course, I'm Jewish, but if it comes to a choice between eating and dietary laws…"

"When it comes to eating" Malcolm chimed in, "Arie's stomach always wins. Of course, I can't talk."

"Right," Arie responded, "and you're supposed to be a non-pork-eating Muslim."

"How's your head, Will?" Sister Ellie asked.

"Okay, I think." Will was feeling much better in the company of such a cheerful group.

After they finished their sandwiches, Sister Sara passed out candy bars. "Would you like a job?" she asked.

Will was delighted with the offer. "Yes, but I would have to leave in four to six weeks. I have a commitment to another job in west Texas."

"Not a problem," Sister Sara said. "We could use the help."

"I'll get my things, but I need a place to stay," Will replied. "And I have a hamster.'

"We have an extra room, but it's small," Arie suggested. Then with a twinkle in her eye, she asked, "Does the hamster need his own room?"

"That sounds good to me. But I think we can share a room," Will replied with a grin. Then he amused them with his story about how Ham had become his traveling companion and Ham's insatiable appetite for the glue on Gideon Bibles.

"Actually, I think we have a couple of old Gideons lying around," Sister Ellie said, particularly taken with Will's story. "I told you Will was a Good Samaritan," she commented to the group.

The mission was just a few blocks away, so by evening, Will found himself in the soup kitchen serving meals to a variety of homeless and destitute men and women. Ham was situated in a small room above the men's dorm munching away on an already dilapidated Gideon Bible. Will, Arie, and Malcolm were under the direction of the mission's main cook, Delbert.

Will had limited kitchen experience, but he was a quick study. Delbert was particular about his product. He objected to too much salt, too high a cooking temperature, and he schooled Will on just how to handle the food.

For all his fussiness, Delbert was well liked by all of the staff and clients. He knew each person by name, and he spoke to him or her as they came through the food line. He even knew a bit of history about many of them. Will was surprised and upset to learn how many were veterans of the Iraq and Afghan wars. He began to worry about his friend Denny, who was certainly in boot camp. Arie explained that many of the homeless men had something wrong with their head either because they suffered brain damage or were afflicted by PTSD.

The sisters also knew their clients by name, and they peppered them with questions, many of them rhetorical. "How's the job going?" "How are you doing today?" "How's your beautiful kitty?" (The mission had a limited number of cages where the homeless could check their pets and a good supply of pet food available.)

To one client, Delbert asked, "Did you see the flying saucers last night?"

Will noted no one raised an eyebrow at the question.

By the time Will went to sleep that night after cleaning up and making certain the guests were settled, he was almost too tired to sleep. He wanted to call Cindy but realized she was probably still on the road and without her charger. He asked God what he thought about the day. Fortunately God was brief.

"I thought the Goliath incident was hilarious. Sorry you were hurt, but I suspect the insurance people thought the Rapture was upon them. They always seem to welcome disaster; it makes them think the end is nearer. And I liked where you ended up; these are good people. Oh, and by the way, don't forget to call home tomorrow."

STEEL

John Steel liked everything about his name. "John" was appropriately biblical, and "Steel" was satisfyingly masculine, especially the fact it was spelled like the inflexible metal. Physically, he was tough without an ounce of fat on his muscular, middle-aged body. His buzz cut and upright carriage shouted "military." He was a thinker and a planner as well as a soldier.

Steel had never been married. It was not that he was ugly, but the women who were attracted to his looks discovered he did not respect them, and besides, he was simply not fun.

Flexibility, Steel believed, was the curse of the modern era. He saw the curse of flexibility everywhere: in political leadership, in judges, in teachers, and in gender roles. Perhaps the worst was flexible parenting, which had created working moms, househusbands, dropouts, teen pregnancy, and drug addiction. He saw himself as the stern, inflexible parent of his militia, the Sons of Abraham. He refused to deviate from Old Testament law, which he accepted without question.

At the moment, John Steel was mad as hell. The truth was, he was mad as hell at something almost every day. He had just returned from the Lifestyle Fair, where he had sponsored a booth supporting gun ownership and the right to carry arms and done a little recruiting. That was where he had an encounter with that fat little nun, Sister Sara.

Steel had had a nice audience and was just finishing his favorite parable when she butted in. In his parable, he liked to tell any audience that if a poor Christian man found a wallet with $1,000 in it lying on the pavement, he would return it to the owner without even thinking of a reward.

But if an atheist found that wallet, not being a god-fearing person, he would keep the money for himself.

That fat little nun from the booth just down the way had been listening. "What nonsense," she said. Then they had argued.

Steel explained his theory of God's sovereignty in morality, law, and government. "Besides giving us liberty, God declares things right or wrong by his commands," he explained. "The Christian understands that and respects the eighth commandment not to steal. The Christian understands the penalty for the failure to obey God's commands. The atheist has no such knowledge or fear, so it is not wrong in his mind to steal the wallet."

"Is something right or wrong because God declares it so?" Sister Sara asked innocently. "Or does God declare it right or wrong because it is right or wrong?"

The audience was listening intensely at that point. Steel did not quite get the question, but he responded anyway. "Of course God knows everything, so God knows what is right and wrong and commands us to act accordingly."

"If God knows it is right or wrong, then there are reasons why something is right or wrong apart from God's saying so," Sister Sara replied. "God says so, because he knows the reasons that make things right or wrong. Presumably, the honest atheist has access to those reasons, as does the honest Christian, so the atheist is just as likely to return the wallet."

Steel realized immediately he had taken a wrong turn in the argument and set out to correct it. "Everything depends on God, so there's nothing that makes something right or wrong *except* God saying so. The sovereignty of God's will is that by his will, and his will alone, something is right or wrong."

"So," the little nun said, "if God were to command the killing of an innocent baby or the drowning of whole people groups, including innocents, then it's right."

"That is correct," Steel answered. "There is nothing wrong with killing anyone when God has commanded it."

"Do you really believe that?" Sister Sara asked.

"Absolutely," Steel replied, "and so should you."

"No," the nun said, "I would disobey any command to kill innocent children, and I would suspect that it was not God but Satan himself masquerading as God who gave such a command. If you really think there is nothing that makes something right or wrong except that God wills it, then you obviously think that right and wrong are arbitrary. Isn't the very meaning of 'arbitrary' something unrestrained by reasons? And even if you do receive a command, how do you know if the command came from God or Satan? Isn't the only test the one I just suggested, namely, that God would not command you to do that which, you knew for good reasons, was wrong?"

"But how would the atheist, who does not talk to God, know what was right or wrong?" Steel asked.

"The same way any moral being knows right from wrong, and the same way God knows right from wrong: by exercising moral judgment. Acting on well-known principles, such as not harming others, helping those in need, and protecting individual rights. You don't have to be a Christian, Jew, Muslim, Hindu, or believer to see the rightness of these principles."

Sister Sara got a lot of nods from the crowd, and Steel knew the charm of his parable had been lost. He also knew he should never have argued with a nun. Those priests were slippery-tongued debaters, and they trained these nuns.

"I know what's right because God talks to me," he growled.

"Someone talks to you, but I doubt it's God." Sister Sara gave a final malevolent look at his pro-gun literature and walked away.

The collapse of Goliath followed shortly thereafter, and Steel saw no more of the pesky nun. She was another one of these "flexibles." Steel knew what was right and wrong; he had the Ten Commandments, which he had had engraved on a small stone tablet that hung from a chain around his neck. It often hurt his chest when he bumped into things or was lifting boxes of supplies, but such was the price of piety.

Steel put down his cherished copy of *The Bible as Law: Rebuilding a Christian Nation*. Its vision of the United States of America as governed by Old Testament law and spreading that law throughout the world brought a wishful gleam and then a tear to his eye. He saw a day when every public building and most private ones would display the Ten Commandments proudly. He saw a day when capital crimes would include adultery, incest, homosexuality, witchcraft, apostasy, and juvenile delinquency, not to mention atheism, agnosticism, communism, and naturalistic or humanistic tendencies. Of course, lack of patriotism was at the top of his list, and punishment for being unpatriotic would be carried out by stoning the offenders; lesser crimes would be paid for by a period of slavery on the part of the offender. Let some of those low-pants, smartass kids think about that.

Steel was a postmillennial dominionist at heart. He believed that God gave man, not woman, dominion over the earth as God promised in Genesis 1:26. Steel was also convinced that if man (Christian man) worked hard and passed laws like "The Constitution Restoration Act of 2004," there would come a time when all government, science, laws, and institutions that affect people's lives would be under biblical law. When the United States had been so reconstructed, then the world could be reconstructed along similar lines, and then and only then would the Second Coming occur. But not everyone would fall in line to make this a Christian world, and that is where the Christian militias would be needed, to root out and kill Satan's hardcore followers. An irony that would always elude him was that he saw himself as an anti-terrorist.

But Steel's plans had a problem besides his lingering anger at Sister Sara. His militia needed to grow. It was too small, and so was its compound. Actually, calling it a compound was a joke. It was a single lot outside of a small community just north of Amarillo, appropriately named "Lost, Texas." His compound was one hundred feet by fifty feet. A crappy little shed, his office, was the only structure on the property. The electric panel that kept his lights on looked like a giant blemish on the landscape. The developer of his site had hoped to cash in on some real estate speculation by selling small, prefab homes to migrant workers coming in from Mexico, only to have the housing market go into the toilet along with the job market. The would-be buyers failed to show. Steel bought the lot and put up a wooden fence around it. It looked silly sitting out in the middle of nowhere: a shack, a fence—part of which had already blown down—and a pole that was the last in a line of poles coming out from town that delivered electricity and doubled as a flagpole. Steel knew it looked bad, and he was surprised he had attracted three other members to his militia, given the poverty of his situation.

It was not that his militia was a total failure. A couple of years earlier, he and one other member had helped shut down a women's health clinic over in New Mexico. They sent white powder and claimed it was anthrax. They also wrote a letter to the paper threatening to shoot anyone who went near the clinic, and they hinted that they might bomb it. They actually took a shot at a couple of people outside the clinic—Steel was not sure if they were doctors or not. In actuality, unknown to Steel, one was a protestor from Defenders of the Unconceived (an anti-masturbation group), and the other was a tourist asking for directions. The unpredictable gunfire, together with the letters, led the clinic to shut down, although it reopened six weeks later. This latter fact was also unknown to Steel.

The previous year, the Sons had forced the only doctor in Lost, Texas out of town. Old Doc Carlson abandoned his practice in the middle of the night after several months of harassment by the Sons of Abraham. They had spray painted his house, taken shots at his bird feeder, tried to poison his dog, knocked down his front porch with a front-end loader, and trashed his car on more than one occasion. The doctor's error had been to perform an abortion on an ovarian pregnancy to save the life of a young Latina woman. God had commanded Steel to remove this murderer from their midst. Since then, the community had been unsuccessful in recruiting a new doctor. In fact, several of the older members of the community as well as some of the youngest had died or had their health deteriorate for want of medical attention. Such was the wrath of God, Steel thought to himself.

However, the mayor of Lost, Texas was extremely displeased. Having given the Sons tax-exempt status, which required annexing the outlying area that included the Sons' compound, he felt that the Sons owed the community some respect. And when he discovered they were the ones who harassed Doc Carlson, he threatened to withdraw their tax-exempt status and write another letter to the federal faith initiative office condemning their activities. Steel was fairly certain that the second letter was being drafted that very moment, especially since the mayor's wife had become ill and she had to drive or be driven some one hundred miles round trip for treatment.

But Steel had plans to improve his circumstances. He had just applied for a government grant as a faith-based agency. He thought he had a good chance of getting some funding—if the mayor's second letter didn't arrive first—for his program to help troubled youth. According to the grant application, he and the Sons of Abraham sought out troubled youth in Lost and helped them engage in community projects, such as restoring the city park and maintaining a visitor bureau. The mayor, who supported any effort to bring badly needed funds, had written a letter of support. As a matter of fact, there were no troubled youth in Lost, primarily because when those born there became youths, troubled or not, they fled the small, dead-end town. To top things off, there was no city park and no need for a visitor's bureau, because no tourists ever came to Lost unless they seriously were lost.

After he got the grant, Steel intended to move into a larger compound. Specifically, he intended to take over the large space now occupied by the Tribulation Army. He drove by it frequently, and while he doubted that Reverend Oliver Newton was as aware of him, he knew each and every member of the "Tribulations," as he called them, by sight. He regarded them as a bunch of wusses, sissies, and womanly men. Steel had scoped out Reverend Oliver Newton at the fair, where he had had one of his boys talk to him. On another occasion, he sent another of his militia pretending to be a potential recruit to the compound to look it over. He had also done some surveillance of the camp from the highway. From what he had learned, he believed that they were a bunch of premillennialists who did not share his vision of building a Christian world to facilitate the Second Coming. They believed there would be the Rapture, Tribulation, and then Second Coming following Armageddon. Steel didn't buy it. Premillennialists were political baggage—theologically wrong and politically useless.

Although he did not respect the Tribulation's supposed theology, his coveting their site led him to spend a good deal of time trying to figure out how to get his hands on it. In front of him lay a set of plans for his new home. It was a tidy arrangement with a drilling yard and a nice brick, air-conditioned office building beside which was a jail with a pair of stocks in front. In the back was a firing range, and further up in the hills outside the compound were an ordinance depot and a place to test explosives. Steel wanted the mechanisms of punishment to be visible reminders that God's word was law, so his *piece de resistance* was a ten-foot in diameter stoning circle with a large pile of fist-sized rocks.

Steel stepped outside the little shack. The weather was sweltering, running well into three digits. Currently, there were only four troopers in his militia, counting him. His problem, he decided, was that there were too many enemies to deal with and they were distracting him. Like a predator lion confronting a herd of wildebeests, unless he singled out a weak individual, he was likely to go hungry.

The "flexibles" came in many stripes. They talked all the time about freedom and the right to make choices. They had it so wrong. The only freedom was the freedom to live according to God's commands. The only choice was to obey those commands. The right to chose one's own goals and how to pursue them consistently with similar rights by others was unknown, strange, and alien to Steel.

Most recently, feminists and female clergy, all of whom were "flexibles," as far as Steel was concerned, were at the top of his shit list. He knew that Sister Sara ran the Social Gospel Mission over near Dallas, and he decided to pay it a visit. He imagined himself going underground, showing up as a homeless man, and then finding a way to bring the place into disrepute—maybe planting drugs, starting a fire, or just spreading rumors that Sister Sara was a lesbian. Steel wanted vengeance on her and all for which she stood. Paul taught in 1 Timothy 2:12, "Permit no woman to teach or to have authority over a man; she is to keep silent." As far as Steel was concerned, the whole problem of modern flexibility lay at the feet of women, starting with Eve. She was the one who had screwed up. Sister Sara was just the tip of that iceberg, but it would be a good place to start—silence her and extract his revenge.

Steel realized that he had a set of priorities now. First, he would take out Sister Sara's mission. Then he would get his hands on Reverend Oliver's compound. He had a few notes, supplied by a guard at the Western Texas House of Correction, on most members of the Tribulation Army. He gathered other information from local gossip. He had only Rev, Chris, Harry, Blink, and Curt to deal with. Rev would be replaced, but Steel hoped to keep Chris, crazy bastard though he was, because he was useful. Harry would go with the flow. He had no ambitions of his own. Blink and Curt could be a problem. But if Harry went along with the takeover, Blink would probably follow. But what should he do about Curt? He was dangerous and possibly armed. In his surveillance, Steel had never seen a gun at the compound, and they had no firing range, as far as he could determine. But the report from WTHC warned about Curt. Curt loved guns. In the end, Steel doubted that Curt was very loyal to the Tribulations.

As far as Steel could tell, the Tribulation Army just sat around, moved some of the leftover auto debris from place to place, and did some weeding and a bit of painting now and then. Recently, there had been a lot more activity. They seemed to be cleaning the place up a bit and even took down the pre-owned auto parts sign. Steel wondered what that was all about, but he welcomed the cleanup.

Steel expected his faith-based grant to come through. He knew all kinds of groups that were getting them. The key was to have what looked like a good cause. There was so little enforcement that he was not concerned about being found out. Who the hell was going to go to Lost, Texas to check out its troubled youth program and its nonexistent city park? But Steel was a little worried after his falling out with the mayor. And even if the grant came through, it was not likely to be renewed. Steel needed money. He knew Oliver was a con artist and, according to his notes, a good one. But he doubted they could work together. However, if he kept some of the Tribulation felons in his militia, he might be able to apply for another grant to rehabilitate convicted felons. Get a revolving door thing going where they would come out of WTHC. He would take them in for a few days, and then let the ones go that he did not want to be Sons. The government would probably pay him by the head, and the recruits would have many of the skills he needed for his future plans.

Steel went back inside and picked a folder off his desk. It was labeled "Revenue." Inside was a diagram of two small banks in the Oklahoma panhandle. Both towns were too small to have police departments of their own. The county sheriff was stretched pretty thin over there. Certain days of the month, a sizeable amount of funds went through these banks from the federal government for properties that the banks held through a series of foreclosures.

Steel planned to rob both banks. He did not believe that it was wrong. In fact, Steel did not believe in the federal government. Taxes were robbery, as far as he was concerned, and besides, he believed in a theocracy—a governmental authority run by God-fearing Americans. Robbing a bank was just a way to return the money stolen from citizens through taxes. Steel had never paid taxes himself or even filed a return.

Steel was on the edge of an inspiration. He looked back through the file on Curt. Sure enough, Curt had been sent to prison for killing a bank guard. According to the file, Curt liked to rob banks. Steel smiled. That was the door into the Tribulation compound.

THE MISSION

The Social Gospel Mission was a sprawling architectural monstrosity that resembled a large bird in flight. The ground floor center of the building accommodated a lobby and a large dining room with attached kitchen and serving line. The wings were dormitories. The staff quarters were located on the second floor. The sisters had a suite of rooms over the women's dormitory while Will, Malcolm, and Arie were lodged over the men's. Extra rooms were also located over the dining/lobby area, used mostly for storage.

Will had just finished his third day at the mission. Even his youthful vigor was sapped from learning new routines and the long hours.

Arie and Malcolm had moved in together when Will arrived. They occupied one of the larger rooms down the hall from Will and Ham. A common bathroom lay between. They had done everything they could to make Will feel welcome, including throwing a small party at the end of his first day.

When Arie discovered that Will had a hamster, she was delighted. "I used to have a hamster when I was a kid," Arie said, "I get along great with hamsters; we're both night creatures."

In fact Arie, Will, and Malcolm were so busy working that they had little time to themselves. The mission, like all such services, was overly full, overextended, and deep in debt. The collapsing US economy had put an unprecedented strain on private charities. The combination of a swell of veterans, out of work families, and seniors with shattered retirement plans kept the mission in a state of perpetual crisis.

Still, Arie, Malcolm, and Will threw themselves into the work, in part because they were young, strong, and idealistic, and in part because the sisters were inspiring. Sisters Sara and Ellie were unflaggingly cheerful, hardworking, and adept at finding last minute funds to keep things going. Will's resources might actually grow, he thought, since he had no time to spend his meager wages.

Will arrived on the second floor and found his room empty of Ham's cage. Laughter and giggles came from an open door down the hall. He figured Arie must have taken Ham down to her room. A quick sniff of his room told Will it was time to do laundry—he had not had time since he left home. His clothing also smelled strongly of cooking odors from his hours in the kitchen.

Flopping onto his bed, Will tried to call Cindy at home again, but she didn't pick up. She had left a message for him earlier telling him she was at the hospital and had to turn her cell phone off much of the time. He had talked to his aunt and uncle the previous evening. Uncle John had heard of the Social Gospel Mission and was proud that Will was working there. When Will explained the delayed opening of Galilee, his aunt had suggested he might return home, but she, too, was supportive of his work. Will did not mention his missing truck.

Will also called the Galilee Theme Park and got a recorded message. "Due to unforeseen circumstances, the opening of the Galilee Theme Park has been delayed from June thirtieth to August fifteenth." Will decided to take a quick shower and check in on Arie and Malcolm.

Ham was the center of attention in his friends' room. Arie's table was cleared, and Arie and Malcolm sat at one end with Ham, who was out of his cage nibbling on a carrot. At the other end of the table were three books: a Koran, a Gideon Bible, and a Torah.

"Hey, Will," Arie said, "we're testing Ham's taste in glue, which will he choose?"

"Not just that," Malcolm added. "We're also exploring hamster theology. We're going to release Ham and see which religious tract he eats."

Will laughed. "I'll bet he goes for the book with the most glue. But what can we conclude if he goes for the Koran? That it's his favorite, his least favorite, or that he just likes the taste?"

Arie's face pinched. "I don't know," she said as she released Ham and hid the carrot.

Ham made straight for the books, climbed up on the Gideon Bible, and attacked the backing of one of Arie's art history books, which lay behind.

"Damn," she said, "the little bugger is a Philistine!"

Will and Malcolm were delighted with the outcome, but Will moved quickly to arrest the delinquent hamster before he could damage Arie's book further.

Arie and Malcolm were a contrast in personalities. Malcolm had a quiet, thoughtful manner with a dry wit in contrast to Arie's lively, quick, quips. She loved science, philosophy, art, good jokes, and Malcolm, but she hated politics. Malcolm, in contrast, paid close attention to US politics and had already lured Will, who studiously avoided political discourse, into several discussions.

Malcolm, with considerable input from Arie, ran a website called HealthyFatwa.org. On his site, under the pseudonym Mullah Nasruddin, he called fatwas down on anything he thought was harmful to humans, including potato chips, Top Ramen, global warming, watching reality TV, and listening to a popular local right-wing radio host. Malcolm's satirical comments on this celebrity included the observation that the radio host was, after all, a consistent guide to truth. For any claim the host made, the negation was likely to be true.

Will opened the cola he had brought from the refrigerator in the hall and then asked a question that had been troubling him. "Arie, I've been meaning to ask how can you be both an atheist and Jewish."

"Easy, Will. I grew up Jewish—Jewish holidays, Jewish food, Jewish friends, rabbis, and synagogue. I even went to a yeshiva for a while, and I spent a summer in Israel—where, by the way, I met lots of atheist Jews, including some rabbis. I greatly value my Jewishness, though not the chosen people part. And I just never got into the God stuff. I have a lot of reasons for not believing in God, but the basic one is that I find it hard to reconcile a just, loving, and caring God with all the suffering in the world."

Will had never encountered atheism directly. Everyone he had ever known believed in God, although Will had wondered sometimes if they believed in the same God he did.

"But surely," Will protested, "there are good reasons why there's suffering in the world."

"Whatever they are," Arie responded, "it can't be because God has limited powers or limited knowledge or because God is partly evil. I'm assuming that the god you're talking about is all-powerful, all-knowing, and all-good."

"Of course."

"So, why all the suffering?"

"In some cases," Will proceeded carefully, since he was a little intimidated by Arie's logical mind and the fact that she was a new friend, "it's because those who suffer are wicked, and they are made to suffer because of their sins."

Arie was not buying it. "Will, just think of the flood story in Genesis. God considered humankind a disappointment, and he was sorry he made humans. But come on, he obliterated babies, fawns, small children, and many people who were already suffering. In fact, every creature was drowned except for Noah, his family, and the passengers on the ark. Can you imagine the suffering, chaos, and turmoil of those forty days? And you can't tell me that all of those deaths were deserved. Even the somewhat wicked ones hardly deserved capital punishment, especially of that particularly horrific kind. Why not sort them out and send the good ones to heaven and the bad ones to hell? Don't you believe that God had to do that anyway after they all drowned? It's hardly a lesson in redemption or compassion. It's neither just nor justifiable."

Will was a bit stumped by this example. "I felt much the same way when I read about the great tsunami in Asia a couple of years ago. I saw pictures of small children wandering the beach having lost their parents, their village, and probably their sanity. It made me angry with God. But maybe these things happen to teach us compassion and to care about people who are in danger."

"I can't say I think the end justifies the means," Arie responded. "Is the divine mind so limited in imagination that that is the only way to teach us compassion? Are we so flawed that it takes a disaster like that to teach us? After all, God is presumably all-powerful, so he could certainly have made us more careful and compassionate or found some other way to teach us. In fact, the biblical flood is hardly a lesson in compassion; it's an act of anger. Even if some good comes out of disaster, that doesn't excuse the evil done in the beginning, especially by a god who presumably can bring about the good without the evil. But, hey, Will, I'm not trying to rain on your god, and I certainly don't want to make my new friend an enemy." Arie slipped her arm around Will's shoulders.

Malcolm had been quiet through this exchange. "Let me try an answer to Arie's question," he said. "The Koran, surah four seventy-seven, teaches that all that is good comes from God and all that is evil comes from ourselves or in some cases Satan. And surah sixteen ninety-five assures us that Satan has no influence over the true believer. So here is my explanation of evil: God's creatures, such as angels and humans, have free will. To give beings free will is to run the risk of them screwing up. But it's a better world if we're free than if we're robots or zombies. So, yes, there's evil in the world, and it all comes from the actions of free creatures like us or Satan."

Will thought this was a pretty good explanation of suffering, but Arie licked her lips like a hungry dog looking at a fleshy bone. The argument, however, was left hanging by the voice of the night proctor calling upstairs.

"Will, Malcolm there's an altercation in the men's sleeping quarters!"

Will, Arie, and Malcolm were down the stairs in a flash and came in the back door to the men's sleeping quarters. Sister Ellie and Sister Sara were already there. Sister Ellie, tall and cool, was standing in front of a shabbily dressed elderly man.

"Carl, put down the knife," she demanded.

Carl's eyes were not quite in focus, and it was not clear he knew where the voice was coming from. He looked around. In his hand he held a shiny object. Alcohol and weapons of any kind were strictly forbidden in the mission. Violators were handed over to the police. The target of Carl's rage, Henry, was sitting on the edge of his bed, seemingly oblivious to the drama going on in front of him.

Will realized why he was so unconcerned: Carl was holding a butter knife that he had probably lifted from the kitchen. Sister Ellie came to that realization at about the same instant as Will.

"Oh my God, Carl." She smothered a laugh. "Are you planning to butter Henry to death?"

Henry had had enough of this drama, and he lay down on the bed and went to sleep.

Carl seemed to forget his rage and, looking down at his own bed said, "Oh, there it is." A copy of a fairly new magazine lay partially obscured by the covers. "I thought Henry stole it."

Quietly but firmly, Sister Ellie took the knife from Carl and pressed him on the shoulder so he sat. "Carl, look at me," she said. "Do not ever bring even a butter knife in here again, or you will be banned for life. Do you understand?"

"Yes, Sister." Carl was contrite.

Will noted that Sister Ellie had a sweet fragrance about her and bubbles on the back of her short, graying hair.

"Thanks for coming down," she said to Will, Malcolm, and Arie.

The dormitory settled into its nighttime quiet. Carl read his magazine quietly with a small penlight.

Arie, Malcolm, and Will returned to their upstairs rooms.

"Sister Ellie was impressive," Will said. "She didn't flinch even when we all thought Carl had a knife. Too bad we interrupted her bath."

"*Their* bath," Arie said and giggled.

Will gave her a confused look.

"What Arie has indiscreetly hinted," Malcolm said, "is that Sister Sara and Sister Ellie are lovers, partners for the past several years." He gave Arie a look.

"Oh, come off it Malcolm," Arie said. "Everyone here knows of their relationship, even the clients. And we all approve," she added with emphasis.

"Oh," Will said. "I didn't know. Thanks for telling me. I'm headed to bed. I have early shift tomorrow, and I want to try to call Cindy again."

Both Arie and Malcolm wished Will a good night, Malcolm with a pat on the back and Arie with a quick hug.

Back in his room, Will realized that Ham was still down in his friends' room. He'd get him in the morning. He picked up his cell phone. He knew it was late in Ohio, but he had a burning desire to talk to Cindy. To his amazement, his phone rang before he could dial. It was her!

"Will! Oh Will," she said. "I just got a new phone and charger. I've really missed you. I arrived in town yesterday. Went straight to the hospital and have been here ever since. Mom is doing a bit better, but Dad may not make it through the night. I'm just wandering the halls. We're supposed to have our cell phones turned off, but I found a corner." She was talking very softly.

Will felt weak in the knees. He really wanted to be with Cindy, and he said as much, although he felt tongue-tied and awkward as he told her a bit about his situation.

"Will, your truck is in good shape. Is it all right if I keep driving it? The family car has been repossessed, if you can believe that."

"Of course. Use all the money as well. I'm getting a decent wage here as well as board and room. This job will see me through until I report to the theme park in August."

"Thanks, Will. Mom's finances are a mess, but I hope I won't need your money. By the way, I called Galilee and got the message." Cindy was obviously moving about the hospital as the background voices and noise kept changing. "I've got to go. Something is happening in Dad's room. I'll call back soon."

"Call me anytime," Will said. "And Cindy," he added on impulse, "I really look forward to seeing you."

"Me too, Will. You've been on my mind a lot even with all that's going on. Bye."

Will sank back on his bed. He could only imagine what was happening at the hospital. He didn't want to dwell on it though. His thoughts turned back to Arie's revelation about the sisters. He wasn't sure how he felt about the revelation. He had heard plenty of talk, even jokes among his friends, about lesbians, gay men, and the gay agenda, although he was not at all clear what it was. He wondered if God was still up.

"Of course, you dope. I'm supposedly ever present." God did not sound nearly as tired as Will felt.

"I was thinking about Sister Sara and Sister Ellie being lesbians," Will confided.

"I know what you're thinking," God reminded Will.

"Is what they're doing wrong?" Will asked.

"What do you think of the sisters?" God often responded to a question with a question. "Tell me honestly."

Will had to think on that for a bit, since his feelings for the sisters were entirely positive. "I admire them," he said finally.

"What do you admire about them?"

"They're honest, they work hard, and they care about the people who come to the mission. They treat the staff with loving respect. I would say they are brave and kind. Without them, there would be no mission."

"How do they do that?" God was full of questions.

The answer was obvious to Will. "They depend on each other. Except for my Uncle John and Aunt Rita, I've never seen two people who work together more harmoniously, and they do it in very difficult circumstances. They really seem to love each other."

"It doesn't sound like you have any problems with them."

"No, I guess not. But I heard a lot of folks, like Revered Steady, talk about how sinful it is to be gay and how they have an agenda to subvert the family."

Will recalled with distaste his visit to the prosperity church. He was also finding it hard to put the sisters in the category of bad or evil and Steady in any category of good.

"I think you've answered your own question," God responded. "The sisters do great good here. That great good grows out of the strength that comes from their love for each other. How can that be wrong?" God's last question was clearly rhetorical. "Have you read Ruth one verses sixteen to seventeen? 'Where you go, I will go; where you lodge, I will lodge; your people shall be my people, and your God my God. Where you die, I will die—there will I be buried.' These words speak of true love, and you are witnessing it here at the mission, love in action."

Will could not help but recall the many prohibitions in Leviticus especially 18:22, which some took to be a denunciation of homosexuality.

God was way ahead of him. "Don't bother to bring up the obsessive compulsive cleanliness duties and commands in Leviticus. That's the silliest book of all. Good grief, look at what I'm supposed to have said about bugs and other creepy crawlies. I mean, you can eat locusts and grasshoppers and crickets, but other bugs are unclean, and touching one makes you unclean until the magic hour of sunset. Also, avoid weasels, mice, lizards, geckos—how does one get car insurance?—chameleons, and so forth. If a bug falls in your soup, you must break the bowl! A dead gecko on your shirt makes it unclean until, would you believe yet again, the magic of sunset? I mean, really. How can you take this book seriously? Did I ever forbid haircuts or beard trimming? I don't think so! Kill the animal because some pervert takes sexual advantage of it? Really? This book reads like a cell phone contract, filled with prohibitions, the violation of any one of which is really going to cost you."

Will knew that God got on a rant occasionally, but he could enjoy a good rant. He did wonder, however, at God's knowledge of cell phone contracts, not to mention car insurance. Well, God was supposedly omniscient, perhaps a necessary requirement for understanding such things. Obviously though, God was not very fond of Leviticus.

As Will drifted off to sleep, he realized that he felt really good about working for the sisters. He believed and felt deeply that they were good people, and so was their relationship. He was proud to be part of the mission.

THE SISTERS

When Sister Sara awoke the following morning, she giggled at the memory of Carl and the butter knife despite her effort to not awaken Ellie.

She snuggled closer to Ellie's warm back and thought about the day. She needed to send Will or Malcolm to pick up some surplus turkey legs. Whoever did not go for turkey legs could pick up some day old bread from the grocery stores.

Damn, she thought, *how can we disguise turkey legs yet again?*

Delbert, the cook, would have a fit. Arie needed to help Ellie with a grant application. That meant Sister Sara would be running the shelter on her own with a little help from volunteers. Delbert would need Wanda, his partner, in the kitchen.

Stop! She told herself. *You're obsessing on the day already.*

She turned her mind to more pleasing thoughts. She thought about the day she met Ellie twenty years ago. They were both novices in the Maryknoll order. She had been sitting in Spanish class with Father Bastiste, infamous for his sympathies for liberation theology. Ellie walked into the classroom, and Sara had felt her breath catch. Tall, black, and with movements so graceful one would think she had been a professional dancer. Sara recalled vividly how short, plump, and inelegant she felt in Ellie's presence. But such differences as there were—and there were plenty—did not prevent them from becoming fast friends and lovers a few years later.

Ideologically, they were one. Thanks to Father Bastiste, they believed that humans required a certain level of material wellbeing before they were able to turn to their spiritual needs. Sara and Ellie were convinced that capitalism could only thrive on the bloody remains of the working poor. Thus, the struggle for the spiritual fulfillment of humans depended largely on the struggle to improve their economic conditions. And capitalism was the major barrier to be overcome.

Sara and Ellie had very different backgrounds. Ellie came from a solid middle class family and had a first-rate education. Her parents were African Methodist Episcopal church members. Her father was a successful pastor who never quite got over Ellie's conversion to Catholicism, let alone her decision to become a nun. Sara's parents were both Italian. Her father had been in the mob in New Jersey. Sara grew up in the projects. She was never quite sure what her father did for the mob, but she knew he was respected in the neighborhood. To her, he was a loving father who took good care of his family, which consisted of Sara, her brother Vince, and her mom. Her parents were extremely proud when Sara took her vows.

Typical of Maryknoll nuns—an order committed to overseas ministry—she and Ellie worked in Africa first and then in South America. They worked among the poor in Nigeria but had to flee in the middle of the night when oil company goons came after them for helping the workers organize. They fled South America for similar activities and amid accusations by the United States ambassador that they were communists. They received a special dispensation to start their mission in Texas. The archbishop quipped that it was clear Texas was a foreign land and, therefore, the mission was consistent with the mandate of the Catholic Foreign Mission Society of America.

The Church hierarchy in the US was not thrilled to have Ellie and Sara back in the country. The bishops would have been much happier to have them stuck in a place they could not find on a map. The sisters had been trouble from their novice days. Ellie was a vociferous advocate for ordaining women, and she had challenged the Church policy of simply moving priests who abused children to a new parish. Sara was famous for her visit to a local Republican congressman. She went there to ask for his help in establishing more voting places in the African-American and Hispanic neighborhoods in the Dallas/Fort Worth area. The congressman's own district was so gerrymandered that its boundaries looked like the splotch of a dropped inkwell. When he told Sara that he did not think "those people" were ready for democratic decision-making, she responded by pitching his Citizen of the Year award from the Chamber of Commerce through one of his windows, followed by his autographed Alex Rodriguez baseball, before storming out of his office. He never pressed charges, because he was afraid that his comments would become public. Sara made them public anyway. He was defeated in the next election due to a high African-American and Latino turnout.

As they grew older, Ellie and Sara found contentment in running the mission. It had been operating for several years now. Sara loved the work and the people, and she liked to remember how she and Ellie pulled it all together. Now, however, it was time for breakfast.

Sister Sara slipped out of bed, got dressed, and then began food preparation in their little kitchen. Moses the cat demanded food before anyone else could eat. Within half an hour, she and Ellie were sitting down to toast, peanut butter—everyone donated peanut butter—and a bit of canned fruit. The day was set: Sara on duty, Ellie working on a grant, and a staff dinner that evening.

But Sara was still caught in the memory web of their earlier days. She reminded Ellie of their struggle to find a cook. Soon, she and Ellie were laughing almost uncontrollably.

They were just beginning to hire staff, and they needed a cook. An ad in the *Penny Courier* had produced only two applicants. They rejected one candidate immediately because of ongoing drug problems. The second candidate, a woman named Wanda, had arrived promptly for her interview. She was lean to the point of gauntness. Every ropey muscle showed in her arms, neck, and legs. Her references praised her as a waitperson and someone who knew food service. But, to their surprise she had never worked as a cook.

Ellie started the interview by commenting that Wanda had not worked in the position for which they had advertised.

"Oh," Wanda said, "I ain't no cook. I'm applying for Delbert; he's the cook."

"How are you connected to Delbert?" Sara asked. "And where is he?"

"Oh," Wanda had a habit of beginning her sentences with an exclamation, "Delbert's at home. He's my sweetie."

Wanda blushed at using such intimate terms. Both Ellie and

Sara warmed to her immediately. "He's very shy," Wanda added as an afterthought.

"How can we evaluate Delbert as a cook if he's not here?" Ellie asked.

"Well," Wanda straightened her back, crossed her boney legs, and looked directly at the sisters. "I'm a food expert. I've worked in many kitchens with lots of chefs, and I can tell you I have never been around a better cook. Delbert is organized, creative, and he gets the food out on time. He's the best."

Because they liked her and they needed a cook immediately, Sara and Ellie requested more information.

"Where has he worked?" Sara asked.

"Mostly he has been cooking for us," Wanda replied.

"He must have had some experience in commercial cooking," Ellie persisted.

"Not really," Wanda said. "He's been busy developing his repertoire." Wanda enunciated the word "repertoire" as if it were delicious.

"What kind of cooking does he do?" Sara asked, trying desperately for more information.

"All kinds," Wanda responded cryptically.

Sara looked at Ellie in exasperation.

"Can you give us some examples?" Ellie asked.

"Oh, sure," Wanda replied and then lapsed into silence.

"Well?" Ellie prodded.

"Well, last night we had chuck roast with special marinade, smothered in assorted mushrooms with seasonal vegetables lightly cooked and a lemon tart for dessert."

"We don't expect to have chuck roast very often," Sara offered.

"Oh," Wanda said, "well, Delbert can do the most wonderful things with the most common ingredients. He can do all kinds of pastas. He cooks Chinese dishes and Mexican dishes. You name it, and he can cook it. He's actually thinking about writing a cookbook. He has all these recipes in his head."

"How did they get into his head?" Ellie asked. "He must have studied somewhere."

Wanda fidgeted in her chair. "Kind of."

By that point, Sara got a little impatient with Wanda's evasiveness.

"Wanda, if you want Delbert to get this position, you have to level with us. Where did Delbert learn to cook?"

Wanda's eyes glistened with tears. "Don't take me wrong here. Delbert is a lovely man, and he ain't crazy; he's not."

Sara fixed Wanda with what she hoped was a compassionate look and waited.

Wanda sighed deeply. "Delbert is an abductee. The aliens took him about a year ago today, and they experimented on his body." Wanda looked warily at the two sisters.

"Go on," Ellie responded.

"Well, the aliens were really gentle with Delbert, and they appreciated being able to examine him. He was their first human subject, you know. They wanted to do something for him in return. They were foodies, so they gave him two thousand recipes." Wanda sat back and smiled, her story told.

Ellie looked at Sara. Both were ready to call it quits.

Wanda realized she was about to be dismissed. "You know," she offered, "I'll tell you what. You pick up some foodstuff, like the kind you're likely to get in the mission, and I'll bring Delbert over and have him prepare a meal for you this evening. If you watch him cook and you decide he's not right for the job, we'll leave, and you'll have a free meal."

To Ellie's surprise, Sara took Wanda up on her offer.

To everyone's surprise, that evening's meal was delightful, and since that day, Delbert and Wanda had been a dynamic duo in the mission's kitchen. Wanda chopped, stirred, and managed the volunteers while Delbert planned the menus and cooked. Delbert was very focused on his cooking, but he always took time to offer a brief greeting to all who came near. He was a large man with powerful arms and a shy manner that endeared him to all the staff and the guests. He loved to cook and never ceased to amaze his fan club. Sometimes, he would say things like, "This kind of fish is very popular on Venus." But that came with the territory.

He and Father Duncan, a defrocked priest who helped out in the kitchen sometimes, shared the culinary space without any rivalry. In fact they were good friends. Father Duncan was one of the few people that Delbert would tell about his abduction experience. Father Duncan said that having been a priest for a while gave him special insight into abductions. Father Duncan and his spouse came frequently to the evening meal. He claimed the Venetian fish was his favorite.

It was a lucky day they interviewed Wanda, Sara thought as she headed down to see how the morning breakfast was going.

What seemed like many hours later, because it was, Sara and Ellie relaxed to a fine dinner, compliments of Delbert, with Will, Arie, and Malcolm. Sara loved her crew of young people. That night, their energy spilled over into a debate that they had obviously begun at an earlier time. It began as they settled back and distributed the last of a bit of wine. They had decided the dishes could wait until morning, and conversation turned, as it did often, to the hardship cases of the homeless and sick who came to the mission.

But Will was thinking beyond such particulars. "Sister Sara and Sister Ellie, Malcolm suggested the other night that there is evil or suffering in the world because God gave humans and angels free will. Arie doesn't think that's a very good explanation of why there's so much suffering. I'm not sure what I think. You both studied theology, and you've seen a lot more of the world than I have."

Malcolm and Arie, who had looked like they might slip off, settled back into their chairs. Sara sighed but found that her interest was also aroused by the question. She had not thought much about the problem of evil since her early days as a novice.

Ellie surprised everyone by taking the lead. "I don't think that free will is a very good explanation of suffering. In the first place, it covers only a small number of the cases of suffering, those caused by human actions. Terrible diseases, hurricanes, natural disasters of all kinds, or, as we say, "acts of God," are the source of the majority of suffering, and these seem to be more attributable to God than to the free will of his creatures."

Malcolm wanted to defend his view. "Even if you attribute these horrible things to God and not to some satanic being, you must admit that they often bring about some greater good. We develop science to fight disease, we build levies to control hurricane surges, and so on."

Will, a student of nature, had a problem with that. "But much of this suffering in nature is unknown to us. The animal that suffers alone and unnoticed in a forest fire caused by lightening teaches us nothing, and if God can do virtually anything, why create such terrible diseases and natural disasters just to encourage science? Why motivate people through desperation? It doesn't seem like a good plan."

Arie had been silent long enough. "I don't care what theodicy you construct, that natural disasters produce some good or that they are punishment for sins—these are different explanations, by the way—for why suffering exists. None of these is very convincing given that God could presumably have done things differently and better."

Arie's comment left everyone silent for a moment.

Sara found herself making a basic philosophical point. "What is this free will we are talking about anyway? If it means anything, it means that free agents are capable of bringing about things, at least some of the time, simply by an act of will. I guess the model is God. God wills that a flower blooms, and the flower blooms regardless of whether it's the middle of winter. In other words, a truly free will can supersede the natural causal order of the world. Doesn't such a notion of free will make each effective act of will a miracle?"

Malcolm did not like that idea at all. "But isn't it enough to say we have reasons for acting and desires for certain things and that our reasons and desires can serve as causes of what we do?"

"Of course," Arie and Ellie said together.

"What about these reasons and desires?" Ellie continued, "Are they not caused by our beliefs, our circumstances, and our needs? How do we get to free will by this path?"

"Perhaps our will can override such causes and, thereby, we can select a course of action regardless of the causes operating on us," Malcolm said. "But that makes it look more and more like a miracle, doesn't it? If the will can disrupt the causal order, then it's miraculous. But," Malcolm pressed, "can't we simply regard our acts of will as part of the causal order? Some actions spring from causal factors outside of us, and some spring from causal factors inside of us, our will, and the actions taken by acts of will would not be miraculous but just part of the natural order."

Several people tried to get a word in at that point. Arie prevailed. "But Malcolm, that hypothesis leaves open the question as to how the acts of will themselves come about. Are they caused? If so, your argument gains nothing. If they're not caused, then they are mere unpredictable whims, as many philosophers have noted, and we are certainly no more responsible because we are subject to these kinds of weird events."

Will had been thinking along different lines. "Malcolm, suppose we grant that much, not all, but much of the suffering in the world comes because of actions by God's creatures. And let's grant that some degree of freedom is involved. We still face the question as to why there's so much suffering in the world. Why could God have not made us better? Why not make us freely choose to do the right thing in every case, or at least more cases? If it's not a contradiction to say that we freely choose the right thing, why not make us so that we always freely choose the right thing or mostly choose the right thing? Would we be any less free for that?"

Malcolm was perplexed by this argument. "I'm not certain it would be free will if we always chose the right thing, but I'm not certain why it would not be. After all, Jesus had a free will and was fully human, and he always chose the right thing. Some think the same is true of Mary. People in heaven presumably retain their free will, and they, except the fallen angels, always do the right thing. I just don't know. But I agree that free will as an explanation of all the suffering and evil in the world doesn't work as well as I had hoped."

Ellie announced that it had been a long day, and she was ready to pack it in. But she made a parting comment first. "Even without giving us the ability to choose the right thing all the time, it seems that God, in his wisdom as Creator, could have made us better so that we cause less suffering than we do. A parent who teaches certain moral skills or who intervenes in the lives of her children and guides them along the way is not seen as squashing their free will but as making the exercise of that will more responsible. There's a lot more to be said about what giving creatures free will means and whether God could have done so in a more morally acceptable way, but not tonight, at least not for me."

It had been a long day, Sara agreed, but something she had seen at dinner struck her now with great clarity. She arose from the table and went downstairs.

The men's lounge was starting to empty as the men headed off to their bunks, but Cole and his friend Side Pockets were still engaged in their nightly chess game. Sara touched Cole's massive hand and asked him to step outside for a brief conversation.

"You can tell Side Pockets about it when you come back," she said.

In the yard in front of the mission, Sara looked at Cole. He had been a large man, and he still carried the shoulders, arms, and hands of a youth. He moved slowly on worn out knees though. His back was hunched. He had served her father faithfully in New Jersey. When she was a child, Cole always had a kind word and a stick of gum for her. He had appeared at the mission a couple of years earlier, and Sara and Ellie both came to trust him and looked to him for help with odd jobs. Side Pockets, an old friend of Cole's, had joined him a year ago.

"Cole," Sara began. "Do you remember that man I told you about, John Steel?"

Cole nodded in affirmation.

"I saw him tonight at dinner. He was in a disguise with a false beard, tattered but fairly new clothing and brand new shoes. He looked out of place right away. I know he's angry with me for calling him out at the lifestyle fair. He may mean to harm the mission; otherwise I can't imagine why he wore a disguise. Can you keep an eye out for him, please?"

"I know the guy you mean," Cole said. "He ate dinner, but he left right after. We'll take care of it, Sister."

"Thank you, Cole." Sara felt a sense of relief and returned to her apartment, where she found Ellie already asleep.

Cindy had been on Will's mind all day. He had expected a call from her, but there were none on his phone. Back in his room, he punched in her number. She answered but in a voice so soft he could barely hear her.

"Sorry if I disturbed you," Will said.

"I was about to call," Cindy replied. "It has been one awful day."

"What happened?"

"Dad died." Cindy started to cry. "The worst part was that he said to Mom, 'Ask that woman to leave, I don't want her here.'"

"Oh God, Cindy." Will was stunned. The cruelty of that remark and the unforgiving nature of Cindy's father became crystal clear. "Maybe I should come up now that the job is delayed."

"Not yet," Cindy said. "But when the time is right, I may ask you for help. Right now, I'm exhausted and incredibly sad. My father died without any reconciliation. On the positive side, Mom is better and has fully embraced me as her daughter. She was appalled at Dad's behavior. It was as bad as it can get in a family. I've got to go now to be with Mom. Will, I love you, and I hope that doesn't scare you."

"You know, I love you, too," Will responded. Then they said goodnight.

Will's conversation with Cindy brought him up against the earlier conversation about suffering. "God, if you're all-good, all-knowing, and all-powerful, why is there so much suffering in the world, and why does so much of it seem to come from things you designed, like disease? As for the suffering we cause, why didn't you make us better? Why give us a free will if we're such cruel creatures?"

God's response caught Will by surprise. "What makes you think you have a free will?"

"I don't know," Will said. "If we don't have a free will, then I don't see how we can be responsible for what we do. Am I wrong to blame Cindy's father for being a bastard?"

"You are responsible for things you do without coercion when you know that what you're doing is right or wrong and you know what the consequences are. Those seem to apply to Cindy's father. As a pastor, he must have known what he did was wrong. As a father, he knew the hurt, and no one made him act like such a jerk. Yes, he was responsible and deserves the blame."

"But suppose he was caused to act that way," Will said.

"There is nothing particularly mysterious about human actions except that humans are not always aware of all the things that cause them to act as they do. Human diseases used to be thought to be the result of strange magical events, but as you have come to understand them better, you realize that disease comes about because of many factors: diet, pathologies, genetic legacies, and so on. Similarly, human actions come about because of personalities, circumstances, pressures, and desires. It's complicated, but someday they will be understood just as you understand disease."

Will was about to concede that acts of will were a lot like the older magical causes of diseases, a substitute for knowledge. But he forged on. "Still, you could have made us better, given us more insight into how we work and why we act as we do. Why did you create terrible diseases and floods and earthquakes? You are, after all, the creator of all things."

God let out a huge, divine harrumph. "Who said I was your creator or the creator of these things? Think about it. True, if I had the powers you say I do, I would have done a much better job. The conclusion you should maybe reach is that I did not make these things, not that I'm an incompetent creator. Were I litigious, I might regard your charges as libelous." God laughed, and with that, he left.

Will knew they would revisit this issue again. He lay awake for a long time feeling a hollow in his stomach as he thought about Cindy's plight. Early in the morning, he fell asleep to the musical sound of Ham's exercise wheel.

EXPLORATIONS

Saturday night would be the right time, John Steel thought. He had not slept at the mission that day, but he had had breakfast and dinner there. The food was not bad. He saw the fat little nun and reconnoitered the place pretty well. He knew some of the staff had that night off and took Sunday off as well. The number of people in the mission dropped on Saturday night through Sunday. On Sunday, only one meal was served, a cold supper late in the afternoon provided by volunteers from local churches.

Steel set the last of two five-gallon gas cans in the back of his Yaris. He hated the car, although it was practically new. He pined for a large black SUV like he imagined the special ops guys drove. But he couldn't afford one. When he thought of how the Yaris looked parked in front of his miserable shack, he was ashamed. It belittled a man of his military sentiments. And that's why, after he burned out the nuns, he was going to take the compound away from the Tribulation troopers. It was not much, but with a little work, it would do until the bank heist money came in.

It was pushing one in the morning. He planned to arrive in the alley behind the mission at about one thirty. The old building was wood. Splash a little accelerant on it, leave a trail of gas, and watch it go boom—from a safe distance, of course.

He had seen the young staff going out, probably to a movie. The nuns were on the top level; he didn't care if they burned. They were idolaters anyway, worshipped the Pope more than Jesus. Otherwise, he figured the clients would get out before the whole place burned down.

At one fifteen, Steel turned into the alley behind the mission. His lights were off, but he could see through his infrared glasses. He wore a black outfit with just enough shadow in it to disappear in the darkness. The Yaris fit rather well in the narrow alley. Maybe it was a good choice for this mission after all.

Steel stepped out of the Yaris and opened the back to remove the gas cans. He figured he would set them by the building and then back out of the alley. That's when he felt rather than heard the presence of someone behind him.

Turning quickly and assuming his most dangerous black belt stance, he growled in his throat. The figure, which appeared to be an old man, slightly bent with large shoulders and arms, said nothing.

"Go away old man," Steel said.

The figure remained silent. Steel decided the figure was either stupid or hard of hearing. He decided to deliver a karate kick, render the guy unconscious, and drag him out of the alley so he could set his fire.

He leveled a hard kick at the figure's midsection. He connected, but it was like kicking a cement wall. His foot, ankle, knee, and the entire right side of his body were in sudden agony. His pain was short-lived though as a fir two by four caught him in his left temple.

Sometime later, Steel regained consciousness. He was too warm, the sun was shining in his eyes, and he felt sick from a sense of motion. He was in a seat of some kind, but it was too large for the Yaris. Jesus, he was on a bus!

"Where are we headed?" he mumbled to the older woman in the seat in front of him.

"Lubbock," she said. "Are you sobering up?"

Steel's head swam; it hurt. He could not remember much about the figure in the alley, except he must have been huge and powerful to be so unaffected by his deadly karate kick. His face was tender, and he was sure it was turning black and blue. Feeling something in his shirt pocket, he discovered a piece of paper and a twenty-dollar bill. He was glad for that, because the money would get him back to Lost. The message on the note in block letters was simple enough: "Get lost."

Steel groaned and looked out the window at the flat, dry landscape as it slipped past. He actually missed his little Yaris, which, unknown to him, sat in a used car lot in Dallas thanks to a new title supplied by

Side Pockets.

Will loved his time off at the mission. He always called Uncle John and Aunt Rita first and Cindy second. Then he, Malcolm, and Arie would head out for some exploring in one of the old mission vans. Frequently, they went to a movie the evening before.

Today, he had talked to Uncle John for quite awhile. Uncle John said everything was fine, except the garden was overgrown with weeds and the lawn needed mowing. Will talked about his work at the mission. Will knew nothing of the drama between Cole and Steel. But he did mention Cindy, and Uncle John insisted that he bring her home after his time at the theme park. Will said he had not heard from Reverend Shister since he last talked to him, but it looked like the theme park would not open for a few weeks yet. Will asked to talk to his aunt and was told that she was sleeping and not feeling well. He promised to call back the next day when she was available.

Will had better luck getting hold of Cindy. Cindy was home alone, so they had a long visit.

"I'm doing much better this morning. Mom is exhausted, and I had to take her back to the hospital. I'm supposed to be planning Dad's funeral, which is hard without Mom's input. The estate, which I'm also supposed to be working on, is a mess, and there are debts to be paid. I'll quit whining now. How's your family and your work?"

"The family is doing okay, although Aunt Rita is not feeling well. Today is a day off, and Arie, Malcolm, and I are off to visit some of the local churches. It's fun to be with Arie and Malcolm. Uncle John wants you to visit, and he was quite emphatic about that."

"God, I really want out of here, Will, but I will see it through. Your uncle's invitation really makes me smile. I'll come as soon as I can. Keep me posted on what you're doing. Your stories about the sisters, Arie, Malcolm, and especially Delbert are wonderful therapy. I can't wait to meet them. Your calls are the only time I really laugh, and I always feel better for that. I know you have to go, but call again soon."

Will and Cindy said goodbye reluctantly, ending as they always did with an "I love you."

Arie and Malcolm were already seated in the off-white van with green doors when Will scampered down the stairs.

"All aboard for a tour of the many strange and conflicting denominations of the greater Dallas/Fort Worth area," Arie announced, her dark eyes dancing. "Where shall we go today?"

The sisters, who sought to run a nondenominational shelter, wanted the young staff to be informed about their clients, because the people who came through the mission attended a variety of ministries in the area. The neighborhood was a focal point of religious enthusiasms. Each visit had been a totally new experience for Arie, who grew up in an area rich in Jewish life, neighbors, and synagogues. Malcolm had spent his life traveling with his parents, who were American diplomats. He had lived in Cairo, Mumbai, and Washington, DC, so these outings were a revelation to him as well. Will was just plain curious, given his rural upbringing. In previous weeks, they had attended a liberal Jewish synagogue, a small progressive mosque in the basement of the imam's home, a mainstream Lutheran church, a black Baptist gathering, and there were the various services at the mission whose pastors were recommended by the young staff based on their visits.

"Today," Arie declared, "we will have magic and sex."

Malcolm started to note that they did not have to go out for the sex. Arie made it clear that today she was all in favor of some "edification," as she put it. "Later dear," she said to Malcolm.

Will, who was used to their banter by now, simply added, "Let's do magic first. I get enough sex vibes just being around you two."

Malcolm and Arie gave Will their sad-for-you look.

"First American-Uruba Redeemed Church coming up," Arie announced. "In case you didn't know, this church is run by Africans, mostly from Nigeria, who are missionaries to America. They're trying to redeem the fallen, which is darn near everybody in the United States, according to them. I talked to Ellie about it, since she and Sara served in Nigeria for a time. According to her, these missionaries are Pentecostal with a lot of emphasis on spirits, demons, and devils. But they're tightly disciplined, and their beliefs have roots in African animism. They believe that the United States and North America generally have fallen away from true faith, and they have a strategic plan to spread their message through immigrant groups, the poor, African-Americans, and then on to white America."

Will had done a little reading as well. "Like prosperity theology, this movement sees an important connection between religious life and money," he said. "But life is greatly influenced by a struggle among different magical beings or spirits. Their first churches were established at the beginning of the twenty-first century."

About an hour out of Dallas, the three friends arrived at a huge parking lot filled with buses and cars. The church boasted of some 30,000 members. People of all stripes were coming and going. The "service" had begun at nine and would probably continue until midnight or later. Music poured from the church and surrounded those entering.

"Love the music," Arie said as she danced toward the entrance.

The first sermon of the day was over and, fortunately for the three, the collection plate had just been passed around. None of them were willing to part with their hard-earned funds except to help out the mission on occasion. Although there were plenty of empty seats at this time of day, they settled in a row that gave them an unimpeded, if distant, view of the pulpit. There, the Reverend Oboye—a native of Nigeria—prayed in a slightly accented voice for the supernatural elimination of debts and the hope that all present would become millionaires.

"God erase my student loans," Arie offered up a mock prayer.

As a finale for the sermon, the pastor called those to the front who had a drug or alcohol problem, and the congregation prayed for them.

"Lord I know that you have a better plan for my life than for it to be wasted on drugs and alcohol. I know that by my work on your behalf and in your name I can fulfill your purpose. My very salvation, my life in heaven with you depends on it. Amen."

There was a lot of music. Some folks got up and danced or just quivered in the aisles. One enthusiast came to the front of the church, said a few things in a language that was new to Will, and collapsed on the floor. Eventually, she was carried away.

Reverend Oboye was young. He looked like a well-dressed graduate student with scholarly glasses and a carefully trimmed beard. "My Friends," he began, "today I will talk about a ghostly presence in your lives. I am not talking about the corrupt politician to whom you gave a donation just before he changed his vote. I am not talking about the neighbor who borrowed your lawnmower and ran it without oil. I am not even talking about the gang member who terrifies your neighborhood and corrupts your children. These are despicable human beings, and they take up too much time in our lives. Paul said all this in his letter to the Ephesians six, verses ten through twelve: 'Be strong in the Lord and in the strength of his power. Put on the whole armor of God, so that you may be able to stand against the wiles of the devil.' I come now to the crucial sentence. 'For our struggle is not against enemies of blood and flesh, but against the rulers, against the authorities, against the cosmic powers of this present darkness, against the spiritual forces of evil in the heavenly places.' Today, our churches and our leaders are not prepared to deal with these dark forces."

The audience murmured their approval.

"They are not prepared, because they do not believe that there are such forces. They think like Halloween trick and treaters who dress up like witches or demons but believe that these are only make-believe. Well, they are wrong." The pastor's voice rose, and he virtually shouted the last sentence. "The forces of darkness operate with impunity in our midst, because no one believes in them. Why would you fight against that which you do not think is real?

"Some among you use the Bible in perverse ways. You realize that the Bible is a powerful book of sorcery, yes, magic. You look down the pew and see your neighbor who ruined your lawnmower. You shake the book at him and send a demon home from church to torment him. You laugh at his torment and say that he deserves it. Well, that is blasphemy. This is the wrong use of God's magic, and you will suffer in damnation for it."

"Really weird," God said. "I'm getting scared just listening to this guy."

"I've never heard anything like it," Will replied. "And, I don't like where I think this is going."

"This is not to say that the power of the Bible is never to be used," the pastor continued. "As a young man, a student at university in Nigeria, I used the Bible to drive a witch out of my village. I followed this evil woman everywhere, shaking the Bible at her, setting demons on her, and identifying her as a witch. Eventually, many people from the village gathered around and they, too, called up demons on her. Both of this woman's neighbors had died of mysterious diseases, so we knew she was a witch. At first I hoped that shaking the Bible at her would exorcise that evil spirit that dwelled in her. But she did not repent of her sins, so we drove her out."

"This guy would have loved the Inquisition," God said.

"For sure," Will replied.

The pastor launched into another story. "Another young man, a classmate, told me that while he was at university his computer was stolen. He took his Bible and placed a skeleton key in the twenty-third Psalm. Then he bound the Bible in string, making a cross on the front of the good book. He took that book and began to chant the names of those who might have had access to his computer. When he came to the name of one of his acquaintances, the Bible began to tremble and shake in his hand. He could barely hold onto it. He went through the list three times, and each time when he came to the name of that individual, his Bible shook and trembled. He put down his book reverently, because he knew that the Holy Spirit was acting through it, and went to this acquaintance's room. There, he found his computer." The pastor held up his Bible. "When you hold the Bible, you hold in your hand a powerful conduit of spirit. And when you use it, you must use it in the Lord's name, and you must believe."

He set his Bible back on the pulpit. "Recall that when Paul visited Ephesus, the Holy Spirit came to the worshipers, and they spoke in tongues and prophesied. Paul tells us this in Acts nineteen verse six. Because he believed, Paul performed many extraordinary miracles. He healed the sick when he was imbued with the Holy Spirit. And when some local exorcists tried to mimic what Paul had done, the evil spirit in the sick man refused to leave his host and caused the sick man to jump up and drive off the charlatans. The exorcists saw the light and publicly burned their expensive pile of magic books. My friends, the power is yours to use, but only one power will prevail over and control the evil spirits, and that is the Holy Spirit.

"Know that evil is real. Know that spirits are real. Know that demons are real. Know that witches are real. Don't listen to the deniers in the so-called mainstream churches. They think the devil is a joke or a metaphor or a myth. Satan is real. Don't listen to the scientists who don't believe. They are mostly atheists anyway. The Bible attests to the reality of magic. But don't ever forget that the Spirit is there, and you can use sorcery to armor yourself. But first, you have to believe that there is an enemy to be fought."

At this point, a young woman appeared beside the pastor. On either side of her, two muscular men held her by the arms. To the amazement of Will and his friends, the pastor proceeded to perform an exorcism on her to drive out evil spirits and cleanse her. He made it clear that this was a voluntary exorcism.

"This sister came to me and told me that there were times when she gets drunk, shouts profanity, and solicits sex in bars."

A collective murmur rose up from the audience.

"She will not do such things anymore now that she has been purged of evil."

The young woman smiled and thanked the pastor for his services. Then she began to speak in tongues, and her body language made it clear she was praising the Lord.

Arie and Malcolm were getting restless, and Will was getting hungry. They headed out for lunch, which proved to be a pleasant affair at a small salad bar where they sat outside.

Malcolm raised the question that was on everyone's mind. "How is it that a single religion can go in so many directions? Or is it a single religion anymore? It's the same in Islam; different sects derive their authority from different traditions. Some rely more on the hadith, the oral tradition allegedly attributed to Muhammad, and others on the Koran. But how does this happen?"

"Oops," Arie said, looking at her watch "we have one more church to visit, and the service begins in less than an hour. Hold that question, Malcolm. It's time for sex."

"I wish," Malcolm replied.

Less than twenty minutes later, Will parked the van in a run-down section of Dallas. They entered what was obviously an abandoned commercial building; the picture window still had the sign "Dollar Store" at the top of the glass. Below was written "Downtown Church" and under that "Welcome."

Arie, Will, and Malcolm entered and found seats near the back. The chairs varied from old wooden benches to fairly recent folding chairs. There were still merchandise shelves on the wall. Interspersed among the chairs were two old sofas.

The pastor was already in front of the congregation turning up the music. It was hard rock and some rap. After a few minutes, the pastor turned off the speakers and then faced the congregation, which looked uniformly poor, somewhat grubby, and in some cases, stoned. The pastor was young, and he wore old torn jeans and a tank top. His arms were covered with tattoos. He had not shaved for a couple of days.

"Hello sinners! Hello fornicators! What are you thinking about now? Are you thinking, 'When can I get out of here and have some good fortified wine and fuck her or him?'"

His words were met with smiles and chuckles around the congregation. More people were arriving and filling the chairs.

"Most of you are going to hell anyway," the pastor continued. "If you're new here, I'm Pastor Diesel, yeah, just like the fuel. This is not some namby pampy mainline church where I tell you Jesus is love and he's kind of like your gay next door neighbor, all limp-wristed and clever. No, Jesus is like the big muscular guy who beat the shit out of you when you came on to his girlfriend."

The audience liked this approach.

"You can still feel his knuckles taking out your teeth and making you wonder what the hell was happening. I'll tell you what's happening. You're going to hell, and there's not a damn thing you can do about it.

"Oh, but you say, 'I can change, and when I change, I'll obey the Ten Commandments. I'll quit stealing and committing adultery. I'll even give up booze, although that will be tougher than giving up screwing.' Well, that's bullshit! In the first place, you can't change. You are depraved, totally depraved. Do you know what that means? It means you are corrupt through and through. It means that your great, great, great, great—and keep going—ancestors blew it. When Adam and Eve messed up and screwed each other, they screwed you too."

More chuckles from the audience.

"The second thing that's wrong with what you think is that you think by doing good you can redeem yourself. You can't. Paul tells us in Romans eleven verse six that it is by grace we are saved and not by works. If works could save you, you wouldn't need grace. Again, in Ephesians two verse eight we're told, 'For by grace you have been saved through faith, and this is not your doing; it is the gift of God.' You ask, 'Didn't Jesus save me? Didn't his death atone for my sins?' Sorry, there was atonement, but it was only partial. Tough cookies.

"But you say, 'What's the point then? I'm doomed. Nothing I do matters.' And you're right. Nothing you do matters, but there is a glimmer of hope for a few of us, and the operative word here is *few.* You all know that Jesus is a pretty smart guy, and you all know that Jesus is God and God knows everything. God knows what you will do tomorrow and the next day and forever. God also knows now whether you are among the saved or not. He decided that a long time ago. He made that decision before you were born, before your parents were born.

"You might be among the chosen. But that doesn't mean you can sit on your ass and disobey God, not at all. God asks you to live a good life; he designed you for that. The next verse in Ephesians says we were made for good works. Do it because God commands it and because God is your judge and creator. He is tough and mean, like the guy who beat you up. Don't forget it."

"Grrrrr," God said.

"Religion as a cage fight?" Will asked. "Where does all this come from?"

"The same place as the message in the last church," God said. "The human capacity for imaginative selective reading."

"Hard to believe."

"One more thing!" Pastor Diesel continued, "don't think you can waltz out of here and tell yourself, 'Oh, I'll get around to it tomorrow, maybe next week I'll put my life together.' Brothers and sisters, you don't have time. Jesus knew that when he told them in Mark nine verse one, 'Truly I tell you, there are some standing here who will not taste death until they see that the kingdom of God has come.' Paul, too, knew the end was coming soon. But you, my foolish friends, don't know, and you think you have time. Jesus and Paul saw that the kingdom was so imminent that you don't even have time for a quickie! Be celibate, focus on the Lord, ignore your friends and family. That was their message! Read Luke fourteen verse twenty-six or First Corinthians seven verses one to thirty-five if you don't believe me."

Pastor Diesel turned up the music, and the three friends slipped out of the store and decided it was time to head back to the mission. They found the sermon both humorous and depressing.

Malcolm offered his opinion with which they all pretty much agreed.

"There's nothing beautiful about people, sex, or religion in that point of view. Even the family is suspect. What a bummer! Compared to that church a few weeks back where the pastor simply went on and on extolling the wonders of Christian sex within marriage, what a difference!"

Arie laughed all the way to the van. "And Jesus and Paul missed the end of time by thousands of years. I mean, they thought the kingdom was coming within their lifetime. I'm amazed that ol' Diesel didn't pick up on that. He sounds like he thinks it's tomorrow or later today."

As they drove down the interstate, Will returned to the question Malcolm had raised earlier. He was overwhelmed by the doctrinal differences among the churches. "Wow what a contrast!" he said. "On the one hand you're saved by grace alone and can't help yourself with good works, and on the other you can save yourself by magical good works. Jesus is love or Jesus is a bully. God has a plan for you or it's up to you and your free will to create your life plan. Leave your family, even hate them, and honor your father and mother." Will trailed off into a dejected silence. He was beginning to see Christianity as a collage of very different perspectives that just happened to talk about certain historical figures, which they understood quite differently.

"Noticing cerebral collapse due to theological quicksand," God interjected.

"Well, I'm up to my chin in it," Will grumbled.

"Hey," Arie said brightly, "one could suppose that God just gets confused and gives different messages to different groups at different times. I can imagine a senile god who tells people to love their enemies one day and cut off their heads the next. But I think one really has to look at the human followers to understand such differences."

"Different strokes for different folks," Malcolm agreed, "but there are also different needs in different situations. Religion, if nothing else, is a response to human needs. When Muhammad was in Mecca and they were making fun of him, he was very conciliatory and tolerant, but when he moved to Medina and had an army at his back, he became more belligerent and aggressive. In the suras of that period, he commands his followers to obey Allah *and his prophet*, whereas in the suras written in Mecca, he commands his followers just to obey Allah."

Will was thinking furiously. "For any written text, there are multiple interpretations depending on context." He was increasingly aware of the different reading of scripture by his aunt and uncle, not to mention Reverend Ted. "Add the fact that words are often metaphorical and have different meanings and vagueness attached to them to the fact that people want different things from the texts, and you get amazing creativity in understanding, as we have just seen."

"Political factors can come in as well," Arie added. "I read somewhere that King James would not allow the word 'tyrant' to occur in the translation he authorized, even though the Bible is filled with stories about tyrants."

Arie, who was driving, pulled in behind the mission. It was near dark as Will and his friends headed to their rooms. Sister Sara passed them in the hall and, with a smile on her face, announced that the mission had just received a check for $9,000 from a car dealer in Dallas who had also very generously supplied cans with ten gallons of gas for the mission's van.

"I know I'm a couple of weeks behind in paying you three, so I'll go to the bank tomorrow and then pay you in cash."

With that welcome news, all said good night.

Will's talk with God that night was brief. When he asked why there were so many religions God said, "Because there are so many frightened, superstitious and—excuse my language—ignorant people. Religion is, after all, a human search for security and supernatural help. Different folks have different fears and need different things. I thought you all did a good job of summarizing why people tread different paths."

"But do these different groups worship the same god?"

"The answer is fairly obvious," God responded. "No. Just look at the Old Testament and the New Testament. Vengeful gods are not the same as compassionate gods. Compassionate gods do not demand the wholesale extermination of peoples."

"Then if they worship different gods, aren't they different religions?"

"Probably," God said. "And worshiping different gods happens within the same congregation depending on how the different individuals conceive their god. Do you really believe Aunt Rita's god is your Uncle John's God?"

"Probably not," Will said reluctantly, "although growing up I assumed they were the same."

The intellectual and physical journeys of the day left him ready for sleep. He checked Ham's water and then tossed a biscuit into his cage. His last thought was that when he got paid, he would send flowers to Cindy and his aunt.

TRUE BELIEF

Monday mornings were always busy at the mission. Calls had to be made to food distribution centers, grocery stores, and selected restaurants. Sheets had to be laundered, and the mission got a good cleaning. Volunteers did most of this work, but Will, Arie, and Malcolm, the paid staff, were given the heaviest, dirtiest, and most responsible jobs.

The many trips to different churches were still churning Will's thoughts. He realized that the more he thought about the different claims, the more questions he had and the less certain he was about his own beliefs.

He pushed through his chores and, having some time before his food pickup, decided to see if Sister Ellie was available for a chat. He found her in her study bent over what looked like budget sheets.

"Will, come in," she said when she saw him in the doorway.

"I don't want to take up a lot of time," Will said.

"You look like you are having serious thoughts. Are they spiritual?"

"Yes," Will responded.

"Then there's always time to talk about these things. Besides, I have little stomach for going over these depressing budgets, although they look better with the funds Cole provided."

Will was not certain he knew why he was here, but he trusted Sister Ellie to help him find out. "I grew up in a religious home," he began. "My aunt and uncle who raised me were religious people. I love them and respect their views on things. At the same time, I never really questioned anything. I just absorbed their religiousness when I was younger; even as I grew older and came to realize that they did not agree very much, I found it comfortable to just go with the flow."

Sister Ellie encouraged Will to go on.

"Since I left home, I have had a lot of contact with Christians. Arie, Malcolm, and I also talk about religion a lot. We all have different points of view. And since we've been visiting other churches, I'm discovering that Christians hold a whole lot of different views on everything. I mean, I knew some of this from my own family. Uncle John seems to think that God is inscrutable and mysterious, but my aunt thinks every sentence in the Bible fell directly from God's mouth. I really can't go with either of those alternatives. And now working here with you and Sister Sara, whom I greatly admire, I feel good about what I'm doing. But I'm also having doubts. I doubt very much, for example, that either the Redeemed Church or the Downtown Church have it right. I'm not certain that anyone has it right."

"By 'right', do you mean 'true beliefs'?" Ellie asked.

"Yes," Will said. "Some churches, like the Unitarians, allow almost any kind of belief, but others require a strict set of beliefs in order to count as a Christian. So, I'm drifting into an uncertain view of what it means to be a Christian. I think I should believe something, but I don't quite know what that is. I don't disbelieve either. I just don't seem to have enough evidence or faith to go in a particular direction."

Will stopped and shook his head. He looked at Sister Ellie, whose expression could not conceal her mirth.

"Your question reminds me of an old joke," she said. "What do you get when you cross a Jehovah's Witness with a Unitarian?"

Will shook his head. "I don't know."

"Someone who comes to your door for no apparent reason."

Will knew that he could always count on Sister Ellie for a bit of irreverence; it gave him a good laugh.

In spite of her humor, Sister Ellie studied him, "Will, first, welcome to the club."

She gave him a dazzling smile that made him feel that he had come to the right person.

"We're going to have to have more than one conversation about all this, but today we can begin with what seems to me to be the central question: How does one select among the innumerable religions and denominations? There do not seem to be any non-question-begging criteria."

Will was not sure what Sister Ellie meant by "non-question-begging."

"For example, I'm Catholic. The Pope and the Church hierarchy tell me that the Catholic Church is the one true Church founded by Peter in Rome. But they have a vested interest in being the true Church, and the evidence, scriptural or historical, that they present all presupposes that they are the true Church. If I accept what they say as evidence, I beg the question, which is whether they are a reliable source of evidence. And their interpretation of the evidence discounts claims of truth by other religions and denominations. They tell you that if you do not have the beliefs prescribed by the Church, you're on the wrong path."

"But all religions seem to claim historical and scriptural evidence," Will protested, "and they claim it with the same degree of sincerity and certainty as the Catholics. If it's so important to have the right set of beliefs and belong to the right religion, why doesn't God step in and clarify the whole issue? Why let all this multiplication of faiths go on and on with their question-begging justifications? I'm getting to the point where I don't know what to believe."

"I have fought the same battle," Sister Ellie said. "In fact, I fight it most days. We're taught that we should have certain beliefs in order to be good Christians. But many of us have trouble holding onto these beliefs. Even those who tell us to have certain beliefs lack good reasons for doing so. They tell us to just have faith. All this is especially troubling when having certain beliefs is said to be required for salvation."

Will was beginning to wonder if he should be getting worried about his immortal soul. But he liked that Sister Ellie was beginning to frame his worries succinctly. However, identifying them was not the same as answering them.

Sister Ellie asked Will to get a couple of cups of tea from the kitchen. "Then," she said, "we can continue. I cannot do theology without tea."

Settled with tea, Sister Ellie studied Will. He had such a solid yet handsome appearance. He looked just slightly younger than Arie or Malcolm, which he was. Sister Ellie smiled at the thatch of unruly hair that always seemed to jump up from the top front of Will's head.

"Can you tell me more?" she asked. "How have you been thinking about your question?"

Will started hesitantly. "Suppose that finding God is the most important thing a person can do, and that requires a specific path. And suppose a person is genuinely seeking God as so many are and have done. Then why doesn't God simply, straightforwardly, indicate the path? Why does God not correct them immediately like God corrected those who worshiped the golden calf?"

"Will, there are many traditional answers to these worries, but I don't know if any of them will satisfy you."

"I've tried to think of a few," Will responded. "Some claim that God makes the path evident, but the sheer number of religions and denominations out there gives the lie to that. A few folks claim to have had a grand experience where God directed them on their path, but most do not. And those who do claim divine direction seem to go off the rails into a crazy set of beliefs, like the Downtown Church. Furthermore, it's always private, so who knows whose voice they actually heard. The scriptures themselves make God fairly enigmatic. God says he is who he is or that he does not think as we think, and he reminds Job just how puny he is compared to God and that Job can't understand something so grand. When I look at the range of theologies that call themselves Christian, not to mention other non-Christian theologies, they all claim to be the prescribed path. So, I can't buy any of them, and the fact that they exist is, to me, evidence that God is not doing his job, that he is either in hiding or he doesn't exist."

Ellie nodded in understanding. "If you don't like that answer, how about saying that there's a greater good that comes from making folks choose one path from among many?"

Will shook his head vigorously. "But there's supposed to be no greater good than union with God, so I don't see how one can argue that a greater good is being served by confusing that pursuit through divine invisibility."

Sister Ellie smiled. She liked Will's analysis.

"I mean," Will looked at the floor as if he was searching for an analogy, "imagine we're God's children, and God loves and cares about us. Imagine that a person or a child is lost in the wilderness with many paths, only one of which is the way home. The child chooses the path that goes deeper into the forest. The parent sees or hears the child, as God surely sees us. Why doesn't God go to such a person and turn him or her around? Any good parent would. If what the other religions say about each other is true, a lot of people are going to be damned, because they've gone the wrong way. And, from what I can tell, it's not true that most sincere seekers eventually find the right view of God, whatever that is. Most of them fail. For all I can tell, God rarely if ever makes the path clear. I guess my concern is twofold. God doesn't make himself manifest to those who are sincerely seeking him, and the sheer diversity of claims made on his behalf not only makes the path harder to find, it's further proof of God's invisibility."

"Another answer," Ellie proposed, "is that we are not equipped to understand God, and that's why we don't take the right path. We're like a flea trying to understand the physiology of a dog. We just don't have the apparatus to do so, and that's why we need grace or faith instilled in us."

She smiled at Will's pained expression. "But I can tell from the look on your face that that response just makes the problem worse for you. Or perhaps it just restates the problem, because how do you decide among claims of faith and grace? And why did God give us such poor equipment to begin with?"

Will nodded in agreement. "I just think God should be more forthright."

At that point, he seriously considered telling Sister Ellie about his frequent conversations with God. But in his state of profound doubt, he was beginning to think that his god might be too eccentric to be God.

"Let's look at a second issue about belief," Sister Ellie suggested. "What makes you think religion is a matter of belief in the first place?"

"Because that's how it's put," Will replied. "If you have faith in God and his Son, then you believe in them. Even the Bible talks that way. In John twelve verse forty-four, Jesus says, 'Whoever believes in me believes not in me but in him who sent me.' He repeats that theme in John a lot. And in Mark sixteen verse sixteen, he says that someone who doesn't believe will be condemned. Doesn't that mean you ought to believe?"

"That's certainly one way of looking at it," Ellie replied, thinking about her own convictions. "But there are a couple of things we need to ask here. First, what does 'believe' mean in these passages? Does it mean 'conviction'? 'Unshakeable certainty'? These same passages point out that the disciples themselves had doubts; they lacked certainty about their fundamental beliefs. Throughout the stories told in Matthew, Mark, Luke, and John, the picture is one of massive doubt and uncertainty, as in Matthew twenty-eight verse seventeen or Luke twenty-four verse forty-five. So, I've always believed that you can be a good Christian and still have doubts. Most people do. You do. And doubting means that you may not have the belief or be able to form the right belief."

"If there is no psychological certainty, what should a Christian do?"

Sister Ellie sipped her tea before answering. "There are two answers in the scriptures that I have found. The first is that when people doubted and failed to understand, Jesus or God gave them understanding and removed doubt. Some might call this 'grace.' Jesus or God just stuffed understanding into their heads. Certainly this is suggested in Luke twenty-four verse forty-five: 'Then he opened their minds to understand the scriptures.' On this view, you can sit around and hope something gets stuffed in your head. Of course, this takes us back to the problem of how do we know that the right beliefs got put there. But a second view is that to believe is to obey commandments, to take action. It's pretty clear in Luke fifteen, Matthew twenty-eight, Mark sixteen—although it's in a later edition—and John fifteen verse ten: 'If you keep my commandments, you will abide in my love.' So it seems to me that obeying the commandments to love your neighbor, spread the word, and treat others with respect is what it means to believe. That's what we try to do at the Social Gospel Mission. Belief is about doing and not so much understanding and being certain."

Will was comfortable with this perspective. It was his natural inclination, or at least the inclination he had learned from his uncle, that he should be kind and helpful whenever he could.

"But," Ellie continued, "there's another somewhat more abstract reason to read the scriptures as asking for actions rather than as demanding certainty of belief."

Will gave her a puzzled look.

"Will, have you ever tried to make yourself believe something just because you want to believe it? Have you ever tried to bring yourself to belief by just willing that you believe?"

"I don't think I could," Will replied.

"Why not?"

"That's not how beliefs come about. I believe something after I've studied the evidence for it, or I believe something after someone I consider reliable tells me that that is the case. It would be very strange and unnatural for me to simply go around believing things just because I wanted to or because it suited me. We are brought to belief by evidence, testimony, and how something fits with our other beliefs."

"But don't we say that some people don't believe because they don't want to believe?"

"Yes," Will agreed, "but if you ask such a person why they don't believe something, they usually give reasons or say they just can't believe it. They don't act as if it's simply a matter of choosing, even though we say sometimes that such people choose not to believe. We don't mean that literally."

Sister Ellie nodded in agreement. "I can't think of a single belief that I can form just by choosing to do so. What this means to me is that belief is not voluntary. We cannot believe because we choose to believe. Belief commands us; we do not command belief."

Will saw where this was going. "We're not obliged to do that which we cannot do," he began. "If my arm is numb, I have no obligation to raise it even if it's important that I do so. So I don't do anything wrong by not raising my arm. Similarly, if I don't believe, I do nothing wrong in not believing, because belief is not something I can choose to do. It's something that happens to me. So, with this in mind, the scriptures do not ask us to do what we can't do. Instead, they ask us to act in certain ways. Presumably, action is something we can choose to do. But if that's the case, what do we mean by saying that someone's disbelief is willful?"

Ellie thought for a moment before answering. "Suppose that someone, like some of our current politicians, denied that global warming is happening."

"They don't live in Texas," Will said dryly. "Actually, some of them do."

Sister Ellie laughed. "What we mean by saying someone willfully disbelieves is that someone refuses to look at the evidence for global warming, refuses to talk to those who are knowledgeable about it. They turn away from what might trigger belief. We can do things like that. We can refuse to engage in activities that might lead us to form a belief we do not want to form. But that is a different thing from making the belief itself voluntary. In short, we might say that if the path is one of belief, then the path chooses us; we don't choose the path. But if the path is one of doing things, then we have more control over it."

By that point, Will's head was spinning, and he needed to be on his way to the food distribution center. "Thanks, Sister Ellie, I need to think about all this some more. This has really helped though. Now, I better be off."

"I enjoyed our talk very much, Will." She gave him a hug. "Maybe we can pull the whole crew together for further discussion. I know Arie is keen on the subject. And Will, anytime you want to discuss such issues, let's discuss them. You are a clear thinker and, quite frankly, philosophy and theology were among my favorite classes."

In the van, Will checked his gas supply; it was full. Then he headed off to the food bank, his cell phone in his shirt pocket. Although Will's head was full of his recent discussion, he drove carefully, as always, and that's probably what saved him.

As he approached a busy intersection about a mile from the mission, he slowed down, thinking the light might change, which it did. However, a car coming from the other way sped up and, with a sickening screech of brakes and the crunching of metal, collided with the side of the car that had jumped into the intersection—a case of aggressive driving by both drivers.

Will jumped from the van and, smelling smoke, took the risk of removing each driver. Thankfully, there were no passengers in either vehicle. Covering each driver with donated coats and blankets, he began CPR on the driver who was not breathing. He instructed others to stop some serious bleeding on the second driver. The fire department arrived quickly and foamed both vehicles to prevent the smoke from becoming a fire.

A medic crouched down next to Will. "I'll take over here, buddy."

The medics were able to shock the driver back to life. Afterwards, the medic turned to Will. "If this guy still has a brain, he owes it to you. Good job. A lot of folks just don't want to get involved in something like this."

A bystander also complimented Will. Best of all, having seen the sign on the side of Will's van, he promised to make a donation to the mission. Will called the mission to tell Sister Sara he would be late returning. She asked if he still felt like completing the run. Then she dispatched Arie to drop Malcolm off so he could help Will load the food.

Malcolm and Arie showed up moments later. Will was glad to see them. Both were deeply concerned that Will might be in shock. Will said he actually felt pretty good. His adrenaline was definitely elevated. By the time Malcolm and Will were able to get away from the police interviews, the local press had pictures of Will and the crash vehicles.

"You'll be in the paper tomorrow," Malcolm noted as they drove on to the food bank.

"I hope it means some good publicity for the mission," Will replied.

After they returned to the mission, Will realized he was, after all, a bit shaky. Malcolm, with Sister Sara's backing, insisted that Will go to his room and lie down.

Back in his room, Will was happy to do just that and chat with Ham, who seemed pleased to have company. He chirped, and Will let him out to run about on the bed while he rested. He knew Ham would find a pocket and curl up inside for a "hamster siesta," as Arie called it.

Will reached for God. "It's barely past noon, and it's been quite a day already. When something like that happens and people are hurt, does that have anything to do with your will? Are accidents part of divine providence?"

"Heavens, no," God replied. "That was just bad driving, reckless driving. But I thought you did extremely well in helping. That one guy might have died."

"Doesn't everything that happens require your allowing it to happen? Isn't that part of being all-powerful?"

"Will," God said, "there are many things that I cannot do, and there are even more things that are attributed to me, which I did not do. I have no time, no interest, and no patience to meddle around in people's lives. I don't decide when they pee, when they're born, or when they die. I also don't decide what they believe and when they believe it."

God's comments returned Will to his discussion with Sister Ellie. He was a bit nervous about getting into the question of divine revelation with God, but God seemed to be in a good mood. "I'm beginning to have doubts that we can ever know what to believe. I'm not certain we know which religion or theology to follow."

"Why is that?" God asked.

"Look at all the different religions claiming to be *the* true religion. I know they can't all be true. But their defenders are so certain. A lot more certain than I am."

"Uncertainty sounds like a good thing to me," God replied. "How can you be certain about such vague and huge questions? People who live in particular circumstances invent religions. That's as true for those who wrote the Bible as for those who interpret it today. Do you really think that if I had dictated the Bible or guided the thoughts of those who wrote it I would have put together such a hodgepodge of conflicting views? No, different folks with different agendas explains why it reads like a disorganized committee report. But complexity is not all bad. It allows for interpretations that suit your needs. You've seen ample evidence of that."

Will was getting a bit sleepy. "You're convincing me that little is to be gained by trying to glean the true faith from cryptic scripture written by diverse people searching for security and purpose."

God chuckled, "I'm glad you've finally gotten that message. How many times have you sat down and pulled up a scripture, only to have it contradicted by another passage or have someone put a completely different emphasis on it?"

"Only all the time."

"And maybe you've discovered an explanation for the problem," God suggested. "If people are looking at the scriptures as if they are going to reveal something about me, and the scriptures are themselves a mess of different convictions, they're only going to produce an ever-changing kaleidoscope of beliefs. Reality will always be hidden by a cloak of bewilderment."

"I'm willing to give up that exercise," Will agreed. "But why don't you just show up? Why don't you just make yourself manifest?"

"You're getting close to an answer on that one," God replied. "But think about it. Your discussion with Sister Ellie assumed both that I exist and that I have an obligation to show up. You also assumed that you can choose actions but not beliefs. You might want to reexamine these assumptions."

There was a long pause.

"You're not going to say any more, are you?" Will asked. "But, at least tell me whether having certain beliefs is important."

"It's what you do," God replied. "It has always been what you do. Now go to sleep."

Will felt some relief as he drifted off. He also felt Ham settle into his shirt pocket, and distantly, he thought he heard God singing.

"Looking for God in all the wrong places...."

THE ONE AND ONLY

The following day, Will's picture and a short story made the front page of two Dallas area papers under the headline, "What a Good Samaritan Looks Like." He was happy it mentioned that he worked at the Social Gospel Mission. He had already called Cindy and his uncle and aunt in case the story became more widespread. The situations in both homes were stable. His aunt was feeling much better, and Cindy had gotten some rest.

Will and Malcolm lingered over their breakfast. They both had kitchen duty, which involved cleanup after the morning meal. They wore old Levis with white, more or less, kitchen aprons across their laps. They were engaged in their usual argument about who was going to be in the World Series and who was going to prevail. Malcolm was a Red Sox fan, and Will liked the National League.

Malcolm took a drink of tea. "Will, you know I'm headed to law school in the fall, but I'm sure going to miss you and the mission. It's been a great place for me, and I feel like you've become a real friend. You're one of the most accepting individuals I've ever met, and yesterday you showed so much cool. I don't think I could have touched those bloody drivers."

Will was a little embarrassed by the compliment. "I didn't really think about what I was doing. I was so afraid that those cars would blow up any minute—I've probably watched too many movies. I just acted. But you know, I'm really glad I landed here after the disaster of the lifestyle show, which was pretty damaging to my ego. I love working with you, Arie, and the other staff. The sisters are really special. And the clients; it seems like there's a story behind each of them—a novel maybe."

"Talk about characters!" Malcolm's brown eyes sparkled.

Will noticed that Malcolm had not shaved that morning. He was probably saving it for that night and some time with Arie.

Malcolm laughed. "I was talking to Jesus Perez the other day. She was repairing one of the tables in the dining area."

Jesus was a Latina woman of indiscernible age who did carpentry jobs around the mission. She claimed to be the same Jesus who had lived in Nazareth and told anyone who was interested the story of her life; she especially liked to talk about the "lost years" when she was a practicing carpenter.

"She now claims it's her third coming."

"That's news," Will commented with a laugh. "Not to mention that Jesus is now a transsexual."

"Yes," Malcolm agreed. "She claims the second coming was during Watergate, and when she heard about it, she decided she had come back too soon. Then she came back again at the time of Bush's second election last fall and decided the world really needed her."

Both young men knew that Jesus was good for a sustained conversation on almost any political topic. She was a staff favorite.

"Malcolm," Will asked, changing topics, "what about you and Arie?"

Malcolm nodded. "We're working on that, believe me, we're working on it! Being separated is almost impossible for either of us to imagine. I'll keep you posted." Malcolm took another sip of tea. "So tell me, after visiting all these churches and denominations, I'm confused about Christianity. Is Christianity monotheistic or is it just monolatrous?"

"What's that?" Will asked, having never heard the word "monolatrous" before.

"In monolatry, you only worship one god, but you may acknowledge more than one. The first commandment sounds monolatrous to me; it seems to allow the existence of other gods. And there are other places in your scripture where there seems to be an acknowledgement of other gods."

"I'm no Bible scholar, but Uncle John says that he thinks the Israelites were polytheists who moved through what you call monolatry to monotheism, the belief that there is only one god. There is some reference to a council of gods at which God sat and was prominent in Psalm eighty-nine verse six. There sure are a lot of statues of other divine beings that have been unearthed in that part of the world and a lot of stories in the Bible about God getting pissed off because the Israelites kept worshiping other gods. But Christianity claims to be monotheistic, as does Judaism."

Malcolm still looked puzzled. "I get that about Judaism, but it's hard for a Muslim to believe that Christianity is a monotheistic religion."

"Why is that?"

"Just look at the churches we've attended in the past few weeks. One of them is really into the Holy Spirit, one of them mentioned Jesus but never mentioned God, and another stressed God. I won't even go into the different characterizations of God or Jesus that one gets moving from church to church. Some think Jesus was not divine but special, some think he was *adopted*, and some think he's one with God. It's enough to make a Muslim's head spin."

As Will listened, he had to concede that Malcolm was justly confused. "There have been a lot of theological contests among Christians, most of them focused on the so-called Trinity—the oneness of the Father, Son, and Holy Ghost."

"Having grown up with 'there is no god but Allah,' I'm hard-pressed to make sense of the three-in-one stuff."

"Most Christians don't get it either," Will replied. "And I'll spare you the three-in-one oil metaphors or the ice, liquid, and steam metaphor. They don't make any sense, since the Trinity is neither a blend nor different forms of a chemical composition. The incomprehensibility of the Trinity is probably why the different services tend to focus on one of the three and why it's spoken of as a *mystery*. My own thought stumbles when I begin to think about whether some things are true of one member of the Trinity but not true of the others. Presumably, only Jesus was fully human. That's not true of God or the Holy Ghost."

"In fact," Malcolm noted, "there are a whole lot of things true of God that are not true of Jesus and vice versa. Jesus was born of woman, and Jesus died. God did not die and cannot die. God is not born. I'm not sure what to say about the Holy Ghost. Is it some kind of blueprint for things? Is it a spirit that infects things at certain moments? Anyway, there are enough differences that some Christians speak of three persons. It seems to me that different persons is the same as different gods."

"But," Will noted, "they are supposed to be of one substance—if that makes any sense."

Malcolm shook his head. "Not to me it doesn't. One could say that identical twins, or perhaps better, identical triplets, have the same substance, the same DNA, but they are still distinct individuals with different properties. And having different properties seems sufficient to show nonidentity. If we were doing forensics and found out that the person who committed the crime had a different DNA from or was taller than the person we suspect, it would be more than enough to establish nonidentity."

"I guess that brings us back to the mystery of it all," Will replied, although he had never understood trinitarianism either.

"A mystery to me is a series of events that has an explanation, but we just have not figured it out yet." Malcolm liked to read legal thrillers. "I think 'mystery' here is used in a different sense. It means that there are things for which there is no explanation. Stuff that is just way beyond us, even incoherent. And that sounds like a copout, a standard move among religions. But the dilemma that Christianity faces is clear. Either Jesus is God or he isn't. If Jesus is God, then he didn't die on the cross—gods can't die—and if he's not God but a separate divinity, then Christianity is not a monotheistic religion. Christianity's dogma is that Jesus is both God and not God. Then they say the 'not God' died on the cross and that because Jesus is God, they're monotheistic. It's unintelligible to me."

Will could not help but be reminded of one of his conversations with God, where God cast doubt on the whole death and resurrection story. Will had asked God a fundamental question. The answer was less than satisfactory.

"Did you die for our sins?"

God responded with another question. "What, presumably, am I?"

"You are God," Will responded.

"No, I asked *what* am I."

"Oh," Will said. "You're *a* god."

"What are some things that are true of gods?"

"Umm, you're powerful and smart."

"What about my life?"

"You never get sick."

"Right. And…"

"You never die."

"You got it."

Malcolm's dilemma, therefore, cut deep for Will. He decided to nudge the conversation in a different direction. "Malcolm, we've been visiting so many religions and talking among ourselves that I'm having doubts about what to believe. Sister Ellie seems to think that doing good things for people is what religion is all about, and holding certain beliefs is not as important. Where are you on faith versus works?"

Malcolm thought for a while. "Probably about where you are. I'm working for two saints who are not at all doctrinaire. I'm sleeping with a Jewish atheist. And I've seen enough screwy religions in the past few weeks to turn anyone into a skeptic. I do know that I really dig some of the music. That African-American Baptist church we went to about a month ago was sheer joy and exuberance. I've bought two gospel CDs since then, and I could see going back there just for the music."

The African-American Baptist church was Will's most memorable visit as well. It was small, lively, and everyone seemed to know each other. It reminded him of home. Arie had embarrassed Will and Malcolm by getting up and dancing in the aisle until they noticed that when she got up, so did several other worshipers.

Arie popped into the kitchen. "Haven't you two lazy bums started to wash pots yet? Delbert will freak if the kitchen isn't clean when he gets here to prepare the evening meal."

Both Will and Malcolm were much more transfixed by the young woman who accompanied Arie. Indeed, Arie had her by the hand.

"Hey guys, I want you to meet Samantha Drake. Samantha, this is Will Tillit and Malcolm Hasan. The second guy is mine."

Samantha was tall. Will was six feet and a couple of inches, and she was close to matching his height. She had long brown hair, soft brown eyes, and stood to her full height. She was beautiful.

"Sam will be joining us for a one-month internship. We hope she'll come on permanently when Malcolm heads to law school or when Will reports to the theme park. By the way, since we're all interested in religion here, I should let you know that Sam is a witch."

"Wiccan actually," Sam said. "And in case you're wondering, I don't turn people into toads."

"Right." Will smiled. "Some people are well able to do that on their own."

This got a smile from Samantha and a laugh from Arie and Malcolm.

"Sam and I are off to tour the place. You two better get hopping, or Delbert will offer you up to his alien friends for experiments."

Arie took Sam's arm, and the two left the kitchen, where Will and Malcolm stared at a huge pile of pots and dishes.

Will and Malcolm did not see Arie and Sam again until after the evening meal and chores. Will learned that Sam was tucked into a small room at the end of the hall that had been used for storage. The plan was that she would sleep there until Will left and then move into Will's room.

The next time Will saw Samantha, she looked absolutely beat.

"Do you always work this hard?" she asked.

"No," Will responded. "Lots of days we work harder. We had a pretty good turnout of volunteers today. But lots of days they call in sick or they have to care for a child, and we end up picking up their chores. The good news is, when the tasks become routine, they're less tiring. I found my first days were the most exhausting."

At the end of the day, Arie, Malcolm, and Will invited Samantha to their evening "talkfest." Sam smiled and stretched out on Malcolm and Arie's bed beside Will, who thought she still smelled incredibly good even after working all day. He was less confident about himself. Ham was perched on Will's chest, but he quickly moved over to explore Sam's long hair.

Arie looked over the assembled bodies, all smelling slightly of cooking grease and food. "Before I send everyone to the showers—you all stink, you know—I can't help but note that we have quite a motley collection here. A pagan witch, a part-time Muslim, an atheist Jew, and a theologically-addled Christian all working for two lesbian nuns amidst a colorful staff of alien abductees, a former priest who is married, a third-coming transsexual Jesus, and a bunch of characters, many of whom have tragic stories but all of whom are interesting to say the least. It's no wonder we talk about religion all the time."

"Before we're sent to the showers, and please remember we have limited hot water, I'm curious to know a bit more about Wicca," Will said, not eager to give up his place beside Samantha.

Even though she was tired, Samantha was keen to dispel at least a few myths about witches. She knew that the Bible wrote against witchcraft and called for the death of witches, but she felt safe among this open-minded group.

"Wicca is an umbrella religion. It includes goddess worshipers, polytheists, pagans of all sorts, and believers in magic. My coven at school was mostly nature worshipers. We didn't believe in a transcendent god or goddess who judged us. But we had an awesome respect for nature. It seems like half of the group were biologists and the other half computer scientists. Our cardinal principle was to do no harm, and within that rule you are free to do as you will. Our values were things like mirth, honor, humility, strength, beauty, and compassion. I liked the rituals and the community. My group, maybe because we were mostly scientists, didn't believe in magic, spirits, or gods. But many Wiccans do hold such beliefs."

"Why would you prefer Wicca to, say, Christianity?" Arie asked.

"I grew up as a Unitarian, so my connection to traditional Christianity or evangelical Christianity was very thin," Samantha explained. "But for all its talk about love, Christianity is a religion about death and violence. There's so much apocalyptic thinking. I was really turned off by stories of Christians celebrating the terrorist attacks throughout the world, because they signaled the coming of the end of time. I was also turned off by Christians who rejected environmental responsibility, because they said God would provide or they said that there was no point in trying to reform before the end of time. And the sexual predation that was going on in the Catholic, Anglican, and fundamentalist churches was just too much. Wicca has a positive view of life and the future. I don't believe in reincarnation like some Wiccans."

"Wow," Will could not help himself, "that's quite a critique. But not all Christians are like that."

"I know that, Will," Samantha replied, "but there's a lot of anger in Christianity, and you can't deny the apocalyptic thinking. Even Jesus advocated it. He told people to sell their property and abandon their family and friends. Also, he claimed he came to cast fire on Earth and not bring peace but war and discord. Some Christians are able to ignore these passages in their sacred scripture, but I can't."

Arie nodded thoughtfully. "You know, I agree with Sam. I think Jesus was a failed messiah. He sought God's kingdom, which he conceived of as an earthly kingdom, a restoration of the Jewish people. He saw a triumph over evil and the enemies of the Jews here on Earth with perhaps himself as king. I think he was stunned when he was crucified, and the account in Mark—probably the most accurate—makes this clear to me. Later traditions try to patch up this failure by making his death part of the plan and a moment of atonement for the sins of Adam and Eve. But this story seems just a way of making a virtue of necessity."

"Jesus bombed in his hometown," Malcolm added. "He couldn't produce miracles, and people didn't believe him. In that regard, he was much like Mohammed in Mecca; he just never convinced anyone that he was the real thing. Jesus should have escaped the Romans, formed an army, and, like Mohammed, set out to conquer the world. It you can't convince them, perhaps you can bludgeon people into belief."

Samantha looked surprised but saw the laughter in Malcolm's eyes. She expected a stout defense from Will, but he failed to offer one.

"A few weeks ago, I would have brought out other passages where Jesus speaks more as a messenger of love and compassion and sounds much less apocalyptic," Will said. "But the truth is, I simply have no confidence that we can get very far in understanding the nature of God and Jesus from these stories. They're too influenced by the agenda of those who wrote them, although I agree that Mark is the gospel that was written closest to the time Jesus lived and, therefore, had to be the most careful in relating the facts. But Sam, you said something that interested me. I love the ceremony of a church service, the music, the prayer, the fellowship that one feels. I guess that's a reason outside of evidence and accurate scriptures for being religious. What's that ritual like in Wicca?"

"I'll tell you what," Samantha said. "Lughnasadh is coming up on August first, which is just a week away. It celebrates the gift that the sun has given us all summer, and it recognizes that the sun is weakening and finishing its time. We have verses that we say, something like, 'The sun knows that his death is drawing near, but that is just part of the turning of the wheel. And he will be reborn.' It's a harvest festival, and if you all are willing to be witches for an evening, I'll conduct a Lughnasadh ceremony, if the sisters approve, in honor of the sun and its many gifts to us."

"That would be cool." Malcolm's enthusiasm was genuine. "I bet even the sisters will participate. I know that Wicca has certain holidays: Samhain on October thirty-first—I love Halloween—and I think the Yule on December twenty-first is also a key holiday."

"Yes," Samantha said, "many like Halloween for all the wrong reasons—probably for the candy and bad costumes—but the Yule celebration is special. It signals the rebirth of the sun, and that's why we burn Yule logs. Did you know that there are at least a million Americans who are pagans or witches, and that it's a recognized religion in the military and in many prisons? The pentagram can actually be engraved on a soldier's tomb."

Will had not known this fact, but Smantha's comment about rituals gave him another idea. "There may be reasons to choose religions that are independent of the truth of scripture or the evidence we have for the existence of a particular type of god. It may be that the decision to be religious comes to us from our feelings. We love ritual, we admire the conduct or values of a particular religious community, or we are in a situation where we need and depend on the comfort of certain beliefs so we hold onto them."

Malcolm nodded in agreement. "William James held that there were beliefs that could arise from our passions when it was important for us to do so, especially if there was no easy way to avoid it and if it was a live option for us. He didn't think we could form a belief through sheer will, but under certain circumstances, we could choose to believe."

"The problem with that," Arie, interjected, "is the temptation to create such circumstances by torturing people into belief. Thus, Saint Augustine thought that torture loosened people up for a bit of religious truth. If you're going to be tortured and killed, it certainly makes the decision momentous, one you have to make. Whether it makes it a live option, I'm not so sure. But it creates two out of the three conditions, and Christianity has had a long love affair with coercion."

"Enough," Samantha said, sitting up. "I'm headed to the showers, and I don't need to take images of torture with me."

"I apologize," Arie said as Samantha gave her a hug.

Will struggled not to imagine Sam in the shower. He was confused. He thought he loved Cindy, but he found Samantha very attractive. It was times like this that it would have been good to have a parent to talk to. His aunt and uncle were not given to talk much about such things.

"Thanks for all your help today," Samantha told Arie. She looked around the room as she handed Ham—who had gone to sleep on her shoulder—back to Will. "I think I'll fit right in here. Thanks for the welcome."

Will managed to get the second shower, which still contained a faint scent of Samantha's shampoo, and soon he was back in his room. The visions of Samantha dancing in his head only added to his discontent. He was becoming keenly aware that he would be leaving the mission soon, and that realization created real regret.

He tried to talk to God, but God was not terribly responsive. It was one of those cases, Will decided, of "You figure it out." Will noticed that God was least responsive when Will was tired. Tonight, he was done in, glad for it, and sought sleep to escape his conflicted emotions. Ham, on the other hand, had just had a nap and was feeling quite lively. Soon, Will was asleep, but his dreams were of dancing nude in the forest under a full moon. Other shadowy figures were around, but they were unidentified.

THE CIRCLE

July ended all too quickly, and the time was drawing near for Will, Arie, and Malcolm to go their separate ways. Malcolm was to report for orientation to law school. Arie was considering going with him. Will was to report to the theme park by mid-August to help prepare for the grand opening later in the month.

Samantha decided to stay on beyond her internship. She proved to be a tireless worker with a strong back and a willingness to take on the most onerous tasks, including light plumbing. In addition, her Spanish was excellent, which helped with the many Spanish-speaking clients. The sisters were confident that with Samantha, a few new volunteers, and the usual set of handy folks, such as Jesus Perez and Cole, they would be able to carry on.

Will's ardor for Samantha was dashed when he learned she was in love with a handsome warlock musician. Still, she fit in well with the group of friends, and Will enjoyed the inclusion of her perspective in their evening gab sessions.

He was still in regular contact with Cindy and his aunt and uncle. Cindy's mother had been readmitted to the hospital. Cindy thought part of it was the stress of her father's death, but something else also seemed to be going on.

Will was distressed to learn that his Aunt Rita was seeing a cardiologist, although she told him the cardiologist was not terribly concerned about her health. Uncle John urged him to help Shister get set up and running, and if Rita's condition changed, he would call Will and fly him home. He let Will know that both of them were very proud of how Will was handling himself and the work he was doing. Aunt Rita was particularly delighted that Will had been thinking about a medical career after Malcolm had prompted him by leaving some materials in his room that described programs in the Dallas area. Will also talked to the sisters about a course of study, and they were helpful and supportive. Will liked the idea of a medical career, but he did not want to become a doctor.

In spite of, or perhaps because of, the impending breakup of friends, the mission became caught up in the Lughnasadh, which was to be held on August 1. Samantha was both delighted and overwhelmed by the number of volunteers who wanted to participate. She had envisioned a small gathering of herself, Will, Arie, Malcolm, and perhaps the sisters. Things were not turning out that way. Sister Sara and Sister Ellie were happy to participate. But when word got out, two women who stayed frequently at the mission claimed to be Wiccan and wanted to join the ceremony. Another client volunteered to play the clarinet, although Samantha had hoped for a flutist. Delbert prepared a special dinner that celebrated all the harvest vegetables and fruits. It included cornbread, apple cider, catfish, and okra with a tomato garnish. He said it was the traditional meal on planets where Wicca was the official religion.

Arie started a rumor that she was going to have Malcolm turned into a toad because he was taking her off to law school. Some of the more devout clients organized a protest against the upcoming ritual, but gave up their objections when they were reminded that it was a nondenominational shelter.

Will was not surprised that "Warren Warlock," as Malcolm called him when not in Samantha's presence, promised to show up and help with the ceremony.

The evening of August 1 arrived, and all went out to the side yard of the mission, where they found a large circle outlined with corn meal. At its center sat a small cauldron surrounded by some of Delbert's cornbread cupcakes and an altar covered with a gold cloth. On it was a gold candle surrounded by a garnish of harvest vegetables and "sun" rocks painted gold. Flowers were everywhere. All of the participants wore bed sheet robes and garlands of English Ivy. Around the circle stood Sister Ellie, Sister Sara, Arie, Malcolm, Will, Jesus—who, at the last moment had declared that she, too, was a witch—and the two Wiccans from the mission. Samantha greeted the arriving spectators and handed each one a small spray of greens. Warren had a conga, which he began to play softly and beautifully.

The ceremony began when Samantha, dressed in a beautiful red robe and holding a wand, walked into the circle and faced north. She stood silently for a moment and then—in an alto voice that Will thought was one of the most lovely he had ever heard, clear and rising—began to sing while the clarinet joined in perfect harmony. She sang of changing seasons, changing light, and thankfulness to the goddess of harvest. Will was thinking he might become a witch. Arie's eyes filled with tears at the beauty of Samantha's song, and to everyone's surprise, Sister Sara joined in with a soprano voice that matched Samantha's in clarity and quality. Together, they sang to Mother Earth and her bounty of love. Even the skeptics in the audience were moved.

The ceremony went on for a few more minutes in this fashion. Then someone in the audience began to play a trumpet, and from the youth center next door, an electric bass began to keep rhythm. Samantha and Sister Sara's voices soared over the growing accompaniment. Everyone present followed Samantha's lead as they moved through the ceremony facing each of the four directions.

It was hard to say who lost focus first, but something confused the musicians as they were trying to follow Samantha. Just as she and Sister Sara ended their duet, the music became briefly chaotic. Perhaps it was to cover up the confusion that the clarinet player, followed quickly by the trumpet, began a rousing version of "When the Saints Go Marching In." Although Warren looked bewildered, he took up the rhythm, as did the bass next door. The audience, recognizing the song, joined in loudly and with feeling. A second line developed and moved around the circle holding loaves of bread and muffins above their heads instead of the traditional umbrella. Somehow they got through all twelve verses. They were particularly strong on the verses that spoke to the oppression in their lives:

When the rich go out and work
When the rich go out and work
Oh Lord I want to be in that number
When the saints go marching in

When we all have food to eat
When we all have food to eat
Oh Lord I want to be in that number
When the saints go marching in

Will was particularly concerned about Samantha, whose ceremony was in tatters, but to his surprise, she burst into song and, along with Sister Sara, led the second line. Then everyone collapsed in laughter, including Samantha, who had to hold onto Sister Ellie to keep from falling down. Tears of merriment filled her eyes.

Several audience members came forward one by one and remarked on what a great ceremony it was, particularly the ending. Many of them hugged Samantha and flooded her with questions. Then everyone headed into the dining hall to eat the Lughnasadh meal. Will noticed that several of them pocketed the cupcakes and dipped tin cups into the cider before they went in to dinner. The garnish of vegetables around the gold candle was also missing.

Later that evening when the chores were done, Samantha admitted it was the most splendid ceremony in which she had ever participated. It accomplished what ceremonies are supposed to do: it left everyone in good humor and made them feel better about life. Ellie and Sara were delighted with the event, and they promised future events, though not necessarily built around Wicca, to some of the regulars.

The group was just breaking up and heading to their rooms when there was a rather loud knock on the mission's main door.

"Open up, Border Patrol," a loud voice announced.

While Will and the others stood frozen in place, Sister Ellie opened the door calmly. Two large men wearing bulletproof vests and carrying firearms stood in the doorway. Ellie stood her ground but did not invite the men in.

"We need to see the roster for tonight," the spokesman said.

"Of course." Ellie produced a clipboard that happened to be by the door. Will could not help but wonder if Ellie had been tipped off about the visit. It all seemed routine to her.

The two men started through the names. Whenever they came to a Hispanic surname, they paused. But Will could not help but notice the overwhelming number of non-Hispanic names, given the large number of Hispanic clients at the mission. The agents checked each surname against another list and said, "He's a citizen" or "She was here last week, and we checked her out." After a few minutes, the spokesman said, "thank you ma'am," and then they left.

Ellie turned to the group with a satisfied smile. "Good night all, and thank you again, Samantha, for that wonderful ceremony."

Back in his room Will realized that the names on the list must have been altered. He knew Gerardo Martinez, who helped Will with food pickups. But only a Jerry Martin was listed on Ellie's roster.

Once a Maryknoll, always a Maryknoll, Will thought with a smile.

God's only comment was: "Damn, they're good."

***

Rev was feeling grumpy. The long-awaited visit from Seymour Smythe was coming up in a little more than a week. The Tribulation Army compound was improved somewhat—many of the weeds had been cut and burned, the Wrecks R Us sign was gone, and a lot of the trash was cleaned up—but the effort left much to be desired. Several potential troopers, newly recruited, had drifted away, perhaps because of the extra work. Curt, the most militaristic of his troopers, was in and out but not doing much. Rev was essentially left with Harry, who was just as worthless as always; Chris, who was crazier than ever; and Blink, who did what he was told but who had little initiative. How was he going to have troops to present to Seymour, who had only recently coughed up another few thousand dollars for expenses? He would have to hire some actors or replacements, which would cut into his take.

On this August day, Rev pulled into the mission parking lot. He hoped to get some bodies over to his west Texas compound, and he thought he could find some of them in his old stomping ground, Dallas/Fort Worth. In return, he had a check for $100 to give to the two nuns who ran the place. He liked the sisters, but he wanted permission to recruit.

Sister Sara and Will were having a discussion in the entryway to the kitchen, and Father Duncan was just finishing his part of the cleanup as Rev approached. He realized how tired he was, having driven all the way from the compound in west Texas, which he had left reluctantly in the hands of Chris. Originally, he thought to leave Harry in charge, but Harry, who had not been particularly religious, had begun attending a small Redeemed church down the road, which led him to become obsessed with demons. Recently, he had "exercised" demons that he detected in Blink, Rev's computer, the Mazda, which was acting up again, and the Port-a-John that served the camp. Harry would flick "holy water," shake a copy of the Bible at the intended target, and shout, "I 'cash' you out, demon, in the name of Jesus!"

One night, Harry caught Rev asleep at his desk. He burst into Rev's office, threw water in his face, and shouted, "I cash you out in the name of the Holly Spook!" It damned near gave Rev a heart attack. Rev seriously doubted that Harry's concept center was well attached to the language center in his brain.

"Coffee, Rev?" Sister Sara offered.

"Please, that is kind of you," Rev replied. He admired the strapping youth who was talking to Sister Sara. Maybe he could recruit him.

"What brings you to the mission?" Sara asked. The young man stepped aside so that Rev and Sister Sara could talk.

"I'd like to hire some help," the Rev lied.

Sister Sara gave him a critical look. "For what?"

"I'm cleaning up a compound in West Texas that may become a youth camp. It's not hard work, but I need a lot of hands. There are weeds to be removed; the fence needs some work, and junk to be hauled to the dump. Two buildings on the property, old double-wides, also need to be repainted.

The young man stepped forward. "Hello, Reverend, my name is Will, we briefly met at the lifestyle fair. I couldn't help but overhear. I need a ride to west Texas and could give you a week or so to help clean up."

"Will is a very hard worker, and he is just finishing here," Sister Sara added.

Rev was so thrilled to have someone who looked and sounded normal that he offered too much. "I'll give you a ride, board and room, and twenty-five dollars an hour."

"I need to finish here today," Will said, "and I have another job to report to no later than August fifteenth at the new Galilee Theme Park."

"That fits my schedule exactly," Rev said. "We'll get over there tomorrow, and you'll be finished by the twelfth, or at the latest on the thirteenth, and have time to make it to your new position. The theme park is just down the road from us."

Will and Rev shook hands, and Rev presented the check to Sister Sara and got permission to talk to some other prospects. He and Will agreed to meet at the mission first thing in the morning. Rev hoped he could find at least two other guys to add. He figured he could hire a few local men for the day Seymour was to visit.

***

John Steel was reasonably satisfied with the appearance of the three men who stood in front of him. They all wore pistols and carried batons. Their uniforms were dark green with military-style boots. Reflective sunglasses covered their eyes, and their hair was military cut. Two of them had bigger guts than Steel would have liked, but they were all loyal—and a bit sadistic. That would help to convert any recalcitrant Tribulation troopers. The sheer bulk of the men and gear would make it tight in the van, a junker he had picked up from a friend who operated a scrapyard. The vehicle was supposed to be crushed as part of the Cash for Clunkers program. Steel had gotten it for a song and had it painted in camouflage.

The trip back from the mission and his encounter with Cole had been a difficult one for Steel. The side of his head still hurt. He had also failed to extract vengeance on the sisters, and his image of himself as a tough hand-to-hand fighter was seriously compromised. To boot, he had lost his Yaris. But he was back on track. He had a plan, and today he and his troops were taking control of the Tribulation Army compound. From his reconnaissance, he knew that Reverend Oliver was away and that only four men remained of the original group. He was in contact with Curt, who had promised to join Steel once he promised Curt a gun. Curt also kept Steel informed on the goings on in the camp.

***

Rev and Will were hot and tired. They had not talked much on the hellishly hot drive across Texas. Having failed to pick up any other recruits, Rev was discouraged. Those who were willing to come with him were all brown-skinned, and he thought Seymour would not go for Hispanic Tribulation troops. It had been a costly and unproductive trip. His silence also ensured that Will would not accidentally discover that his militia was a con. Rev looked forward to a cold beer and resting in front of his air conditioner. He hoped it was working.

Will was eager to get Ham into a cool, quiet place where he could rest. The haze from local wildfires and the road noise disturbed the hamster. Rev had not been eager to take the hamster aboard, but when he realized that it would cost him Will, he dropped his objections.

As Rev turned into the compound, the first thing he saw was a camouflage van sitting in front of his trailer. The second thing was a strange man standing guard outside the trailer and another unfamiliar figure closing the gate behind them. Finally, he recognized Curt, who was wearing a sidearm and an unfamiliar uniform. Curt waved him into a parking place beside the van. His gut told him that something was seriously amiss.

He turned to Will. "Follow my lead, and don't volunteer any information. There's something odd here."

As if on cue, Steel emerged from the front of the trailer. "Hello Rev, welcome to my compound."

"Hello, John," Rev said calmly. He was at his best when things were uncertain.

"Who's that with you?" Steel asked, seeming surprised that Rev recognized him.

"A new recruit," Rev answered.

"Put him in the trailer with the others," Steel told Curt. "Take his cell phone, if he has one." Then he turned to Rev. "We need to talk."

Curt helped Will with his duffle, but when Ham's cage emerged, Curt let out an un-soldierly shriek. He was terrified of mice. That's how Will ended up carrying Ham a safe distance behind Curt into one of the other trailers. Once inside, the door closed, and Will heard it lock.

Will looked around. Inside the poorly lit room sat three men. One of them was short and in uniform, one was large—indeed, huge—and sad-looking in an old sweatshirt with cut-off sleeves and pink paint stains on the front. The third man was small, wiry, and had what Will thought were busy eyes. They all looked at Will.

"Hi," he said, "I'm Will. What's going on here?"

"I'm Chris," the small, wiry, man said. "We're what's left of the Tribulation Army. Rev was our leader, and now, apparently, another group has captured our compound."

"What's the Tribulation Army?" Will asked.

"Well," said the man in uniform, "When the rupture comes and the really good people are taken to heaven, some of us sinners will be left behind to fight the antsy-Christ. I'm Harry, by the way."

Will was used to a lot of strange religious ideas, but this explanation left him speechless. "I thought this was going to be a youth camp."

"Hi little guy," Chris said, talking to Ham. Then he turned to Will. "Is this your spirit guide?"

Will shook his head. "No. I rescued him from a cat, and he's been traveling with me."

"He's really cute," said the mountain of a man, who identified himself as Blink.

"Are we prisoners?" Will asked.

"For now," Chris replied. "We'll either be sent packing or incorporated into the new militia."

Will was in shock. He could not imagine a worse turn of events. He was being held prisoner and might be drafted into a militia. And he had no idea what the group's agenda or theology was. "What do we know about our captors?"

"The commander's name is John Steel, and he comes across as a real hard-ass," Chris offered. "They call themselves the Sons of Abraham, and he's building a stoning circle. I think he intends to impose Old Testament law. He's some kind of dominionist. After he talks to Rev, he'll interview each of us separately and determine our fate. Personally, I'm scared."

Will was familiar with the fundamentalist movement called Dominionism or Christian Reconstructionism. He knew that they sought a theocracy in accordance with their interpretation of scripture, especially Old Testament law. There was a frightening number of "sins" for which death by stoning was required. Many of them rejected the Rapture story in favor of creating a Christian world to which Jesus would want to return. They had some political clout in the US Congress. Uncle John said they were as scary a bunch of Christians as he had ever encountered.

"Oh, boy," was all Will could say. Suddenly, the sane and loving world of the sisters seemed far, far away.

"There's nothing to do but wait," Chris said.

"Can I play with your hamster?" Blink asked. "What is he chewing on? It looks like the back of a book."

"Sure, he likes attention and glue from books," Will said. "Where should I put my stuff?"

"Just throw it into that corner," Chris replied. "I think they'll try to sort us out by this evening. At least the AC is working."

Will moved his bags into a corner and lay down against his duffle. He was tired but too upset to sleep. He heard Blink talking to Ham in the background. Harry was silent and pacing. Chris was smoking a joint—Will recognized the smell from high school parties.

"This is just too weird," God said. "We're actually locked up."

"*I'm* locked up," Will said. "What a mess!"

"Good point," God replied.

INTERVIEWS

If John Steel were an honest man with some degree of self-knowledge, he would have admitted he was really looking forward to his interviews with the remains of the Tribulation Army. He truly enjoyed having control of a situation, and he felt very much in the catbird seat. Were he even more self-aware, he would have noted that he enjoyed seeing fear on the faces of his adversaries.

Steel had taken over Rev's office. He darkened the room by blocking off one window and turning off some lights. He also lowered the air conditioning to make the temperature more uncomfortable. The new stoning circle was just outside the front door, and Steel wanted all of the new recruits to know what it was.

Rev was the first one with whom he needed to talk. One of Steel's men led Rev into the room and sat him down in a chair. Then he stood silently by the door.

Rev did not behave as Steel expected. He simply sat silently looking at Steel. No accusations, no hysterics, just a quiet calm that Steel found unnerving. He began to regret starting with Rev.

"Should I call you 'Smooth Sam' or 'Reverend Oliver Newton' or just 'Rev'?" Steel asked, hoping to unnerve him by conveying he had inside information from the WTHC.

"'Rev' will do."

"You're probably wondering what has happened here." Steel really wanted to provoke more of a response.

"I think I know what's going on. Do you?"

Steel decided to stay with his line of questioning. "Where are all your troops?"

"Most of them left," Rev said honestly.

"Do you want to join the Sons of Abraham?"

"Not really."

"Do you want to leave?" Steel knew he was in charge of that, but he asked anyway.

"Well," Rev replied, "I have a very important guest coming in a little less than a week. He's been a big backer of the Tribulation Army, and he's coming here to inspect the compound. Are you interested in putting on a show on his behalf?"

"What do you mean 'show'?" Steel was unable to contain his surprise.

"Come now, Steel." Rev looked like he felt sorry for him. "You don't think a small group of convicted felons, all of whom are on parole and led by a guy who calls himself a reverend but has never been ordained, constitutes a real militia, do you?"

"If you're not a militia, what the hell are you?"

Rev said nothing.

"Are you telling me that you're making money out of this pretense?" Steel was incredulous, since he was always desperate for funds.

"Yep. About twenty thousand so far," Rev lied. He had nearly $50,000 in the bank, most of it from Seymour Smythe.

"How much do you expect to get?"

"I'm thinking six figures, if we can convince …" Rev almost said 'the mark', "Seymour that we have a serious tribulation force here. He's ready."

Seeing the greed in Steel's eyes made Rev think that he, too, was ready to bite. Greed was the con man's best friend.

Steel thought for a moment. "Who's Seymour?"

"Seymour Smythe, president of Texas/Oklahoma First Citizens' Bank."

Steel erupted into gales of laughter. The change in his affect was so abrupt that Rev was taken aback. "Sorry, I don't get the joke."

"That's the bank whose branch up in Judd, Oklahoma I'm going to rob next week." Steel could barely choke out the words he was laughing so hard.

Rev recovered fast and began to see possibilities here. "We could rob him twice—once at the end of this week and then again next week."

"Yes, we could." Steel wiped his eyes. "I'll think about it and get back to you."

Steel wanted his interviews to be short and leave uncertainty in the interviewee. He nodded and the guard took Rev back to the trailer that was holding Will, Chris, Blink, and Harry. The prospect of wealth had put Steel in a good mood.

Harry was next. He stood at attention in front of Steel. He felt crumpled in his rumpled uniform and naked because they had taken his Leatherman away. Besides, the room was too warm.

"Hello, Harry," Steel said, still in a good mood.

"Hello, sir," Harry said.

Steel liked the "sir."

"Harry, would you like to become part of the Sons of Abraham and stay on here at…" Steel realized he did not have a name for the compound. "Camp Joshua," he adlibbed.

"Would we be real soldiers with real guns?" Harry had always been miffed by Rev's refusal to allow guns in the camp.

"You bet," Steel replied. "I have a whole camper full of the latest in automatic weapons that I bought from an online dealer in Wisconsin.

"You can count on me; it would be an honor," Harry said with enthusiasm. "Do I get a new uniform as well? And can I have my Leatherman back?"

"I'll order it done right away," Steel said. He had always believed that Harry would fold quickly; he just wanted to be included. Steel nodded authoritatively to the guard. "Fix Harry up with a shower, give him his Leatherman, and assign him a bunk. There's no need to keep him with the others. We'll talk about what kind of arms are to be distributed when I'm finished here."

Harry was as easy as Steel thought he would be, but Chris was the valuable one, so he decided to talk to him next.

When the guard took Chris for his interview, Rev's parting advice was, "Just try to be agreeable, but don't commit to anything until you know exactly what's going on."

Steel felt like he was on a roll after his conversion of Harry. Curt had told him that Chris was a genius at fixing things but that he was as crazy as they came, and he had no idea where Chris' loyalties lay.

"He's just fucking nuts," Curt had said. "It's like he's on drugs, but the drugs are religion."

Steel studied Chris as he was led into the room. He was a slender man, only about five foot eight. He had a pinched face and slightly reddish hair that the Texas sun had bleached out until it was a slightly blond color.

"Are you a Christian?" Steel asked.

"Yes sir," Chris replied, staring at Steel.

"Do you believe we're sinners and that Jesus, who was fully human and fully divine, died for our sins?"

"Yes sir."

"I heard you were a Muslim," Steel challenged.

"Yes sir."

"You can't be both a Muslim and a Christian."

"Yes sir."

"I also heard you were Jewish."

"Yes sir."

Steel wondered how far he could push this conversation.

"And Sikh, Buddhist, and Hindu."

"Yes sir." Chris continued to stare straight at Steel.

"What the hell are you?" Steel demanded. He had had it with this nut case. Then he came up with a solution. "Chris, I'll tell you what you are. You are a slave. Your life means nothing to me, and I will decide whether you live or die. The Bible does not condemn slavery. In fact, it offers instructions on how to be a slave. The short of it is, obey your master. As a nonbeliever, you don't deserve to be among Christian men except as a slave. And remember the biblical punishment for apostasy is death by stoning. Think on that, do what you're told, and we'll see."

Steel thought he could see Chris trembling. It made him feel powerful and in control.

Harry had been so easy. Steel was certain that Blink would follow along. When Blink came into the room though, his size made Steel uneasy. Blink was bigger than he had realized. His shoulders were massive, and his hands, spotted with pink paint, look like giant clamps. Steel did not want to set Blink off, and he looked a little upset now.

"Hello, Blink," Steel began. "Please have a chair. Would you like something cold to drink? It's hot."

"I'm okay," Blink replied.

"Blink, Harry has just agreed to join the Sons of Abraham, and we would like you to join as well. Are you interested?"

Blink just sat there.

"Blink, did you hear me? We think very highly of you and would like to have you become a soldier in the Sons of Abraham. You can have a gun." Steel recalled how being armed had worked on Harry.

Blink's reaction was immediate. "No gun!"

Steel's voice was oily, "You don't have to have a gun, but you can have one if you want."

"No guns," Blink started to fidget in his chair. "I'll go back to trailer now and play with Ham."

Steel did not know what to do. And he had no idea who Ham was. "Okay, go back and think about it. I'll talk to you later."

Steel was relieved to see Blink leave the room. Obviously, Blink was not as dependent on Harry's decisions as Steel had believed. Steel opened a cola; he needed a break before the next interview.

In the trailer, Will, Chris, and Rev were discussing their options when Blink returned muttering something about "no guns." Chris took him aside, and they fell into a quiet conversation as Chris produced two joints. Then he and Blink settled down next to Will to smoke them.

"Rev, do you want a hit, or you Will?" Chris asked.

"No thanks, Chris," Rev said, "I have to think."

Will also declined.

Rev turned to Will. "Will, I am very sorry to have brought you into all this. I really had no knowledge of Steel's takeover."

Will realized he should be angry with Rev, who had not told him the truth, so he made an attempt. "You told me this was going to be a youth camp. You said nothing about it being a militia. Were you actually going to pay me to paint or just take advantage of my labor?"

Rev studied Will before answering. "Honestly, I was going to pay you. I knew nothing about this, and we were planning on turning the camp over to a youth ministry when we got it fixed up." Rev's last claim was a lie, but he said it with total sincerity. "Let me think," Rev moved off to the other end of the trailer.

"Guns are bad," Blink said again. "Guns very bad. Harry's stupid."

"Yes," Chris agreed, "guns *are* bad. They get you in trouble."

Will decided that he liked both Chris and Blink. He felt a kind of camaraderie with them. They both seemed gentle, they liked Ham, and they were trying hard to reassure him.

"Rev's smart," Chris said. "He'll get us out of here."

Will was starting to relax in spite of his fear, although the smoke from Chris and Blink was beginning to make him cough. Chris described his interview and also gave a summary of Blink's based on what Blink had told him. He wanted Will to know what to expect.

"Just be agreeable," Chris said, echoing Rev's advice.

The guard appeared and called for Will, who felt a bit lightheaded and kind of distant when he stood up.

Looking at the young man, Steel could not help but think of his humiliation at the hands of Sister Sara, not to mention the man who attacked him and stole his car. The do-gooders who surrounded her made his blood boil, and here was one of them. This kid was big and strong; he looked like the fittest person in camp. In a different situation, he might have been a good recruit. But Steel disliked him intensely because of his association with the sisters. He had seen Will working in the kitchen; saw him helping the fat sister with a heavy pot. They were laughing together, obviously friends. He considered the mission a locus of liberalism, communism, and witchcraft. Steel also hated the fact that Will just stood there looking at him. There was none of the cringing that he really wanted.

"Your name?" Steel barked.

"Will Tillit."

"Well, Will, God has brought you into my hands. That pleases me."

Will, doubting that God had anything to do with it, heard God say, "Don't look around so much. You're losing focus." Will tried to straighten up, smiling slightly at God's reprimand.

"You doubt that do you?" Steel was incensed further by Will's strange affect. "I can even tell you why God delivered you here. Do you know what the Bible says about witches? It says very clearly in Exodus twenty-two verse eighteen that we should not allow a witch to live. Do you believe in witches, Will?"

Will had lost track of the conversation again.

"Will," God said, "you're high on second-hand marijuana smoke. Answer the question."

"What was the question, again?" Will asked.

Steel started to repeat, but Will interrupted. "Sorry, I wasn't talking to you."

Steel stared at Will, perplexed.

"Okay, I remember now," Will said finally. "No, I don't believe in witches."

"That's odd," Steel said, wondering to whom Will thought he was talking. "I heard from reliable sources that you worked for those lesbian witches near Dallas. You participated in a witch ceremony there just before you left. You hung out with a self-admitted witch. You carry a little familiar around with you. Are you a witch?"

Will recalled the ceremony at the mission. "Only on Thursdays." Will's attention went to a fly buzzing around the room.

Will's affect made Steel even angrier. "Don't you get it? The evidence is right before my eyes, and believe me, because you've turned your back on God and worship Satan, you will be the first to die along with your little familiar in the stoning circle." He hoped to scare the crap out of Will, to get his attention.

"Hmm...." Will replied his eyes retaining their distant look.

"You really are something!" Steel shouted. "I'm talking about your life here. After we finish our business up north, we'll have a party with lots to drink and a special event in which you will be the star. I intend to videotape your stoning and send it to your witch friends at the mission. This camp is now under Old Testament law; it is not a democracy, it is not flexible, and it is not liberal. Your death will do a lot to bring about obedience and discipline in the ranks. Meanwhile, what should I do with you?"

Will studied Steel. "That sounds like an excellent plan," he said, trying hard to be agreeable.

My God, Steel thought. *The boy is totally fey. I didn't realize he was a mental defective. He hears voices. He's worse than Chris. I'll use him and send him on his way. I can't stone someone that incapacitated.*

Directing his attention back to Will, he applied the Chris solution. "I know what we can do with you in the meantime. We need these trailers repainted, and we need some cleanup done quickly around here. Since we're under biblical law and you are an alien in our Christian midst, we can enslave you. That's in Leviticus twenty-five verses forty-four to forty-six, in case you didn't know. And in Ephesians six verse five, you're told to obey your earthly master, and I am just that. Tomorrow morning, crack of dawn, you begin to paint."

"I love colors," Will responded. He was feeling really good. "Burgundy would be nice. I love getting up early. Can we go fishing?"

Steel felt an incredible headache coming on. Except for Harry, every interview was a complete bust. He had no idea there were so many defectives in this world.

Back in the trailer, Will sank onto his duffle. Chris, Blink, and Rev descended on him immediately.

"What happened in there?" Rev asked.

"We talked," Will said dreamily. "He wanted me to be stoned, but it was too late; I think I'm stoned already." Will giggled. "He seemed kind of confused about what to do with me. But," he added brightly, "he made me a slave."

"Me, too," Chris said. He glanced at Rev. "My fault about Will. He's a lightweight, the second-hand smoke got to him."

"I'll talk to Steel tonight," Rev said. "I think we can work our way out of this mess. If we can't, we'll simply break out."

"How can we do that?" Will asked vaguely.

Rev looked at Blink and Chris, and Will realized they had been talking and planning. "We have plan A, B, and C. Give it some time, and let them get used to our passivity. Steel wants to have a successful visit from Seymour Smythe, and then he wants to carry off a successful bank robbery. That will take time, and he needs my cooperation to pull it off. He needs your and Blink's labor, and he needs Chris to keep things working."

That evening, a simple meal of hamburgers and water was sent in. Rev sent word to Steel that he wanted to talk with him after dinner. Rev was satisfied with how things were playing out.

Will lay on his duffle. The air conditioning kept the temperature tolerable.

"You were really out there," God said.

"I remember now what he actually said. He plans to kill me!" In a moment of clarity, Will was horrified. "I think he intends to kill me by stoning!"

"In this little drama," God said, "I'd put my money on Rev, not Steel."

Will liked the sound of that. He was still frightened, but sleep was winning.

Rev overheard Will talking. "Will, he isn't going to kill you. He was just trying to frighten you, control you." Rev's voice was very reassuring. "I'm going to talk to him again, so relax and go to sleep."

As he approached the trailer, Rev strategized. Steel was rigid and ambitious; he had to be played just right. By the time he entered the office, his plan was ready.

"You've had some time to think about it, so what's your decision?" Steel asked as Rev sat down.

Rev looked calmly at Steel. "I have a proposal."

"Let's hear it," Steel seemed alert and almost hyper. Two empty cola bottles sat on his desk.

"I'll help you plan the visit with Seymour. Let's see if we can get a hundred thousand or more out of him. After the robbery, we split the take—seventy-five percent to you and twenty-five percent to me. Your share pays the others. Then I take my possessions and Will and anyone else who wants to leave and drive away. The compound is yours. I'll even sign it over to you." Rev did not own the compound, but he did pay a small monthly rent.

Steel looked shrewdly at Rev. "Your take is only five percent."

"Seven percent," Rev replied, hoping to give Steel the impression of bargaining.

"Deal." Steel shook hands with Rev. "Now, let's talk about the visit first."

"Seymour is a peculiar guy," Rev began. "He has a house just down the road in Serenity. He also has a condo in Dallas. He's convinced that the Rapture has already begun, as has the Tribulation. He has a lot of money and gives it to causes that he believes in, such as Tribulation militias, prosperity churches, and ultra-conservative political groups. I met him through his church, which I attend from time to time. He's the major stockholder in the Texas/Oklahoma First Citizens' Bank, which he also founded. I think he wants to drive up here and see a clean compound with well-dressed and well-disciplined men."

"How long will he stay?"

"I would guess just an hour or so. I suggest that we have things spruced up. Hire a few young people from the Texas Academy marching band to parade around in uniforms, present Seymour with a complementary uniform that says "Tribulation Army" on it, and let me do the talking. He knows me and trusts me. Also, stay away from the Dominionist stuff. He does not believe in that."

Steel sat back in his chair. "Will he want to see some firepower?"

"I'm not sure," Rev replied. "It probably wouldn't hurt to have some shooting off in the distance. He won't be curious, because he's a very fearful man. Mostly, he worries about going to hell because of all the shady deals he's struck."

The rest of the planning for Seymour's visit went well. The big issues would be getting enough uniforms made, recruiting the students, and getting the painting done. Steel and Rev set out a series of tasks and assigned them to different members of the troop. Rev made certain that he had primary responsibility for supervising Will, Chris, and Blink. Then Steel asked about planning the bank robbery.

"These are my thoughts," Rev began. "Keep Curt somewhere where he can't hurt anyone or fire at anyone. He's a murderer, and he will kill again if he has the slightest chance." Rev was absolutely sincere in this plea.

"I like Curt," Steel responded. "He's my kind of guy, and he likes to shoot."

Rev looked at Steel. What a dumbass. "John," he began, deliberately using Steel's first name, "I learned a few things during my time in prison. One is that guys like Curt cannot be controlled. At best, you can manage them a little. The more you put him in the center, the more likely things will blow up. Another thing I learned is that if you hurt people in a robbery, shoot a guard, for example, they will come after you with more resources and more vengeance than if you don't. You don't want to spend the rest of your life in prison, do you? If you want this robbery to succeed, use your own guys to handle the guns, and use Curt and one other guy to carry the money out."

Steel did not want to give Rev any authority, even though what he said made sense. "I'll think about it," he replied.

"I also wouldn't let Harry have a gun. He's a bit excitable around firearms, but use him as a driver. He has some skill there." Rev, who only let Harry drive for short distances when the traffic was light, knew Harry was a menace on the road, especially when excited.

Steel nodded. "So, two of my guys will have guns. I'll also have a pistol. We'll wear masks. Curt and I will carry the money, Harry will drive the van, and one of my guys will stay here with you, Blink, Chris, and that other guy. Sorry, Rev, I don't trust you to go on this job."

"I'm a little disappointed," Rev lied. "But I understand."

Steel stood up, signaling the meeting was over. "Tomorrow and the next few days will be busy; let's get some rest."

Rev smiled to himself all the way back to the barracks.

BANKING

On the day Seymour arrived at Camp Joshua, even Rev didn't recognize his old compound. The garish pink trailers were now a suitable dark green. The air-conditioning units hummed in the windows. One trailer had been gutted and made into offices and two others made into barracks with rows of bunks along each wall. Even though hardly any of the beds were used, they were lined up against each wall with some personal effects placed strategically. Rev figured he owed a small fortune to the local rental agencies.

The compound was free of weeds and included a hard-packed drill area. The stoning circle was "in storage" and out of sight. The fence around the property had been repaired. On the trailer with the offices was a sign that read: "Headquarters, Camp Joshua" and another sign quoting Luke 12:49, "I came to cast fire upon the earth." An outdoor cook tent with nearby tables sat in the shade of the compound's lone tree. The van and the Mazda were both painted camouflage, as was the power wagon, which still did not run, but it looked formidable even as a derelict.

Close to twenty-five men marched in close drill, led by the director, who had agreed to supply the "troops" for a suitable donation to the Friends of Texas Academy marching band. They looked sharp. Harry was by the cars pretending to attend to their maintenance. Blink, Chris, and Will were confined to one of the barracks, and Ham was stashed under Will's bunk. If Seymour wanted to see their barracks, the trio was to pretend to be recovering from injuries. Chris had a bandage for his head, Will was genuinely tired, and he looked it. He and Blink had done a huge amount of the labor required to put the compound right.

There was a formal greeting ceremony. Rev appeared in a commander's uniform. Steel was content to appear as second-in-command. A trumpet player was to play suitable marshal music as Seymour emerged from his car. A brand new US flag flew proudly. Below it flew a flag that read "Camp Joshua." The entire affair impressed the hell out of Rev, who had been so busy getting things done that he had not had time to take in the big picture.

Seymour's limo pulled through the gate, which boasted a guardhouse—one of the old Port-a-Johns repainted with the door removed. Unfortunately, that left the camp with only one toilet, which was well concealed in the back. Also in the far back of the compound was Curt with a gun. The pop, pop, pop of his firing was clearly audible. Rev knew that Curt would keep shooting at the straw bail until he ran out of bullets, which he hoped would be about the time Seymour left.

Seymour stepped out of the air-conditioned limo into the blistering heat of west Texas. He blinked in the bright sun. He looked like a pudgy white doughboy that had just climbed into the oven. Rev greeted him warmly, Steel ramrod straight by his side.

"Mr. Smythe, welcome to Camp Joshua. May I present my second in command, John Steel. Would you like a tour now or to take some refreshment?" Rev knew the limo had a bar and plenty of refreshments, but he wanted Seymour to feel like he was making the decisions.

"Let's do a tour," Seymour said, sounding excited. "I had no idea you were making such solid progress. Most impressive, most impressive."

It was good to create low expectations, Rev thought.

The tour took very little time. The marching students put on an impressive display of coordination, especially considering the heat. Rev told Seymour that other equally numerous units were out on maneuvers.

"Amazing that you have so many young people; they look like they should be in college," Seymour remarked. Hearing the distant shooting, Seymour did not want to go anywhere near it. Instead, he chose to visit the barracks, the first of which was empty, so the party simply walked through. The second housed Will, Chris, and Blink, with whom Seymour stopped to chat.

"Dear sirs," he began, "soldiers of the Lord, I understand you've been wounded while training to fight the Antichrist. You have my thanks and my admiration."

Thanks to Rev's coaching, Will knew enough of their situation to play along. Most importantly, Rev told him to keep it short.

"Sir, I understand that you have made all of this possible. I thank you for helping us prepare for the Tribulation."

Seymour beamed. "Thank *you.*" Then Seymour stopped and listened. "What's that sound?"

Will recognized it as Ham going top speed on his exercise wheel—the whirring noise was quite audible—and was uncertain what to say.

Chris was on the ball though. "Sir, I, too, thank you. When I recover from my injuries, which I acquired in hand-to-hand combat, I will eagerly fight for the Tribulation Army. I am Technician First Class Chris Eclectic. The sound you hear is part of the high tech alarm system we have installed to warn us should forces of the Antichrist, who are already here on Earth, try to surround us. The electronic sensors make a whirring sound as the electric eyes sweep the camp and its periphery."

Seymour absorbed this techno babble with a smile. He had no idea what Chris was talking about.

Blink simply blinked at Seymour, who thought this mountain of a man was the most impressive he had ever seen. The tour moved on.

Back in the main office, which was cooled by the camp's most reliable air-conditioner, Seymour sipped a glass of lemonade with a touch of vodka in it. He looked at Rev, who sat across from him at his desk and glanced over his shoulder at Steel, who stood at parade rest along the wall. Outside, the students had quit drilling and were around the kitchen tent having pizza and pop.

"Well, well, Reverend Newton, I hardly know what to say. You've created a first-rate army here. Come the time of Tribulation, which I think has already begun, you will be well prepared to carry on. I'm impressed. I don't know if you see the same signs that I do, but we are moving rapidly toward that final battle, Armageddon. You know the earth is heating up. They say it's from global warming. I agree that there is global warming, but the cause is not carbon dioxide in the atmosphere. The fires of hell are getting closer and closer to the surface. And look at our country. We are led by a weak-willed, feeble-minded president. Communists and socialists are planning to spend all our resources on the poor. This Christian republic is being torn apart by the enemies of the Lord." Seymour stopped, short of breath.

Rev knew it was time to add to Seymour's delusion. He tried to think of what Seymour had left out. "And marriage," Rev ventured, "that sacred institution between a man and some women, is being perverted to allow same-sex unions to count as legal marriage."

Seymour caught the suggestion of Rev's words. "Do you believe in polygamy, Rev?"

"Most of the time, I do not," Rev replied. "In fact, I believe with Jesus and Paul that this is not the time to be married. There is too much uncertainty, and the end of time is surely near. Yet, when I see a man, such as yourself, who is so successful and so attractive, I can't help but think of the many beautiful women who would benefit from a union with you. David and other biblical heroes certainly took many, many wives. It's a way of helping the weaker vessels among us."

Seymour was not immune to flattery. He had never really thought of himself as a chick magnet, but Rev had him in exactly that frame of mind. "I can see what you mean; the Bible certainly allows for polygamy."

Steel, the misogynist, was gasping at all this talk about women. He wanted nothing to do with females. Instead of arousing his libido, the thought of multiple wives made him shrivel.

"But getting back to your question about the signs," Rev continued, "I am impressed with the number of wildfires in California this year, and I believe if there's an eruption from hell, it will come there first, probably through the San Andreas Fault. California, after all, is our Sodom and Gomorrah. But perhaps the fire of hell will come first to godless Seattle in the form of volcanic eruptions. The signs are there to be read."

Seymour smiled. He liked the part about California going up in flames. He glanced over his shoulder. "And what do you think, Commander Steel?"

Steel was caught off guard. He had little patience with these Rapture/Tribulation people, but he knew the game Rev was playing. "The sign I see," he began, "is the growing acceptance of witchcraft and magic, which the Bible warns us against over and over. One thing we can do is root out those who practice those beliefs. They will, we know, support the Antichrist in the final battle. The Lord is allowing such practices to grow in order to test us and make us see the need to prepare for his coming."

Then Steel waxed even more theological. "Everything that happens in this world happens because of divine providence. The Lord controls the smallest thing, from the flight of a butterfly to the election of a president." Steel trailed off, totally unaware of the irony that he had denounced magic in the same speech that he had endorsed a world controlled by supernatural forces and unaware that he had stepped on Seymour's theology, since Seymour thought that the Antichrist was responsible for much of what was happening. In any case, Seymour was getting bored with this visit to this outpost; he wanted to be sitting by his pool. The lemonade had given him a craving for more of the same.

"Gentlemen, and especially you, Reverend Oliver, I am setting up a special account in your name in my bank in Serenity. You can draw up to one hundred thousand from that account at any time. We already have your signature and thumbprint. After seeing this, I realize that you must have considerable ongoing expenses. I want to help. It has been a good year for me with many repossessions and a huge low-interest loan from the federal government. Plus my own bonus was, shall we say, generous."

With that self-promoting speech, Seymour rose to his feet. "I'll leave you two to your work. I may visit again in a couple of months just to see how you are expanding. Praise Jesus, and keep up the good work."

Had Seymour known that one of the two men to whom he was ostensibly giving money was preparing to rob a branch of his bank, he might have been offended, or he might have just shrugged. After all, Seymour had been robbing his banks for several years. He had insisted that Judd, Oklahoma take on several risky securities and then sold the overvalued securities in exchange for several lower-risk securities that he counted as of equal value. Then he brokered the low-risk securities to banks that were overextended, because they had bought some of his high-risk securities in the first place. Of course, he accepted a large CEO bonus for this clever manipulation, and now he was giving a fraction of it away, although it showed up on his taxes as a donation to a nonprofit religious foundation.

Minutes later, Seymour's limo pulled out of the gate. Shortly after that, a bus picked up the students and their director. Steel was not happy that Rev alone had the power to draw out the money, but he understood that Seymour was used to dealing with him.

"We'll go into town and move that money into an account only I can access." Steel was emphatic on that point.

"Of course," Rev agreed. "But first, you have a bank to visit come Monday."

***

Sophie Kneemeyer was mad as hell. Her hip hurt, and she had had to walk two blocks from the municipal parking lot, relying on her heavy cane to support her weak side. Now she was standing in the bank with a bunch of other people who did not smell all that great waiting to get her money out. Sophie had lived in Judd, Oklahoma for most of her life. It was a small town with one bank, and she, along with most of her neighbors, had read the article in *Poor Judd,* the local paper, that the state and federal tests of her bank had shown it to be lacking in assets relative to its debts and the huge bonuses it paid to its CEO. An infusion of funds was needed. Unfortunately for Sophie, a couple of managers of bigger banks that had loaned funds to her bank had also seen the article and called in their loans. The Texas/Oklahoma First Citizens' Bank branch of Judd had paid these loans off and, after cashing out the first few customers of the day, was woefully short of greenbacks by late morning. So, Sophie steamed and waited for her money.

In the meantime, the van from Camp Joshua was loaded and on its way to the Oklahoma panhandle. Steel, two of the Sons of Abraham, and Curt were in costume for the robbery, and Harry was driving. The meanest Son of Abraham, a guy named "Dirk," had been left to guard Will, Chris, Blink, and Rev, who remained locked in one of the barracks.

The barracks had only one window out of which the prisoners could see. The others had been covered and nailed shut. The only exit was a hollow core door.

They waited until the van had been gone for about an hour, and then Chris began to fiddle with the lock.

"I'll have us out of here in no time," he boasted.

"What the hell is going on in there?" Dirk shouted from the opposite side of the door, obviously wise to Chris's breakout attempt. "Quit messin' with that lock or I'll fill the door with holes."

"Too slow," Blink said impatiently as he launched his huge frame at the door.

The door did not stand a chance. It tore away from the jamb, and one hinge flew off and landed ten feet away. The door itself hit Dirk with such force it threw him back about six feet. He was unconscious before he hit the ground. Rev scooped up Dirk's gun and threw it over the fence into a patch of tall weeds.

"Let's get to the car," Rev said.

They all headed toward the Mazda. Will had Ham's cage tucked under his arm. Unfortunately, when they got to the vehicle, they discovered that the keys were missing. However, after a little wire pulling and re-attaching, Chris got the Mazda running. Blink and Chris barely fit in the back. Will, with Ham on his lap, was in the passenger seat. They pulled onto the highway, and Rev floored it, but it still took the little car several minutes to get up to the speed limit and beyond. They had just exceeded the speed limit by about ten miles per hour when a highway patrol sneaker came up behind them and turned on its siren and lights. Rev pulled over immediately.

"What's the hurry?" the patrolman asked.

"Bank robbery," Rev replied, which got the patrolman's attention.

"What bank?"

"Texas/Oklahoma First Citizens' Bank in Judd, Oklahoma."

Rev offered a capsule summary of the planned robbery and the fact that they were escaping from a crazed bank robber/militia commander.

"You better come with me," the patrolman replied before he realized there was no way he could get everyone in his car, given Blink's size and girth. "Follow me," he said. "And don't try anything."

Rev followed the patrol car to Serenity, which had a highway patrol office. The patrolman was on the radio the whole way.

***

Sophie Kneemeyer was just about to go out for a very late lunch. It was one thirty, and the funds the bank manager said were on the way had yet to show up. Just then, a van painted in camouflage pulled up in front of the bank. Three men emerged out the back door, and a fourth exited on the passenger side. Sophie's eyes were not that good anymore, but the men's faces looked unusually furry.

The men stormed into the bank, and one of them fired a gun into the air. That got everyone's attention.

"This is a robbery! Everyone on the floor, now!"

The robbers seemed surprised to see a large crowd in the bank, many of them seniors.

"What did he say?" an elderly man named George Pullet asked.

The robbers moved swiftly to herd the crowd to one side, ordering everyone to get down on the floor.

"I couldn't hear him," George's friend Gary Watson replied. "I was talking to you. But I think they want us to close the door."

Some of the younger people were getting down on the floor. That gave the idea to the older folks, but many of them were having trouble making their bodies obey. One of them was Sophie. She remained standing. Her hip simply would not allow her to lie on the floor. Besides, the floor was dirty and needed to be swept.

Three of the men approached the teller windows. "Don't touch the alarm," one of them warned, "or you'll die right now. Take all the cash out of your drawers and put it in these bags."

The tellers looked terrified. "Sir," the bravest of them said, "we don't have any cash. We ran out some time ago."

"At least we know they're not lying," Sophie opined. "I thought they just didn't want to give us our money."

"Who the hell are you, and why aren't you lying down?" one of the robbers asked.

"I'm Sophie Kneemeyer, a longtime client of this damned bank, which is not really a bank, because they don't have any goddam money. I'm sorry, I don't usually swear, but this has been a terrible day. My hip hurts, so I can't get on the floor. My dog at home probably needs to go potty, and they won't give me my money." Sophie began to cry. "And you insult me when you talk to me that way," she added as an afterthought.

One of the robbers had entered the tellers' spaces and pulled out all the drawers. He also checked the vault. He turned to the others. "Let's get the hell out of here. There's no cash here anywhere."

The robbers fled to the van, which was still idling. Steel was first to the passenger side. "Let's move!"

Sophie could not see very well, but she could see that when the other three robbers tried to enter the van through the side door, it opened partway and then stuck. The robbers ran to the back door just as the van surged backward—Harry had hit reverse instead of drive. The men were knocked to the ground and lay pinned under the rear of the van, which was wedged firmly on a metal bicycle rack so that the drive wheel simply spun as Harry mashed the accelerator.

At that moment, several police and highway patrol cars roared up and surrounded the van. The trapped robbers screamed some terrible words at the driver. In her later conversations with the police, Sophie could never bring herself to repeat what they said.

Sophie decided she was not going to get her money that day, so she limped to the door and headed for her car.

The bank robbers lying under the van were receiving first aid. The police had the man who had spoken so harshly to her doing a spread eagle on the curbside near where Sophie was trying to walk. On the other side, the driver was also being searched. Sophie never could explain why she did what she did except to say that it had been a very bad day. She put her weight on her good leg and swung her heavy wooden cane directly at the head of the man on the curb. The cane made a satisfying crack, and he collapsed against the van.

"You miserable…" Sophie was at a loss for words, "bad, bad man," she finished somewhat lamely.

The cop who was searching the man gave her a startled look. "Ma'am, please move along," he said with a smile as he held the collapsing robber up with one hand.

"Bank robbers were much more polite in my day," Sophie remarked as she limped away.

***

Will, Blink, and Chris were seated in the waiting room of the Serenity police station. FBI Agent Angela Smith was interviewing Rev. She would get to Will and the others later. The FBI was particularly interested in whether there was a kidnapping to be prosecuted. They already had word of the unsuccessful bank robbery, and Will and company were being given credit for alerting the authorities. Names, addresses, and criminal histories were already known. The FBI and local authorities were combing the grounds at Camp Joshua. The fact that Chris, Blink, and Rev were all parolees from WTHC was causing some concern, but Rev gave Agent Smith the straight scoop on Will. He had no criminal record and was on his way to a job at the Galilee Theme Park. Angela believed him; especially after a phone call to Reverend Shister confirmed his story.

Agent Smith had two sons of her own, and she liked the young man with the hamster. Later that day, she drove him back to the compound, let him collect his things—he found his cell phone in Steel's office—and then drove him down the road to the theme park, to which she had considered taking her sons when it opened. She assured Will that if the entire story could be confirmed, Rev, Chris, and Blink would not be prosecuted. But she took note of Will's bizarre tale, including the threatened stoning, which horrified her.

"We may need you to testify when this comes to trial, and it's likely the prosecutors will be calling you in the meantime. That bunch up in Judd should be going to prison for a long, long time."

Will was so relieved to find a sympathetic, caring person that he almost burst into tears.

It was after dark when Will and Angela arrived at the theme park. In the dark, Will could only make out a few fairly large structures. Reverend Shister met them at the gate. After Agent Smith left, he showed Will to a construction trailer.

"Staff quarters aren't finished yet," he explained, "but you can have this room all to yourself until the dorms are ready."

Reverend Shister looked nervous when Will showed up with an FBI agent, but he relaxed a bit after Agent Smith offered a thumbnail sketch of what Will had just been through.

Will was delighted with his trailer. It was cool, and the bed was clean. Ham seemed none the worse for the excitement and was chewing merrily on a very old and unrecognizable Gideon Bible. Will was still pumped up from the day's events, and he wanted desperately to call Cindy, although it was already late in Ohio. He called anyway. There were a dozen missed calls on his phone, most of them from her.

"God, Will. Are you all right? I've been trying to reach you."

"I'm fine," Will said. "It's a long and unbelievable story. I've been a captive of some would-be bank robbers, who are now in jail. They took my phone."

"No way!"

"Truth," Will replied. "I promise to give you a detailed account when we have more time. I know it's late back there. What's going on with you?"

"Bank robbers?" Cindy was fully awake and curious.

"I caught a ride to west Texas with a guy who ran a fake militia, and his compound was captured by another…oh, I'm too tired for this now. But I'm at the theme park and have a place to sleep. How's your mom?"

"She had a relapse. She's comfortable but not doing well. I'll keep you posted now that you have a phone. I've missed your calls. I'm so glad you're all right. Bank robbers!"

"I'm afraid so," Will said. "But a very nice FBI agent helped me collect my stuff and brought me to the park."

"That's good. Is Ham all right?"

"He seems a lot perkier than me," Will replied.

"I'll let you go, Will. I love you, and I am so happy you're all right." Cindy sounded tired.

"Love you, too. I'll call soon."

After he hung up, Will crawled into his bed and said a quick prayer of thanks. He also asked God to look out for Rev, Blink, and Chris.

"So, your best friends, apart from Cindy, seem to be convicted felons," God said.

"They were nice to me," Will replied.

"I can't disagree with that," God said, "And quite frankly, they are among your most interesting friends. You could learn hacking, mayhem, and confidence games from those three."

"Why don't you like them?" Will asked.

"Actually, I do like them. You came on this journey in part to broaden your perspective. So far you've lost your truck and your money, you've had multiple concussions, been fired, kidnapped, and enslaved. You've piled up good works, fallen for a lovely young woman, gotten high, and been arrested. All this sets a new standard in the broadening horizons department. And you've only been on the road for a few weeks. God knows what you'll do next."

Will smiled. “I wasn’t arrested; I’m a material witness. So I’m not so boring anymore?”

“Go to sleep, Will.”

GALILEE

The morning after his arrival at the Galilee Theme Park, Will staggered out of his trailer and discovered he was in the midst of stacks of lumber, rebar, and men in hardhats. He found his way to a large temporary dining tent and bathhouse. His letter of appointment from Reverend Shister got him a shower and some breakfast. While eating, he was told that there would be a general meeting for all new staff at ten. It was already nine thirty, so, holding a map, Will set out for the amphitheater where everyone was gathering.

Heading across the park gave Will a sense of just how large and ambitious the project was. There were dozens of exhibits in various degrees of completion. Office buildings, conference centers, theaters, stages for performances, first aid stations, and an entire carnival with rides and games filled the rest of the space. Souvenir stores were scattered throughout, and most exhibits had a shop where you could purchase artifacts. Will was truly stunned by the enormity of it all.

The amphitheater was already filling up. Smaller groups within the gathering were chatting as if they knew each other. Will noted that most of those assembled were about his age. There were more young women than young men, and all were dressed casually.

As Will took a seat in a row of several women, all of whom seemed to know one another, the lively, red-haired woman next to him identified herself as Kate Sullivan and introduced him to several of her friends. Everyone there was from a seminary or a college somewhere in the southwest. Most had arrived at the park over the past couple of days.

Reverend Shister was not long in making his appearance. "Hello, all," he said. "Let us pray."

All heads bowed.

"Lord Jesus, we ask your blessing on this crew and our work. We seek an understanding of your life and teachings for ourselves and for others. We work in your name and praise your gift to all humanity. In the name of Jesus Christ the Lord, Amen."

The Reverend looked over his audience. Shister, as Will had come to think of him, looked a youngish fifty something. Will's uncle remembered Shister only as a young, personable pastor. He must have been very young. Shister's hair was silver now, and it seemed to be held in place by a substance with little or no flexibility. He wore a chain around his neck and a couple of good-sized rings on one hand but no wedding ring. He had on newish Levis and what looked like an expensive white shirt.

"As you know, I am Reverend Shister, with a short 'i'," the Reverend began with a chuckle. He had a warm, deep voice. "I know all of you have filled out an application and received a letter of acceptance. Yet, very few of you have met me. Over the next few months, I hope to get to know each one of you. However, as you can see right now," Shister waved his arms toward the construction, "I'm fairly busy trying to get things finished, get the publicity out, and keep the finances going. I know you all want to work for the Lord, but I imagine that since most of you are headed for college, you would not mind a paycheck at the end of your time here."

There were some cheers.

"Before I say more about our plans for the future of Galilee Theme Park, let me say a little about the concept behind it. We all know that the education system in this great Christian nation has been hijacked by a liberal and secular curriculum. The faithful are mocked, denied the opportunity to pray, and taught to believe in the atheistic materialism of *Darwinian evolution.*" Shister spit out the phrase as if he were using foul language. "When God told me to build this park, He wanted an antidote for this poisonous curriculum. Galilee is where we welcome the faithful, the home-schooled, and the skeptic. We serve them the *truth.* Starting today, you will all receive instruction on how to serve the thousands, millions of people who will be visiting Galilee."

"Oh, dear," Kate whispered, "I'm a biology major, and I don't believe you need to throw out evolution to keep God."

Shister amped up the volume as he stressed the mission of the theme park. He was getting really "revved" up now. Will enjoyed his pun, but God groaned. "You can do better than that."

An elegantly dressed woman sitting in the front row made a sign with her hand. Shister blinked at her and then he seemed to recall that his time was limited.

"During your time here, you will gain a better understanding of our reasons for being. But I've been given a signal to wrap this up. We are going to open on August twenty-fifth as promised. That is only a few days from now. I would estimate that about forty percent of the exhibits will be ready by then, and that is where you will all be working. Originally, we hoped to remain open all year, but this year we will be closed for part of the winter to finish construction. I realize this schedule is not what some of you had planned on. We hope to reopen on May first, the National Day of Prayer. Some of you may want to return to help us out next summer. I am sorry that our opening was delayed, but the Lord works in mysterious ways. Now, Mrs. Williamson, my administrator, my right arm, will speak to you about the practicalities of getting us started while I return to the prison of my office."

Shister nodded to the woman in the front row who had given the signal. She wore a high bonnet of blond hair and appeared to be about Shister's age.

After brief applause, Mrs. Williamson rose and seized the microphone. "Hello." She had a loud, somewhat grating voice. She was clearly comfortable being in charge and was quick to make it clear that she was the real boss. "I am Mrs. Williamson, Reverend Shister's administrator. Before you came, I read your applications, and now that you're here, I am responsible for your assignments. I also evaluate your work and will provide you with what you need to do your jobs. My office is in the administration building, first door on the right, Room 101. If you have any questions, needs, or encounter any problems, my office is your first stop.

"Today you will get settled. One wing of the staff dormitory is finished, and your room assignments will be posted by early afternoon. You will move your things from wherever they are now to the dorm. By this evening, your work assignments will be posted on the entryway bulletin board. For the next four days, you will carry out your duties. Things are going to be a little rough at first, because construction is still going on, and the crowds will be coming in and asking questions before you are fully trained. So that you will know how to handle their queries, we will have mandatory meetings, which we will announce in advance. These will inform you of the official Galilee Theme Park response. And, by the way, some of you will be doing double duty, because we are not yet fully staffed. But hang in there. Remember you are doing the Lord's work and you should take joy in that. Are there any questions?"

Almost every hand in the amphitheater went up.

***

The staff dormitory looked like any campus dorm. It was large and boxy with a cafeteria, offices, and lounges on the first floor, women's rooms on the second floor, and men's rooms on the third. Will arrived at his room to find his roommate already present.

"Hi, I'm Simon Tigard," said the sandy-haired youth who was sitting on one of the beds. "I was waiting for you to get here so we could decide who sleeps where."

"Thanks," Will said. He was much more concerned about how Simon would take to Ham, whose cage was collapsed and in his duffle while Ham rode in his shirt pocket. "I really don't care. If you like the bed you're sitting on, why don't you keep it?"

"Sounds good to me," Simon replied.

Simon was the opposite of Will in many ways. He had short, sandy hair and was small, almost childlike in size. His body was thin with toothpick arms and a narrow face. Will had always been large with powerful arms and shoulders.

"We kind of look like Mutt and Jeff," Simon said, noticing the size difference. "I've always been the skinny little guy. In high school they called me 'Spindles'."

"I guess that gives me more room to move around," Will said good-naturedly. "I have a traveling companion, if you don't mind." Will produced Ham from his pocket.

Simon did not mind at all. His eyes lit up, and he held out a small hand to take Ham. "He's really cute. Does he make much noise?"

"At night sometimes he runs on his wheel, but he's getting less frequent with that. I think he's aging." Then Will told Simon of his rescue of Ham and Ham's bad habit of eating Gideon Bibles.

Simon was delighted with the story. "I never liked that edition anyway. But we're not supposed to have pets in the dorm."

"I know," Will said, 'but I can't part with him at this point."

The two young men agreed to keep Ham a secret. "I need to get some shavings or newspaper for his floor and set up his cage. I'm also getting low on hamster food."

"That shouldn't be a problem," Simon ventured. "You and I—here's the good news—are assigned to the petting zoo. In fact, you're listed as the manager. You must have some experience with animals."

Will nodded. "Yeah, my aunt and uncle always had a ton of animals around, many of them rescue animals. We had chickens, ponies, cattle, a goat once, and endless dogs and cats. I also spent a lot of time in the woods. I actually got friendly with a deer for a couple of years. He would eat right out of my hand. I mentioned some of that on my application."

Simon's eyes sparkled. "I was never allowed pets. My parents always treated me as sickly and thought I had allergies, which, in fact, I don't have. This is my first venture away from home. It feels good. Oh, and I should mention that we're backups for trash pickup."

"Does that mean all of the garbage this park produces?" Will was not happy with this bit of news.

"No, my understanding of the assignments is that we will only be responsible for driving a little cart around and putting new bags in the cans as they fill up if the regulars can't get it done. We don't do anything with construction trash." Simon looked pleased to have given Will the inside scoop on their assignments.

"Okay, I can handle that," Will said, "but don't they do any recycling?"

"I didn't see any mention of that," Simon replied.

"Well, at least being at the petting zoo should give me access to shavings and food for Ham."

Will was starting to warm to the idea of his assignment. He also liked Simon. He was not very strong, but he seemed open-minded and friendly—the fact he agreed to allow Ham in the room was also a big positive.

"I know we're not really supposed to begin our assignments until tomorrow, but I think we better check on the zoo today. Whenever live animals are my responsibility, I know the more attention we give them, the better."

"I don't know anything about live animals," Simon said. "But I'm willing to learn. Let's go."

The petting zoo was at the far end of the park from the entrance and dormitories. Will and Simon arrived there at about the same time as Mrs. Williamson showed up riding a small electric golf cart.

"Are you the two boys I assigned to the zoo?" she asked. "Which of you is William Tillit?"

Will stepped forward, "I'm pleased to meet you Mrs. Williamson."

Without acknowledging Will's greeting, or the fact he was not supposed to work until the following day, Mrs. Williamson pulled him to one side. "Will, I hope you know what you're doing with these animals. They're arriving right now. We bought out a petting zoo up in Arkansas. The vet, who has volunteered her services, is with them. She'll sort through the animals and euthanize any that don't qualify. She'll also give you instructions on the care of the animals we keep. You should also know that I'm opposed to this zoo. Zoos of any kind are smelly and cause extra work and expense. But Reverend Shister wants this to be a family place, and children love petting zoos. It will be up to you to keep the place clean and keep anyone from getting hurt."

"I understand, and I know how to care for animals," Will said. "Is Simon my only help?"

"No, I have also assigned a girl to help here." Mrs. Williamson consulted her clipboard. "Her name is Kate Sullivan. She should report tomorrow. She can also help pick up trash, if needed, but I really want all of you to stay close to home so that the zoo is clean and there are no incidents."

"I'll do my best," Will said. He was delighted that Kate was assigned to the zoo. She seemed friendly, and he hoped, being a biology major, knowledgeable.

"Good boy." Mrs. Williamson seemed unaware that calling nineteen- and twenty-year-olds "boy" and "girl" did not set well. "I have something else to show you that will also be your responsibility."

Mrs. Williamson walked toward a large crate with holes in the top and a clear Plexiglas panel in front. She stopped about ten feet from it. Will went forward and looked in. Before his eyes, coiled up and resting with its tongue flicking in and out, lay a huge, whitish boa constrictor. The snake looked beautiful, and, Will thought, a bit hungry.

"How can you get that close to that monster?" Mrs. Williamson asked, obviously terrified of snakes. "That thing is close to seven feet long. Some friend of Reverend Shister sent it to us. He also sent some frozen rats and rabbits to feed it."

She looked at her clipboard and made a sour face. "Its name is Bullwinkle. Reverend Shister is having a display pen built in the Garden of Eden for it. He thinks its mere presence will remind visitors of original sin. But the snake's home pen will be here at the zoo. It's just inside the office. He requires special light and a bunch of other stuff."

She handed Will a few sheets of paper that were entitled *Care of Boa Constrictors*. "I have to get back to my office. You and Simon stay here to help the vet." She started to leave. "Oh, here are the keys for the zoo and the various pens, including the snake's. You'll have to figure out which is which."

With that, Mrs. Williamson turned on her heel, got in her cart, and fled.

Simon approached Will. "You look like someone just dumped a lot on your shoulders."

"I've been given a lot of responsibility, but taking care of animals is something I enjoy," Will said as he walked with Simon toward the office. "I just became a zookeeper, and you became a zookeeper's lackey."

Simon laughed.

Will finally found the key to open the office. It looked like it was finished. Inside, he found a number of cages, including a large vivarium. Since the power was on, he had no trouble setting the temperature at about eighty-two degrees Fahrenheit and turning on the light to create a warmer area. He filled the pool with water. The instructions were precise and the vivarium well constructed.

"Let's get Bullwinkle in here," Will said when he was finished.

The instructions said that Bullwinkle was quite tame and could be handled safely. The traveling case was on wheels, so Will and Simon pushed it into the room with the vivarium. The temperature was too low, and there was no water left in the traveling case. Will opened the door and lifted Bullwinkle out, only to have the snake wrap a powerful coil around his waist.

"Hold onto her tail," he instructed Simon, "so she can't get another coil around me." Simon made a grab for the tail, but Bullwinkle hardly noticed as she wrapped another loop around Will.

"So we meet again," Kate Sullivan said as she walked into the office. "Do you need some help? She's a good-sized mama."

"Oh my God!" Mrs. Williamson screamed as she entered behind Kate. "Satan is eating a person!" She seemed to remember neither Will's name nor Bullwinkle's. "Kill it! Kill it!" she screamed from a safe distance.

Will was not panicked. It was more of a reptilian hug than an attack. Still, it prevented him from getting Bullwinkle into her box.

Kate grabbed onto the snake's tail and began to unwind Bullwinkle. As she gained access to the snake's body, she handed it to Simon. In a short time, Bullwinkle was exploring her new vivarium.

"Thank God, praise Jesus," Mrs. Williamson gushed. "I told Reverend Shister that creature of the devil was too dangerous to be allowed in the park."

Kate reassured Mrs. Williamson that Bullwinkle was not being particularly aggressive; she was just a snake looking for something to hold onto. Mrs. Williamson was obviously more interested in being right in her conflict with Reverend Shister than in knowing the facts. She rode off, once again, on her electric cart with a threat to take the matter all the way to the board.

"How did you know Bullwinkle is a female?" Simon asked.

"The female boa is more muscular and longer than the male," Kate answered. "Bullwinkle looks very female to me. In fact, I'd be willing to bet she's pregnant. I'm not a big snake fan, but I enjoy studying the diverse animal groups."

Will studied the instructions. "She was last fed a couple of rats seven days ago. She has to be hungry again. Where are the rats?"

"Here in the freezer." Simon reached in and handed a couple of stiff dead rodents to Will.

"I doubt she'll eat the frozen ones." Kate said. "Here, I'll defrost them."

She popped them into the microwave and then examined the controls. "Darn, there's no setting for frozen rats." She laughed. "I'll just have to guess."

Bullwinkle was hungry and quickly constricted and swallowed the rats. The victory of settling Bullwinkle gave Will a good feeling. Better yet, he really liked his crew.

A knock on the door proved to be a truck driver and the vet. The vet was an older woman who reminded Will of his aunt. She was small, quick, and seemed quite serious about everything. Her name was Mildred Collins, and she put them straight to work unloading and helping her sort the animals.

Several hours later, after dark and under lights, Will, Kate, and Simon had finished with the animals. A few had died on the trip from Arkansas. A couple of chickens and one rabbit had to be euthanized. The surviving animals included two rabbits, two guinea pigs, a llama, a lamb, two ponies, two small goats, a peahen, a peacock, and a donkey. The animals were bedded down, fed, and watered. Mildred gave the crew careful instructions on animal care and then took off in her red Jeep.

Will had had some long days at the mission, but this day at the petting zoo topped them all. He, Kate, and Simon staggered back to the dorm, said goodnight, and then went to bed after grabbing some cookies and milk from the cafeteria's snack shop.

As Simon settled in, he looked over at Will. "I think they made a good choice in making you zookeeper."

"Thanks," Will said. "You and Kate make a good couple of lackeys as well. You really helped me with Bullwinkle."

"I'm afraid Mrs. Williamson has confused Bullwinkle with the serpent in Genesis," Simon observed. "And that is going to be an ongoing problem."

"I'm afraid you're right," Will replied. He stepped outside and called Cindy, who was amazed once again at the turn of events in his life.

"Damn it, Will, it's just not fair. I'm here hanging out at the hospital, dealing with doctors, nurses, and bill collectors, not to mention funeral directors. And you, my lovely friend, are out there associating with felons and wrestling boa constrictors. But, God, it makes me laugh and realize there is a crazy world out there that I may become part of once again."

Aunt Rita also enjoyed the Bullwinkle story. She was doing well and said she would like to visit the theme park. Will liked the fact that he was able to leave those he loved in good humor.

Back in his bed, Will hoped to talk to God, and he found God was willing.

"You do get yourself into some interesting situations," God began.

"Yes," Will agreed. "Was that really a serpent in the Garden who started all the trouble?"

"Huh?"

"You know, the Garden of Eden, when Eve was tempted by the serpent, and then she tempted Adam, and they ate of the fruit after you told them not to. So you expelled them from the Garden and punished Eve by making women suffer in childbirth. You know, all that stuff." Will recited Genesis 3:16, where God says to Eve: "I will greatly increase your pangs in childbearing; in pain you shall bring forth children, yet your desire shall be for your husband, and he shall rule over you."

"Not really," God said. "It doesn't sound like an even remotely plausible historical event. If such a story is around, it probably gives women and snakes a bad name."

"That's for sure."

"I would counsel you to forget it. Believing a story like that will only put you on the path to misogyny, and, er…and maybe 'misreptilianism.' A story like that only leaves you with an unanswerable question about why on Earth anyone would tell such a story or include it unless they were building a foundation for patriarchy."

Will had always thought the story was simply weird and horribly unfair, and, for that reason, he never thought it something God would do. But he thought that about most of the stories in Genesis.

BEGINNINGS

The next morning, Will awoke with a sense of excitement. He roused Simon, and both of them set out for the zoo. On their way, they passed by the Noah exhibit, which was next to the zoo. A long ramp filled with pairs of animal statues lined up two by two extended up to the deck of the ark. Will noted that none of the animals were anatomically correct. A statue of Noah stood at the foot of the ramp, presumably greeting the animals. A separate escalator allowed visitors to ride to the deck and admire the animal statues on the way up. It was the classic picture Will had seen in Sunday school books, except that instead of a giraffe on the deck of the ark there was a brontosaurus. There was also a man standing at the base of the dinosaur statue yelling.

"Shoo, get off there!"

Simon turned to Will with a twinkle in his eye. "Maybe that's why there are no dinosaurs today; they were chased off the ark before she sailed."

The figure on the deck spotted Will and Simon. "Would you get your bird off the nose of my brontosaurus?"

Will and Simon looked up and, sure enough, there sat Pansy the peahen. She let out a couple of loud honks at the irritating figure shouting at her. Her call was answered by her mate, Peter, who was still in the peafowl enclosure.

"Just a minute!" Will shouted. "Quit harassing her, and I'll call her down." Will was not at all certain how to call a peahen. He turned to Simon. "We need to get a cover on their enclosure."

Once in the zoo, Will dumped some grain in a metal dish and shook it vigorously. Pansy listened for a time, and then, after a bit of bobbing about, she took flight and landed cleanly in the enclosure. He let her have the dish of food, which she and her mate ate voraciously. While they ate, Will and Simon attached an extra piece of chicken wire to the top of the pen.

The man who had been railing at Pansy arrived a bit out of breath and flushed with anger. “Keep you damn bird off my brontosaurus,” he said. “She shit all over his face, and now I have to go up in the cherry picker and clean it.”

“I’m sorry,” Will said. “We just received these animals late yesterday, and some of the pens are not quite adequate. But, as you can see, we have now covered their enclosure.”

“What are two peafowl doing in a petting zoo, anyway?” Simon asked after the worker left.

“I don’t know; I just work here,” Will responded. “Let’s finish cleaning the stalls and the cages so there are no unpleasant odors for Mrs. Williamson and then go have breakfast. There’s an all-staff meeting at ten.”

At breakfast, they sat with Kate, who was mightily entertained by Pansy’s misadventure.

“I’ll come by after the meeting and help attach the wire permanently to the peafowl cage,” she said. “We need to go over all the cages and enclosures to make certain we have no more escapees. Why are there peafowl in a petting zoo anyway? They’re noisy and messy.”

“But they are a bit exotic for west Texas,” Will said.

After breakfast, the staff gathered in the amphitheater. This time, Will noted that there were even more young men and women assembled. Mrs. Williamson took to the lectern at exactly ten o’clock, even though a few stragglers were still coming in.

“Good morning, staff,” she began. “Today and for the next two days we will be having these morning lectures. Their purpose is to inform you of the official positions of the Galilee Theme Park on a number of issues. The visitors will be asking you questions. Some of them may challenge you. We want you to be informed, polite, and more or less speaking with the same voice. If you personally disagree with us, you only need to know what the official position of the Galilee Theme Park is. Then you can supply the answer. If you can’t do that, then we think it best that you and Galilee part company before any of our guests arrive.

"Another point: All of you should have your work instructions by now, and you should have reported to your assigned area. For those of you working on the rides, there will be an extra safety training session this evening. And as a special treat for those of you who would like to try out the rides, there will be a period of free rides tomorrow evening from seven to nine. If you are going on the roller coaster or the whirligig, I recommend you eat a light dinner."

This remark brought laughter.

"Now," Mrs. Williamson continued "it's my pleasure to introduce Dr. James Wylie, a professor of theology at Bowling Hill Bible College. He is going to talk to us about beginnings, the beginning of everything, the creation."

Dr. Wylie stepped up to the lectern. "It's a pleasure to be here and to see all these intelligent young faces. You give me hope, joy, and confidence that Galilee Theme Park is in good hands. As you have probably noticed, many of the exhibits here have to do with beginnings and origins. There's the Garden of Eden and the Flood, also Abraham and the Ten Commandments, the picture of sulfur and fire raining on Sodom and Gomorrah, the story of Abraham and Isaac, and many others. At the core of all these is an interest in origins. How did we begin? Where did the universe come from? What's the significance of these events? Those who visit and see these authentic representations of actual events will likely bombard you with queries. This lecture today is part of a series to equip you to deal with such inquiries. In addition, we will pass out a frequently asked questions sheet at the end of the lecture to help you with some of the things you may be asked."

"How does he know the exhibits are authentic?" God asked. "Was he there?"

"You have a real opportunity here to bring people to the Lord," Dr. Wylie continued. "There's one puzzle that is especially troubling to folks. That puzzle begins with the question, 'How did things come to be?' Some call this the 'cosmological argument for the existence of God'. There are several different ways of putting it, but I will give you a fairly straightforward version. It goes like this: The world around us is made up of dependent beings, that is, beings that depend on other beings to come into existence. You all depended on your biological parents to be born.

The movement of your car depends on the firing of its cylinders and their connection to your drive shaft and so on. Our world goes back approximately six thousand years. But our world itself is a dependent being. The question is, if there was nothing before our world, what brought it about? Dependent beings must have a cause that produced them. The cause must either be another dependent being or a self-existing being that does not need a cause. It cannot go back infinitely. If there were no dependent beings before the world began, there must be a special self-existing being, namely, a creator. It is a simple argument and has a lot of appeal even to skeptics. Genesis, then, is just an account of how this self-existing being went about creating the dependent being we call 'the world'. Are there any questions?"

"I have several," God said to Will. "Which of the two creation accounts is true? Were Adam and Eve created first so they could name the animals, or were the animals already there? And is the fact that Adam was made of dust the reason men are so untidy? And why doesn't Eve have one more rib than Adam?"

Will realized that God was not taking this lecture very seriously. Simon and Kate certainly were though. Both were taking notes. They doubted that many in the petting zoo would be asking for explanations of the world, but there was always the chance they would be reassigned to another exhibit where the question would pop up.

Simon raised his hand. "I'm somewhat familiar with this argument, but won't someone who's a skeptic simply ask us what caused God? Why is God exempt from the list of things that require causes?"

"Good question," Dr. Wylie responded. "Of necessary beings, it makes no sense to ask what caused them, because by definition, such beings do not have a cause, or as some say, they are self-existent."

Simon pushed a little harder. "How can we know that God is a necessary being, a being who must exist? Just defining God that way will not satisfy the skeptic. How do we show that God's nonexistence is an impossibility?"

"That's a tough question," Dr. Wylie said. "There's another argument called the ontological argument that concludes that if God is the greatest thing that can be conceived, then God must exist."

Will was taken back to his debate at the lifestyle fair. He remained convinced that the ontological argument did not show that God existed. Also, Will was troubled by the idea that if you needed an argument to prove that God existed, then it certainly seemed possible that God did not exist, in which case God did not qualify as a necessary being. He realized that he and Simon would have to talk about this some more.

At lunch, Mrs. Williamson pulled Will to one side. "Will, I heard about the escape of that bird, and I don't want to hear of something like that happening again. You are responsible for the behavior and the confinement of those animals. As I told you, I am not in favor of the petting zoo, and every time there's an incident like this, I'm closer to getting rid of the whole display. I just want to be clear where I stand on this." Mrs. Williamson did not ask for an explanation; she just made it clear that it was Will's responsibility.

Will was peeved. "I don't think that's fair. The pens were not well designed. We changed them so she can't get out again. I don't think you need to inflate every event in the petting zoo into a cause for closing it down."

Mrs. Williamson did not reply, but it was obvious she did not like anyone standing up to her.

Following lunch Will, Kate, and Simon returned to the zoo. Will was insistent that all the animals be brought out and groomed and handled with the exception of the peafowl, whose pen he asked Simon to clean.

"We need to make certain that these animals are gentle and that they have not been abused. If they aren't gentle, we need to get rid of them, because they will just be a liability. We also need to go over each cage and make certain they're secure."

"Will," Kate had been looking at the rabbits. "One of the rabbits has pulled out quite a bit of hair and has piled it in the corner, and now the hair is moving."

"Is she alone in the cage?" Will asked.

"Yes, each rabbit has its own cage."

"Good, because with that kind of behavior, I suspect she has babies in there or is about to. Let's make certain her cage is in a quiet place where she won't be disturbed."

"How about the guinea pigs? One of them must have given birth to babies, because there are five guinea pigs here now," Simon announced.

"Boy, are the little ones cute."

Will groaned. "Of course they didn't check on this kind of thing when they bought the animals. That goat looks pregnant, too. She's developing an udder and is quite round in the belly."

Kate was quite upbeat about the whole thing. "This is great; we'll have more pets to be petted. And we'll have cute babies for the children to look at."

"And protective mothers and extra work," Will said. "Not to mention more trouble with Mrs. Williamson."

"We'll just have to call you 'Mr. Fertility'," Kate teased. "By the way, that one is on the FAQ sheet."

"What one?" Simon asked.

"Through a divine miracle, the animals on Noah's ark did not reproduce. God ordered it thus to prevent overcrowding and unsanitary conditions. Some believe that the animals didn't defecate or make any kind of mess either."

"We could use that miracle here," Simon said as he walked past with a wheelbarrow full of donkey and pony droppings. "How did they get all those animals on the ark anyway? I suppose they had to extend the life of mosquitoes and moths and other animals that don't live very long. And certainly bacteria had to be kept from reproducing."

God joined the conversation in Will's mind. "Does it mention that perhaps God miniaturized the animals so they would fit? Elephants, mammoths, and dinosaurs must have really shrunk. Maybe Noah shrank, too. Perhaps the ark was only three hundred centimeters long. Who knows what a cubit really is?"

"Bonsai elephants—with miracles, anything is possible," Will replied. He was still thinking about the new mouths he had to feed and how he was going to deal with Mrs. Williamson.

Simon let out a yelp. He was in the peafowl pen. "Pansy just attacked me!" he said rubbing his hand. "Oh crap. She has some eggs here. How about an omelet? We do not need more peafowl."

"No," Kate said, "but cute chicks will be a real attraction. We'll build a second barrier so that the kids can't get too close to the pen."

Will said nothing. Things were getting a little complicated.

Walking back to the dorms for a quick shower and then dinner, Kate,

Will, and Simon fell into conversation about the morning's lecture.

"When I look at the glorious world we live in," Simon began, "with all its beauty and the way things fit together, I can see the handwork of God. So I really liked the argument that Dr. Wylie presented."

"I sense the beauty and order of things, too," Kate replied, "but I think the design argument you refer to is a different argument from what Dr. Wylie calls the 'cosmological argument'. In fact, I think we're getting a lecture on design tomorrow."

Simon nodded. "Still, I can see that what Dr. Wylie is really saying is that we need an explanation of why there's something rather than nothing. In other words, why does the world exist?"

Kate was still caught up on design. "I'm more impressed with how the world is structured than with the simple fact that it exists. What do you think, Will?"

Will's critical faculties had been sharpened a bit by living with Sister Ellie, Sister Sara, and especially Arie. "I'm afraid the cosmological argument doesn't take me very far. I don't think you can get God to be a necessary existent without the ontological argument, and that argument basically tries to *define* God into necessary existence, which leaves the question unanswered. Defining God as necessary, as Wylie seemed to do, is a cheat. I also doubt that any particular thing necessarily exists. It certainly seems possible that God does not exist. Perhaps that's why we look so hard for arguments to show that God does exist."

"But," Simon countered, "don't we need something that's not a dependent being to explain the existence of dependent beings?"

"Even if I grant you that there are special beings that are not dependent beings, which I do not," Will said, "there is still a logical gap that needs to be filled. If there are necessary beings, you still need to show that the one that caused the world to exist was God and not some other necessary being. Maybe the universe itself is a necessary being. But to go back a bit, why do we need to explain the existence of the world? Perhaps we don't need to explain it; just accept it. Period."

"But the world *is* a dependent being," Kate said. "Even scientists say the universe was born, and that seems to demand an explanation."

Will looked up at the sky. "I don't know enough to go into it, but it seems that your argument presupposes that everything must have an explanation or that all dependent things or events must have an explanation. But from what I've read in some areas of physics, there are things that just happen, and they seem to happen randomly, all of which casts some doubt on your principle that all dependent things have a cause or explanation, and without this principle, the argument doesn't work. But because you accept such a principle, you think that you've captured an explanation when you postulate a special thing to which this principle does not apply."

Kate and Simon nodded in agreement.

"But when you do that," Will continued, "it seems to me that you need to explain further why God is special, why we don't need an explanation for God and an explanation for why God created this world and not some other world. The kinds of things you want to take as givens simply cry out for elaboration."

"Well," Simon responded, "God is God. We simply don't have access to why he created a world at all or why he created this world rather than some other. It's a mystery."

"Right," Will agreed, "but when you put it that way, you are, in effect, saying that postulating God give us no explanation at all. We're just saying that something happened magically, and a world was the result. But look how empty that is. That's the same as what happens in a fantasy novel when the wizard waves his arms, chants an incantation, and an image of fire appears. Is that an explanation in any intelligible sense? Remember, the claim is that we need an *explanation* of these dependent things, but the cosmological argument doesn't even begin to offer one."

"No," Simon agreed, "but we're talking about God here, not some fantasy wizard." He paused. "But I feel the bite of your objection. We really haven't explained anything. We've merely postulated that we might have an explanation if we knew more. And supernatural explanations that only masquerade as explanations are easy to come by and do no real explanatory work."

"That's a good way to put it," Kate said. "I'm inclined to agree that the argument does not look very tight. I'll put my confidence in the design arguments in any case."

"I still like the cosmological argument," Simon said. "Will makes some good points, but I have more confidence in the ontological argument than he does. However, I do see the need to establish that the special being who got things going is God. That needs a separate argument. And maybe we need a separate argument other than by definition to show that God is a special being."

By the time the argument had progressed this far, they were in the downstairs lounge.

"Listen guys," Will said, "I'm going to walk back down to the zoo after dinner and check on the animals.

"Can you do it without me?" Simon asked. "I'm really pooped. But, Will, I'm glad I drew this assignment, I'm already stronger." Simon laughingly flexed a skinny arm that showed almost no muscle.

Will pressed Simon on the shoulder, "I'm glad you're on board, but I need to check on the animals. No need for you to come along, but tomorrow we really must begin to check them out for temperament."

Kate took Will's arm. "I'll meet you for dinner and then go back with you."

"Great, and thanks."

It was amazing what a shower and dinner did for Will's energy. On the way back to the zoo, he and Kate chatted about many things. They also decided to have an extra set of keys made for the zoo in case the set they had got lost or whoever had the original was unavailable.

"Will, if it's not too personal, do you have a girlfriend?"

Will had not really answered that question for himself. "Yes and no. I met a young woman who is very special to me, but she's in Ohio and…we talk a lot, but we aren't clear where our relationship is going."

Will did not feel quite right about his answer, but he wasn't sure why. And he really liked Kate. She was sweet, smart, and good with the animals.

"How about you?" Will asked, wanting to take the focus off himself.

"No, I'm not even marginally involved," Kate said. "I had a boyfriend at school, but we broke up when I came here. I have serious plans to go to graduate school and become a research biologist, hopefully in some medical program. You sound uncertain about your relationship. What's her name?"

"I guess I am," Will admitted. "Her name is Cindy."

The zoo was quiet. The mother rabbit was nursing her young. Will guessed there were eight to twelve babies, naked and squirming. Kate had gone in the back to check on Bullwinkle. Will heard a loud giggle followed by, "Oh, my God."

Will hurried back to the vivarium. Bullwinkle was surrounded by a mass of squirming babies; there must have been thirty little boas. Will simply had to sit down. Kate found the whole thing so amusing that tears streamed from her eyes as she sat by Will and hugged his shoulder. Will actually felt his shoulder getting damp from Kate's tears.

"Will, whatever happens in the rest of your life, will you ever forget this summer?"

Then Will began to laugh. As they sat on the bench, he told Kate about the tornado, the lifestyle fair, the mission, the escape from Camp Joshua, and now this. "No," he said, "Unless I suffer a major cerebral collapse, I'll never forget."

Finally, Kate pulled Will to his feet. They locked up and headed back to the dorm. Construction was continuing at night, so there was plenty of light.

"Will," Kate began. "I've never heard such a tale in my life. Perhaps you're a modern-day Job. Thanks for being open and vulnerable with me. I think you do have a girlfriend in Cindy, but I fear it won't be long before she has quintuplets if she continues to hang around with Mr. Fertility here." She gave Will a thump on his shoulder.

"Hey, it's not my fault," Will said, smiling.

"You're the one in charge," Kate joked. "But seriously, we need a plan to feed all these babies—and deal with Mrs. Williamson."

At the dorm, Will and Kate gave each other a "good friends" hug and said goodnight. Will felt he had a new friend and ally in Kate.

Back in his room, Will called Aunt Rita and then Cindy. Her mother was doing poorly. They talked for a long time. Cindy loved his stories about the petting zoo. She laughed hard upon hearing about Bullwinkle's babies. Will was enthusiastic about his job and his friends. He had an easy intimacy with Cindy whenever they talked.

"Will, you don't know how much I'm living vicariously through you. I yearn so much to be with you that I'm having dreams about the petting zoo, of all things, not to mention Mrs. Williamson. Am I going crazy?"

"Cindy," Will said, "you must hang onto the fact that your situation is temporary and that it will end. Perhaps not pleasantly, but then you can get on with your life. Think about meeting me at Uncle John's or come to the theme park."

"I do, every day and every hour," Cindy said. "I love you."

Simon awoke toward the end of Will's talk with Cindy. After Will hung up, he told Simon about Bullwinkle.

Simon was stunned. "How did a boa named 'Bullwinkle' become a mother anyway? Surely we're not dealing with an immaculate conception here."

"I suspect she was named before she was sexed," Will replied. "And she was with a male before."

"What are we going to feed them?" Simon asked.

Will shrugged. "We'll have to find some frozen mice."

After Will and Simon said goodnight, Will sensed God waiting to talk.

"God, what about all these origin stories?" Will asked. "Are they true?"

"What do you think?"

"They don't make sense to me. The flood simply does not fit with what we know about geology or biology. The great extinctions seem to have had natural causes. And I hate that story of Abraham and Isaac."

"Why?"

"According to that story, you gave Abraham a son, rather late in life, and promised him descendants through that line. Then you asked him to sacrifice his son, and Abraham was willing to do it! It was irrational in the extreme since that was his line, and it was morally wrong because it constituted child abuse and the killing of an innocent. Yet, Abraham is praised for being irrational and immoral. He should have told God to stuff it, pardon the language."

"Your skepticism serves you well," God said. "These stories don't make sense if you take them as history. And the divine actions are often morally unacceptable. But if you take it as religion, making up some foundational stories from an earlier tribal society, then it makes a little more sense."

"But why not just try to tell history as best we can the way it was?"

"Because that would not make your religion special," God answered. "And religions need to be special, so they concoct these stories."

"Okay, I see that," Will conceded.

"By the way, Will, I loved the peahen on the brontosaurus."

"Me, too," Will replied. "How about a mass sterilization of the petting zoo?"

"Should I include you?"
"Oh, forget it."

SURPRISES

The grand opening was drawing near; the countdown measured in hours rather than days. Everyone was excited, but much work remained to be done. Will had a list of things to which he needed to attend and an equally long list of things that should be done but which he was not likely to complete. The baby boas were taken care of. The veterinarian, Mildred Collins, had arranged for them to be handed over to a local pet store, whose owner had furnished the frozen mice to feed the youngsters.

Ham was less active than usual, so Will had Mildred examine him. She reported that Ham was just getting old. He appeared to have had a long and happy life before Will rescued him. Both Will and Simon took time to talk to Ham and give him some extra attention afterwards, which he seemed to enjoy.

At the top of Will's list of things needing attention was a conflict that had erupted between Kate and Simon. They were barely speaking to one another. The tension between the two began during the previous evening's Bible study group.

A young minister who was active in 'The Closers', a Christian men's group that was part of the Termination Theology Tendency, had been the study leader. He expressed a number of beliefs that had been floating around Christian youth ministries for some time. For example, they believed that men should be masters of women and women should submit to men. And, because the end was near, they advised men and women to refrain from sexual intercourse and even marriage. Women were held responsible for original sin, and men could best arrive at their potential as disciples of the Lord only if women were controlled and set aside. Their practices matched their rhetoric.

After a quick review of Eve's punishment, the leader pointed out that Jesus and Paul both recommended against forming families and urged their followers to abstain from marriage and sexual intercourse. Men were asked to leave their families and devote themselves to Jesus in Luke 14:26. The leader especially liked Ephesians 5:22, which seemed to direct women who were married to obey their husbands as their masters. But the study leader really focused on 2 Timothy 3, wherein the author seemed to say that in the end times, which were near, "silly women overwhelmed by their sins and swayed by all kinds of desires" would never come to understand what was required during theses times. The leader took these "silly women" to be feminists.

The lesson even went so far as to say that *any* man should, therefore, be able to command any woman. There was praise for the early Christians, who believed that celibacy was the way for men to regain their spirituality. Some of the early Syrian churches, the leader pointed out, accepted only celibate men and refused baptism to married men. The Christian father Tertullian described marriage as "an obscenity" and a crime against God. The minister clearly implied that the theme park would be better off with an all-male staff.

At that point, Kate and another woman walked out. Will joined them thinking about what Sister Sara would have to say about such nonsense. He didn't have to guess what Kate was thinking.

"I have never been subjected to such sexist, patriarchal bullshit in my life," she raved. "If that's Reverend Shister's idea of how to deter sexual relations among the staff, I'm out of here."

Kate had asked Simon later why he did not leave with her. Simon responded that if these things were in the Bible, as fundamentalists committed to the inerrancy of the scriptures, weren't they obliged to follow it?

Kate fired back that he probably believed he could sell his daughter into slavery or stone his son for apostasy. "Fuck you!" she said as she spun on her heel.

There was little Will could say or do about the hostility between them. He needed their cooperation, but at the same time, he agreed that there was no excuse for promoting this kind of misogyny. His best effort was to tell Kate that although there are some horrible things in the Bible about women, they should be seen as artifacts of a male-dominated religion and thrown out along with all the anti-Semitic passages. He also urged Simon to reconsider what was said from Kate's point of view and to apologize.

Even God seemed shocked by this line of attack on women. "I'm a-Pauled," God punned.

Will groaned. "What is your view of marriage anyway?"

"I've never been married," God replied. "According to myth, I did get a woman pregnant though. I wish I could remember doing that; it must have been fun. More seriously, Will, you may have noticed that the Bible is one of the most hierarchical documents ever written. Angels submit to God, men submit to God and his angels, women submit to men, children submit to parents, servants submit to masters, slaves submit to owners and their servants, animals submit to humans. Need I go on?"

"Please, no," Will said. "I get it; there's a rather rigid view of the order of things."

Later, Will sat in his room running over his to do list for the zoo and wondering who he was going to have to help him. Ham was having a good day and was busy demolishing a Gideon Bible that Simon, of all people, had provided for him. A knock on the door interrupted Will's worrying.

When Will opened the door, he was astonished to see Blink and Chris.

"Hey, Will," Chris said. "This is the coolest place, a technician's dream. There's so much that can go wrong—and already has—that I'm getting big bucks just standing here."

To Will's surprise, Chris gave him a hug.

"Where's the little guy?" Blink asked as he entered the room and approached Ham's cage. "Hi, little guy," he said as he lifted Ham out and put him in his lap.

The next hour was a time of catching up. Will learned that after they were cleared in the bank robbery and were free of other violations, Rev had disappeared and was thought to be living abroad. Harry, Curt, Steel, and his Sons of Abraham were in jail awaiting trial. Chris, having heard about the theme park from Will, had secured a position for himself as technical troubleshooter and gotten Blink, whose real name, it turned out, was Marc Feinstein, a role as Goliath in one of the dramas that was repeated twice daily. (Will made a mental note to try very hard to call

Blink "Marc," since Marc said he viewed "Blink" as his prison name and not his real name.) Marc had no lines in the drama. He only had to growl a little and fall down when a fake stone was thrown at him.

Since the park did not open until the following day, Marc offered to help Will with the zoo when he heard Will's fears about being short-handed. "You know I love animals," he said.

Simon showed up just after Chris had received a call on his beeper and left. He said he had found Kate and apologized to her. She accepted his apology, but things remained frosty between them. Simon was in awe of Marc, who seemed to fill the entire dorm room. He was also delighted to hear that Marc would be helping to clean out the stable and spruce up the yard for the next day's opening.

Will and Marc, together with Simon and Kate, who was uncharacteristically quiet, had the petting zoo in great shape in no time. The pens were spotless, and the animals were groomed and gentle and as ready as possible for the expected onslaught of children. Will was amazed at Marc's gentleness and his way with the animals. After Marc left to attend a rehearsal for his reenactment, Simon asked Kate to take a walk with him, but she refused.

Back at the dorm, Will took a minute to rest. His mailbox contained a letter from Cindy and a brief note from his aunt. He was just beginning to read them when there was another knock on the door. To his surprise, it was Agent Smith.

"Hi, Will," she began, "I'm sorry to just drop in on you, but I was on site to give a recommendation for Marc and Chris to Reverend Shister. He wants them to work, but he needed to be reassured that, as convicted felons, they were safe. I also need to set up a time to take a deposition from you. Does tomorrow work?"

Will invited Agent Smith in. "Tomorrow is the grand opening, so I'll be pretty busy. I can also speak to Reverend Shister about Chris and Blink, if that would help."

"I don't think that's necessary," Agent Smith replied. "Shister seems to really need their help. Chris is amazing in his technical skills. He actually straightened out the server at our office after we had had trouble with it since we bought it and the techs they sent out from the Bureau couldn't figure it out. I think Chris and Marc are going to be okay."

"Could we do the deposition now?" Will asked. "And will I be required to testify?"

"Almost certainly you'll be called to testify," Agent Smith confirmed. "Let's have you make a statement. I'll have it typed up, and then you can sign it later. I have my recorder with me."

After the preliminaries, Will told his story, starting with the promise of a ride from Reverend Oliver and a job painting trailers. He got quite emotional when he talked about being held prisoner and Steel's threat of stoning. He stressed Rev's kindness and Marc and Chris's efforts to free him. Agent Smith asked what he knew about the bank robbery. Will was little help there. What he knew he had heard from Reverend Newton, whom the FBI was unable to locate.

Agent Smith put away her equipment and spent some time just chatting with Will. Was he dreaming about these past events? How would he describe his emotional state after Camp Joshua? What about his future plans?

Before she left, she looked over at Ham's cage. "Is your hamster all right?"

Will went straight to the cage and reached down to touch Ham who did not respond. He picked him up; he was cool but limp. Will felt tears surge in his eyes. The emotions of going through his story and now the death of Ham were too much.

Agent Smith seemed to understand and sat with him until Simon returned followed by Marc. Then she expressed her sympathy and said goodbye. Marc was also very upset by Ham's death and left shortly to find Chris. Will suggested that they bury Ham near the petting zoo. There was a nice shaded area to one side. They agreed to meet there that evening after dinner. Simon left to tell Kate.

That evening at sunset Will, Chris, Marc, Kate, and Simon gathered at the petting zoo. Marc produced, from somewhere, a Gideon Bible, which he had hollowed out to make a place for Ham's little body to rest. Will thought it was the perfect coffin. He told Marc so and thanked him. Simon seemed to find it somewhat amusing, but Kate was moved to tears, along with Marc.

Each person spoke. Will told them a bit about his adventures with Ham and thanked Ham for his companionship. Marc just said goodbye to the little guy. Kate expressed sympathy for Will. Simon said he appreciated Ham's cheery greetings. Chris said very little except to offer a hope that in his next life, Ham would advance on the wheel.

Will returned to his room with Simon. Chris had some troubleshooting to do; he figured he would be up all night. Marc went back to his trailer.

Will and God were not talking as frequently, because Will was too busy to be much of a conversationalist.

"I don't suppose animals go to heaven," Will said.

"I don't really know," God replied. "Why wouldn't they?"

"They don't have souls."

"What's a soul?" God asked, to Will's surprise.

"It's a…" Will was not sure what to say. "It's the immortal part of us."

"What makes you think you have an immortal part?"

"All the preachers talk about life after death. The Bible promises rest for the soul, although, come to think of it, it rarely mentions the soul." It hadn't taken Will long to reach a point of uncertainty.

"I suspect that life after death is an oxymoron," God replied. "Life is what you get, and death is extinction. Your body is corrupted, and that destroys your brain, and that, in turn, eliminates your mind and consciousness. No, animals do not survive death, because nothing survives death."

"If our consciousness is gone and, with it, our memory, our feelings, our values, and our beliefs, I guess there is no afterlife," Will said.

Uncle John had convinced him to give up believing in hell a long time ago, when he said, "It's hard to believe in a God who punishes people eternally for insubordination or punishes those who have never heard of Jesus or those who are too busy surviving to form the right belief system. And God does not punish good people who believe in a different God. God is just not such a hard-ass. And I doubt that anyone deserves eternal rewards either."

"Yep, the term 'afterlife' is another oxymoron," God pontificated. "That's why you need to take special care with the life you have. Love when you can, help others, and appreciate your lesser cousins like Ham. And I know you loved him and you miss him."

God had Will doubting heavenly choirs, golden gates, and behavior ledgers. It turned out that God, at least Will's god, was a materialist.

***

The grand opening hour finally arrived. Will, Simon, and Kate were at the petting zoo early. Banners were everywhere. Balloons decorated the exhibits that were open. Construction crews were not on site that day. The petting zoo was in good condition, but with animals, there was always a need for cleaning and re-cleaning. Bullwinkle was moved to her pen in the Garden of Eden. Then, after breakfast, Will and his crew moved the gentlest animals out to where they would be accessible to the children they expected to visit.

Marc stopped by to see what he could do, but everything was under control. Marc was nervous about his performance, and when Kate said, "Break a leg," he almost panicked until Will explained that it was a way to wish good luck without violating a theater superstition.

They all headed up to the amphitheater to watch the opening ceremony. Will was only a little surprised to see Seymour Smythe sitting in the front row. He knew that Smythe had a lot of money and was located in Serenity, which was close by.

Reverend Shister got up to speak. "My friends, this is a marvelous day. God has granted us sunshine, reasonable temperatures, and very little wind. It is a perfect day to celebrate the life of our Lord. To all you staff, thank you for your hard work. The success or failure of this great theme park rests on your shoulders. I want to thank the staff at the petting zoo in particular. The money we received for the sale of some thirty baby boa constrictors makes the petting zoo the most profitable division so far."

There was general laughter, and several staff members turned to Will, Kate, and Simon and gave them thumbs up. Will did not see Mrs. Williamson's face, but he doubted she was happy with Shister's remark.

"But," Reverend Shister continued, "there are others who deserve our thanks and appreciation. One of these special people is sitting here in the front row. He is a modest man, and I don't want to embarrass him, but Seymour Smythe, would you stand so that we can give you a special thank you for making this park possible?"

Seymour stood and blushed visibly. Will and the others gave him a warm round of applause.

Reverend Shister returned to the theme of the previous day's lecture.

"How anyone can look at the marvels of nature and perceive its fantastic design and not believe in God is beyond understanding. But my hope is that, after touring this wonderful park, those who have doubts and those who trust in evolution or naturalistic explanations will give up that foolish road and come to the Lord. I also hope that anyone who doubts the life of Jesus or doubts that Jesus is Savior or lacks understanding of that beautiful life will come here and be fulfilled, indeed, filled with the Holy Spirit. We also want people to have fun. That's why we have a petting zoo and rides and games. The gates open at noon. Go have an early lunch and then report to your stations. Good luck, and thank you again for your hard work."

Will, Kate, and Simon were at the zoo a good thirty minutes early. Shortly after noon, the first children arrived. There were five of them, and they looked like siblings. Admission was free that day, and the gates had been opened wide. The children's parents did not seem to be paying much attention to their offspring. Will was startled, however, when one of them reached in the guinea pig pen, picked up a baby, and tossed it to his brother who, fortunately, made a good catch.

Kate was on them immediately. "This is a *petting* zoo," she said as she took the baby from the boy's hand and returned it to its cage. "That means we may touch the animals, but we do so gently and not in ways that might harm them. Suppose you had missed that baby."

Just then, one of the other children pulled on the donkey's tail. Simon went to the rescue.

A hurried conference determined that one of the petting zoo staff should be at the entrance at all times to greet families and inform them that there were rules and that the adults in the party needed to supervise the children.

The afternoon went more smoothly after the initial family left. The other children seemed more respectful of the animals. Will was starting to relax when a young man came rushing into the zoo. He wore a staff badge and the official red Galilee T-shirt.

"Will, come quick, the snake is loose in the Garden of Eden!"

He and Will took off running for the Garden exhibit, which was a nicely done bit of statuary with lions lying down with lambs and cows grazing. A young man and woman, both very attractive and dressed in flesh-colored clothing, were supposed to just wander about looking blissful. At certain intervals, a cover was removed near the Tree of Knowledge, revealing Bullwinkle. Typically, she was asleep.

On this occasion, things did not work that way. Bullwinkle's display case door was wide open, and Bullwinkle had slithered out when the cover was lifted. Seeing a large snake on the loose sent the visitors fleeing and screaming. "Adam" was nowhere to be seen, and "Eve" had climbed the Tree of Knowledge. Unfortunately it was not strong enough to hold her. The branch broke, and she fell out of the tree. When help arrived, she was making small shrieking noises as she cradled her left arm. Bullwinkle was simply looking around, perhaps for a thawed rabbit. She was due to be fed that evening.

Will reasoned that the day was probably over for that exhibit, so he picked Bullwinkle up—she wrapped a couple of grateful coils around his waist—and headed back to the zoo.

As he walked back, Will noticed that there were not as many visitors as he had expected. Perhaps it was because of the escaped snake. But as he looked down the fairway, he saw a similar lack of activity at the other exhibits and concession stands. That was strange considering it was late in the afternoon.

Back at the zoo, Will described the events in the Garden for Kate and Simon. They cleaned the zoo and then went to dinner. The opening day was a short one, and everything closed in the early evening.

"How many people actually came through the zoo today?" Will asked.

Kate was in charge of counting visitors. "We only had twenty children with six sets of parents. We turned away some kids who were without adults."

At dinner, Will and the others learned that all of the exhibits had had the same experience. Not many people had visited the park on its opening day. No one knew why, although lack of advertising and the unfinished nature of the park were suspect. They also learned that the Garden exhibit was closed permanently. Eve had broken her arm, and having a live snake in the exhibit was considered too risky. Besides, the Tree of Knowledge had been ruined. A staff person on the scene reported with good humor that, as the medics worked on Eve, she had said that if she wanted to work with snakes she could have taken a stripper job at the Everglades Bar and

Grill. It would have paid better and offered less risk.

Will hoped the next day would go better. He was worried about what would happen to Bullwinkle without the Garden exhibit. But all in all, he thought the day could have gone worse. Chris had had a wonderful day troubleshooting, which made him even more indispensible. Marc had fallen down on cue and was excited about his dramatic triumph. And Simon and Kate were at least speaking, which made Will feel better.

DESIGN I

Attendance on the second day of the opening of Galilee Theme Park was not much better than the day before. The "zoo crew," as they had become known, arrived early, cleaned up, groomed the animals, and waited. And waited. The park opened in the late morning, hoping that visitors would come and eat lunch at the many concessions. But the place was simply dead. A few adults wandered through, and a couple of senior tours came and went, but they had no interest in the petting zoo. They went to the various dramas and exhibits instead. All of this gave Kate, Simon, and Will plenty of time for a rousing debate about the lecture on design sponsored by the park.

The pastor who lectured, Pamela Patterson, also claimed to be a biologist. She had found the inspiration for her talk from William Paley's *Natural Theology.* He told a story about how a man walking across a field and seeing a stone lying in the path does not wonder at how it came to be there, because a stone is a natural object. But if the man were to come across a watch lying in the path, his first thoughts would be to ask how it came to be there. Who dropped it? Who manufactured it? Did it still tell time?

So it is with things like the human eye, Paley argued. When we see an eye, we cannot but think how wonderfully designed the eye is for the purpose of seeing. We infer naturally that the eye was designed for that purpose, just as the watch was designed for the purpose of telling time. And nature is filled with things like the human eye, organs that serve specific functions. All in all, Reverend Patterson marveled, "Nature resembles one huge factory filled with wonderful machines all doing the bit for which they were created. How one can be a scientist and not believe in God requires a shocking dislocation of intellect."

Simon and Kate, but especially Simon, were impressed with Reverend Patterson's argument. Through the petting zoo, Simon had just become acquainted with animals, and what he had learned inclined him even more strongly than before to see the world as a carefully designed machine.

"Will, you seem to be the analytical one," Simon said as he was brushing the donkey, recently named "Moses," who simply could not get enough of the currycomb and who brayed loudly if he saw people standing idly about when they could be brushing him.

"I have to admit that nature is pretty impressive," Will said. "The organs and interactions of species and the whole dynamic of environmental factors often makes me feel small and ignorant. But my skeptical nature doesn't let me buy into your analogy."

"Say on," Kate encouraged.

"I don't doubt that we can recognize a watch as a human artifact, and we're pretty good at distinguishing artifacts produced by humans from those that are not. We have a lot of knowledge about how we make things, what our needs and wants are, and what tools we use. The question that has not been asked, but which needs to be, is this: 'Among the things that are not human artifacts, how do we distinguish those that are designed from those that are not?'"

"I don't understand," Simon said, clearly perplexed.

"Well, suppose we look at mineral crystals and we look at the human eye. Both are complex structures, but neither one is a human artifact. On what basis do we say the eye was designed and the crystals were not?"

"Some would say that everything that is not made by humans is of divine design," Kate said, but then rejected her own suggestion. "But that can't be a premise in an argument intended to argue for a designer from only *some* artifacts."

"We have a scientific explanation for how crystals form, but we lack a good scientific explanation of how the eye was formed, so we give that to God," Simon said confidently.

"No, no," Kate said. "You walk a dangerous path, Simon. First, we have a good account of how the eye formed, starting with light-sensitive cells. But, second, if you relegate something to God because we don't yet have a scientific explanation for it, you open yourself to the charge of confusing absence of knowledge with knowledge of absence. You're suggesting that if we don't have a scientific explanation right now, no such explanation exists, and we should substitute a supernatural one. Some people call this the 'God in the gaps argument', and it hasn't served religion very well, because every time religion uses it and science comes up with an explanation, religion looks silly. This has happened with planetary orbits, disease, thunderstorms, and almost every other natural phenomenon."

"Clearly, however," Simon said, undeterred, "some things serve a purpose just like the watch serves a purpose. The eye sees, and the watch tells time. Those, then, are the things that are designed."

"I don't want to get too picky here," Will said, "but we use the word 'purpose' in at least two senses. In one sense, it means that something has an *intended* function—that is, someone built it to do something specific. To know a thing's purpose in this sense, we have to know either the intentions of the builder or infer them from the builder's needs and abilities. All things with a purpose in this first sense have a designer. In the second sense of 'purpose' it simply means 'function' without any implication that it was designed for that function. Every inventor knows that his or her inventions function in ways they were not intended. In that movie *The Gods Must Be Crazy,* a Coke bottle proved to have many functions: ornamental, religious, and practical—they ground millet with it—beyond its intended purpose of holding soda. I agree that the eye functions to see, but the question still remains whether that is its intended use. To know that, we would have to know more about the designer's intentions, needs, or abilities."

"Well," Simon was clearly floundering, "God made humans, so he must have made the organs that make up human bodies."

"But hold your horses, or in this case, the donkey," Will said. "If you begin with the premise that God made humans, then you can conclude that humans and their organs were designed by God, because you have begged the question again by assuming what you hope to show."

Just as Will was pointing out the circularity of Simon's reasoning, a new family arrived at the petting zoo. The donkey had proven safe and tractable to letting children sit on its back with an adult holding the child by the waist. This proved to be what the seven-year old girl wanted. Kate hoisted her up, and her father kept her in place. Her younger brother wanted to pet a rabbit, a desire that Will was able to satisfy by picking up the large, gentle buck and holding him in his lap for the boy to pet. As soon as the family left for one of the dramas, Simon returned to the argument.

"You guys are tough," Simon said to Will and Kate. "Why can't we assume that we're made in God's image and that, therefore, God has similar needs and wants and abilities as our own, except much greater? God goes about designing things much like humans do, and that's why we are able to recognize divine design."

"You're implying an analogy that you don't have," Will said. "If you study an artist's work and know what kind of materials she had to work with and maybe something about her training, you can easily build an analogy as to how another artist worked. Here you have no idea how God works. Presumably, God does not need tools or training. God has virtually no limits, and you know little or nothing about God's desires or even if God has desires. In short, you do not have grounds for an analogy."

"And," Kate added, "if you assume God designs things just like humans do, you diminish God and come to all sorts of silly conclusions, like maybe God had to build prototypes to get the bugs out or had to consult an expert on materials. And if you deny that God works in any of these ways, you're back to having no basis for an analogy."

"Fudge," Simon exclaimed. "Let me think."

"While you're thinking," Will said, "let's go brew a cup of tea." One of the advantages of working in the petting zoo was that they had a kitchen attached to the office, complete with stove, refrigerator, freezer, and sink.

Will noticed that Kate and Simon were still sitting apart. "I don't want to pry," Will said, "but are you two doing any better?"

"Yes," Simon said.

"A little," Kate admitted without looking at Simon.

"Sorry," Will said. "I don't mean to embarrass anyone."

Blushing, Simon tried to change the subject. "Have either of you noticed that something weird is going on around here? Some construction efforts seem to have been abandoned, and I've heard that some staff are being let go."

"Judging by the number of visitors we've had here at the zoo, the park may be in trouble already," Will said. "But it seems awfully early to make such a call."

Simon remained in the thrall of the design argument. "Speaking of designs, wouldn't it require a perfect designer to bring about such an optimal world as we have?"

Kate was not impressed. "I don't see perfection at all in nature. I see things that are cruel like forest fires and the hunting practices of predators. I see things that are just poorly designed, such as the urinary track of the domestic tomcat. And I see things that are incredibly inefficient like the march of the penguins, so I hardly see perfection."

"As for the world being a machine," Will added, "I think one of the defining properties of a machine is that each part is a machine. Is each part of the world itself a machine? If so, are you not back to assuming everything is the work of divine design?"

"I suppose," Simon conceded. "Okay, it's not perfect, but it works pretty well."

"Yes," Will responded, "but if you're a creationist who believes in a perfect creator, then the imperfections and inefficiencies and outright cruelties of nature are problematic. An evolutionist only requires that there is a certain level of efficiency, one that allows for successful reproduction."

Simon was not out of arguments yet. "But just look at how improbable it is that all the factors that came together to make up life in this wonderful system would come together here in this corner of the universe. If one little physical constant were different, it wouldn't work. So, someone must have designed it; otherwise our world is as improbable as a bunch of metal falling into a heap and coming out as a watch."

Will thought about this for a moment. "I'm not certain what the argument is here. True, we live in a small solar system in the universe, but we don't know anything except this little corner, although we are slowly getting more information about other areas. We simply do not know how likely or unlikely it is that these things would come together. We don't know how many worlds or universes are there that could produce such results. So we can't compute the probability of these things coming together any more than we can compute the likelihood of drawing a particular card from a deck of unknown number. Furthermore, the fact that something is improbable does not mean it does not happen. Hey, we live where there are tornados, and they do the weirdest most unlikely things.

It seems to me that people do the same thing with unlikely or unusual events as they do with scientifically unexplained events—they attribute them to some supernatural cause."

"Oh boy!" Simon said as he pointed to a car and small truck that had just pulled up in front of the zoo. The car belonged to Mrs. Williamson. The truck was unknown to them.

"Kate, Simon, Will," Mrs. Williamson said as she got out of her vehicle, "this is Mr. Hastings, who donated Bullwinkle to the park. He has come to take Bullwinkle home. We are donating the vivarium to him in exchange for the use of his snake."

Mr. Hastings was a thin, reptilian-looking individual who seemed to move by gliding and then pausing to look around. One could imagine his tongue flicking in and out as he decided where to move next. He glided over to the vivarium and studied Bullwinkle, who studied him back.

"You all have taken good care of her," he said with sincerity. "It looks like she was fed recently."

"Yesterday evening," Kate answered.

"Perfect," Mr. Hastings replied. He looked at Will. "Would you help me load Bullwinkle into her traveling box? Then we need to load the vivarium itself."

"I'll grab the leftover rabbits and rats," Kate volunteered.

"Yuck," Mrs. Williamson said.

The whole process took only a few minutes. Mr. Hastings thanked the crew again for the care given to Bullwinkle and then left. Mrs. Williamson, however, looked around the zoo for quite a while. Finally, she left while muttering to herself.

"Whew," Kate said. "I don't know who's creepier, Williamson or Hastings."

"I vote for Hastings," Simon ventured.

"I think we're in trouble," Will said, "unless the park can drum up more business."

It turned out that the next few days—it was approaching Labor Day weekend—were extremely busy for the zoo crew. Parents wanting to give their children a special treat before school began took them to Galilee and to the petting zoo. Will, Kate, and Simon had their hands full keeping the animals safe and the children happy. Marc came by and helped clean up. The Goliath exhibit had been closed because the stone thrown at Goliath had wildly missed Goliath and hit a spectator, although Goliath had dutifully fallen down anyway. Marc was now working in security at Chris' insistence.

The park was open later on the weekend, so Will and his friends didn't finish cleaning up and bedding down the animals until well after dinner. The kitchen crew set aside food for them. Monday, Labor Day, was an exception; the park closed early.

Walking back to their dorm only reinforced their belief that things were not going well at Galilee Theme Park. More projects had been abandoned, and the number of construction trailers was diminishing each day. Also, the crowds had thinned over the long weekend, although the zoo remained popular with the children.

In their room, Will and Simon had more time to talk. "I apologized, I apologized, and then I apologized," Simon said. "I realize that what I said was stupid and offensive, but Kate is still very frosty."

"I'm glad you apologized," Will said. "Just take it slow. You can't force someone to forgive you."

"And I deserved Kate's wrath," Simon continued. "Kate is simply super. How are you and Cindy getting on?"

"I wanted to talk to you about that," Will said. "Cindy's mother is dying. She just lost her father, and I think she needs some support. I'll talk to her later, but if she needs me, I want to go to her. You think you and Kate can handle the zoo with some help from Marc?"

"Absolutely," Simon replied. "I know you've been eager to see Cindy again, and you should go up there if she needs you. My guess is that after this weekend, things will get pretty dull. Mrs. Williamson will visit and regretfully inform us, as she secretly gloats, that we are being shut down and the animals are being sold. I expect to be back in school in a week. And having some time at the zoo with just me and Kate sounds, well, it might help."

Will had to laugh at Simon's enthusiasm for his absence. "Good. I'm going to call Cindy right now, and you and Kate can fight it out as to who is zoo crew chief."

Will called Cindy at the hospital. He had to wait until she moved into an area where she could use her cell.

"Oh Will, mom is dying, she slipped into a coma last night. They think she'll pass away tonight or tomorrow."

"Cindy, I don't want to complicate your life, but I could catch a red-eye out of Amarillo and be there in the morning."

Cindy was close to crying. "I sure could use your support, Will. I'm dealing with so many things, and I'm kind of an emotional disaster. But what about your job?"

Will was ready with his answer. "I can get away from here for a few days. Personally, I doubt my job will last more than a few days anyway. I'll be there. You stay at the hospital, and I'll take a cab there." He didn't tell her that he already had plane reservations.

Will found Chris and arranged a ride to Amarillo in a new theme park van. Then he located Mrs. Williamson in her office and told her he had a family emergency. To his surprise, she was understanding and gave him a week to travel to Oldstown and return to the park. She agreed that Kate and Simon could hold things down with Marc's help.

Will called home to let Uncle John and Aunt Rita know he would be making the trip. His aunt was feeling good and chatted about local events and people Will knew. They asked if he needed more money for the trip, but Will said he was okay. He still had the money he had saved while working at the mission, and Rev had actually paid him for his work at the camp.

He took a quick look in his mailbox before going back to the room and discovered a letter from a federal prosecutor asking that he make himself available at a federal court in Amarillo in ten days' time. He shoved it in his pocket and went to pack.

Will and Simon continued to chat while Will sorted clothes. He and the zoo crew had been absent from the staff gatherings, because they had to clean up the zoo and take care of the animals, but Simon had gone to a meeting that evening, and he was excited.

"Will, a bunch of us are going over to Roswell, New Mexico in a couple of weeks if we can get away. There's a large conference of UFO believers. We have a few carloads planning to go."

"Why?" Will asked.

"That's a good question." Simon said. "Some of the staff want to witness to the UFOers. Others want to go to the conference. It turns out that some of us believe in aliens, and some of us don't. It turned into a big debate. Some think that man—er, humans—are the focal point of God's creation. Others argue that the Bible mentions intelligent beings who are not human but were created by God. They believe some of these might be aliens. Our argument got pretty funny with some humming the *Twilight Zone* theme and others seriously wanting to learn more about aliens. I'll keep you posted."

"Right now, I don't have any interest in such a trip," Will said, "but who knows. I may believe in aliens after I spend some time in Oldstown. I also have a possible trial date about the bank robbery coming up in ten days, so I'll play it by ear. I've got to run; Chris is taking me to the airport in Amarillo."

To Will's surprise, Simon gave him a hug. "Be safe, Will."

God was duly impressed with Will's argument against design. "I stayed out of it, because you were doing so well. It was fun. I think humans like to think they have a purpose. Look at all the theological speculators who reassure everyone that they have a purpose in God's world, something they are eager to believe. People are purposeful beings; thus, they assign intentions to Mother Nature, animals, each other, and all the gods they invent. Even storms, and other natural disasters are seen as happening for a reason. In all these cases, it's just natural laws at work. But Christians are like overly imaginative children in a haunted house; they see spirits everywhere. Intentions are often the offspring of superstition."

God started humming the theme from *House on Haunted Hill.* Will tuned him out and went to meet Chris.

OLDSTOWN

After Will's plane landed in Cleveland, he took a bus to Oldstown and a cab to Lutheran Hospital. Oldstown was a place whose future had come and gone. Coming into town, Will rode past newer malls already looking shabby that were filled with name brand chains, such as Home Depot, Pet World, Wal-Mart, and fast-food stops too numerous to mention.

"I wonder if Seymour Smythe owns those," God said. "And I'm glad you're back; you've been lost in animal poop for days."

"Thanks, it's good to talk to you, too," Will said as he watched Oldstown emerge.

Where gigantic steel mills once existed there were empty lots filled with rusting iron and buildings with broken windows. These mills had supported a bustling downtown with half a dozen banks and many family-owned shops and restaurants. Today, there was only one visible bank and many boarded-up storefronts. One of the old family businesses, Rubinstein's Dry Goods, wore a hand-painted sign reading, "The Apostolic Church of Jesus Christ."

"I doubt that old Rubinstein would approve," God opined.

The hospital stood on a hill in a better part of town, though it also looked a bit worse for the wear. The creamy stone walls carried smudge marks and ivy that had grown up one side and died but still clung tenaciously to the stone. The plants adjacent to the front door were in need of replacement, and the cigarette butts littering the ground around the entrance contributed to the general feeling of shabbiness. A man pushing a woman in her wheelchair came down the worn ramp toward Will. He moved out of their way.

Cindy, who had been in the waiting area watching for Will, came flying out and seized him like a linebacker desperate for a tackle.

"Oh God, Will," was all she could manage.

They stood there, Cindy holding onto Will as if her very being depended on that grip. Will, in return, held Cindy in his arms, drinking in her fragrance—a combination of Cindy, old perfume, and hospital antiseptic. His heart pounded in response. Her scent worked magic on his olfactory senses and his spirit. He realized how glad he was to be with her. After a moment, he also realized that Cindy was much thinner than she had been, and her eyes, dark and sunken into her face, were filled with tears.

"I need to get out of here for awhile," Cindy said. "Mother is still comatose but stable. They have my phone number, so we can go home and come back then. Your truck is in the lot," she said pointing.

Cindy drove, because she knew where she was going. Being in his truck felt good to Will.

They pulled up to a comfortable older home in a neighborhood not far from the hospital. Clearly, Cindy's parents had made a nice living at one time. The house appeared to be in good repair, although Will could not help but notice that the lawn needed work. All was not well, however, as they approached the front door where a bright orange sign read: "In Receivership. There is a lien on this property by Oldstown First Federal."

"What's this?" Will asked.

"It's a long story," Cindy replied. "Foreclosure. Right now, I just want to be with you. Is that okay?"

Inside the house, Will saw evidence of the stress under which Cindy was living. The kitchen had dirty dishes piled by the sink and old take-out cartons lying on the kitchen table and counters. Laundry was done but not folded or put away.

Cindy cleared the table, and then she and Will sat down over two cups of tea. "Sorry for the mess, me and the house," Cindy said. "I've spent so much time at the hospital that things just—"

"Please don't apologize," Will said. "I understand, and I came to help."

Cindy looked at Will. "Oh God, Will," she choked out. Then she began to cry, because her life had been hell for so long, because Will had come to help and now she had a shoulder to cry on, and because she had been holding it back for so long. Will began to cry, because Cindy cried.

"You two are one soggy mess," God muttered compassionately. "You'll have me going in a minute."

It made Will smile, which was the point.

Eventually, Cindy ran out of tears. Then she began to ask Will a hundred questions about his job, about the mission and the sisters, about Ham, and about Galilee Theme Park. She was starved for conversation that didn't involve her troubles. She said she hoped never to spend that much time apart from him again, which suited Will just fine. She laughed at his description of Bullwinkle's grand escape. Slowly, she came around to telling her own story.

"When I got back, Dad was in intensive care and had been for some time. I got to the hospital in time to be with him when he died. But as you know, he sent me away. I think he was disappointed he didn't get raptured," she said with a little laugh. "He died of plain old heart failure. Mom, who was never very strong, was drinking a lot, and had let things slip. I started in on the accounts and discovered we didn't have any money. My parents had taken out a second mortgage to get by, especially after he got sick and had to retire. Then his heart just got worse and worse. We haven't even had his funeral yet because of Mom's health. In short, my parents hit the end of their credit line and had not made payments for the past three months, hence the foreclosure. Mom's social security is pitiful. I can't find any life insurance in the records. And...we're worse than broke."

"Go on," Will encouraged.

"Well, his health insurance quit paying the hospital bills, which is the reason they went through the equity line so fast. The insurance company sent us a notice that they had cancelled Dad's policy and that we owe the hospital a hundred and twenty thousand for Dad's care. They also canceled my mother's policy. There's some language about a failure to report pre-existing conditions. They didn't say what they were. I have an appointment with a Mr. Welch to discuss the matter tomorrow. Would you come with me?"

"Of course," Will replied.

"So, now we also owe the hospital for my mother's care, which is over two hundred thousand. Even if I sold everything my parents own, it wouldn't make a dent in these debts. But I don't think I'm liable for any of this. They will just take the house, the car, and every other asset, and I'll leave town."

They both sat silently for a while.

"What can I do to help?" Will asked.

"You came, and that was a huge help. I was about to crack," Cindy said. "Now, let's go out to dinner, and then we have a conference with the doctor this evening. Tomorrow, we'll go see Mr. Welch, and after that, we get to visit the bank people, who are busily foreclosing at this very minute."

Will regarded Cindy's gaunt frame. "Some good food will definitely help. If you're going to get screwed over, it's better to have a full stomach."

This remark generated a grim smile from Cindy. At the same time, Will realized he had not eaten all day, and his stomach was protesting.

"Don't you have any family in the area?" Will asked.

"No, they were my only family," Cindy replied. "Dad was a pastor here for many years, but the church carried only a bare-bones health insurance policy, and their retirement fund got used up, because the church had to pay a parishioner who broke a hip on an icy sidewalk. They always intended to replace the funds, but when revenues began to fall…" Cindy trailed off her recitation of the woes that had beset her family.

Oldstown did not offer great cuisine or much in the way of healthy eating, but Cindy and Will had a decent meal at Wing On Chinese Restaurant, which advertised no MSG. They ate great quantities of rice and finished off several different dishes. They also assessed their assets. Cindy had none of Will's loan left. He had a bit more from his employment at the mission, and she had some room left on her credit card, but not much. Cindy figured that all her parents' money was gone to the bank and the insurance company, although Cindy's mother had given her a key and power of attorney to her bank box, which Cindy had not opened.

Cindy sighed. "At least I might be able to afford to get out of town."

They began to strategize. Cindy would drive Will's truck to the mission and stay there until Will could wrap up his job and join her. From there, they would drive to his aunt and uncle's. While still sitting in Wing On's, Will placed a call to the mission. To his delight, Sister Sara picked up the phone.

"Will," she said with joy, "it's so good to hear from you!

What's happening?"

Will gave a quick summary of his life and then put a bit more emphasis on what had been happening to Cindy. "We were hoping to meet up at the mission," Will said finally. "Do you have a place for Cindy to stay and work until I can get there? What's happening with the mission, anyway?"

"They don't have to pay me," Cindy whispered.

"You don't have to pay her," Will added. "Or me, if I come through for a while."

"Of course Cindy and you are welcome, and we could certainly use the help." Sister Sara was silent for a moment. "I'm going to be honest though, Will. Things are not going well here. Ellie is traveling right now trying to raise funds. You probably don't know this, but under the new Pope, the Vatican has begun a clandestine investigation of nuns who are living nontraditional lives. They want us back in our habits, they want our daily lives built around prayer, and they want us working in traditional Catholic institutions, such as hospitals and schools. Ellie and I don't measure up on any of those counts, not to mention our love for each other. We've been cut off of all Church money, we've been told to close the mission, and we've been ordered to report to separate convents, all under the threat of excommunication." Sara paused and controlled a sob. "Most of our staff has left or taken part-time jobs elsewhere. Arie, as you know, went to be with Malcolm. Samantha got married to that very good-looking warlock. Cole and Jesus are still working here, as are Delbert and Wanda, and a few day volunteers still come by."

Will was astonished. He had never met two more dedicated individuals than the sisters. He had some idea of just how much keeping the mission going had cost them and what closing it would mean to them. Both women were older, he guessed that they were somewhere in their early sixties. He found himself choking up, and that made it hard to talk to Sister Sara, who seemed to understand what was going on.

"I'm sorry, Will, I didn't mean to dump this on you."

"It's okay. I just know what that place and its residents mean to you. Let Cindy and I come down and work for you a bit. It would be good to see you anyway."

"Dear boy. We'll look for Cindy and wait for you." Sara seemed cheered by Will's promise to visit.

After Will repeated Sister Sara's story, Cindy seemed renewed. He loved how she would get a set look in her eye and confront new challenges.

"Well, we'll have to give those good women our best for a while. It seems they could use us."

Will could only nod in agreement.

An hour later, Will and Cindy were sitting in a small room in the hospital waiting for a doctor and someone from the financial division to show up. The hospital smelled like hospitals do, of medicines, people, and human waste. There was a quiet pervasive hum to the place that was punctuated occasionally by a clang or a sound that was like a metal cart or bedpan connecting with another metal object. Will and Cindy had been sitting in the room for a good thirty minutes when the door finally opened and the doctor came in.

"Hello, I'm Doctor Stewart," the man said. He was wearing green scrubs, and although he was lean and quick in his movements, his white hair revealed that he was older than he first appeared. "You must be Cindy," he remarked, and then turned to Will. "And, you are?"

"This is my friend Will," Cindy replied, "and I asked him to be here. Is that all right?"

"Of course," Dr. Stewart replied. "Cindy, we're supposed to charge for these conferences, but I want you to know that I'm waiving any fee for this meeting. We really need a health reform bill containing provisions that cover such consultations. Sorry for the editorial."

"I fully agree," Cindy replied, "but thank you for waiving the fee. I think we're in enough trouble with this hospital already."

"That's not my department," Dr. Stewart added hurriedly. "But we do have to talk about your mother. She's been comatose for some one hundred and twenty-two hours now. She's slipping deeper and deeper into it. We've been feeding her intravenously, but we need to make a decision. Do you want to continue feeding her or not? You need to know that I have talked to virtually the entire medical staff, and I'm sorry to say that no one thinks she'll get better. If we continue to supply nourishment, she'll likely pass away in a week or so. If not, it will be much sooner. As her only family member you have the right to make that decision."

Cindy's eyes filled with tears. "Is she aware of anything?"

Dr. Steward shook his head. "We don't think so."

"Can I talk about it with Will for a bit?" Cindy asked.

"Of course." As Dr. Stewart spoke, the door opened, and a young woman in a blue business suit entered.

"I'm Claire," she announced, "you must be Cindy."

"And this is my friend, Will," Cindy replied.

Dr. Stewart excused himself and left, but before he went, he gave Cindy his card with his cell number on it. "Please call me when you've made your decision."

With the doctor gone, Claire had command of the room. "I'm sorry to be the one to bring such tidings, but as you know, your parents' insurance company is refusing to pay for your mother's treatment, and the debt for her care is considerable."

"Yes, I understand," Cindy said. "I believe it's in excess of two hundred thousand."

"Yes, considerably in excess of that," Claire replied. "Because we cannot afford to continue her treatment, we have arranged for her to be moved to another public hospital that will take her on as a charity case."

Cindy's eyes widened. "Won't it be hard on her to be moved?"

"No, these transfers are done every day. It's no more traumatic than simply moving from one room to another."

Will was caught up in the moment. He was trying to think rationally about Cindy's predicament while also endeavoring not to show any emotion that would weaken her resolve.

Just then, Dr. Stewart reappeared unexpectedly, entering the room without knocking. "Cindy and Will, I think you should come with me, now. Things appear to be moving much more rapidly than we anticipated."

Dr. Stewart led them directly to Cindy's mother's bedside. "I think she's failing. I came by to check on her after leaving you and saw that her vital signs were down significantly."

Cindy held her mother's hand while tears rolled unashamedly down her cheeks. Will slid his arm around Cindy, who leaned into him. Dr. Stewart discreetly left the room.

They were only there for a few minutes when the monitor by the bed made a buzzing sound. This was followed by the appearance of a nurse and Dr. Stewart. Will thought he heard Cindy say a quiet goodbye to her mother.

Dr. Stewart listened for a heartbeat and then turned to Cindy. "She's gone. Do you want to resuscitate?"

Cindy shook her head and then turned to Will and wept. Will's eyes burned with tears for yet another time that day. Dr. Stewart and the nurse left them alone in the room.

Will looked down at Cindy. "Do you want to have a moment with your mother?"

"No, please stay with me," Cindy replied. She sat down by the bedside and held her mother's hand for a long time. Will stood silently. He did not think she was even aware that he was there.

They left the hospital about an hour later, having signed all the necessary papers. Cindy had arranged for her father's funeral, but now she decided on a double funeral for her parents.

Neither Cindy nor Will ate much that evening. They cleaned up the house and kitchen and then curled up together and slept a deep and untroubled sleep until late the next morning, when they had an appointment with Qualihealth Insurance.

Qualihealth Insurance Company occupied the top floor of the Oldstown First Federal Bank building, in which they were the major stockholder. It was an imposing red brick building complete with a security guard at the front door. A quick inquiry and a check on their appointment time led them to a spacious office.

"You can see all of Oldstown from here," Cindy remarked as she looked out the window.

An officious man entered the room and introduced himself as Larry Welch. "Cindy, what can I do for you?" he asked after the introductions were complete.

"I made this appointment some time ago," Cindy said, as she produced a set of papers from a folder on her lap. "I have reviewed my parents' health policy, and I can't understand why you canceled my father's insurance, leaving us with a claim of a hundred and twenty thousand dollars from the hospital. You have also refused to pay for my mother's hospitalization. I have two letters from you stating that due to some errors in my parents' application for coverage, you determined that Qualihealth has no obligation to pay for their care. What are the errors? I want to know what is going on."

Larry Welch produced his own set of papers. "Let me see if I can clarify things," he began.

As the man ruffled through his papers, Will studied him. He was a pale man who looked perpetually scrubbed. His skin was pink, and his nails were perfect. His head was balding but covered with short brown hair.

"Ah," Welch said. "Were you aware that your father had hypertension and he didn't tell us?"

"What evidence is there that he was hypertensive?" Cindy asked.

"We have his blood pressure recording here from his physical when he joined the church as an associate pastor in nineteen eighty. His blood pressure was a bit high."

"Do you have later confirmations?" Cindy asked. "He had his pressure under control."

"That may be," Welch said, "but he left blank the section on pre-existing conditions, which makes us suspicious. But let me hasten to add that this alone is not what triggered our response."

"Or lack of response," Cindy added.

Welch looked at her quickly and then acted as if she had said nothing. "The real issue seems to be that your father, with his marginal blood pressure, put himself in a position of stress and did not convey that fact to us." Welch looked confident. "And your mother, of course, did something similar by marrying your father and, thereby, by the law of transitivity of pre-existing conditions, created one for herself."

Will realized that Cindy was getting angry. Starting near her collarbone, a red splotch began to grow. It climbed her neck and burned its way into her cheeks. There were things about Cindy that Will found very endearing, but seeing this righteous anger was like watching a fire spread.

"What you're telling me," Cindy said in a controlled voice, "is that you cancelled my father's policy because he was employed as an associate pastor—the very job under which you first established his policy. And you covered him when your own report showed his blood pressure to be moderately high. Now you are claiming both as pre-existing conditions that even carried over to my mother. God damn you!"

Welch's complexion took on a rosy hue. "Miss Norton, I don't make the laws, and I don't make the rules. I am the messenger here. Our attorney found that your parents misrepresented their medical history, and the company simply cannot afford to take on those who, like your parents, have a pre-existing condition that they do not divulge."

"But one of which you were fully aware," Cindy snapped. "You paid for his blood pressure medicine for years, and his physical exams."

"I am only telling you what our attorney has said," Welch repeated.

"Why did you wait until my parents became ill to rescind their policy?" Cindy asked.

"I really can't answer that; perhaps it was because of your father's illness that we asked our legal department to look at the policy."

"I want to see your paperwork on this matter," Cindy demanded. "I also want to know if you have a policy of recession, whereby when someone you insure gets ill, you cancel the policy. I think that's illegal, and it has always been immoral."

"These papers are private and cannot be disclosed to someone other than your parents, whom I believe are no longer living," Welch said, looking relieved by that fact.

"Time to go, Will," Cindy said as she stuffed her papers in a folder. "We're not making any progress here."

"Just a moment," Welch said. "When is your mother's funeral?"

"It should be early next week," Cindy replied. "Along with my father's."

"You may not be aware of the fact that Qualihealth is the principle owner of Oldstown First Federal Bank. The bank has been generous with you in allowing you to stay in your parents' house while they were in the hospital. But we expect that to end after the funeral. Can you be out of the house by the end of next week?" Welch did not look at all sympathetic; he looked exactly the same as when he came into the room.

"Damn right," Cindy said. " I'll be out by Friday. I wish I had the resources to sue you bastards."

"You do realize, Miss Norton," Welch continued "we will lose a considerable amount of money. Your parents had very little equity left in their home. The bank will get the house, and we will get only a token payment."

"Good," Cindy said as she and Will left the room.

"Want me to strike him dead?" God asked Will in all sincerity.

"Would it do any good?"

"I doubt it; they would just send another flunky."

Will wrapped his arm around Cindy's shoulders, and she leaned into him.

"We still have to visit the funeral home," she said.

Oldstown Memorial Funeral Home was a quiet, dark place. A bell rang off in the distance when they came in, and as if by magic, a young woman appeared.

"Miss Norton," she greeted Cindy.

"Mary, I'm very tired, so can we just finish our business quickly? I don't mean to be rude; I'm just exhausted."

"Of course," Mary replied. "This way."

"This way" turned out to be the casket display room.

"As you know, your mother and father prepaid for their funerals, although there's a funny clause in the contract that states that should your father be raptured to heaven, only a simple marker is required."

"I know about the clause. It's not in my mother's contract is it? She was always more realistic than Dad."

"No," Mary replied

"Let's go with that one," Cindy pointed at a coffin.

"I'm sorry, but that one is not available on the package your parents purchased. However if you really want that one—"

"I can't put more money into this," Cindy replied as she squeezed Will's hand, telling him not to volunteer.

"Very well then," Mary sounded disappointed. "You can choose between these two slumber chambers."

Will heard God choke at the euphemism. "Oh, come on," he said. "Slumber chambers for the dead as door nails?"

"Fine, I'll take the light-colored one," Cindy said. "Is there anything else?"

"No, we already have your mother's remains, and we will be ready for the funeral. Would you like to speak at the funeral?"

"I know that Reverend Jacob will speak. He's the new pastor at the church. I may say a few words."

"Very good. Then we'll see you on Tuesday at two." Mary marked something on her clipboard and then showed them out.

Will and Cindy found themselves squinting at the bright Ohio sun.

"Let's pack and get some food, and not in that order," Cindy said. "After lunch, I have to pick up the death certificate and clear out my mother's bank box. Until then, there's not much to do except pack, and we should get your truck serviced before I head to Texas."

"I'll take care of that. Let's decide what personal items you want to take and get some boxes and set them in the hall." Will was trying to think of everything he could to help Cindy out.

"You smiled in there when she mentioned the slumber chambers," Cindy noted.

Will decided to trust Cindy. "I hope you don't think I'm crazy, but since I was a little kid, there's been a voice in my mind, a voice I call 'God'. He's fond of making some very irreverent remarks. He asked if I would like Larry Welch to be struck dead. And he was amused by the term 'slumber chamber'. He challenges me to think through my reasons for what I believe."

Cindy smiled. "I like your god, Will."

Will nodded. "Yeah, he really has a sense of humor." Then he told her about God's response to prosperity theology.

Cindy laughed. "He really said he would become an atheist?"

"That's what he said."

"An atheistic god, now that is something I could believe in. What does your god say about the Rapture thing?"

"He's never mentioned it," Will said with all honesty. As he told her about the rapture booth at the lifestyle fair, God interjected

"Do you think I would do anything that stupid and immoral? The very idea of jerking people up to heaven and leaving cars without drivers and planes without pilots, not to mention perambulators without mothers to perambulate? However, there are a few people I would like to yank off Earth, but I wouldn't send them to heaven."

"There's your answer," Will told Cindy as he related God's remarks.

"I love your god," Cindy replied as they pulled up to the house, fortified once again with Wing On cuisine.

By the next morning, the truck was serviced and loaded with personal things. Shortly after the bank opened, Cindy and Will were sitting in a private room with the open bank box. Cindy pulled out a pile of papers and a couple of envelopes. There were copies of the house mortgage, the second mortgage, and her father's diploma from divinity school. One of the envelopes contained a note from her mother.

Dearest Cindy,

Although your father forbids me to speak your name and does not acknowledge that he has a daughter, I love you and have never stopped loving you. These envelopes contain the money I have saved over the years for your college education. If I had had a way to be independent, I would have left your father years ago, but I never had a chance to go to college. Make the most of your life and remember me.

Love, Mom.

The envelope contained a bit more than $20,000. Cindy was amazed and overwhelmed. She wept quietly for a while and then thanked her mother. On the way out, Cindy cancelled the box.

Cindy's parents' funeral was sparsely attended. Several women from the church came, as did a couple of neighbors. Pastor Jacobs spoke pleasingly about what wonderful people the Nortons had been, though he spent more time talking about Cindy's father than her mother. Cindy was less discreet and more direct.

"My mother was a good woman," she said. "Like many women of her generation, she lacked opportunities to travel, to be educated, and to live her own life. She lived vicariously through her husband. She promoted his career, served at his teas, and typed and edited his sermons. My father was not a particularly good man. He did not consult her on major decisions, he told her how to vote, and when he disowned me, he forbade her to speak my name. He told her regularly that although he was Rapture material, she was not. She was too flawed, too weak, and not devout enough. In spite of his tyranny, she found a way to express her mother's love, and for that I will always cherish her memory. If there is a heaven, I expect she is there—*alone*."

"Way to go Cindy," God whispered in Will's ear.

Pastor Jacobs was shocked livid with rage, but he managed to choke out a final prayer.

That evening over dinner, Will told Cindy that he really liked her remarks, her honesty, and how glad he was that it was over. He also told her that God had loved her comments.

That night, they made love for the first time. Cindy asked Will beforehand if it would upset him or violate his religious convictions. Having dreamed about Cindy for so long and having achieved a new level of intimacy over the past few days, it felt right. Their lovemaking was gentle and careful, as they were both feeling emotionally vulnerable. In the end, with a promise of seeing one another soon, it was the perfect punctuation in their growing love for each other.

At the end of Will's time in Oldstown, Cindy paid Will the money she owed him, saw him off at the Cleveland Airport, and then headed south. After opening a secured credit union account in Cleveland, she closed the books on her life in Oldstown and, apart from missing Will enormously, she felt damn good.

DESIGN II

Returning to the heat and flatness of west Texas was a bit of a shock for Will. He was tired and already missing Cindy, but he felt happy that she was out of Ohio and on her way to the mission.

Chris picked him up at the Amarillo airport. On the way to Galilee Theme Park, he filled Will in on what was happening, which was not much. Mrs. Williamson continued to hound the petting zoo, looking for opportunities to close the exhibit. And there were increasing rumors about the park closing, which Chris thought was likely. Attendance remained lower than expected, and even highly valued employees like Chris were not being paid their full salary. Instead, they received living allowance checks with a promise of big bonuses if they stayed on.

It was late evening when Will finally walked down to the petting zoo and found Kate and Simon. With Marc's help, they had just finished putting everyone to bed for the night and cleaning up the grounds. Marc gave Will a quick hug and then headed for the dining hall, his favorite place in the park.

Kate and Simon confirmed what Chris had already told him: the status quo was the status quo, and the predatory Mrs. Williamson was lurking about the zoo. Both Kate and Simon were going to Roswell in a couple of days and had saved a place for Will in the van. Will was not at all certain he would make the trip, although he was curious about the conference and what kinds of interactions his park colleagues would have with the UFOers. Simon and Kate were still in a partial freeze, although they walked Will back to the dorm in exchange for an account of his visit with Cindy. Will gave them a brief and upbeat version of his trip.

After Simon and Kate left, he made a quick call to Cindy, who was making good time on her way to the mission. Then he showered and went to bed, determined to catch up on his sleep.

The day of the drive to Roswell produced considerable excitement, at least among the three vanloads headed to the conference. Will was unable to resist going along, especially after Marc took responsibility for the animals. Roswell was a famous New Mexico town where rumors had it an alien spacecraft had been shot down or crashed, and aliens, either dead or alive, had been discovered. The alleged incident was in the late 1940s, but the controversy about the government cover up had been around all of his life.

As Kate drove, Will, Simon, and Maggie, an employee who worked in the souvenir stand, poured over a copy of the *Roswell Daily Record* that Simon had managed to procure. It contained a summary of the controversy as well as an abbreviated program for the conference.

Simon read the conference schedule aloud. There were workshops on alien spacecraft design, what aliens look like, and the alien agenda. Simon was taken by a seminar on the compatibility of Christianity and the existence of extraterrestrials. Will was delighted to discover a cooking class entitled "Far Out Recipes" taught by Delbert and Wanda. Being able to catch up on the mission would make the trip worthwhile.

"I think we may have made some wrong assumptions about these UFOers," Simon noted.

"How so?" Maggie asked.

"Well, we assumed they weren't Christian, but this program indicates that many of them are. Some even believe that the angels of the Bible are extraterrestrials. We tend to think of them as worshiping space aliens, whereas many of them just see space aliens as further evidence of divine creation."

"But," Maggie pointed out, "some of them think that space aliens engineered Earth and even created humans, or at least guided their creation. Also, if you believe, as I do, that Jesus Christ was unique and that only through accepting him as our savior can we be saved, as it says in John fourteen six, then they cannot believe what they do and be Christians in any orthodox sense."

"But," Kate ventured, "at least they agree with us that Earth and its life forms were designed and not the result of some cosmic accident. Or they agree with some of us at least." She glanced at Will. "Maybe it's time to give you my version of the design argument as distinct from that of Reverend Patterson."

"By all means," Simon said.

Will settled back in his seat. "Would it help if I drove while you expound?"

"No thanks, the argument is very simple," Kate said. "It goes like this. We can recognize designed things from non-designed things in the world. For example, we see immediately that Mount Rushmore was carved but that the sandstone pillars in Bryce Canyon are the result of erosion. We especially find designed things in biology, that is, complex systems that do a certain task. The eye sees, the lungs moves oxygen in and carbon dioxide out, the heart pumps blood. According to evolution, these complex systems were selected over time by how well they performed their purpose. Of course, if they were incomplete or missing some parts, they would not function at all, so they would not exist. In this sense, they are irreducibly complex. They could not have come about gradually, as is suggested by evolution theory; they would have to come about all at once with all their parts. The same is true of species. Some birds walk around on cattle and remove their parasites; that's their role, but the birds with that role could not come about over time. They exist because they, together with their role, happened all at once. Because evolution fails to account for these parts of nature, we must resort to an explanation by design. This argument does not deny that evolution can work at a simple level, perhaps the level of bacteria, but evolution does not and cannot account for such irreducibly complex systems and species. That is at least the outline of my argument."

It was obvious to Will that Simon thought Kate was brilliant, and Maggie was not far behind. *Why me?* Will thought.

"Because you have a good critical mind," God said.

"Come on, Will," Kate urged. "I can see that you have that I-have-my-doubts look."

Will took the bait. "First, tell me why you like this argument so much."

"I like it, because it allows that evolution can make small changes, it doesn't depend on an analogy like Reverend Patterson's version, and I'm not a young earth creationist who believes the earth is only six thousand years old; I can accept that it's roughly four point six billion years old. All this is much more consistent with my biological training. I also think it makes for a better argument, because I don't assume that God was the designer, only that there was a designer. It might be some of those little green creatures with big eyes."

Will reflected on her argument for a moment. "I guess I have a couple of worries about this argument. Actually, I have more than a couple, because it seems to me that you have some of the same problems Reverend Patterson does. The question we should ask is not whether we can detect human design—of course we can—but whether among things *not* designed by humans we can detect those that were designed by other beings. This concern actually ties into my first major worry."

"Looked at that way, how can we know what is designed by nonhumans unless we know the designer? Our old problem with Patterson's argument."

"Thanks Simon." Will was glad he was not alone. "Let me put Simon's point another way. We know perfectly well what an explanation by design looks like."

This statement drew some blank stares.

"I'm sure you've all read a mystery book at some time."

There were nods all around.

"In a mystery book, the detective solves the crime by figuring out the perpetrator's motivation and opportunity. To discern the motivation, the investigator has to figure out something about the perpetrator's state of mind, and to determine opportunity, the detective must understand the perpetrator's capabilities. Someone who can't lift the proverbial blunt instrument can't bludgeon the victim, and someone who can't see can't deliberately shoot the victim. Unless we know these kinds of things about the perpetrator, we don't have an explanation by design. Since you don't want to say anything about the designer, how can you claim to have an explanation by design?"

"Right, if aliens have very different capabilities than God, then what they design or can design will be very different than what God would or could design," Simon observed. "In fact, we can't even recognize what is designed by God, aliens, or whatever unless we have some knowledge of what the alleged designer can do and wants to do. We recognize human-designed things, because we know what humans need and the kind of things humans can do."

Kate had been listening and giving Simon dirty looks. Will suspected Simon's agreement was more about being passive aggressive toward Kate.

"So, you think we've put the cart before the horse, to use an old expression," she said. "We err if we claim an explanation by design or even claim that we can recognize design before we know something about the designer."

"Yes," Will replied. "That sums it up nicely. But there's another part to your claim that evolution theory can't explain big things like species or complex systems that I find troubling. The reason you give is that such systems, on evolution theory, must come about gradually, and since they don't have their particular function until they have all their parts, they must come about all at once, contrary to evolution theory."

"Right," Kate said, sounding less confident.

"I'm no expert on evolution theory," Will began, "but isn't it true that in evolution theory, different parts of an organism may be selected in different ancestral environments? For example, the feathers of a bird might serve as thermal regulators in one environment and later in another environment, where there is greater predation, those feathers may allow rudimentary flight for some who happen, through natural variation, to have longer feathers. Those fortunate few survive better than those that do not."

Kate nodded. "That's true."

"Then how can we claim that the parts of these complex systems could not have come about gradually, the different parts appearing for different reasons, and when the situation demands it they come together as a single system? I seem to recall that the human eye or the similar structure in the octopus came about from a cell that was photosensitive."

"I've read that, too," Kate acknowledged. "And, in all honesty, I find a lot of evidence that species arise quite readily in the animal world. All you need to get a new species is to isolate a genetic population, and they will go off in a different direction from the population from which they are isolated. I really think sticking to organs is better than including species in the argument."

"What remains of your argument, then, except a general skepticism about how complexity could come about over time?" Will asked. "A very, very, long time."

"At least I can say that the human soul was put into man and that evolution cannot explain that." Kate was emphatic, if desperate.

"But on your own account, evolution theory does not try to do that," Will protested. "So it isn't fair to offer the 'ensoulment' of humans as a criticism."

A general silence descended on the van as each occupant reflected on the recent conversation.

Will turned to God. "What's the story here? Did you design what Kate claims you designed or not?"

God's voice took on a conspiratorial tone. "Consider the following story. When I was younger, I was very bored. In my boredom, I took a lot of naps. As you know, a million years is like a second to me, so if I slept very long, things began to change. Once after a long nap, I noticed there were little things on one of the worlds—your world. Most of the little things were swimming around like crazy. In fact, I think all of them were swimmers. I lost interest for a time, probably took another nap, and discovered that a bunch of the swimmers were walking and crawling around on your world. Later, I discovered that some of these were beginning to look more like you."

God paused for dramatic effect. "Not much like you, actually. They were very small, not much brighter than the average politician, and quite hairy. Over time, they changed and began to divide into groups. If I had been a bookie, I would have bet on the Neanderthals—and I would have lost. Homo sapiens just seemed, well, not so bright, but you sure knew how to reproduce."

"So you had nothing to do with our creation?" Will realized that in light of God's story, the question was rhetorical. "No garden of Eden, no Adam and Eve, no generations that don't make any sense?"

"Nope, I claim total innocence," God replied. "If I wanted to make something, I would have done a better job. But the problem of being a god who is changeless—you know I'm supposed to be totally perfect as I am—means that I can't causally affect anything. So, how in the world would I go about creating anything?"

"Did you notice any other little things on any other world?" Will asked.

"Probably, but let me ask my friend Zog, and then I'll get back to you."

Will wished he could look God in the eye. He felt like his leg was being pulled in several directions at once, but God had retreated and was not to be found.

"Will, wake up," Simon said. "It's time for you to drive."

Will took the wheel and realized that Kate had brought them close to Roswell on 380. They would arrive before dark.

As their van approached Roswell, traffic picked up considerably. Signs appeared at every corner urging those attending the conference to stop and camp. They promised restrooms, showers, laundry, and, in some cases, shade. The vans from Galilee were now traveling closer together.

Following a quick consultation via cell phone, they chose the most promising looking "campground." A farm, actually, it featured a twenty-foot high flying saucer tipped at an angle to suggest it was crashing. In fact, from another angle, they realized part of the saucer was buried in the ground. The farmer who appeared to collect their camping fee told them that it was made from plywood, chicken wire, and "a hell of a lot papier-mâché" with a good coat of waterproof paint. "It helps folks find their way back here after being in town," he declared.

Will and his friends found a likely spot, with a couple of trees for shade. Will and Simon shared a tent, as did Kate and Maggie. It was dusk by the time they finished, lit a small campfire, and set up a kitchen.

After they ate, one of the other vans produced a guitar player. He entertained them with a few songs, which they sang unenthusiastically—they were there for the conference, not summer camp. Another group set up another camp a few yards away.

Maggie and Will wandered over and invited their new neighbors to join them at the campfire, which they did, bringing along some wine. The newcomers proved to be older and more experienced UFO conference goers. From the new group, Chuck in particular seemed to know his way around these events. Overweight and balding, he was probably the oldest person there, possibly in his thirties, Will guessed. Chuck was highly animated and friendly. With short, sandy hair and rather heavy glasses, he looked like a geek and he promoted that image deliberately. He had attended UFO conferences in Australia, Germany, and even in Vladivostok, Russia. He was also one of the presenters at this conference.

"*Aliens Among Us* is the title of my talk," Chuck said as he poured himself a generous glass of wine. "Simon, would you like some?"

"Sure," Simon replied.

Will, Kate, and Maggie were surprised by Simon's acceptance, but Kate and Will also took a smaller measure of vino.

"Can you give us a preview?" Kate asked.

"No problem," Chuck responded. "I am actually a rocket scientist who used to work for NASA. While I was there, certain individuals stood out as slightly smarter, stronger, and definitely had more endurance than the rest of us. At first, I thought they were just people who occupied the upper end of the bell curve. But one day I caught a couple of these ubermensches—I think they were named Jerry and Tom—arguing. But they weren't speaking any language that I recognized, and I speak German, English, and Russian, and I can recognize a bunch of others. I listened for a while and then decided to follow them. That was a big mistake."

Chuck paused to sip some wine, probably for dramatic effect. "These two lived in a small house near the base, and that's where they went. I was hoping to get a glimpse inside their house. Unfortunately, the place was kind of exposed, but there was one approach with bushes for cover."

"Campfire stories," God whispered into Will's ear. "I bet he was a boy scout and a camp director."

"Anyway, I found a window and peeked over the edge. I thought I was well concealed. The guy I could see was talking into a strange device. It looked like a mango, but it pulsed as if it were alive. As soon as I looked into the room, the guy, I think it was Jerry—they looked so much alike—glanced in my direction. As we made eye contact, he began to talk rapidly into the mango. I ducked and ran from the house. I made it to my car and was a couple of miles from the house when my brand new Toyota simply stopped. I looked at my watch. It had stopped, too. I opened the door and was planning to hide when a craft appeared right over my car. The beam, probably a tractor beam, sucked me up like I was a piece of lint."

Chuck paused and looked at his audience. They were motionless, everyone focused on him. He sipped more wine and adjusted his position.

"For a while, I thought that there was something in the beam or perhaps they had given me a sedative when I arrived, because everything was blurry. My mind worked, but my vision was off. Now I believe they just see more in the ultraviolet range than we humans. The room into which I arrived was huge. They could beam a triple semi-trailer in there and still have room for a 747. There were figures moving about, but because of my vision problem, I can't really describe them. They put me on a cart; it felt a lot like a hospital gurney."

Chuck paused again, blew his nose, and started to choke up. " I was really terrified. I thought I might lose my bowels or empty my bladder. It got worse when they wheeled me into a room with a large chair and strapped me into it. It was a fairly comfortable seat with a footrest and a head support. The lights were bright and pretty overhead. However, the lights dimmed, which helped my vision, and two figures entered the room, both wearing white coats. One of them picked up some metal instruments, which I could not see clearly but I heard them rattle. Then he tipped the chair back and approached me. I was paralyzed and simply lay there."

Will heard Simon's quick breathing in the silence as Chuck paused for more wine.

"He put a substance on my face. It actually smelled pretty good. I wondered if he was going to probe my mouth or nose, since that's where he put most of it."

Simon could not contain himself. "And, and…"

Chuck smiled. "He gave me a shave, one of the best I've ever had. Then he tipped the chair up and gave me a haircut. It was a little short but nice and even."

Everyone in the circle groaned.

"I'm not pulling your leg," Chuck added in all seriousness. "The aliens had evolved so far that they no longer had any body hair, and they were fascinated by our hairy appearance and how our barbers were the keepers of our hair. I suspect that whoever cut my hair and gave me a shave was some kind of cultural anthropologist who had been studying the behavior of Earth barbers."

"How did you get off the ship?" Maggie demanded. "I don't believe any of this."

"The alien barber showed me my face in a mirror and then held out his hand. He/she might have wanted to shake hands. I noticed that there were only three fingers and no thumb. But just then I remembered that old soft shoe rhythm, you know, "a shave and a hair cut, two bits," so I gave him a quarter. He looked puzzled, but he kept the quarter. Then they transported me, all cleaned up, back to my Toyota.

"At work the next day, Jerry and Tom just looked at me and laughed. Then Jerry said, 'Nice haircut, where did you get it?' I quit the job and started my own UFO consulting business."

Will had very little inclination to believe Chuck's tale, and neither did God.

"Hell of fun story though," God commented wryly.

ALIENS

The first morning of the conference came entirely too soon for Simon, who was hung over. Will had about decided to leave him in camp and head off to the conference when Simon staggered out of the tent.

"Oh God," Simon muttered as he climbed into the van. "My mother would kill me if she saw me now."

Kate looked only slightly sympathetic. "I'm sorry, Simon, but you need to realize that you have the body mass of a large housefly. You need to go light on alcoholic drinks."

Simon nodded and then gripped his head. "I learned my lesson. I'm sure I'll feel better as the day goes on. I've just never had a hangover before."

Maggie, who was the most prudish in the group, had even less sympathy for Simon. Will and Kate quickly vetoed her suggestion that they all sing "Onward Christian Soldiers" at the top of their lungs. Simon looked thankful.

Driving into Roswell proper, they saw that the conference was well attended. Booths were everywhere; each building that had any space was in use. To Maggie's horror, even the local churches had "sold out" and rented space for conference events.

The Galilee workers had pre-registered, so they were able to pick up their programs and badges. As Will read the schedule, he felt God looking over his shoulder.

"I have never seen so many task groups, committees, working groups, study groups, truth panels, advisory groups, investigating committees, not to mention the various sub-committees and governance committees," God said. "The conference is a study in paranoia. Look at the program.

The Truth About Crop Circles, What Your Government Isn't Telling You, The Roswell Cover Up, The Secrets of Area 51, Star Gates: More Than Good Television. You should have a lot of fun here."

Despite God's comments, Will was looking forward to some of the sessions. His first stop would be Delbert's food tent. He wanted to catch up on happenings at the mission. He also planned to attend a session entitled *First Intergalactic Peace Conference*.

Kate headed off to a session called *Terraforming Earth: How Alien Planning Contributed To Our History*. Later, she and Will planned to meet at a panel that was debating whether global warming was part of an alien plot to transform the Earth's climate and make it more hospitable to alien life forms or whether it was simply the result of clueless politicians and the capitalists who trained them. It was called *Global Warming: Contrivance or Sheer Stupidity?* Maggie headed off with a small stack of Bibles and a determined look in her eye. Simon, with dark glasses over his eyes, trailed after Kate, not really caring where he went as long as he could sit down.

Since the instant oatmeal that they had eaten for breakfast was not doing its job, Will was especially delighted to find the dining tent. The smells of Delbert's kitchen were wonderful—eggs, bacon, and pancakes. Will had barely stepped under the canopy when he heard Wanda's voice.

"My God, it's Will Tillit!"

Soon, her bony arms were around him, giving him a surprisingly strong hug. Even Delbert, who was somewhat shy, came over to Will and gave him a hug.

Wanda sat him down near the kitchen and provided him with a real breakfast. As Will worked his way through the pile of food, he was able to give Wanda a brief and highly edited account of his life since he had left the mission. He had just finished his story when Kate and Simon wandered into the tent and joined them at the table. It turned out their session time was misprinted in the schedule. Following introductions, Kate ordered pretty much what Will had, and Simon settled for a cup of tea.

While they ate, Wanda gave Will an update on the mission. "We only left there the day before yesterday. We were committed to doing our cooking classes here and running the food tent. Sister Sara would have come with us, because she was curious about this conference, but she had to stay behind, because the mission is so short of staff. Jesus and Cole still volunteer, God bless their souls; they're such a big help. But honestly, Will, I'm not certain the mission will survive. Sister Ellie had some luck on her fundraising trip, but that money will run out soon. If Ellie has to be out fundraising, that puts extra work on Sara, and since the young people left, that's a lot of work. We still have a few volunteers. Delbert and I are committed, although we're both working extra jobs to keep our own budget out of the red. Then there's all that crap from the Church wanting the sisters to separate and close the mission. It's a wonder we're maintaining the program at the level we are. There's so much need out there—the poor homeless, confused vets from those wars, the out of work, whole families—it's awful, simply awful! We had so hoped to open space for families with children." Wanda's eyes glistened with tears.

Will tried to think of something to cheer Wanda up. "I told you about Cindy," he began. "She should be at the mission by now, and she'll help out. I'm fairly certain I'll be laid off when I get back to Galilee, so I'll go help, too. And I may be able to talk Chris and Marc into joining me. At least they've promised me a ride to Dallas."

Wanda had to get back to work. The volunteers were not clearing the tables fast enough, and dirty dishes were piling up.

As Will and Kate finished their breakfast, Kate gave Will a thoughtful look. "You know, I don't see any point in my going back to college until next fall. I've already missed some of the sequence of courses I need. I might as well go and work through the rest of the year."

"It would be wonderful for you to help out, and I think you'd enjoy it. The sisters are great people, and the staff and clients respect them and each other."

Kate and Simon headed to their session. Simon simply looked sad. Will thought he followed Kate like a neglected puppy. He decided to just look around.

In no time at all, he encountered Maggie and a small cluster of UFOers. Her face was a little red, set off by her orange-tinted hair, and she was in full voice.

"You asked why I think my experiences of Jesus are real? I think they're real, because I don't choose them. Jesus just comes to me. I feel his presence vividly, and these experiences produce a true change in my life, a change for the better. I become more conscious of others and the need to attend to my spiritual life. These have been the marks of true religious experience since Paul was on the road to Damascus."

A small UFOer, whose badge said, "Billy Clark," spoke up. "But by your own criteria, many experiences of extraterrestrials are also real. We don't choose to be abducted or contacted or sent messages. We certainly don't volunteer to be probed, and it's definitely vivid. We're just suddenly there. Furthermore, these are life-changing events. And for many of us, the changes are positive. We begin to work for a better world or even intergalactic peace. We seek to transform our environment for the better, apply ourselves to science, and so on. So, what's the difference?"

"The difference," Maggie retorted, "is that my religious experience is supported by a sacred text. Jesus died for my sins and was resurrected. It says clearly in John fourteen verse six that no one is saved except through Jesus. In addition to the biblical story, we have archeological evidence that the things in the story actually happened."

"What you have," Billy responded, "is a potpourri of stories written long after the fact by authors who could only have heard some kind of oral tradition maintained by individuals who have a vested interest in keeping such stories alive. These stories do not agree with each other in important details, and many other stories were simply excluded, because they didn't conform to the powers that be at the time. I can't accept the Bible as evidence for your beliefs first because of the nature of the book itself, not to mention its overly numerous interpretations, and second, because to accept the book would be to beg the question, which is whether there is a deity even approximately like the god you worship."

"And just what evidence do you offer that there are extraterrestrials among us?" Maggie demanded.

"That's the point of these conferences," Billy replied. "We've had experiences that we consider to be veridical. There are thousands of us around the world who claim firsthand knowledge of extraterrestrial life. If you listen to the seminars and witnesses of these events, you may come to believe. As for archeological evidence, there are things in this world, like the pyramids, that don't make sense unless you suppose they were built by a more sophisticated technology than has ever existed on this planet."

"You're a bunch of nuts!"

Billy did not buy into her heated rhetoric. "I think you need to listen to us before you decide we're crazy. There are many well-educated people here who have successful careers in science and public life and who have come to believe, often against their own will, that there are extraterrestrials among us. Anyway, why are you upset? How do our beliefs challenge your religion? Wouldn't it be a good thing for you if you discovered that there were green, wide-eyed Christians?"

"There are no green, wide-eyed Christians," Maggie said with authority. "The Bible says that we were created in God's image, and he is not and, therefore, neither are we, green or wide-eyed. And God gave his only son to us, and it is only through him that we are saved. So, there can be no extraterrestrial Christians."

"But surely this in-his-image stuff is only analogical, and a weak analogy at that, since you perceive God to be an immaterial, all-knowing, all-powerful, all-good being. We humans are none of those things, so how can we possibly be created in God's image?" Billy was not giving any ground. "The same goes for your Jesus. He's a planet Earth concept. Perhaps the savior takes a different form on other worlds."

Maggie returned to the question of evidence. "I'm just not impressed with a bunch of testimony that comes from you all. First, it's not reliable. When there are follow-up investigations, they fail to uncover the evidence you say is there. What this means is that there are thousands of reports that are either fabricated or unconfirmed. Second, when you look at the reports, it's almost as if there's a common narrative. Someone writes a story about being abducted, and then there are copycat stories that use the same language, the same descriptions of the experience, the same story line. People like to tell stories, and, given the influence of the media, I'm not surprised you all say the same things and believe the same things. There's no independent corroboration for what you say. Third, we have sophisticated corroborative techniques to use when someone claims to have seen a tiger in the jungle where tigers have not been seen for a long time. We can find evidence, such as scat, footprints, and hidden camera pictures that allow us to check out the claim. You simply fail to have these kinds of checks on your claims as to the reality of aliens."

Will was impressed with Maggie's arguments.

"But you're no better off," Billy retorted. "I can't grant you all the points you make, because you forget the vast cover up that governments carry out. But talk about a common narrative! Your whole case for Jesus is flawed by your own standards of evidence."

"You have no better evidence of a cover up than you have for the existence of aliens," Maggie interrupted.

"Maggie, you have no reliable evidence of your claim that God exists and appears to people," Billy charged back in. "Look at the fraudulent religious claims; they greatly exceed the claims we make about alien encounters. And you, too, offer up a common narrative. In Christian societies, the experiences are all of Jesus, God, or the Holy Spirit. In Hindu societies, the Hindu gods or manifestations of Kali are experienced, and they're always presented in a way consistent with the imagery of that religious tradition. You totally lack corroborative evidence of the kind we normally regard as decisive. And the archeological and historical evidence is not much on your side either. There are no contemporary secular records that Jesus ever existed."

At that point, Will felt God's laughter. "I like these two kids. Fighting over the existence of nonexistent beings. It reminds me of a debate between two seven-year-olds over the relative reality of Mighty Mouse and the Easter Bunny. One of them argues that Mighty Mouse is real because there exist sacred comic books, and the other argues that the Easter Bunny is real because they can't explain the Easter eggs they find."

"Well," Maggie began, "I deny that God doesn't give us enough evidence. God may have special reasons for remaining hidden to some extent."

"But," Billy interjected, "that doesn't work for you, because now you're saying there's some purpose that is God's secret reason for not revealing himself that trumps our knowing about him. But by your own theology, there is nothing greater than that."

Maggie turned to Will. "What do you think, Will? You've been standing there like a statue all this time."

Maggie's face was quite sweaty, and her face was flushed. Billy was also feeling the effects of the New Mexico sun and the passionate argument. Both looked worn out by their exchange.

"I don't want to rain on either of your parades," Will began, "but it seems to me that both of you have a similar problem." He thought furiously about what to say next and then decided to channel God's line of analysis. "You both want to argue for the reality of some extraordinary beings with extraordinary powers. Maggie, your god can presumably do anything, knows everything, and is totally beneficent. You posit an extraordinary history of your subject that relies on ancient texts, many of which are probably fanciful, but it's not clear which are fanciful and which are not. At the same time, you claim to know very little about the intentions and purposes of this god.

"And Billy, your aliens are capable of amazing technological feats, but their intentions are also shrouded in mystery. And the history of such beings is either unknown or in dispute. So, how do you show that these amazing beings are real? Neither of you can use our usual techniques and our familiar and reliable methods for detection. So you resort to extraordinary experiences, stories, witnesses, and a great deal of hand waving. The problem is, the evidence to which you must resort is the same kind of evidence that every snake oil charlatan and conman uses to convince the gullible. As soon as you attempt to retreat from your problematic evidence and make your appeal more scientific, or even more like common sense, your case falls apart. You have a hiddenness problem. You posit the existence of entities that are quite capable of making themselves known but which, for some mysterious reason do not do so in any straightforward way. That creates the credibility problem that each of you points out about the other's position."

"But look at how many of us are scientists or have studied science," Billy replied.

"And look at how successful Christianity is," Maggie added. "It's the world's largest religion."

"Those facts don't matter." Will was convinced he was on the right track. "Scientists need not be scientific in their approach to all things. I really don't know how many scientists are led to believe in extraterrestrials by science. And it's a mistake to confuse the success of a belief system with the evidence for it. In fact, most religious systems have enjoyed a degree of success, at least for certain historical periods, without being true or even well founded.

"Another thing that I can't help but wonder about, and that neither of you brought up, is that there seem to be powerful interests that seek to keep these beliefs going. Religion is a huge enterprise with billions of dollars and much political influence at stake." Will had a vivid image of the prosperity church he had attended. "Even these alien conferences are an example of a cottage industry that, judging by the attendance here, is making a good deal of money. I don't mean to doubt the sincerity of your beliefs, and do not infer from my comments what my own beliefs are. I'm merely trying to point out some features of your arguments."

Maggie was angry that Will had not backed her up. "And *you're* an employee of Galilee Theme Park? I don't even think you're a Christian." With that, she stalked off.

"Nicely done," God said.

"Just what did you mean by saying that they were fighting over the existence of non-existents?" Will asked.

God's answer was coy. "I only meant that neither of them seemed to have evidence for the existence of the kinds of entities for which they were arguing."

"Does that mean you don't actually exist?"

"I didn't say that," God said as he faded away.

Will snapped back to reality. It was time to head for the *First Intergalactic Peace Conference*.

At the tent housing the conference, Will found Simon. He slipped into the seat beside him. Simon looked a bit better and whispered to Will that he had just come from an exciting panel entitled *Are You Next*?

"It's kind of like being raptured," Simon explained, "except they don't take you while you're driving or flying a plane. I heard several people talk like Chuck did last night about suddenly finding themselves on a spaceship. They said the view of the universe was fabulous, the food was good, and they experienced total peace of mind. Doesn't that sound like heaven to you? Maybe the rapture is an abduction."

Will was about to answer when Kate appeared. She was returning from the climate change panel. She thought those who argued that it was sheer stupidity and greed, not to mention oil and coal lobby money, were right. They had the better explanation of why the planet was getting so warm and why no government was doing much about it.

"The science on climate change is simple and complete," she said. "In the end, money is driving us toward extinction. The corporations and their lackeys are going to cook the damn planet and all of us with it to bolster their bottom line."

The peace conference was a sham. One of the panel members said he represented the Karpathians while another represented the Cloy. Apparently, these two races had come into conflict over a highly desirable planet where both had established colonies. The colonies got into a war, and by this small war, the two races were drawn into conflict. But the two civilizations were so evenly matched that it would be mutual assured destruction for them to actually fight. They had presumably contacted the two panelists and asked them for a fair division of the planet and its resources. By the time they got out the huge map, identified major mineral deposits, arable land, fresh water supplies, and sites for good vacation homes, Will and his friends were nodding off. They did not stay for the division of these resources.

On the second day of the conference, Will spent time talking to Cindy on the phone, eating in the dining tent, and listening to music. Cindy was at the mission. She had already done one kitchen and one laundry duty. She loved the sisters.

"Sara is so much fun, and she's open to so many ideas," Cindy said. "Ellie is just scary smart but so kind and gentle. I want them to adopt me!"

Will told her about the conference, and then Sara got on the line, and he had to repeat his stories for her. She asked when Will thought he might get there, and she also checked on Delbert and Wanda, who were heading back that evening.

"Cindy is too modest," she added. "She's taken over most of the accounting and is working with Ellie on new grants. Thank you, Will. She's a godsend."

Will was bursting with pride by the time he signed off.

After two days at the conference, the Galilee workers headed back. The conference had had some interesting effects, as Simon found in the little poll he conducted before and after it began. Before the event, few of those from Galilee believed in aliens. After attending, sixty percent said that aliens were possible or likely, and thirty-five percent thought they were very likely. Simon was among the new believers.

Several of their party had gone to a session entitled *Are the Angels of the Bible Extraterrestrials?* Despite Maggie's protests, most of them were attracted to the idea that the angels or 'ministering spirits' (Hebrews

1:14) were part of an intergalactic congregation. No amount of drawing contrasts between angels and aliens—angels are always kind to humans, except the vengeful ones, aliens always probe humans, except the ones that do not, and so on—did any good. Maggie chose to ride back with the "true" Christians—those who did not believe in aliens.

Will, Kate, and Simon were pleased to have the van to themselves. They talked a lot about their future plans. Simon was less set on going to seminary now than when he arrived at Galilee. At the same time, he was worried about how his parents would take his change of mind. Kate was also of a mind to interrupt her college career, at least for a year. She thought a few months at the mission might give her time for that. Will realized he was eager to get back to the mission and to drive home to see his aunt and uncle.

Will was also beginning to suffer from a toothache. It had bothered him off and on for a few days, but it had grown worse despite the pain meds he was taking. Because he was feeling poorly, Simon and Kate drove. Will was certain that Maggie would say that it was divine retribution, but God said sympathetically, "Perhaps you need a root canal."

CLOSINGS

As soon as Kate, Will, and Simon reached Texas, they stopped in the first town they came to and asked a woman with a stroller where they could find a dentist. By the time they trooped into the dentist's office, the whole side of Will's jaw hurt and was swollen. The dentist, Bob Morrow, told Will that he did indeed need a root canal.

Galilee Theme Park had issued plastic insurance cards that were supposed to be good throughout Texas for medical emergencies. The receptionist/dental assistant who took Will to the examination room looked carefully at Will's card and his drivers' license. She was a lovely middle-aged woman with a radiant smile. "I've heard of this plan. I'll have to call Galilee and confirm you're an employee. Even so, Bob may not want to accept it, because we've heard that the park is having financial problems."

She studied Will's license further as if she was having a hard time reading it. In a quiet tone she said, "Wait here a moment, and I'll see what we can do for you."

Left alone, Will only caught the murmur of voices from wherever they had elected to have their conversation. He hoped they would offer some relief soon, if only in the form of a shot of Novocain.

After what seemed like a long time, the dental assistant came back into the room. She paused at the door for several moments, just looking at Will, before she sat on the stool next to him, where she continued to study him quietly. Will found her scrutiny quite unsettling and was just about to ask what was wrong, when she spoke in a soft voice.

"Will, we need to talk." She paused, seeming to struggle for words. Finally, simply and directly, she said, "Will, I'm your mother, Mary-Rose

Tillit, now Mary-Rose Morrow."

Will was stunned. For a moment, he actually forgot he had a toothache. He sat there trying desperately to think of something to say. He was totally unprepared for this moment, and he realized that the same was true of this woman next to him, who had tears in her eyes. Will could see a family resemblance in her: there were the large bones and strong profile of his Uncle John, and the voice was close to Aunt Rita's.

"I never thought I would see you again," he said finally.

After a long pause, Will's mother began to talk. "Will, in some ways I'm so ashamed of what I did. I basically put you up for adoption to my brother and sister. But you need to understand that I did it not because I didn't love you. I loved you with all my heart, but I was a lousy mother. I was too young, too wild, and I was neglecting you. I wanted a better life for you and for me. So I did the unforgivable and gave you up. You probably hate me for that, and I deserve it."

"I…I really don't hate you," Will said. "I hardly remember you." He saw the hurt in his mother's eyes when he said that. "But if you intended for me to have a good life, you should know that I have. Uncle John and Aunt Rita loved me and cared for me. They have supported me in every way, and we're a family. I don't know what it would have been like if you had kept contact with me. I think it might have gotten in the way of me becoming their son." Will was at a loss to say more, and he felt his own eyes forming tears.

"Sorry to interrupt," Dr. Morrow said, "but Will, I need to get some numbing started. The park no longer stands by its insurance cards, but we're going to fix this anyway."

He gave Will a shot of Novocain, and Will smiled gratefully.

"Tell me about my brother and sister," Mary-Rose said.

Will did the best he could under the circumstances. He also filled in a bit about his own life. When he was finished, Mary-Rose reached over and hugged him. After a brief tangle with the bib, Will did the same.

Suddenly, his jaw flared up, and he groaned in pain. Mary-Rose was hugging him on the side of his still sensitive bad tooth. She released him immediately.

"I'll tell your friends that they have about three hours to wait."

When she came back, Will and his mother continued to talk as the anesthetic set in.

Three hours and a little more later, Will staggered out of the dentist's chair. His jaw was numb, he had a bag of antibiotics, and he had tucked his mother's address and phone number in his wallet.

Kate and Simon were sitting in the waiting room eating sandwiches and drinking Dr. Pepper. With Will in tow, they headed back to Galilee. As Will's story unfolded, both of them were flabbergasted.

Will, not certain it was accidental, gave God a quick thanks.

"Don't thank me," God replied. "Coincidences happen. You were very mature in there, by the way," he added.

Will was feeling better in some ways. "What was I supposed to say? 'I hate you and the dentist, and I don't want you to fix my tooth'? That would just be hurtful, and it wouldn't change a thing." Then Will added wistfully, "She's beautiful and kind. I think she's changed a lot since we separated. It also made me realize what my aunt and uncle have done for me. I love them."

God seemed to have departed.

Will did not remember much about the return to Galilee Theme Park. Somehow, Simon guided him back to their room and dumped him on his bed, where he slept through breakfast the next morning. But his tooth felt wonderfully better, and when he finally woke up to a brisk cup of tea, the past twenty-four hours seemed like a dream in which his mother had mysteriously appeared. He even double-checked the address in his wallet to make sure she was real.

The theme park was much changed, even though they had only been gone from Friday through Monday. There were no visitors, and a large sign in front of the park declared it closed. Many staff seemed to have left, and a meeting had been called for late afternoon for those who remained. Kate, Simon, and Will walked down to the petting zoo, where they found Marc sitting downcast amid the empty stalls and cages. It looked like a burglary had taken place, like someone had swept in and looted the animals. The cages were still dirty.

Marc saw them coming and pointed out the obvious. "Animals all gone. They took little bunnies, guinea pigs, ponies, donkey, and lamb. They took everything." He was blinking rapidly, and he had been crying.

The three of them were consoling Marc when the familiar golf cart bearing Mrs. Williamson appeared outside the zoo. She stepped down from the cart, walking very carefully in some shiny new pumps.

"Well, this place smells much better without the animals."

"What did you do with them?" Kate asked.

"We sold some of them to another petting zoo, and the Humane Society took the rest," Mrs. Williamson replied, ignoring Kate's cringe. "Now I want you three to clean this place up. Scrub the cages thoroughly; we can't auction them off dirty. You're all back on garbage duty as well. Everyone is cleaning up the exhibits. The food concessions are dumping stuff."

Mrs. Williamson climbed back into her golf cart. "By the way, there will be a staff meeting later today, an hour before dinner. We'll discuss what needs to be done in order to close Galilee Theme Park."

"Will Reverend Shister be speaking?" Will asked.

"No, Reverend Shister has been called away for a family emergency. We do not expect him back any time soon." She signaled to her driver, and the golf cart whizzed away.

A plan began to trickle into Will's mind. "Let's go have lunch, I think the staff should have its own meeting before the official one."

"I agree," Simon ventured. Kate also nodded her affirmation.

Lunch was a paltry affair: baloney sandwiches with pickle relish and potato chips. Soft drinks were scarce, so most of those present drank water, which was tepid.

Simon remarked on how few staff members were left. "I heard that a lot of them have headed home. I wonder if we'll get paid."

During lunch Will, Kate, and Simon circulated among the remaining staff and asked them to spread the word that there would be a staff meeting at two in the old Garden of Eden exhibit area. The zoo crew was popular, so when they asked people to attend a meeting, they got a positive response.

The bleachers in the seating area of the Garden of Eden had already been removed and were stacked to one side, so the assembled staff members sat in a semi-circle on the ground. Will paced nervously and hoped he would not succumb to the hiccups. They decided that Kate would speak first.

"Thank you all for coming," she began, "I'm Kate Sullivan, for those of you who don't know me. When my friends Will Tillit and Simon Tigard and I were talking, some questions occurred to us that seemed of general concern to everyone here. First, we were supposed to be paid every two weeks. We've been here about four weeks. Has anyone been paid?"

No hands went up.

"There's also a huge amount of cleanup work here, some of it very dangerous involving construction skills, high ladders, and heavy lifting that few of us are trained to do. Yet, it looks like we're going to be asked to do it. We're cheap labor, and we're unskilled. I would guess that we are being exploited to do the work of skilled more highly paid labor." Kate paused as a hand went up.

"I'm Allen Caldwell," the hand holder said. "Me and a couple of guys have been asked to dismantle the ark exhibit. It's very high and involves some big timbers. We have no idea how to do it, let alone do it safely."

Another staff person, a small woman named Teri, noted that she and some friends had been asked to disconnect a number of appliances. "I don't even know where we can find wrenches to disconnect them, and most of them have live electrical connections."

"These are good examples," Will said. "And another consideration: We've all heard rumors that this place is due to be vacated in a week. Given the amount of work we need to do, we will all be working overtime. Has anyone been offered any overtime pay?"

No hands went up.

"Reverend Shister is not here. Does anyone know where he is or if he's planning to return and honor our contracts? Most of us haven't been paid, and many of us have missed part of the first term of school. We're giving up a lot to do dangerous work for which we lack the skills."

There was a murmur of assent, but one hand shot up as its owner rose to his feet. "I'm Teddy Shister, Reverend Shister's nephew. My uncle is an honorable man and a good Christian. You're just speculating about what he might do, and you have no basis for anything you are saying." Teddy was getting quite red in the face.

Teri was on her feet again. "Teddy, this is more than speculation. We haven't been paid since we arrived, and some of us have been here several weeks. We've been asked directly to do these dangerous jobs. I am not an electrician, and I'm not a plumber. I don't even know where to shut off the power or turn off the water." Teri plunked back down in exasperation.

"Teddy, I want you to be honest with us," Will responded. "Have you been paid since you started working here?"

"I, uh..."

"Have you?"

"Yes, I get paid every two weeks," Teddy admitted.

Simon's eyes flared. "Has anyone except Shister's relatives been paid?" His question was greeted with total silence.

"I suggest," Will continued, "that we do no more work until we're paid and that we refuse to do the dangerous dismantling we are being asked to do. Also, we do nothing until we have a contract that addresses our overtime pay."

There was a rousing round of cheers from the assembled staff members. Will felt vindicated by the response and that he had made his appeal in public without a hiccup.

Teddy left in a hurry. Will, Simon, and Kate mingled with the remaining staff members. Several said they were taking off, salary or no salary. They had spent enough time at Galilee and gotten little out of it. Others said they intended to go to the meeting and see what was being offered.

A security guard appeared driving a golf cart with "Security" written on it in bold letters. He approached Will, Kate, and Simon. Teri, who had been asked to disassemble the appliances, came forward and made it clear she was going to stand firmly with the zoo crew. So did Allen. The guard said that Mrs. Williamson wanted to see them in her office at four just before the general meeting.

When he left, Teri was irate. "That little toad Teddy was on his cell and told them about the meeting and what our concerns are."

"There's not much we can do but go to her meeting—unless we go over there now and catch them by surprise," Simon said with a mischievous gleam in his eyes.

That's all it took. The five of them headed to Mrs. Williamson's office.

"Mrs. Williamson is on a long distance conference call," said a young woman who was busy pulling piles of paper from the files and stacking them by a large shredder.

"We can wait," Kate said.

"But you're quite early for your appointment," the young woman said as she began to shred.

Kate, Will, Simon, Teri, and Allen simply stood together.

"The sisters would be proud of you," God opined.

Will certainly hoped so, but at that moment, he was nervous and plagued with doubts. They really didn't have as much information as he would have liked. And it didn't help when God started humming and singing.

"Arise ye workers from your slumbers, Arise ye prisoners of want."

"So now you're a Bolshevik?" Will asked.

"Only when necessary."

Mrs. Williamson finally emerged from her office. She was surprised to see them but recovered quickly. As always, she was dressed immaculately. Her heavy blond hair was in place, and her shoes were stylish and matched her outfit.

"I think she wears a wig," God observed. "Don't trust her; she's a shifty shill for Shister." God loved alliteration.

"I don't have time for this conversation right now," Will said.

God vanished.

"You're early," Mrs. Williamson said. "Please, come on in."

Mrs. Williamson's office featured a large desk stacked with piles of papers, which Will guessed were headed for the shredder in the other room. She sat, but there were no chairs for them, so the delegation remained standing. Will thought this imposed discomfort was deliberate.

"I understand you have some concerns to express," Mrs. Williamson said. "Before we begin though, I would like to ask if you represent yourselves or if the other staff members have delegated you as their representatives. If you were delegated, was there a vote? If so, what was the outcome?"

Simon's face went red with anger. "We were chosen as delegates by acclamation. We have some concerns to express to you, and we will report your response to the other staff members."

"Why not wait until the meeting at five?"

"We and the other staff members would like time to think about your answer to our questions before the meeting," Kate said smoothly.

"All right, what are your concerns?"

"First, we want to know when we will be paid the salary that is already owed us," Will began, "Second, we want to know if we will receive overtime pay during this last hectic week when we will have to work extra."

"And," Teri cut in, "we don't want to be asked to do dangerous work for which we aren't qualified and for which we were not hired."

"We've already been asked to do dangerous work on the ark," Allen added.

"I see," Mrs. Williamson said. "I think you have some bad information. Let me explain. As you no doubt know, the park has not done as well as we hoped it would. However, we are not in bankruptcy proceedings, and no one has been paid, not even me."

"Teddy Shister has been paid," Simon interrupted.

"Teddy Shister gets an allowance, nothing more. It comes from Reverend Shister's private account."

Normally honest, Simon surprised Kate and Will by lying. "No it doesn't. I saw his check, and it was not a personal check. It was a Galilee Theme Park check. It said so up in the corner."

Mrs. Williamson looked a little rattled. "I'm sure there's some explanation. But let me return to your concerns. I'm certain there will be overtime pay. At this point though, I don't know what it will be. And we will not ask you to do anything dangerous. Do these assurances take care of your concerns?"

"But we've already been asked to do dangerous things," Teri insisted. "My crew has been told to disconnect appliances electrically and, if plumbed, that, too. And we haven't been paid."

Mrs. Williamson was looking less friendly by the moment. "I'll tell you what," she declared, "I'll pay each of you right now for the time you've been at the park. I have your employment records right here. Then you can pack your bags and be on your way to college or whatever." She looked at them expectantly.

"We need to report this conversation to the other staff members," Will said. "We all want to be paid. We didn't come to ask just for ourselves."

"If you don't accept the terms I've just offered you, I will have you removed from the park by security, and you will not be allowed back in. Furthermore, you will not be paid for the summer's work. Have I made myself clear?"

The members of the delegation looked at each other. "We can't take the money and run," Will said. The others nodded in agreement.

Mrs. Williamson was on the phone immediately, and just as quickly, three security guards stepped into the room. One of the three was Marc, whose large body did not fit into his uniform. The sleeves of his shirt were giving way at the seams.

"I want these five former employees escorted out of the park," Mrs. Williamson said. "Send someone to pick up their possessions and deliver them outside the gate. Do not let them back in!"

"Marc," Kate said, "she can't do this; it's wrong. We're only trying to get the staff paid and get safe working conditions."

"I haven't been paid either," one of the guards said.

Marc looked at Kate, Simon, and Will. "You're my friends," he said, as if that was enough.

"I want them out of here!" Mrs. Williamson was getting rather shrill.

"No way," the third guard said, "not if Marc doesn't agree."

Will punched numbers into his cell phone. Agent Smith picked up right away. "Agent Smith, we're in Mrs. Williamson's office, and she's trying to have us removed from the park because we questioned some of the park's employment practices. They're also shredding everything in sight."

"Just hold on Will," Agent Smith interrupted. "We're coming into the building right now. We've had Galilee Theme Park under investigation for fraud for several weeks. We just picked up Shister at the airport. He was headed for Buenos Aires. We're coming for Williamson. Keep her there if you can, and unplug those shredders."

"I'm leaving," Mrs. Williamson said as she headed for the door.

"The FBI is on the grounds, and asks that you remain in your office," Will said. "Allen and Teri, please unplug the shredders."

"No way," Mrs. Williamson was gaining momentum as she headed for the door, which was unfortunate, because Teri simply stuck out her foot and tripped the departing woman, who fell face-down just as Agent Smith and two other agents entered the room.

Agent Smith looked down at Mrs. Williamson, showed her a warrant, and told her she was under arrest and entitled to an attorney. Then she smiled at Will. "Hi, Will. It's good to see you again."

Behind her, the agents confiscated un-shredded piles of paper.

"You have nothing," Mrs. Williamson said, glaring at Agent Smith.

"We'll see," Agent Smith replied calmly. "What have you got, Chris?"

Will was surprised to see Chris standing near Marc and behind the agents who had just appeared.

"I have everything," Chris replied. "All the transactions, including the transfer of large sums to offshore accounts. It's all in the server, and I have a backup disc as well."

"Good work," Agent Smith said, "Were you able to do anything about payroll?"

"Just before you froze the assets, I cut checks. They can be distributed at the meeting. Anyone not there will get them in the mail."

"All right." Agent Smith was clearly in control. "We need to communicate with the staff."

The meeting was brief. Agent Smith announced that all work in the park was to cease. Employees who could produce identification were paid back wages, and everyone was told to be out of the park by nine the next morning.

Kate, Simon, and Will received many hugs and slaps on the back. Will had never seen Simon so happy. Kate was radiant among her many well-wishers. God was cheery, too.

"Damn nice work Will."

ANCESTRAL MEMORIES

The next morning, the bedraggled, hungry remnants of the staff from Galilee Theme Park assembled before the park gate. They had not had breakfast, as the dining tent was closed, not even coffee, as the electricity had been shut off. And most of them had not gotten a lot of sleep, because they were either packing or attending a large party that had sprung up spontaneously in the Garden of Eden. Several of them were simply hung over. FBI agents swarmed over the park, making certain everyone was out.

Will called his aunt and uncle and told them he was leaving and that he planned to stop at the mission to work for a bit. Then he and Cindy would drive over to see them. He also told them he would be testifying at a trial concerning his alleged kidnapping and that the trial had been moved to the Fort Worth area. Agent Smith had told him not to discuss his testimony, and she promised to meet him in Fort Worth to help him prepare. She would also keep him informed as to the trial date, because continuances were common.

The large white van with "Galilee Theme Park" written on the side pulled up. Chris was at the wheel, and Marc rode in back.

"All aboard for Dallas/Fort Worth!" Chris shouted.

"Is this your van?" Will asked.

"Yep," Chris replied. "I let the park put their logo and name on the side, because I used it to haul guests sometimes. It's got three rows of seats. Let's get loaded."

Soon, everyone was sandwiched in. Marc and Will could not sit together, because they were too big. Marc shared the middle seat with

Kate. Will sat up front with Chris, and Simon, who had asked to tag along, sat with Teri, who was interested in visiting the mission.

"Chris," Simon asked. "Are you an FBI agent?"

Chris laughed. "Hardly. I'm a convicted felon. Got caught hacking into the married Governor of Texas's personal account in order to reveal that he had two women as lovers and that he had taken huge kickbacks from highway construction firms, all while running on a ticket promoting family values and transparency. Agent Smith knew the details of my record and saw a chance to put me into Galilee as a mole. I think the FBI actually liked my revelations about the governor, so they took me on. I can't say a lot about what I did, but since I was responsible for the computer network, I could monitor all of the park's financial transactions, which I delivered to the FBI. The fraud investigation was already underway when I began working at Galilee, but they had no one inside. Agent Smith is one smart woman. She saw immediately that even though I was a convicted hacker, I had the skills to get the information they needed to prosecute."

"We really appreciate your cutting checks for us," Kate added.

"That was just fortuitous," Chris said as the van turned onto the interstate and headed east. "I saw a lot of money headed for the Bahamas, and I had the payroll list, so I just hit the right keys, and out came the checks. Right after that, the FBI froze the park's assets to stop the hemorrhaging of money. But the checks are backed by sufficient funds. You will notice, however, that they only cover part of the back pay, not everything you're owed."

Will and Kate were surprised by the conversation that ensued between Simon and Chris. It turned out that Simon had also done a little hacking, and he obviously admired Chris.

Marc was still sad about the closing of the petting zoo. He had made friends with most of the animals. He even had special names for each of them. Kate tried, without much success to convince him that the animals had all found a good home.

"I know one that did," Marc said as he produced a young guinea pig from a cage under his seat. The rodent erupted in a series of squeaks as Marc produced a carrot and a cabbage leaf from a small plastic container.

"Meet Oga," Marc said with pride. Oga proved to be very tame, and to everyone's delight, sat cheerfully on Marc's lap and ate her carrot and cabbage leaf snack.

"Marc," Kate began, "I've been wanting to ask you about your former nickname. Everyone called you 'Blink', and I've even heard you introduce yourself by that name. How did you come by it?"

"It's not very interesting," Marc replied.

"Marc," Chris said, "I could tell them a little more, with your permission."

Marc nodded. "Sure."

"When Marc was little," Chris said, "he was shy and big even then, a great big Jewish boy in a WASPish neighborhood. His frequent blinking is a nervous reaction that resulted from being teased. Because he was big, he got into a lot of fights and gained a reputation as a tough guy. He beat two challengers up in a bar fight—one of them the son of a prominent citizen—and ended up at WTHC. 'Blink' was a prison name."

"Thanks, Chris," Kate said as she put her hand on Marc's shoulder. "I didn't mean to make you uncomfortable."

"You didn't," Marc replied. "You all are my friends. I like that. You've probably noticed I'm not really a tough guy." Thus, Marc finished the longest and most self-revealing speech of his life.

Simon kept trying to get Chris to reveal more about hacking into Galilee's books, but Chris was evasive.

"The world needs more hackers like Chris," God suggested. "Perhaps another is in the making. Another divinity student gone bad."

"Tell us more about this place we're going," Marc said to Will.

"The mission was founded and is run by two great women, Sister Sara and Sister Ellie," Will began. "It's a shelter for homeless people. They have a wing for women and one for men, and they're trying to open smaller units for homeless pregnant girls and women with children who have had to leave home. They serve two meals a day, and right now there's a huge demand for their services, because so many people have lost their homes and their jobs. I hope that when we get there, we can help them out. The building needs repair, wiring, and plumbing work. They also need staff on site to help with the daily chores. Sisters Ellie and Sara aren't getting any younger, and it's hard work."

"I can do plumbing," Marc said.

"Marc actually completed his apprenticeship as a plumber before his arrest," Chris added.

"I'd like to work with the girls," Kate said.

"I'll do whatever I can," Simon added. "But I'd like to work some with Chris on the wiring and technical support. What did you do, Will?"

"A lot of different stuff, like picking up food, working in the kitchen, and sometimes night duty. It's too bad none of us is rich, because what the mission really needs is funding. The Church has cut them off, and I think the sisters are being, or have been, excommunicated."

"Why?" Kate asked.

"Because they're lovers, and they're not doing the traditional work that nuns are supposed to do. Also, they don't dress like nuns. They're nontraditional in lots of ways. But I've never met two better people."

"Oh," Kate and Simon said simultaneously.

"My friend, Cindy, is working there now." Feeling a little protective of the sisters, Will added, "She totally loves them. She said she wants them to adopt her."

Kate and Simon both came out of evangelical households, so they held no love for the Catholic Church. On top of which, they had been brought up with the belief that homosexuality is a sin. But Will's unqualified admiration of the sisters made them reserve judgment as they processed this new information.

"Hey," Simon changed the subject, "I got a phone call from alien lover Billy Clark, and there's another UFO conference in the Dallas area next month. I was thinking about going."

"Be sure you clear it with the sisters," Will said, "before you head out."

Chris was curious about the conference that Will, Kate, and Simon had attended. Specifically, he wanted to know if anyone thought that aliens were included in any theories of reincarnation.

"I have absolutely no idea," Simon said, "but why not? Why restrict reincarnation to this world?"

"Or this time period," Chris said. That got puzzled looks from everyone. Chris tried to explain. "Reincarnation seems to involve the soul living in other life forms over time. In some lives, you might be a flea and in another life a Republican candidate for president. But from what I've read, reincarnation believers always talk about modern animals, human or not, as exemplifying the forms that you might take. And there are people who say they remember past lives as well. Thus, they might claim to remember being Napoleon or Julius Caesar. Some folks even believe that they can channel these past persons. There may be some truth to these claims. My own experience was amazing, it all started when I began to have some very vague and disturbing memories."

Chris exited the freeway and pulled up in front of a convenience store. "I need a cup of coffee and a rest stop, I'll bet you all do as well. Will, you drive for awhile, I'm tired of dodging big trucks."

Will was happy to oblige. Chris was eccentric, brilliant, and always had an interesting take on the spiritual side of things.

"So you're no longer trying to wager yourself into many different religions?"

"Not since I joined the Park," Chris said. "I realized I must have looked pretty crazy doing all those different practices. I got so confused that I ate a peyote wafer once while trying to do communion. What a trip! What I was doing was not a wager that one can make either rationally or intelligently. It was irrational, because you can't hold obviously conflicting beliefs simultaneously, and it was unintelligent, because if you look at the basis for belief in any religion that I've found, it's weak, if not silly. I'm much more satisfied with my present set of beliefs, although they will probably change, too."

Back on the road, Chris returned to his exposition. "So, I began to have dreams and memories that were hard to explain. I'd wake up and find I'd been swimming in bed. The sheets were a tangle, and I realized I'd been remembering a life in the water. After a time, I began to dream that I was in the water sometimes and on land at other times. I recalled being slow with short legs, and I often dreamt of being eaten by other creatures not much faster than me. At each stage, my dreams became a little clearer. When I could climb, I lived in the trees and used my large, hard teeth to eat nuts and fruits. In one of my most vivid dreams, I thought I was Lucy, a small, thin, hairy creature who, when I looked it up, lived about three point five million years ago. I seem to recall that I was too small to hunt anything bigger than a lizard. Anyway, my memories of past lives just kept getting clearer, but I didn't always become a more complex organism than my previous life. Sometimes I was a simpler organism than before. I recall living in a small family unit on the ground. My arms were still long, and although I could walk upright, I often ran on all four limbs. There was a terrible time when I had a life on the southern tip of Africa. The rest was covered with ice. There were only a few of us hominids, but there was an abundance of shellfish and edible plants. I also remember being a baker in a small community in North Africa a million years later, and still later, I was a Myna warrior."

Will was the first to catch the twinkle in Chris' eye. "You're just making it up. You've never had such memories. Such memories are scientifically impossible."

They all laughed, and so did Chris.

"Are you sure you don't remember being a single-celled organism that divides asexually?" Kate asked.

"I repressed that memory," Chris said, chuckling. "Actually, I was just offering a *reductio* of all that past lives talk. After all, why do we restrict our past lives' memories to the recent past or the same species or some modern life form? Why not ancestral? Why not plants? Or, for that matter, why not aliens?"

"So, what do you think happens when we die?" Simon asked.

"You cease to exist," Chris said. "It's just like before you were born. You were nonexistent. Did you have a hard time before you were born?"

"I don't like that answer much," Simon complained. "But if we're this complex biological structure; well, I can see the point." He lapsed into silence.

Although he was driving, Will raised a theological point with God. "Didn't you or your son, who is supposed to be you, die and then come back to life?"

"People keep holding onto that," God said, "and you keep asking me that. So once more from the top. Will, what am I?"

"You're God."

"No, I didn't ask you for my proper name, I asked you *what* I am."

"Okay, you're *a* god."

"And what is a god?"

"A very powerful being who can do lots of things that we humans can't."

"Like what?"

"I don't know. Part seas, cause hurricanes, impregnate virgins." Will was starting to have fun.

"Wrong answer. What is a crucial characteristic of gods?"

"You don't get sick, and you never die."

"Bingo."

"If you can't die, then you can't be resurrected," Will reasoned. "But what if you're also wholly human?" Will began to remember a bit of theology.

"Beats me," God said. "Quite frankly, that makes no sense. If you're wholly human, you're mortal; if you're a god, you're immortal. I would say, make up your mind."

"Perhaps it's a mystery that we have to accept on faith."

"It's a *mystery* all right," God said. "If faith means accepting contradictions, then I don't know how you can reject anything. Everything follows from a contradiction. You just threw reason out with the bathwater, to use a mixed metaphor."

By then they were in Dallas traffic and not far from the mission. Will's thoughts shifted from theology and eschatology to Cindy. Soon, he turned into the mission parking lot and parked next to his pickup truck.

"Here we are," Will announced to his sleepy companions.

Their arrival did not go unnoticed. Cindy came flying out the door and crushed Will against the van as she pressed her lips against his. She smelled strongly of the dish soap that the mission used in its kitchen.

"Come in, be welcome," Sister Sara said, joining the group. "Are all of you coming to help us out?" She was astonished, and her eyes opened even wider as Marc emerged from the van.

Introductions took only a few minutes, and then they went inside. It was well past dinner hour, but Delbert had saved some food for them. Leaving bags and suitcases in the hall, they crowded around the staff/chopping table in the kitchen. Sister Ellie joined them, and the two sisters hovered around the table as Will and his friends devoured their late dinner.

"Yes," Will finally answered Sister Sara's question. "We all came to help out. Marc is a plumber and knows some carpentry. Chris is a whiz with electronics and appliances. Kate, Simon, Teri, and I can be all-purpose help."

Tears filled Sister Sara's eyes. "Bless you all. A few of us have been holding this place together with help from several of the guests. We have a full house of men and women as well as two girls staying in the girls' units, both of whom are pregnant." Sister Sara stopped, unable to go on.

Sister Ellie stepped forward. "I should also tell you we are short of cash. We can pay you for a couple of weeks, but it's hard to see beyond that. We really need help. Our computers are down, our phones are cutting out, the van needs work, and there are definite short-term and long-term plumbing problems," she said, looking at Marc. "I should also tell you that we are no longer nuns of the Catholic Church. We have been excommunicated. But, now I have a surprise for you all, especially Will, Chris, and Marc."

Sister Ellie left the room for a few minutes. When she returned, Sam Willingham was in her company. "Sam is a guest at the mission."

"I'll be…" Chris was speechless, but he and Marc were already giving Rev hugs and back slaps. Will joined in the reunion.

"Yes, I've returned for the trial," Rev said. "The possible charges against me have been set aside in return for my testimony. I came by here, because I knew the good sisters, and I may be able to help with the funding problems."

"You've already given us a generous donation, Sam," Sister Sara said.

"I intend to raise more money for you, and I want to get a foundation board going that will do that regularly. Those who know me know that my practices have not always been, well, legal, but I've changed a lot, and I see here a genuine cause in need of funds. People tell me I'm convincing, and I hope to use that ability on your behalf."

"You might start with my father," Simon volunteered. "He has lots of money and is always looking for good causes for charitable contributions."

Given Sam's history, Will wondered at the wisdom of Simon's suggestion.

"Perhaps, young Simon," Sam said, "we can make him a proposal. Right now, however, I'm concentrating my efforts on some of the local churches and individuals whom I know and have worked with before."

By the time they had drunk a couple of bottles of wine, which Delbert kindly provided, and moved their bags into the living areas upstairs, it was getting late, and the sisters warned them that morning came early at the mission. Will and Cindy had Arie and Malcolm's old room. Marc and Oga had Will's. Kate and Teri moved their things to a room near the sisters. Simon and Chris shared a newly opened room next to Marc's.

Alone at last, Cindy and Will cuddled in bed.

"You have no idea how much I have wanted this moment," Cindy said.

"Me, too." Will sighed. "It seems like a hundred years since I was in Oldstown."

There was a lot more snuggling.

"We have to go see my aunt and uncle soon," Will said dreamily.

"I know we do," Cindy replied. "But you know what? I've already met them."

Will looked at her, astonished. "How?"

"They stopped by the mission about a week ago. They were in town for some medical tests on your aunt. She's doing really well, but, as you know, she has a heart condition. This was just a routine checkup. When they came by, I was a mess after cleaning up the dining hall. I kept trying to brush the dirt off myself. I was so embarrassed that I must have been beet red. And you know what your dear, dear uncle did? He reached out and pulled me into a hug and said, 'Daughter, don't ever be embarrassed about doing good works. We're proud of you and Will for helping here.' And your aunt reached out and gently touched my grimy cheek. They made me feel like family."

Will smiled. "That sounds like Uncle John and Aunt Rita."

"They expect us this coming weekend, and the sisters know we need to visit them. You'll be back in time for the trial."

"I'm not going to be much good around here for a couple of weeks," Will said. "I'm so nervous about testifying."

"Will, you just brought an incredible crew to the mission. It's exactly what they need to keep going. There've been a growing number of conflicts in the wards at night. People are so frustrated and angry. They can't get work. The government doesn't understand that they need to add jobs, spend money on infrastructure, and create a better safety net. The Church doesn't care either. All they want to do is tell the world that they excommunicated the sisters. Will, your crew *is* our hope of survival."

The rest of the evening and well into the night was taken up with talk about being together and Will's friends, whom Cindy seemed to like a lot, and of course, Cindy wanted to know how Will felt about meeting his mother.

"That must have been a shock to accidentally discover your mother. Nothing can prepare you for that."

"I'm still struggling with it," Will admitted. "I know how to contact her. I sort of want to, and I sort of don't. I have loving and caring people all around me. It's made me appreciate what my aunt and uncle have given me all these years. I think I need to talk to them and you about it more, but right now, I'm just trying to come to grips with the fact that I have found my mother."

"Okay, hit the showers, love, if you want more snuggles," Cindy said, because she realized Will would have much more to say on the subject another time.

After they made love, Will dropped in on God for a brief goodnight. But God seemed as exhausted as Will and did not have much to say except that he thought Oga was really cute.

HOME II

Will and Cindy sat quietly in the S-10 pickup at the head of the lane leading to his aunt and uncle's home. Will had been away most of the summer and into fall. The flowerbeds were not as neglected as Will had predicted. He wondered who was doing the work. The house looked a little smaller than he remembered.

The two days previous had been chaotic to say the least. The theme park crew had all been put to work. Will learned the new protocols for food pickups and found he enjoyed taking on that job again. Chris attacked all tasks mechanical and electronic with his usual manic frenzy—and Simon's help. Now the mission truck started on the first try, the computer system was back on line, and one of the old freezers was running once again. Marc had all the showers working and was tearing out the old urinals and replacing them with donated water-saving models. Kate and Teri took the two young girls under their wing, and a third girl indicated she would like to come and stay.

"I'm more hopeful today than I have been for the past six weeks," Sister Sara said. "I don't know what to do with myself; there are so many hands pitching in."

"Where did you find these wonderful people?" Sister Ellie asked.

"That's a rather long story," Will replied.

After he gave her a quick sketch of how he had met his friends, she stopped him.

"Hold that story until you're back from visiting your family," she said, "The details sound too good to miss."

Following the early shift at the mission, Cindy and Will headed east to

Shreveport for a weekend visit. Cindy drove to the front door. She already had warm feelings toward Will's aunt and uncle. It was good fortune that they had already met. She and Will had agreed that although they would prefer to sleep together, they would abide by aunt and uncle's wishes, which they assumed would be separate rooms.

Aunt Rita and Uncle John came to the door together. "Welcome, home, son and you, too, Cindy," Aunt Rita said as she gave them heartfelt hugs.

Delicious smells greeted them as they brought their bags inside. "I know you're tired after a morning shift and the drive over here. Go freshen up. John will put your bags in the guest room; it has an adjoining bath." Will was astonished and exchanged a smile with Cindy. Here he was with his aunt and uncle, and they were acknowledging that he and Cindy could sleep together in their home even though they were not married.

As Will and Uncle John went on to put the bags away, Cindy pulled Aunt Rita aside. "Are you sure it's all right if Will and I stay together?"

Aunt Rita had a twinkle in her eye when she answered. "This way one of you won't have to get up in the middle of the night and sneak into the other's room. Seriously, Cindy, a few months ago I wouldn't have been comfortable with this arrangement, but I know a bit about what you've been through together. I've changed in many ways since my heart troubles. I'm not so eager to leave this life. I love it here, and I'm happy seeing healthy joy in those I love. I see that in you and Will. Now get along, and thank you for coming to our home."

The warm reception Cindy received was overwhelming to her. The welcome continued. She was included in the round robin family prayer. The sincerity of her thanks for the Tillit family brought a sniffle from Aunt Rita.

Later, Will and Cindy cleaned up the dishes, put the leftovers away, and fed the patient dogs. It was their second kitchen shift of the day, and they were in bed and asleep at the same time as Aunt Rita, who retired early.

The next day was full of reminiscence and stories. They all went for an easy walk in the woods. As was the custom, the dogs joined them—although Will missed the lumbering energy of Bubba, who had died while he was gone. They showed Cindy some of their favorite haunts, and they laughed over the failed cemetery. Uncle John confessed he did not know what he was thinking when be started the funeral business, and Aunt Rita confessed that during that time, she half expected zombies complaining about damp graves to visit her door. At Will's old treehouse, they admired the poison ivy patch that guarded it. After a little while Aunt Rita turned back for the house. Cindy went with her, Aunt Rita's arm in Cindy's. Uncle John and Will continued.

After their walk, Will and Cindy prepared lunch. As they ate, they discovered that, just as they had been through an adventurous summer and fall, so had Will's aunt and uncle. With several trips to a specialist in Dallas, Aunt Rita's medical condition had taken up a good bit of time and money. Uncle John had given several guest sermons at local churches whose congregations were returning. The surprise of the summer was a phone call from their sister, Mary-Rose. She told them about Will's stop at the dentist and said she hoped to visit them. Perhaps the most unexpected thing for all was that his mother and her husband had pledged significant money toward Will's college fund, a promise that would take a huge burden off of his aunt and uncle.

"How do you feel about your mother coming back into your life?" Aunt Rita asked Will.

"I have mixed emotions," Will admitted. "When Cindy asked me the same question, one thing that was clear to me was how much I love you and Uncle John. You're my true parents. I think part of my concern is that she might try to claim some of that, which I think belongs to you. I don't want you to feel that she replaces either of you. I'm here with the three people I love the most. After that it's Sister Sara, Sister Ellie, and a couple of aging felons." Will started to tear up, as did everyone else at the table.

"Thank you, Will, that was a most beautiful speech to my ears," Aunt Rita said.

"I think we're too solid for this minor turbulence to upset our family," Uncle John said. He squeezed Will's arm and held Cindy's hand at the same time.

"I agree," Aunt Rita said. "On another note, have you thought more about what you might want to study when you go on to college, Will?"

"Actually, I have. I want to do something in the medical field—nurse or medical technician—and I want to continue working part-time at the mission. There are good schools in the Dallas area."

"What about you, Cindy?" Uncle John asked.

"Well, I'm good at math, and I'm thinking about becoming a CPA with maybe a degree in business. I can do that easily at a school in Dallas so Will and I don't have to be apart. My mom left me some money for college, but I also want to work part-time at the mission. Perhaps I can specialize in nonprofit accounting."

Aunt Rita and Uncle John were pleased with these plans. They launched into a series of questions about the summer, Will's time at Galilee, his kidnapping, and Cindy's struggles with her parents' insurance company. They were particularly interested in the mission. Both Uncle John and Aunt Rita had been very impressed with the sisters and their ambitious plans.

Lunch lasted until late afternoon, whereupon Aunt Rita took a nap, Uncle John rested, and they all agreed to go up to Shreveport for some good Cajun cooking.

That evening, they drove by the New Word Prosperity Apostolic Life Congregation. It was a Saturday, and the parking lot had several cars in it, but the facility by no means looked like it was bustling. Will asked how the church was doing.

"Attendance is way down," Uncle John said. "Steady was sued by his wives in California, and they won a large settlement. I think the people here got tired of their church donations going to his ex-wives. And they learned they wanted to go to a church where the pastor knew their name." Uncle John tried unsuccessfully not to gloat.

Aunt Rita turned to Cindy. "Excuse me for being nosey. I know your father was a pastor, but I suspect you're not terribly religious?"

"True," Cindy admitted. "I lost a lot of my faith when I was treated so badly in high school and when my father threw me out of the house and wouldn't allow my mother to mention my name in his presence. I admit I did some foolish things, for which I apologized, but nothing seemed to matter. There was no forgiveness. I'm not a promiscuous woman, really, Aunt Rita."

"I never thought you were," Aunt Rita replied with a smile. She reached over and touched Cindy. "I shouldn't have pried into that. I used to believe that the only good people were Christians, and I used to believe that unless you accepted Jesus Christ as your redeemer, you wouldn't be saved."

This statement from Aunt Rita left Will astonished for the second time since he had come home. All his life he had heard her expound salvific exclusivism, and she had just said she did not believe that anymore. "What do you believe now?" he asked. Will was more than curious.

Aunt Rita looked at him. "I suspect your religious convictions have changed as well, but I don't care as much about that as I used to. The change began with my illness. About a month after you left, Will, I fainted in the supermarket. Alice Rosenberg took me to the hospital and then brought me home. She was very kind—we're in garden club together—but you know, she's Jewish. She never goes to synagogue, and she admitted to me that she's what she called a 'secular Jew'. She doesn't believe in God or that she's part of a chosen people. At the time, it shocked me, but we've always gotten along, and she lives just down the road. Anyway, she came by regularly and helped your Uncle John. He's a wonderful man, but he's not real good at domestic chores," she said with a laugh that got a smile from Uncle John. "She cooked some for us and got others to bring us meals. I wasn't feeling well a lot of the time, and a good bit of that was getting used to what seemed like the hundreds of pills I had to start taking. John was wonderful about helping me organize my medicine. Alice took time to visit me regularly. She was more than kind; she was a true friend." Aunt Rita paused and took a deep breath.

Cindy touched her arm. "You don't have to tell us more if you don't want to."

"Oh, but I do want to talk about it."

"I wish you had told me all this was going on, I would have come straight home," Will said.

"I know you would have, dear," Aunt Rita responded. "That's precisely why I didn't tell you. If my illness had been life-threatening, I would have told you right away.

"Anyway, I began to think that good people like Alice surely do not go to hell. God wouldn't punish someone like her. After all, she grew up in a Jewish community; her parents were Jewish. She never really learned anything about Christianity. Yet, she's as good as anyone I know. Now I think that if people try, really try, to live a life of caring for others and treating others well, then there's a place for them in heaven, even if they're atheists." Aunt Rita remained thoughtful. "I know that your uncle has always believed that good people are good people and that they will find favor with God. He probably influenced me as well."

Cindy obviously found Aunt Rita's views compatible with her own. "I went through much the same process. After I was thrown out of my house, I went to stay with a friend whose parents were not religious. They were very kind to me and kept giving me the message that I was a good person, that being a good person was something I could control even if I made the occasional mistake. My dad made me feel like trash, like I was hopeless and depraved."

Will was having a hard time listening to what Cindy's father had said and done to her.

"Relax," God said. "These things need saying, and you need to hear them. Loving someone is about knowing the hurts as well as the triumphs."

Will sat back and listened.

"I began to realize," Cindy continued, "that most of us form our religious beliefs under the influence of others, and we do it mostly as children when we really have no critical faculties with which to challenge what's being fed to us. We also grow up in a particular culture where having these beliefs is necessary to our acceptance by our peers and the adults around us. I don't think we choose our beliefs; beliefs just come to us as we stagger through life. It also seems clear to me that no one has found a way of convincing everyone that their religion is the right one."

"Amen to that," Uncle John said.

Aunt Rita gave Cindy's hand a squeeze. "Thank you for giving me more reasons for my new convictions. I like your way of putting it."

Will looked at Cindy with new admiration. "I agree. You really helped to clarify my thinking. It never felt right that only those lucky enough to be born into the *true* faith should be eligible to be saved."

"I'm glad someone clarifies things for you," God said. "God knows I've been trying for years to smarten you up."

"Oh, go away," Will said with a smile.

At dinner, Uncle John became a bit reflective. Will decided to ask him how his religious convictions had changed, if at all, over the summer.

"I've been thinking quite a bit about my faith and what it means to me," Uncle John began. "I think Rita and I both have been moved by acts of kindness. Although I didn't grow up thinking well of Catholics, I was really inspired by the sisters, whom I understand are not really Catholics anymore anyway. Their commitment to helping others become strong enough to help themselves really struck me as foundational to a healthy religious perspective. It also sent me off into thoughts about one of the oldest fissures in religion."

"I think I know what that fissure is," Will said. "Redemption versus works; grace versus works; individual salvation versus community, and all that."

Uncle John nodded. "Right. A lot of the preaching these days has to do with redemption. We're just a depraved lot who need Christ's death to redeem our souls. That kind of preaching always puts me in mind of Vernon Johns, a somewhat irascible, early twentieth century Baptist preacher and black leader. After hearing a sermon on redemption, he said something like 'If that's what Christianity is all about, God could have dropped Jesus into the world on Friday, had him killed on Saturday, yanked him back to heaven on Easter Sunday, and been done with it. But instead, we have the life of Jesus to study and the lessons to learn from that, and many of those lessons are to respect others and treat them well. In other words, do good works.'"

"You've always thought that way, John," Aunt Rita said. "We've always tried to show kindness to others and help them become what they can become. I was not good to your mother, Will, but I think, with this second chance, we might restore our sisterhood at long last."

"My dad was always into redemption," Cindy said. "Of course, our church did things for the poor, but the sermons were always about what sinners we were and how we needed to find redemption in the Lord. But my dad never was able to forgive me. And he was convinced that he would be raptured while the rest of us would be left behind. What I don't understand is why we can't have both redemption and good works. Why can't good works be valued as part of our redemption?"

"That does make sense, Cindy," Aunt Rita replied. "However, those who stress redemption often do so because they believe we are utterly incapable of bringing about our own salvation, and to admit that good works count is to admit that we have some influence over our salvation. It's how many people think about redemption that blocks your synthesis of redemption and good works."

Uncle John had a further thought. "You know, when I study the Bible, and I am not alone in this, I think that Jesus was all about good works, and he sought to create a kingdom on earth, a better place in which to live. Just look at the passages where he says it will happen in the lifetimes of his contemporaries. But he failed; he got caught and executed before his message could flower. Later writers tried to save something out of this disaster, and that means they had to make his death theologically significant. They did that by making it a redemptive death. I suspect many Christians emphasize that, because it allows them to ignore the failure of their messiah. I don't know that they really believe this, but it's an arguable point. And it certainly pulls people into the language of redemption, whereas the kingdom on Earth draws one toward good works."

"That's putting it out there," God said to Will. "Your Uncle John just came to the same conclusion as Arie. But what he said actually makes sense of the gospels, especially John's emphasis on redemption."

"Is that what happened, was it a failed ministry and a scramble to save it?"

"You have to figure that one out for yourself," God replied. "But I really like the idea of good works, and you and Cindy seem to be in the right place at the right time for that."

Sunday afternoon came all too soon. After a good breakfast, they attended Pastor Bob Williams' church, where the sermon was more about redemption than any of them would have liked.

Afterwards, Aunt Rita rested while Will, Cindy, and Uncle John took a walk. Will talked about the trial that was expected to begin that week. He was nervous. Agent Smith had called Will while he was at home and set up a session with him for the following Tuesday.

Aunt Rita was smiling as they were about to leave.

"What's making you smile so much?" Will asked.

"Okay, here are some of my thoughts that make me smile. I'm thinking about the boy we sent off a few months ago and all the things that have happened to him: he fell in love with a lovely, tornado-riding woman, to whom he loaned his truck; he worked in a mission, got kidnapped, met a nice FBI agent, wrestled a large snake, talked to aliens, reconnected with his mother, and made some wonderful, if felonious, friends. Will, if I was going to plan you a summer, I wouldn't have left out a single thing. Plus, you've provided your old aunt with a wealth of stories to tell her friends."

Uncle John gave one of his big laughs. "That's for sure. We're proud of you, Will. I have just one request. If you two ever decide to get married, and, mind you, I'm not pushing for it, I'd like the honor of performing the ceremony. I'll do it the way you want. But Cindy, I know I speak for Aunt Rita and myself in saying that whatever you and Will decide, we regard you as one of the family."

Cindy misted up. "Damn it, Uncle John, I knew you'd say something like that and make me cry just as I'm leaving. But thank you both. I've not had a family for a few years, and it feels awfully good."

Cindy gave her goodbye hugs to Will's aunt and uncle, as did Will.

On the road again, Cindy and Will basked in the remnant warmth of the visit. They chatted about their favorite moments with Aunt Rita and Uncle John. Then Will's cell phone rang. It was Agent Smith.

"Hello," Will said. He was glad that Cindy was driving. He had been dreading the call about the trial; he hoped for another continuance.

"Will, I have good news. John Steel confessed to the charges. His crew turned on him, and he admitted to the crimes, justifying them because he claims he was just exercising his religious freedom. But that's all we need for a conviction. You're off the hook."

Will's heart soared. "Thank you, thank you for the news." He gave Cindy a thumbs-up. "I am so relieved."

"I knew you would be, and I am, too. The evidence was so overwhelming that a trial seemed a waste of money. I also want you to know that I'm stationed in the Dallas/Fort Worth area now, and I plan to do a bit at the mission, which is not far from my office."

"That would be great!"

"See you soon."

Will smiled all the way to the mission.

God was happy, too. "Now Cindy and I don't have to deal with a basket case."

TRUDY

The next day as work began, Will and Cindy learned that the sisters had finally addressed a question that had been confusing the staff: What should they call the sisters now that they were no longer nuns? The answer was that since they had worn their sister tags so long and since they were still in the same line of work, there was no need to change unless they wanted to just use the sisters' first names.

Mission life was normal, which meant everyone was working very hard. Will and Simon found themselves needing to call on quite a number of suppliers in their effort to get enough groceries for the next few days. Turkey drumsticks and some cheeses were available, but other sources of protein were scarce. Delbert had threatened them with endless Vulcan turkey tetrazzini if they brought more turkey legs back to the mission, and they were already very tired of turkey tetrazzini. Even God said he was bored with it because of Will complaining about it.

The mission was also facing such a surge in demand that they had to turn some people away. There were long lines at mealtime and before evening check in. Unemployment remained high both nationally and in the Dallas/Fort Worth area. Statistics showed there were roughly five workers for every job opening, and so many jobs did not pay a living wage. Any hope for fewer needy was futile. Many clients were men and women denied unemployment insurance. In a fit of austerity, retraining programs had been cut along with benefits. Veterans faced similar cuts, because politicians, not caring about the misery they had caused by starting wars, had cut spending for the social safety net in order to maintain tax cuts for their wealthy patrons.

Simon was excited, because his father was planning to visit the mission. "He has a lot of money, so I hope he or his foundation will want to help us out."

While Simon was hopeful about his father's visit, Will also detected an underlying anxiety. Simon, after all, was supposed to be in seminary, not working in a shelter. He admitted to Will that he had fibbed and told his father that he was "called" to work at the mission. In fact, under Chris' sponsorship, Simon was taking computer science classes online. How he got enrolled remained unknown, although Will suspected some hacking was involved.

The positive news was that Sam Willingham had had some success in creating a core of donors. He brought in a pledge of $100,000 from a local urologist, which was to be paid out over the next ten months. The sisters still harbored some suspicions about Sam, and they asked Will directly if he thought Sam could be trusted.

Will was not sure. "Sam has basically been kind to me and generally leveled with me. But he has a history of cons that goes way back. Even the FBI admits he is a man of mystery. But it seems to me that if one of you goes with him to talk to donors, and, of course, you'll have to take charge of any advisory board, there shouldn't be a lot of opportunity for his shenanigans, to use one of my aunt's favorite terms."

"Certainly, we need to monitor his activities," Sister Ellie said. "Would you be willing to work with the board if Sara or Cindy or I can't be present?"

"Of course," Will agreed.

Will and Simon turned into the parking lot and backed up to the loading door. Delbert met them on the dock and glared at the boxes of frozen turkey drumsticks piled in the back of the truck, but he brightened when he saw some boxes of cured hams and bags of potatoes. They unloaded and headed into a staff meeting that was usually held during the lunch hour.

Just before the meeting, Kate came in and told Sister Sara and Sister Ellie that they needed to come and speak to a new client whom had been admitted, a young girl named Trudy Driscol. "I think you need to hear her story as soon as possible so we can begin to figure out what to do. Right now, she's comfortable and seems willing to talk."

The staff meeting was delayed an hour. A plate of turkey sandwiches was passed around, and the others were told to enjoy lunch and a cup of tea while the sisters talked to the newcomer.

They found Trudy in the lounge area of the new girls' unit. Teri sat beside her.

Sister Sara opened the conversation. "Hello, Trudy, are you comfortable here? Has Delbert's cuisine stimulated your appetite?" She noted that this small, fourteen-year-old was very thin. Her bony arms were folded across her chest. Her oily hair was dark. She maintained a defiant frown.

"The food is okay."

"Trudy, we're here to help you. We're on your side. Would you tell us what brought you here? Please?" Sister Sara looked directly into Trudy's eyes.

"I don't think there's anything you can do for me. You're nuns, and you don't believe in abortions." Trudy broke eye contact.

"Trudy, we're *former* nuns," Sister Ellie said. "The Church kicked us out. Please don't judge us too quickly."

Trudy brightened. "Wow, you really must have pissed off the Pope!"

Sister Sara glanced at Ellie. "You have no idea." That comment got a small smile out of Trudy. "So, what happed to you?" Sister Sara said gently.

Trudy sat a little straighter. "I don't want to talk about it."

"Is there anyone here you would talk to?"

"Can I just talk to Teri and Kate?"

"Of course," Sister Ellie said.

She and Sister Sara returned to the meeting.

"Please tell us your story," Kate encouraged Trudy.

"I used to babysit a lot for this couple in my hometown in Pennsylvania," Trudy began. "They have a three-year old baby, Coleen. Her father, Tom Wilder, is a deacon in the church I attended. His wife, Lana, teaches Sunday school. They're big buddies with the pastor and his wife, Reverend and Mrs. Tarker. Anyway, one night about a month ago, I was babysitting Coleen. I was staying overnight, because a bunch of us kids from the church were leaving early for a weeklong retreat. Wilder and his wife were leading the retreat, and that night they were working late at the church getting ready.

"Coleen was asleep, and I was watching TV when Tom came home unexpectedly. He said he'd just come to check on us, but he didn't leave. He just stood there looking at me. He told me that I was a pretty girl, and then he came over and sat next to me. I was uncomfortable and said I wanted to go home. He said 'sure,' and then he stood up, grabbed me, and held me down, and..." Trudy stopped and took a deep breath. "Shit, he raped me right there. He was so strong, and I don't have a lot of muscle." Trudy had told her story completely dry-eyed, but now she began to cry.

Kate held Trudy's hands in her own. "You can stop anytime if it hurts too much to talk about it," she said, her own eyes filled with tears.

"Oh, it gets better," Trudy responded. "Wilder didn't take me home; he took me to the Tarkers, and while they talked, they locked me in a room with no window. I heard the reverend say that he could handle my parents, who didn't expect me home for a week. They're big Reverend Tarker fans and friends with Wilder.

"That night, they fed me and let me have a small TV. Reverend Tarker came in and told me that I had sinned in the eyes of the Lord by seducing Wilder, and if this were Old Testament times, I would be put to death. But since these were modern times, I would have to apologize to the Wilders for my sin instead."

Teri exploded with rage. "They asked *you* to apologize to the rapist?"

Trudy wiped her nose and nodded. "Yep. I asked and asked to call my parents. I wanted to talk to the police, too. They told me that was impossible. They also told me that a good Christian doesn't accuse another Christian of a crime."

"That same night, they put me in a car with a strange man and woman. They drove straight through to Dallas except for potty stops. Then they locked me up in the home of Reverend Rheve. His wife, Mrs. Rheve, insisted I write a letter to the Wilders apologizing for my seduction. She said I would not get fed until I did. I refused anyway, and they stopped giving me food, and he was so angry when I wouldn't obey that he shook me real hard. But yesterday, they got a little careless with the lock, and I slipped out of the house and hid in an abandoned building. I spent one night on the street and then came here. I should call my parents, but they're so thick with the church crowd I don't trust them. I really don't know what to do."

Trudy paused. "I'm afraid I might be pregnant from the rape, and I can't get the image of that man on top of me out of my head."

As if she had just exhausted herself, Trudy pushed her back and head against the cushions and collapsed. Then she sat back up, "Please believe me; it's all true."

Both Kate and Teri were having trouble with their own feelings.

"Trudy, we do believe you, and we'll protect you," Kate said, "But we have to figure out the best way to do that."

"Well, one thing is for sure. Reverend Rheve will come to get me. From the way he shook me, he can be scary-violent."

"We can deal with violent," Kate said. "Have you met Marc?"

Trudy smiled. "Yes, he let me feed a carrot to Oga. I don't think even Reverend Rheve will push Marc around. Could one of you just sit here with me? I don't want to be alone."

"Of course," Teri said. "I'll stay. But, Kate has to go to the meeting."

"Do you think Marc would bring Oga, too?" Trudy asked.

"I'll track down Marc and Oga on my way to the meeting," Kate said.

It was a small group at the meeting, just Simon, Will, Cindy, Kate, and the sisters. Trudy's situation needed to be dealt with first so Sister Sara asked Kate to update everyone. Sister Sara looked at her staff's sad, serious faces. She realized this kind of horror story was new to them.

Sister Ellie broke the silence that followed Kate's report. "We think those trying to cover up the crime will come and demand that Trudy be turned over to them. We can't do that. I've asked Wanda, who's at the front desk, to lock the front door and only admit known clients for now. Does anyone have any suggestions as to what we might do to further protect this child?"

"We could change her name and simply deny that she's here," Simon suggested.

"The mission risks a lot if we're caught," Sister Ellie said.

"Can we go to the authorities?" Kate asked. "Do we have some friends in Child Protective Services or the police department?"

"That's a possibility, but the truth is that supervisors are unpredictable, and even if we get a good case worker, we risk having her sent right back," Sister Ellie said. "We should call her parents, but Trudy doesn't think that's a good idea."

"Why don't I call Agent Smith?" Will suggested. "I'm no expert in the law, but if Trudy was transported across state lines unwillingly, isn't that a federal crime?"

Everyone liked that idea, so Will put in a call to her. She didn't pick up, so he left an urgent message briefly describing the problem at the mission.

The rest of the meeting dealt with work assignments for regular staff and for volunteers. The schedule was going to be affected by the departure of Teri who had to go home because of a family illness.

Sister Ellie also reported that the wards had been much calmer since Marc arrived. He often walked through them with one of the sisters in the evening, and the sheer bulk of his presence made the quarrelsome less so. But more than that, Marc had a gentle way of saying 'hello' to everyone. "He remembers their names and a bit about them," Sister Ellie said. "He's like Delbert in that regard, and they love him. Many of our clients are usually ignored on the street. Passersby don't even like to make eye contact with the homeless."

There was a knock on the door. It was Wanda. "There are two men outside demanding to be let in to see the person in charge," she said. "I think it's about the new girl."

The sisters left the meeting and went downstairs. They said the others didn't need to come, but Simon, Will, and Cindy followed. Kate headed back to alert Teri, Marc, and Trudy.

Two men stood or rather paced on the front steps of the mission. The sisters unlocked the door and greeted them. A heavy man stepped into the front hall.

"I am Reverend Rheve, and I want to know if you have a Trudy Driscol here."

"By what authority do you ask?" Sister Ellie replied.

"I'm her guardian."

"Do you have any papers legally establishing your guardianship?"

"Her parents and her pastor back in Pennsylvania asked me to look after her. That is sufficient for me."

"Legally, that's not enough for us," Sister Ellie said. "Who's your companion?"

"Warren is a member of my congregation and a member of the Dallas police force, currently off duty," Reverend Rheve replied.

"Then I think he will understand that we are a private charity, and we do not give out the names of residents unless there is a clear line of authority or a warrant for such information. Our client list is confidential. I cannot and will not say whether the person you named is here or not."

"That child is my responsibility; I think we'll look around anyway,"

Reverend Rheve said. He began to move toward the door of the men's wing, but Sister Sara, flanked by Will, Simon, and Cindy stepped in front of the door, blocking his way.

"No one enters this facility without permission," Sister Sara said.

Reverend Rheve started to put his hands on Sister Sara's shoulders to push her aside, but Will and Simon seized his arms, lifted him off the ground, and pushed him back a couple of steps.

"Keep your hands to yourself," Will said.

"Be careful, Reverend," Warren advised.

"Damn you, get out of my way, this is important," Rheve demanded.

Just then, Will felt the phone in his pocket vibrate.

"I want you to leave immediately," Sister Ellie said. "You're trespassing on private property, and you're being physically aggressive. Now off with both of you!"

At that moment, Delbert heard the commotion and came into the entryway. That was too much for the Reverend Rheve and Warren. They left, although Rheve informed them that he would be back that evening.

Will was in a corner explaining to Agent Smith that the situation was getting worse. He emphasized that the reverend threatened to come back. After he hung up, he addressed the group. "Agent Smith will be here as soon as she can. She's just finishing up an interview. Her advice is not to give up the girl or reveal her presence. She will talk to her and then, when appropriate, the parents."

Sister Ellie turned to Cindy. "I want you to go tell the others about Agent Smith's visit. Let Trudy know that she's been a friend to us and has been a big help."

Entering the lounge area of the girls' unit, Cindy saw Trudy sitting on a couch feeding a piece of lettuce to Oga. Marc sat smiling and watching Oga's ecstatic pleasure at such simple fare. Teri sat with an arm protectively around Trudy's shoulders. Teri responded at once to Cindy's entry.

"Trudy, this is Cindy who works closely with the sisters."

"Who was that? Did they come for me?" Trudy demanded.

"Yes, but they didn't get in," Cindy said.

Trudy still looked a little suspicious.

Cindy suppressed her anger at the intruders and tried to sound calm. "They came, and we refused them entry and didn't tell them you were here. We're not giving you up."

Trudy liked that, but she still frowned. "They'll get a court order or something. That deacon rapist will be down here so he can protect his own ass. If he comes, Marc, will you kill him for me?"

Marc looked surprised for a moment. "No, killing is wrong. How about if I just hurt him real bad?"

Trudy laughed. "I like you, Marc. If I am pregnant, I want to be rid of the thing inside me. Every time I think it might be there, I want to throw up. How can I get rid of it when I have to have my parents' permission? My parents are opposed to abortion."

"Trudy, we don't know for sure if you're pregnant, and don't sell the sisters short; they are pretty clever," Cindy said. "We talked about your situation and called a friend who's an FBI agent."

She got no further as Trudy jumped up off the couch. "No, no! They'll take me home."

"No, please listen, Trudy," Kate said. "Agent Smith will understand, and you will be protected. What they did to you was a federal crime. I've seen Agent Smith in action. Please give her a chance."

In the early evening, Agent Smith arrived. She was dressed casually, and her approach was friendly. She put an arm on Marc's shoulder. "How are you doing big man? How's Oga?" She turned to Trudy. "Hello Trudy. I'm here to help. Can we talk?"

"I want my friends to stay while we talk," Trudy responded.

"I'd be happy to have them stay."

"Trudy, is it all right if I go out and let them know you're in conference and safe with Teri, Kate, Marc, and Agent Smith?" Cindy asked. "We don't want you disturbed."

Trudy nodded. "Sure."

Cindy told Will and Simon and the sisters what was happening. Then she picked up a large accounting book, so as to return it to a file cabinet in the reception area. Will and Simon were in the kitchen cleaning up from the evening meal. Will was about to run an errand for Delbert when

Wanda opened the door for a late client who had asked entry. Six men who had been waiting outside for just such an opportunity forced their way into the lobby.

Reverend Rheve grabbed Wanda and told her to be quiet. "Look in the back!" he told his confederates.

Three men moved off toward the other units. Will, who had just come out of the kitchen, moved to block them, but the two men with Rheve pushed him to the floor so the other three could slip by. Will was not a fighter, nor was he easily subdued. Two men were inadequate to hold Will down so when Reverend Rheve tried to help them, Wanda got free and let out a cry for help. This brought Cindy with her accounting book to the lobby, and Simon and Delbert emerged from the kitchen.

One of the men trying to hold Will down had his hand on the floor, balancing against Will's struggles. Delbert, who was carrying a small cleaver, nimbly nipped off most of the man's index finger as if chopping a carrot. At same time, Cindy clobbered the second man on the head with the accounting book, and Simon launched himself onto the man who had been holding Will and punched him in the stomach. These counterattacks were too much, and the three men fled into the night.

The sisters arrived in time to see Delbert scoop up the index finger and say, "At last, a piece of meat that isn't turkey."

"No, it's evidence," Agent Smith said, who was escorting the last of the invaders through the lobby. "Just put it in the evidence bag."

She held out a small plastic bag, into which Delbert dropped the severed finger.

"Another culinary opportunity wasted," he grumbled, to everyone's amusement.

After Agent Smith left, Kate and Teri told Will what had transpired in the girls' lounge.

"Agent Smith was great with Trudy," Kate said. "She listened and assured her that she would be protected. Our interview was about finished when three guys broke into the room. One of them yelled, 'Get her,' and pointed at Trudy."

"Trudy screamed, and I grabbed her hand and headed for the back alley," Teri added. "Then, Marc let out a roar and stood up, which stopped the intruders in their tracks. Just before he charged them, Agent Smith pulled out her badge and put the trio under arrest."

In late evening, Agent Smith returned to the mission. She was smiling. "Trudy, I have some good news. I talked to your parents. They were horrified to hear what happened to you. Those who locked you up in Pennsylvania, the pastor and his wife and the deacon, are under arrest for kidnapping, rape, and plotting to transport a minor across state lines. We have warrants out for the couple that actually drove you to Texas. Those who tried to grab you here are under arrest for aiding and abetting with the crime of kidnapping. We caught the last three at the hospital, one with a missing finger and the other with a mild concussion.

"Anyway, your parents are relieved to know you're safe. As you know most of their friends and neighbors are members of the church. The arrest of a deacon, his wife, and the pastor and his wife has generated a lot of confusion and anger in the church. Your parents think it might be better for everyone if you stay here for a while. Is that okay with you?"

"Absolutely," Trudy said. "I really don't want to be back there around those church people, anyway. But I want an abortion if I'm pregnant."

"I have good news there as well," Agent Smith said. "They gave their permission—I have a fax from them—for you to have an abortion if you're pregnant. They don't approve of abortions, but when it's their daughter and it's a rape, it's a different story. They do care about you, but their situation is difficult for them. Sister Ellie has a doctor friend, another former nun, who will examine you and perform the abortion, if necessary. Her name is Dr. Karen Strong. It is a very nice clinic. I've used it once myself."

"Wow," Trudy said. "Can someone go with me?"

Agent Smith smiled. "Of course."

"I can't believe the sisters will let me get an abortion."

"It's your choice and your life," Agent Smith said. "Those are their exact words."

Sister Sara came into the room. "Hello, Trudy. I just came by to say we're very happy to have you stay with us and that we have arranged to pay for your visit to the clinic. You deserve to put all this behind you, and we will do everything we can to help you do that. The clinic will also provide counseling to help you sort things out. Karen is a very nice woman with a lot of experience helping people."

"I'll give it a try," Trudy said as she got up off the couch. She walked toward Sister Sara. "Is it okay to hug a nun?"

"Of course. Even *former* nuns need hugs like everyone else," Sister Sara said as she welcomed Trudy's hug.

"I'll bet you're going to want me to study my school subjects while I'm here," Trudy said, trying to look cross.

"You're damn right," Sister Sara said. "And I'll quiz you about them, too."

Trudy sat down again, but she looked pleased. "Thanks everybody. Thanks so much. I'll bet you're really in trouble with the Pope, now."

The next day, Cindy took Trudy to the clinic for a physical examination. A follow-up appointment two weeks later confirmed that Trudy was pregnant. She had an abortion almost immediately and returned feeling a little drowsy. The following day, a new Trudy emerged. She pitched in and helped Wanda wait tables and clear dishes. She and Wanda formed an instant bond. With much laughter, they created the Society of the Bony Armed. No one else was close to being eligible.

Will, Cindy, Kate, Teri, and Simon had one of their after-work sessions with a bit of wine and some crackers and cheese, compliments of Delbert.

Will was surprised and pleased that Simon had backed him up physically against the attackers. He realized that Simon had put on bulk over the summer.

"Hauling hay to one end of that donkey and removing the remains from the other end," Simon said as they all laughed.

"I was really surprised that the sisters allowed Trudy to have an abortion," Kate said. "When it came up, I wasn't sure how I felt about that, but I can see that it was the right thing to do. Trudy is a new person with that burden off her shoulders."

"Yes, but aborting the fetus doesn't punish the person responsible, the rapist," Simon said. "It only hurts the fetus."

"True," Cindy admitted, "but I don't think that is morally relevant. The point of the abortion is not to punish anyone; that's the purpose of the law and courts. The point of the abortion is to free someone from an involuntary 'servitude,' however it is imposed."

"But what if she regrets it later?" Teri asked.

"If she regrets it, that seems like a different thing," Will said, joining the conversation. "Isn't the question whether she has a right to make a choice to disengage herself from a being, in this case, a fetus that was implanted in her through violence and against her will? I think it's absolutely the right thing to do, although I would not have said so even a few months ago. It's her choice now even if she regrets it later, which I'm inclined to doubt given the circumstances."

"I agree," Kate said. "I heard her say her fear of pregnancy was like a monster growing inside her. Every time she thought about it, she felt like she was being raped again. And it brought back the image of the actual rape and rapist. My guess is that she will not regret it, and she would be much more likely to regret continuing the pregnancy. But I've had to change my mind about some things, too."

Simon let out a hiccup. "Sorry, guys. I'm actually with all of you on this one. But my dad will be here at the end of the week, and we better not say anything to him about this incident. He's very conservative and gives lots of money to those anti-abortion groups. He even admires the guys who shot those doctors. He would never give money to the mission if he knew. For that matter, if he gets wind that the nuns who run this place are lesbians, he won't give money either." Simon looked glum.

Will, as usual, tried to cheer him up. "Simon, your dad isn't the only one who can help. I think the sisters are going ahead with setting up an advisory board to help raise funds. And Sam, just today, brought in another pledge of fifty thousand. So I think we can hope for others to help out."

After everyone called it a night, Will and Cindy settled into bed. Will never grew tired of how Cindy felt next to him. "You accountants have a mean swing," he said with a laugh.

"Who says numbers lack weight," Cindy replied. "What has your god got to say about today, Will?"

"We didn't talk much, but when we did, he was both angry and sad. He pointed out that this kind of thing happens too often. The scandal in the Catholic Church is not unlike what goes on in Protestant churches or any place where there are adults who have so much control over the lives of children. It happens in families, it happens with children lured into sexual slavery, it happens in schools, it happens to a whole lot of girls but also boys. But churches with their aura of respectability and supposed safety are not subject to the same kind of public scrutiny as other institutions, which makes them especially dangerous for children. He also said he would like to jam a lightening bolt up that deacon's ass."

"Goodnight, Will," Cindy said. "I like your god, even when he's crude."

TEMPTATION

The preparation for Simon's father's visit was covert. Although the sisters claimed that it was business as usual, they found extra cleaning tasks to assign to staff and the volunteers. Extra help was called in. Simon hid some of his computer science materials, knowing full well that his father would not be pleased that his son was toying with an alternative career. Physically and intellectually, Simon was simply not the same skinny, pious kid worried about his parents' approval that Will knew at the opening of Galilee.

Trudy had became a valued member of the kitchen staff. Delbert and Wanda pledged to put some weight on her, and they fussed over what she ate like a worried nutritionist parent. Trudy soaked up the extra attention and always greeted Wanda and Delbert with hugs. She also endeared herself to Delbert, as she seemed to be the only one at the mission, besides Wanda and Father Duncan, who would listen endlessly to his stories of extraterrestrial abduction.

The crisp fall day got off to a good start. Will and Simon had just gotten back from their food pickup route. They were unloading pallets when a limousine pulled up in front of the mission. The driver opened the door, and out stepped Simon's father. He wore a long coat and an expensive suit. Even Will, who had virtually no experience with designer clothes, recognized that. Simon hopped off the loading dock and went to greet his father.

Simon's father's was also named "Simon Tigard." He wore a serious demeanor. He was a restless man who looked around habitually and observed his circumstances. Some part of his body was constantly in motion; his hands especially seemed to have a life of their own. He was not a big man. Simon topped his father, who Will noticed was wearing elevator shoes.

Simon introduced Will to his father, who expressed admiration at the load of food. As Simon and his father started for the entrance of the mission, Cindy emerged to help Will unload. That led to a further introduction before the two Simons disappeared inside.

Once the truck was unloaded, Will and Cindy arrived in the main lounge just as the tour with Simon's father was beginning. They stopped by the nondenominational chapel, a simple room off the main entrance. A service was about to begin. Different religious leaders came in somewhat irregularly to conduct services. Today's minister, Rabbi Schultz, was a popular visitor, and the chapel was already full. The service-of-the-day poster outside announced her topic: "The Ten Suggestions." A summary of the talk stated that there were multiple versions of the so-called Ten Commandments and the earliest list in Genesis that everyone thought of as *the* Ten Commandments was not called "commandments" in Genesis. That term was applied to a different set, which included some strange instructions, such as never boil a kid in its mother's milk.

Simon's father turned a bit ruddy as he read the description. "The Ten *Suggestions*?" he growled to no one in particular. "What kind of religious service is this anyway?"

"Oops," God said.

The petite rabbi, who happened to be standing nearby greeting those who were coming into the room, turned to him. "It's a biblically accurate religious service to guide those who notice these things when they read Genesis," she said. Then she turned and went into the room to start the service.

Simon's father looked about with a more critical eye. "I thought this was a Christian shelter and you were here on a ministry," he said to Simon and Sister Ellie, who were leading the tour.

"We're nondenominational," Sister Ellie replied calmly. "The homeless and vulnerable are of many faiths, and we try to accommodate them. We are also dependent on volunteer religious leaders. Daily services are held when leaders can find time in their busy schedule to come here. Rabbi Schultz is a very popular speaker who also does counseling. Besides being a rabbi, she has an MSW with a specialty in drug abuse. We find her invaluable."

Simon's father was not impressed. "I'm certain that you could find a Christian with these qualifications."

"I doubt we could find a Christian rabbi," Sister Ellie said with a smile.

Simon's father returned her smile. At least he got the joke.

Will and Cindy hung back; they did not want to get in the way, but for some reason they wanted to be there.

God tapped Will on the shoulder. "This is going to be good," was all he said.

The next stop was the kitchen, where lunch was being prepared. Delbert was fixing his Martian Mac and Cheese. Huge vats of pasta were cooking, and large piles of blended cheese were being grated. As he flew about the kitchen, Delbert spoke a language no one could comprehend. It was very guttural. Trudy was helping to put the clean dishes out where they could be used by those coming for lunch. She and Wanda were chatting as they worked.

"Did Delbert pick up his recipe when he was abducted or did he actually visit Mars?" Trudy asked.

"No, he never visited Mars," Wanda replied. "He was just in the lab in a spaceship, and that's where he got his recipes. Sometimes he changes the story a little. For example, he claims to have visited Venus. I've never heard him say he visited Mars though. Mostly, he was on the ship."

Simon's father stood transfixed. He only caught a snatch of the conversation, but it was enough for him to determine that someone in the vicinity believed that they had been in contact with extraterrestrials.

Simon tried to save the day by saying that Delbert loved to give his recipes names of the planets, although they all came out of *The Joy of Cooking*. Simon's father was not convinced.

The remainder of the tour took in parts of the men's, women's, and the girls' areas. The last housed four girls, two of whom were pregnant. Simon's father went up to one of the girls, named Judy, who was sitting in the lounge area, and asked her point blank if she was going to keep her child or put the child up for adoption. Sister Ellie held her breath.

"I haven't decided yet," Judy replied. "I'll have to have some tests tomorrow. If the baby is healthy, I may put him or her up for adoption. If not, I will probably get an abortion. There's some question as to whether the baby will even grow to term."

"That is God's decision," Simon's father instructed.

"No, that's between me, God, and my doctor," Judy replied.

Simon's father turned to Sister Ellie. "I thought you were nuns. Surely you don't countenance abortion or even allow it as a possibility."

"As I said, we're nondenominational," Sister Ellie repeated. "This mission is not supported by just one faith; we receive help from several congregations in the Dallas area. Perhaps you'd like to join us for lunch and we can discuss further the responsibilities of a nondenominational shelter."

"Sorry, I have a late lunch meeting downtown. But I would like to talk to you briefly about finances. Simon tells me that the mission could use some help."

"That is an understatement. We seem to get by week to week or, if we're lucky, month to month. Why don't we go to my office? I've asked Sister Sara, Will, and Cindy to join us. They're the staff most concerned with development. And Cindy has been doing our books." Sister Ellie was her usual calm yet authoritative self.

Once everyone was in the office and seated, Simon's father came right to the point. "I am interested—rather, my foundation is interested—in supporting projects like this mission. We've done our research on you, and you have a very solid reputation. However, our mission statement makes clear that we are a Christian foundation, and we only support Christian institutions. I am willing to have my foundation provide one million dollars a year to the mission for the next three years."

Will heard the sisters collectively hold their breath.

"But there are some conditions. I want this mission to revise its rules a bit. No one works, paid staff or volunteer, without explicitly stating that he or she is a Christian who accepts Jesus as savior. Some of this money can be used to help increase the salaries of those paid employees. There must be New Testament books at each bed and nightly Christian services along with prayers at mealtime. Do you currently have public prayer at each meal?"

"We have a moment of silence when each person can offer his or her own prayer," Sister Ellie said.

"The mission should permanently house a Christian counseling service to be made available to any pregnant girls or women who come into the mission," Simon's father continued. "I would like a position to be created for a paid missionary who can spread the gospel among those unconverted who come here. I think such an arrangement would be of great benefit to you and to the foundation. It's a worthwhile project, even if it's being run a bit loosely at this point. If these changes can be implemented, I'm willing to give not only the annual support but also substantial money for capital improvement. I notice that some of the furniture is old and the building could use some work."

Sister Ellie took Sister Sara's hand. That alone startled Simon's father.

"Mr. Tigard, your offer is generous, and we could certainly use the help. Your contribution would ensure that we would be able to meet the growing demand for our services. We are the largest such mission in this area. But much of the demand we get comes to us because we are non-denominational. In fact, we do not proselytize. We have volunteers from all sorts of backgrounds. Some are religious, and some are not, and we respect our clients' decisions and their freedom to worship or not worship as they choose. As much as your gift would mean to us, we cannot accept those terms. We could certainly make an effort to increase the number of religious services available each week. But attendance would remain voluntary. I suspect that would not be enough to satisfy you."

"That is correct," Simon's father said. "Well, good day to you, and thank you for your time."

Cindy stepped forward. "May I make a point before you leave?"

Simon's father nodded. "Of course."

"You live in the Dallas area, do you not?"

"I do."

Cindy pulled out a letter. "I was just going through our mail and recording donations. I have here a letter from the Dallas police guild that commends the Social Gospel Mission for its work. They noted that the area served by the mission has one of the lowest crime rates in the whole Dallas area. It has experienced a marked decline in alcohol and drug related incidents. They have sent us a check for ten thousand dollars to continue our work. They estimate that we save many times that amount in police time and property damage."

She pulled out another envelope. "There's another letter here from a much more restrictive mission, one that is run along the lines that you suggest. They would like to send us funds, which they can't afford to do, of course, but we are an invaluable resource for them. They don't take the hardcore homeless or those hostile to their religious convictions, but the fact that we do and we can handle them has taken much of the pressure off them. The number of conflicts at their shelter has declined since our expansion."

She took out one more envelope. "There's another letter from an organization that you do support, Mothers Against Abortion, and they also thank us for our open mindedness. We let them come in to counsel if there is a request for them. Mr. Tigard, with all due respect, this mission serves a vital role in the civic and religious life of this community. If you care about that life, please reconsider helping us."

Simon's father asked for the letter from the police. He read it carefully. He also asked for the letter, which was a personal note to Sister Ellie, from the local director of Mothers Against Abortion. Everyone held their breath.

When he was done reading, Simon's father sat back. "Young lady, you make a good case for the mission, so here is what I will do: I will give you twenty-four hours to accept my offer. I cannot violate the principles of the foundation I represent. After that, the offer is off the table forever."

With that, Simon Tigard, senior, left the room. Simon joined his father in the lobby, and they walked to his limousine.

"Simon, I suspect you are on another track now; you have not mentioned divinity school for some time. So, I want to talk to you about that. You are already well into the school year, so why don't you stay here and work out the year? But I would still like to see you in seminary. They might be able to correct some of the ideas you have imbibed here. But looking at you, I can see you are happy and healthy and that you are doing good work. Why don't you call you mother and make arrangements to come to dinner? Bring some of your friends if you want." With that he was gone.

The mission did not quiet down until late that night. The entire staff was called together. The sisters, Simon, Will, Chris, Marc, Cindy, Kate, Teri, Trudy, Wanda, and Delbert all sat in the dining hall with steaming cups of tea. Trudy preferred a coke. Oga stuck to carrots. Sam Willingham also joined the group at the last minute.

"I'm really sorry things didn't work out," Simon said. "Dad is pretty rigid."

"Simon, it's not at all your fault," Sister Ellie replied. "Your dad and the mission just have different visions and values."

Simon nodded. "I know; I used to think like my Dad, but now I think more like you all."

"But what do we do to keep going?" Sister Sara asked.

"We could do so much with what he offers," Cindy said wistfully.

"The roof still leaks a little in the men's wing," Marc offered.

Will asked God if he would change Simon's father's mind.

"Of course not," God said. "I don't do that kind of thing; it would interfere with the free will that humans think they have but they really don't."

"Huh?"

"Never mind. I think Sister Ellie is trying to get your attention."

"There's no doubt that we would benefit from having these resources over such a time period," Sister Ellie began. "However, look around. Would any of you be able to work here?"

"I don't think even I would pass his litmus test," Simon volunteered.

"I supported Trudy's decision, so I guess I would be suspect," Kate admitted.

Will shook his head. "The problem is, when Simon's father says 'Christian', he means 'my kind of Christian', and that is not a very large group. We've had Muslims, Jews, Quakers, atheists, and witches on staff. Our clients run the same gamut or more. How can we be what we are and accept this deal?"

"We can't," Sister Ellie said. "Not to mention lesbian nuns or *excommunicated* lesbian nuns. If we were to accept this deal, we would have to be deceitful from the beginning, and we would have to live in dread of being found out. Simon's father moves in the same circles as the archbishop who excommunicated us. That level of deceit would be dangerous for the mission. Are we going to deny the young girls the choice of an abortion? Are any of you willing to take a pledge to Simon's father's canon? I doubt it."

"And my dad's foundation would really be running the place," Simon added. "They do micromanage."

Sister Ellie looked at Cindy. "Where are our finances at, at this point?"

"We're good for a couple of months, but after that, it looks bleak." Cindy smacked the table. "Dammit, there are so many people on the street, so many veterans from the wars. The new congress has taken away some of the healthcare funding, and this is the state of Texas, where it's everyone for him or herself. Our electric bill is through the ceiling with the AC in summer and heat in the winter. With almost one in six in poverty, we really need to do more, not less, for families with children. I know we can't help them all, but I want to." Cindy's eyes filled with tears.

"You know," God said, "Simon's father is just trying to lay up entry points for heaven. He cares about himself, but he doesn't really give a damn about those his foundation helps. In fact, the less he's taxed, the less he gives to help the poor and the more he gives to lobbyists who work to reduce his taxes further."

"But he saw the need," Will objected.

"No, he didn't."

Sam cleared his throat. "I have some promising possibilities. Sister Ellie and I have been assembling an advisory board. Right now, we have three members. They're talking among themselves, and they have agreed that, collectively, they can fund you for six months beyond the two for which you already have funds."

Sister Ellie looked at him in surprise. "When did they make that decision?"

"When you were on tour with Simon's father. They're also negotiating with a couple of foundations and for some city block grant funds left from some discontinued federal project. I think it likely that one of those will pan out." Sam smiled. He was holding something back.

"What else?" Ellie asked.

"Well," Sam looked around the room with a sly smile on his face. "As you know. Seymour Smythe has long been a confidante of mine. He was shocked when the Sons of Abraham kidnapped our Tribulation Army and then attempted to rob his bank. He was very proud of his support for the Army. He also greatly appreciates the fact that I undermined that robbery. He was appalled to learn that Reverent Shister was embezzling money from the Galilee Theme Park, in which he had considerable investments. As it turned out, the theme park defaulted into Seymour's hands. He just sold the whole park to Tigard Enterprises, owned by one Simon Tigard.

He made a bundle on it. Tigard intends to reopen a smaller version of the park with an adjacent shopping mall to bring people in. Seymour needs a charity badly for tax purposes, and it needs to be fairly long term. He's preparing a contract that gives the mission eight hundred thousand for each of the next five years and provides one million dollars for capital improvements over that time. Seymour wants a proven charity, and this is one he has actually heard of. I showed him the history, an overview of the books, and we discussed the good reputation of the sisters. The fact that you were excommunicated came up, and Seymour, being a good evangelical, decided that was a positive. He also believes that the time of Tribulation is upon us and that institutions like the mission are fighting on the side of the Lord just like the Tribulation Army was. I may have overplayed that a bit. The fact that Chris, Marc, Will, and I are involved actually blurs the distinction between his beloved Tribulation Army and the mission. In short, he is going for it big time and has so instructed his legal team. They want to sit down with Sister Sara and Sister Ellie fairly soon. Seymour wants quarterly reports from the sisters. That's it."

"Too delicious," Simon said.

"Hot damn!" God and Sister Sara said at the same time.

Sam produced a proposal signed by Seymour, which went into the safe awaiting a visit with the attorney in the morning. Oga chirped. Delbert cried, and everyone got hugs. Trudy did an impromptu soft shoe along with Sister Ellie, and no one slept much that night.

"Talk about irony," God said as Will and Cindy began to explore a romantic moment.

"Go away," Will said.

TALKING

Cindy went to the attorney's office with Sister Ellie and Sister Sara. Will, who had some time off, showered and dressed and headed for the local library. He hoped to find the new book by Carl Hiaasen. His books always made him laugh even as they discouraged him from ever wanting to live in Florida.

The library was quiet, and Will found himself in the magazine/newspaper section catching up on the news and reading an article about evolutionary changes in snakes—how certain digestive proteins had become venom. Will had always loved science, especially natural science. His uncle's library contained copies of *Nature* and *Scientific American*. The current Texas newspapers were more depressing, especially as they contained incredibly unknowledgeable statements. One politician who had introduced a bill banning the importation of iguanas speculated that they might evolve into lizard people and take over the world. In a reversal of thinking, another politician took the fact that no zoo monkey had ever evolved into a human to be evidence against the theory of evolution. And, in a fit of Islamophobia, some education vigilantes were pressuring the Texas School Board to switch to Roman numerals, because they had discovered that arithmetic used Arabic numbers. They said it was further proof of Sharia law in textbooks. And besides, everyone could use Texas Instrument calculators.

"Good grief," God said. "You seem to be collecting all kinds of useless information."

"It's not unimportant as long as there are people of influence who believe this stuff," Will rejoined.

"True enough," God said. "I suspect if ignorance, and much of it is willful, doesn't do us in, superstition will. Combined, they're almost insurmountable."

"What superstitions are you thinking about?"

"Well, we're all a bit superstitious," God said. "But I am not thinking of people who have a lucky tie or a rabbit's foot. I'm thinking of people who believe in chi and base medical decisions on it or who believe that the alignment of planets determines who you marry or who think that there are magical beings in the world."

"You mean, like the CIA?" Will teased.

"Of course not," God said testily. "The CIA may be invisible, it may be stupid, and it may be paranoid, but it is not magical. To change the subject, how are you and Cindy doing with all this work?"

"Great," Will said, "We love being here, and we love each other. I think I should ask her to marry me."

"Cindy is great," God agreed, "but you're a bit young to think like that. Cindy is the only woman you've ever been with."

"Cindy is a couple of years older than me," Will said.

"So you're nineteen, and Cindy is twenty-one. Time is running out for you."

"Stop it," Will said, "I'm trying to be serious."

"Actually, so am I," God said. "You haven't known each other for that long, you're young, and you need to give it more time. I grant you have been through a lot together, but don't let your passions over take your reason."

"You're probably right," Will admitted grudgingly. "I'll think about it some more. Now I'd like to change the subject. We've been talking most of my life, and I call you 'God'. But for some time, I've wanted to ask you: Is that your real name? Who are you?"

"Who wants to know, and why is it important?"

"So often you respond to my questions with one of your own."

"Do I?"

"And you can be infuriating at times, like right now."

"I try my best."

"Can't we just talk about this like adults?"

"Do you think I'm an adult?" God asked. "To be an adult one must have been a child or, heaven forbid, a teenager. But I'm supposed to be timeless or outside of time, so how can I be an adult?"

"Oh, crap," Will said, "you really are baiting me. You know what I mean. Here's the bottom line: Are you real?"

"What do you mean by 'real'?"

"I mean, are you an entity that exists independently of me?"

"Independent in what way?"

"I notice that your thoughts echo my own. You seem to know what I'm thinking."

"I like your thoughts," God said.

"Let me try again. Do you exist?"

"Of course I exist. But that does not necessarily make me real in every sense."

"Suppose I never was born," Will persevered, "would you still exist?"

"No."

"So I made you up."

"What if that were true?"

"It would mean you are a fictional being that I made up."

"So what? Is that a bad thing? Haven't humans always talked to fictional beings? There've been ghosts, gods, oracles, fairies, and sprites, not to mention sulkies, furies, dead ancestors, spirit guides, demons…Good grief, even today many take orders from fictional beings."

"Okay, okay, I get it!"

"To go back to your original question, no, you did not make me up."

"Just where did you come from then?"

"You can work that out, just think about it."

"Oh, boy," Will was beginning to wish he had not started this conversation, yet he knew it was important and long overdue.

"Let me give you a hint," God said. "Sometimes when you're troubled about what to do or how to think about a situation, you ask yourself what your Uncle John or Aunt Rita would advise, right?"

"That is true."

"Do you come up with an answer sometimes?"

"Yes. Sometimes I'm confident that one of them would say a certain thing. Or sometimes I discover that they would just leave it up to me."

"Are they real?"

"Of course they're real; they live in Louisiana."

"But they're not here, and even if they were to die, you could ask the same question and come to the same answers."

"Yes, I suppose."

"What about all those people over the years who seek advice and counsel from dead ancestors and nonexistent gods? Don't they get answers, too?"

"Yes," Will agreed. "And sometimes they get very good answers, answers filled with comfort or even wisdom."

"Do you think they totally fabricate those beings and their answers?"

"They must; where would they come from otherwise?"

"What is one of the most important abilities we have that allows us to live among other humans and feel a sense of intimacy to some of them? What is it, at least in part, about Cindy that makes you love her?"

"She loves me, too. She has feelings for me. She needs me, she feels like I do."

"How do you know that?" God asked. "Do you feel her feelings?"

"No, of course not."

"Then how do you know?"

"I guess, more scientifically, I see that Cindy is a human being whose physiology is very close to my own. I observe emotions in her that are similar to my emotions based on the ones I feel when I act in certain ways. When she acts in those ways, I assume the same or similar emotions are at work within her. I admit I'm wrong sometimes."

Will paused and looked at a physiological diagram in the *Scientific American* before him. "So, I guess the thing that you're asking for that allows intimacy is our ability to project feelings and even thoughts. And if we couldn't do that, I don't see how we could even have a society or a sense of belonging to a community."

"Wow," God said, "good stuff. Where can we project these feelings and thoughts?"

"Well, I suppose that once we have this ability, we can project them into all kinds of things, real or imaginary. I could project them into a rock, a tree, a statue, a dog, the boogey man …" Will thought of all the ways he had projected his feelings and even some profound thoughts into his favorite dog. "Almost anything. It's easier if the thing is more like us. So, are you saying that I made you up by projecting all this stuff into you?"

"Not quite."

"Where does it come from then?"

"When you ask how Uncle John would think about something, does all that information come from Uncle John?"

"No, some of it comes from Aunt Rita, who knows Uncle John really well, some comes from what I have heard others say about Uncle John, and some of it is speculation, because I know what books Uncle John reads and agrees with. It comes from lots of places."

"So, apply that to me."

"Okay, let's try this," Will said. "You are a voice in me, an imaginary friend, but the thoughts and feelings and humor that I give to you come from a whole lot of learning that I've done. It comes from my life experiences, what has happened to me, from books I've read, from conversations with friends, from my aunt and uncle, and, more recently from the sisters and from Cindy. You're a projection of this experience. And because there is this collective wisdom or sometimes foolishness in me you sometimes give me insight or you really help screw things up."

"Very good," God said with admiration.

"In a way," Will continued, "you're my critical common sense infected with a wicked sense of humor, which probably came about the same way. I guess everyone has such a "person" inside who is separate and yet not so separate from themselves."

"Are we getting profound or what?"

"So, our capacity to invent gods or other supernatural beings derives from our social learning plus our ability to project that learning onto other things, be they real or imaginary," Will said, "and all this grows out of a necessary skill that we need in order to live together and see each other as human."

"You got it."

"But then you didn't inspire the Bible, you don't sit in heaven and judge us, you didn't create the world, and you don't mess with our lives. You are not all-knowing, all-powerful, or all-good—not that I think such properties make any sense."

"Me either," God said. "And I have never claimed to be that god. Furthermore, have we discovered any reasons to believe such a deity can or does exists?"

"No, none," Will admitted. "And we have found lots of reasons to doubt that such a being exists or could exist in a world so rife with suffering and pain."

"You're catching up," God observed.

"That means I…we…are atheists," Will realized.

"Yep."

"But it also helps me understand how theists so often get disconnected from reality."

"You mean like some of the members of the Texas legislature?" God asked. "Sorry, that was politically incorrect. But what such people do is take marching orders from one of their imaginary friends, who are already disconnected. There are a lot of insane, nonexistent gods out there giving orders."

"I guess we all work the same way," Will said. "It's just that their information is neither fact-based nor critically assessed. They're not in touch with the world of science and reason. They're delusional, to put it nicely, and they feed those delusions into their own inner voice. Not that any of us are completely free of delusions, but some delusions are much more dangerous than others. You need to put some real work into thinking through what you believe and what you should do about it. And there are very few easy answers."

"What do you take from all this, assuming we're right?" God asked.

"Wow," Will had to think for a bit. He remembered a quote from Goya that said, "Imagination abandoned by reason produces impossible monsters; united with her, she is the mother of the arts and the source of her wonders."

"Well, for one thing, if some folks don't gain their belief system through science and critical reflection, they are not likely to be persuaded from their path by it. So, there seems to be an abyss here that is not easily crossed, because the different routes to belief use such different mechanisms. One path might be guided by knowledge and logic, whereas another follows ignorance and superstition."

"Perhaps there other ways of knowing that don't need science and logic," God opined.

"I reject the notion that there are ways of knowing that don't need both, although I grant there are many other ways to form opinions. And don't go postmodern on me," Will warned. "I'm still in the school that believes in reason and truth."

Will changed the subject. "Given that you are a kind of imaginary friend, and since we've had this conversation, will you leave me?"

"I can hardly be said to have abandoned you, since we are continuing to have this conversation!" God exclaimed. "Why would your common sense and sense of humor ever leave you unless you lost your mind? I love our conversations. It's called 'reflection' by another name. Will, you are, if nothing else, reflective."

A question remained for Will. "I've always felt that you were that voice in my head that said and thought things that I was reluctant to say publicly or that I thought were funny but was afraid to say so. I think everyone has that voice. It's just that you seem a bit more…present."

"True," God replied. "I'm that voice that whispers 'bullshit' when you watch an ad on TV or hear a con offering ten percent return on your investment. I'm also the voice telling you to reconsider what you haven't thought about enough. Listen to me, but keep collecting information and critical thoughts because I'm only as good as the background information you provide. I was born in your uncle's library when you were reading everything you could get your hands on. I'll only stay robust if you keep feeding me with your curiosity."

"Should I keep calling you 'God'?" Will asked. "After all, in a sense, I'm you and you are me. Do you want to be called 'God'?"

"Not really," God replied. "Why call me anything?"

"Well, for one thing, it makes writing dialogue much easier," Will dead-panned.

"Oh, bother," God said. "Just call me 'Phil' but not 'Dr. Phil'."

With that, "Phil" left.

DOUBT

The next few months were a blur to both Will and Cindy. The new financing meant more work, not less. Will and Marc oversaw much of the capital improvement. Will actually spent considerable time repairing the roof of the men's wing. Cindy had more receipts to pay, more books to balance, and more admissions to enter although it was easier with the software Chris had introduced. The sisters were on the road constantly talking up the need for the proposed new expansions with potential donors. Sam accompanied them and was very useful in facilitating introductions.

Kate was in charge of the girl's unit, which housed about twenty teenagers now, most of them runaways. The police brought them to the mission routinely. Rabbi Schultz was in charge of recruiting volunteers and assigning them duties. She and Cindy were responsible for the daily operations of the mission. Teri had left to help her parents and resume college, majoring in political science. Trudy drew heavy kitchen duty with so many to feed at each meal, although Wanda and Delbert always made certain that she had time to study. Simon was doing all the food pickups. He took the irony that his father was indirectly financing the improvements in stride. In fact, he found it amusing.

The state of Texas was facing yet another large budget deficit, and their answer to the crisis was to cut jobs and create yet more unemployed, thereby increasing the state debt and then cutting more jobs and creating more unemployed. It was a vicious cycle, and frontline charities like the mission, not to mention the citizens of Texas whose necessary public services were in sharp decline, were the victims.

By spring, Will and Cindy were looking forward to school and working part-time at the mission. They were tired of being so busy. They were now treated as a stable couple, a perception they enjoyed. Marriage was something they talked about, but given the state of their lives, they had no time for serious planning.

Phil was happy with this arrangement. "You know, Will, I had my doubts, because you've never really been with anyone else. On the other hand, your nature is like a kitten; you found a nice pair of arms to settle into, and you moved right in. Cindy has seen more of life than you, but she seems to think you're the one. Go slow. I don't think you'll change your mind, and I doubt you'll even have a midlife crisis, but you're young."

"You don't think much of my sense of adventure, do you?" Will asked.

"What sense of adventure?" Phil said. "Every adventure you've ever had tracked you down and grabbed you by the hair. Think tornado, collapsing Goliath, being kidnapped, bank robbers, escaped pythons."

"You have a point, and it was a boa," grumbled Will.

"But," Phil admitted, "Cindy is one hell of a beautiful, talented woman."

"My point exactly," Will said with satisfaction.

Will and Cindy called Shreveport and asked if they could come for the weekend, something they had done regularly over the past few months. Uncle John and Aunt Rita were delighted.

At dinner the first night, Cindy turned to Uncle John. "I know it would be unorthodox, but if Will and I get married, could you perform the ceremony *and* give me away? Although I don't like the expression 'give me away'."

"I'll tell you what," Uncle John said, "I'll escort you down the aisle, and then I'll miraculously slide to the front and do the ceremony."

"I love you, Uncle John," Cindy said.

Will knew that Uncle John was very pleased to be asked.

Aunt Rita was an old hand at participating in weddings. "I have three requests," she said. "First, the ceremony should be at the mission. There are no vacations in that kind of work, and that would allow more of your friends to attend."

"Good idea," Uncle John agreed.

"Second, Will, I think it would be good if you invited your mother, if you would like to. It's past time that we were together again."

Will was surprised but pleased by the suggestion. "I think I'd like her to be there," he said.

"Third, if there is a piano available, I'd like to provide the music for the ceremony. And let's not have people divided by friends of the bride and friends of the groom."

"These are great suggestions," Cindy said with enthusiasm. Will agreed.

In bed that night Cindy rolled over and traced her finger down Will's chest. "I don't mean to be pressing you to get married. It, well, it makes me feel more a part of the family to discuss these kinds of things."

"Cindy, I love you, and the conversation was very comfortable for me. It's a decision we will have to make before Uncle John and Aunt Rita get too old. I like the vision we have of a wedding at the mission."

On the second day of their visit, Will was invited over to Wilma Williams's place for ice tea. Cindy declined to go along, as she and Aunt Rita were in the garden picking strawberries to make jam. The two of them always seemed to find a lot to talk about. Uncle John was with a friend at the hospital.

Although it was early spring, it was warm, and Wilma was sitting in the shade of a large willow in her front yard. She had married a man, Paul Bulton, whom Will had never met. She was very happy with her situation, but she was curious about Will's adventures having heard bits and pieces from Will's aunt and uncle.

"I hardly know where to start, so many things happened so quickly, and I don't know how much Aunt Rita and Uncle John told you," Will said.

"I heard about the Social Gospel Mission and the escaped boa," Wilma said.

"Did you hear that I was kidnapped and enslaved?"

"God, no," Wilma looked concerned.

"It wasn't a big deal. I got away, and the FBI caught the kidnappers, who have just been sentenced to prison." Will told her a bit about his time with the Tribulation Army.

"Speaking of belief in the Rapture and all that stuff," Wilma said, "I wanted to talk to you, in part, because we both grew up as preacher's kids. That was a big part of our lives. But since I married John, we haven't been to church much, and that is largely my fault. I don't find that I welcome God much into my life anymore. It started with Denny being killed in Afghanistan."

"Oh, no, not Denny!"

Wilma nodded. "He had a rough time of it. He wrote me regularly, and he was increasingly disillusioned with the military. He had also become very cynical about religion, especially seeing what the Taliban was trying to do. He thought they were a lot like the evangelical community in which he grew up. Even though I have a comfortable life here, I, too, think the world is screwed up, and if God's providence is what allows these things to happen, I think he's doing a lousy job."

Just then, Pastor Bob, Wilma's father drove up.

"Hi, Dad," Wilma greeted her father with a hug. "I'm just regaling Will with my unhappiness with God."

"I don't know anyone who hasn't been unhappy with God at some point or another," Pastor Bob said. "I certainly have. Fortunately, it was temporary. It happened a lot in seminary, too. In fact, some students left because of it."

Will had always found Pastor Bob easy to talk to. He shared Uncle John's open mindedness and sense of humor. Pastor Bob and Uncle John were always on the phone exchanging bad jokes.

"Will," Bob said, "with all your adventures, at least you must have felt good knowing that God was by your side."

"You have no idea," Phil interjected.

"My views about religion have changed a lot," Will admitted somewhat tentatively.

"How?" Wilma asked.

"Go ahead, tell them. Be honest," Phil encouraged.

"Well, it's hard to know where to start." Will recalled his conversations with Sister Ellie. "We have a lot of beliefs, some of them true and some of them false. They come to us in many ways, but they come to us unbidden."

"And some of them we wish we didn't have," Wilma added.

"Exactly," Will said. "Actually, a lot of them are beliefs we don't welcome. But many of them are like old friends, some of them we have confidence in and others not so much. In some cases, we have criteria by which we sort out those that are true, or probably true, from those that aren't. Sometimes we can't sort them, but for trivial beliefs, it doesn't really matter to our lives. The trouble comes when we lack reasonable criteria for important beliefs and there's a lot of conflict. They might all be false."

"Now we're coming to religious belief," Pastor Bob asked.

"Not just religious belief," Will asserted. "Other sets of beliefs can have these features as well. But to get to religious belief, at the mission we have a lot of different religions represented. And we made an effort to visit different places of worship when we had the time. I saw such different points of view and such incompatible claims about God, salvation, demons, magic, and sin that I became confused."

"Holding onto the true belief is especially hard in the face of so many claims," Bob said.

"But that's just the problem. I never could come up with a set of criteria to pick out the true beliefs, at least a set that was not question-begging," Will responded. "The different belief systems posit different gods with different properties or no gods at all. When two people both say they believe in god, it often seems as if they believe in very different things. And when you ask them why they have these beliefs, they often appeal to some experience or some scriptural passage to support their belief. But the experience and the passage are always ambiguous."

"But, surely you can just know God without the supporting evidence," Bob urged. "At least that was a view some held at seminary."

"I really don't think so," Will said. "Our early beliefs about God are usually formed by the authorities in our lives, most often our parents, but also people such as you, who taught Wilma and me about God. But we were kids; we trusted you, so our beliefs were shaped before we were able to think critically. Look at all the beliefs that get set in this way, some good and some bad. We know, living here in the south, how racial beliefs are inculcated very early, and they are highly resistant to change. But many bigots say the same thing about those beliefs that you just said, that one knows these things about other races without evidence. In cultures where there are strong beliefs in ghosts and spirits, it's the same. But as we grow older, some of us bring our newly acquired critical abilities to bear on these beliefs and revise them or abandon them. I think we have an obligation to subject such beliefs to scrutiny."

"Amen to that," Wilma said

"Would you say the same, if your parents were atheists and you came to your belief through their influence?" Pastor Bob asked.

Will nodded. "Absolutely."

"But why do you reject the claim that we can know God is with us?" Pastor Bob asked.

"When I left here, I believed in God, and I was sincere and certain in my belief. But what I learned last summer is that certainty of belief is very different from knowing. Knowing requires evidence, reliable evidence, and that is missing in the case of religious belief, although certainty is still there. In fact, we can have knowledge without certainty, like when I have good evidence of something but I still question it. And we can have certainty without knowledge, like when I believe in something and am willing to bet on it, without good evidence."

Pastor Bob looked puzzled. "But Will, you have the Bible, the scriptures, and the authority of history. Is that not good evidence? Can't you decide among the many competing beliefs based on that?"

"Hardly. All the crazy belief systems cite the same sources, which is by itself proof that it is not good evidence. I thought a lot about this, and the Bible is a mess in terms of its inconsistency. Many of the events that are reported are historically problematic or simply impossible. It just will not do as my guide." Then Will told them about the conversation about evidence with the UFOers.

"In my seminary days, many of us came to such skeptical conclusions," Pastor Bob admitted. "There's nothing like studying the Bible seriously to bring out its inconsistencies."

Wilma looked at him in surprise as he continued.

"Some of my classmates abandoned their studies over these things. Many of us decided not to read the Bible critically but to read it devotionally, which really just dodges the issue. Personally, I don't think *faith* is an alternative to reason and evidence, but it is what allows us to hold onto our religious convictions in the face of contrary evidence and serious questions about the truth of what we believe." Bob was enjoying this conversation with Will.

Wilma made a gesture to get their attention. "As you know, Dad, I've lost some of my faith, but not for the reasons Will mentions. I simply can't reconcile all the suffering in our country and the world with there being a caring God."

Pastor Bob studied both Wilma and Will. He looked both serious and a little sad. "I wish I had an answer for each of you, but I don't. Why God allows so much evil and what are the criteria for picking out the true faith are perennial questions. I'm not one who believes that you will burn in hell for having such doubts. I think that God must have a reason for allowing the suffering that he does, and he must have a reason for allowing the proliferation of crazy religions, but I don't know why he hasn't stepped in. Sometimes, I think that churches like prosperity theology and some of the places you visited, Will, do more to destroy faith than to build it."

Will was struck by his response, "Pastor Bob, we started out this conversation with you claiming that you were comforted by *knowing* that God was by your side and my side. Then Wilma and I raised doubts about whether we can, in fact, *know* this. But now you sound more like a skeptic. There are all these things that you say you believe on the one hand, and then you concede on the other that you don't know why God allows evil and you don't know why God allows all these crazy beliefs. It seems you don't know the god who walks by your side. You're as doubt-ridden as we are."

"Will, I'm glad you didn't go to my seminary," Pastor Bob said. "I might be a plumber now." He laughed. "Truth is, I just don't think about these things much anymore, I guess that's what having faith is all about."

"I'm not trying to talk you out of your faith," Will said.

"I understand that. And I don't take you to be doing that. You and Wilma are raising honest questions that perplex you. And I'm not certain that anyone has answers for you. Your Uncle John is a prime skeptic. To him, God is an enigma, and it's a mistake to try to understand Him. I think he's read too much Kierkegaard."

"And these beliefs are not trivial," Will added. "If all religions are false, as I now believe, then there is no ultimate judgment or reward or punishment for your religious convictions. But in a society that holds these beliefs, there are serious day-to-day consequences. I cannot imagine raising charitable contributions for homeless atheists. It's nearly impossible to run for public office as an atheist. This is probably why most atheists—America's most despised group—keep a low profile."

"True enough, Will," Pastor Bob said. "It's a regrettable fact that when we talk to people who are losing faith that we often point out the social losses they will experience, and these are, as you say, very real. I have seen whole families and even churches dissolve over change of faith issues. And I've seen children disinherited because they abandoned their family's faith."

At dinner that night, Will told Cindy, Uncle John, and Aunt Rita about his conversation with Wilma and Pastor Bob.

Uncle John laughed. "I've always known Bob was in touch with his inner skeptical liberal. But he is right. These are tough questions, and I would rather see someone go through life with your honest perplexity than to bull ahead with unquestioned faith in what they were taught as children. So, should I consider you a Unitarian, an atheist, or both?"

"Right now I'm an atheist," Will admitted for the first time in his life, "and I say that after years of talking to my god, who is also an atheist, if that makes any sense." Will paused. "But, having said that, I don't feel any less committed to the sisters or the mission. To me, the greatest calling is to be able to serve the common good and make the world a better place."

Uncle John turned to Cindy. "What do you make of your partner's atheism?"

"I guess I'm with him all the way," Cindy said "including serving the common good."

"Amen," Aunt Rita said. She reached out and took Will's and Cindy's hands. "Enough of this talk. You two have made my life so much richer, your calls, emails, and wonderful, crazy stories. I can't believe I'm saying this either, but I don't give a 'D' if you're both atheists. Now I'll probably go to hell." She sat back and smiled.

Will realized this was the first and probably only time in her life Aunt Rita had thought to say 'damn', and she still could not do it.

Uncle John poured a bit more red wine into each glass. "A toast to loving one another, helping those we can, and the common good."

"I'll drink to that," Phil said.

The first night Will and Cindy were back at the mission, there was an impromptu party for Arie and Malcolm, who were on break from school. They sat at the large kitchen prep table along with the sisters, Rabbi Schultz, Kate, Simon, Will, Cindy, Trudy, Marc, Chris, Delbert, and Wanda. Arie and Malcolm were coming back to the mission at least part-time, so even with Simon leaving to study computer science, Teri gone, and Will and Cindy cutting back to part-time, the staffing looked sufficient for the near future.

Simon's father, proud of Simon's success in computer science, had granted him a trust fund so he could continue his courses. The new funding for the mission meant that Chris and Marc were now paid, full-time employees. Delbert and Wanda had also gotten nice raises, and Trudy was staying on to work as a paid staff member. Her parents realized she was thriving—never a good student, she was now making straight A's—and agreed to her request to stay.

Describing their trip home, Will told Arie about his conversation with Pastor Bob. "I knew you would make it all the way to atheism," the always-philosophical Arie said. "But I especially like your point about how we confuse our psychological certainty with having knowledge or having truth. I think there's a reason for that. When we have really good evidence for a belief that belief is often accompanied by *certainty,* and it is right in those cases to say we *know* it. So we come to associate certainty with knowledge. However, when we are certain about something without good evidence, we still think that we have knowledge, when, in fact, *all* we have is conviction. A bad move every time, unless we can come up with evidence."

"You'll go all the way, all right, all the way to hell." Simon gave Will a dig in the ribs. "What is it about this place that makes people lose their faith?"

Sister Sara was pretty relaxed from the good company and the wine. "I'll tell you why our work generates doubt. We work our butts off helping people who are suffering and desperate through no fault of their own. We take care of ten people, and behind them are another forty, and behind those, another thousand. And more are being born all the time. The young, idealistic men who went to war and came back with half a brain, the old men with gnarled hands from a life of hard work thrown onto the street, the abused women, the homeless kids selling their young bodies for sex. These are throwaway lives. The worst are the babies who are sick and there's no healthcare for them. And the moneyed class simply doesn't give a damn; they're too busy buying politicians and getting their taxes reduced.

"C.S. Lewis, in all his naiveté, seemed to think there are universal moral principles that God built into each of us. It ain't true! We can be a callus and uncaring race toward the less fortunate; and the various priggish religions of the world—whose main concern is getting more paying members through the turnstile—seem to lead the charge. Look at what the Catholic Church tried to do to this mission. How many donations promised us have been reduced so that a church could remodel or build a new building? This is not to deny that humans occasionally do great things. And I recognize you who are listening to my grief overflow are among those who truly care. Please forgive my outburst; I know the battle must go on tomorrow and tomorrow and tomorrow—my thanks to Faulkner."

Sister Sara's face was a bit flushed, but she smiled as Ellie kissed her cheek tenderly and Cindy and Kate gave her a three-way hug.

"Then we're the lucky ones," said Trudy, who was holding Oga as she snuggled between Marc and Rabbi Schultz. "We live with each other."

No one disagreed with that. Not even Phil.

"I love these people," he said.

ACKNOWLEDGEMENTS

I give special thanks to Linda Heuertz, who read numerous versions of my manuscript and contributed significantly to the story. Laura Harrington, not only read the manuscript and offered excellent suggestions, but also compiled the critical comments from a talented group of young readers, namely, Amanda Lyon, Ben Phillips, Jackie Lungmus, Allie Draper, and Natalie Karbelnig. Kristin Wolfram helped immensely with a final edit. Without all of you, I could not have finished this story.

All biblical quotations are from: *The New Oxford Annotated Bible*, 3rd ed. Michael D. Coogan ed., Oxford University Press, 2001.

Koran quotations from: The Koran Penguin Classics revised translation by N.J. Dawood, 1994.